MAGIC The Gathering®

Experience the Magic

MAGIC
The Gathering®

A MAGIC: THE GATHERING Anthology

THE
SECRETS OF MAGIC
A N T H O L O G Y

Edited by
Jess Lebow

The Secrets of Magic
©2002 Wizards of the Coast, Inc.

Distributed in the United States by Holtzbrinck Publishing. Distributed in Canada by Fenn Ltd.

Distributed to the hobby, toy, and comic trade in the United States and Canada by regional distributors.

Distributed worldwide by Wizards of the Coast, Inc. and regional distributors.

Made in the U.S.A.

Cover art by Kev Walker
First Printing: March 2002
Library of Congress Catalog Card Number: 2001089470

9 8 7 6 5 4 3 2 1

UK ISBN: 0-7869-2731-3
US ISBN: 0-7869-2710-0
620-88552-001-EN

U.S., CANADA,
ASIA, PACIFIC, & LATIN AMERICA
Wizards of the Coast, Inc.
P.O. Box 707
Renton, WA 98057-0707
+1-800-324-6496

EUROPEAN HEADQUARTERS
Wizards of the Coast, Belgium
P.B. 2031
2600 Berchem
Belgium
+32-70-23-32-77

Visit our web site at **www.wizards.com/magic**

Table of Contents:

Part I:

Ancient History

A long, long, time ago . . .

For Want of Ink
Paul B. Thompson

Pharon was dying.

It was an incredible thing to say aloud or even think: *Pharon was dying*. The great wizard had stood at the right hand of the kings of Kjeldor since the nation was founded four centuries ago. A man of matchless wisdom and power who had evaded the clutch of Death so long was not meant to expire wheezing in bed like an ordinary man.

Rumors of the mage's illness were the talk of Kjeld's taverns and markets, and they depressed spirits and raised prices at the same time. People stood about in small groups, discussing the wizard's health in grave whispers. Speaking of his death was like contemplating losing the sun—all that could follow was darkness.

Paul B. Thompson

Could the kingdom survive his loss? The court was as worried as everyone else. A royal decree was hastily enacted, making it a crime to speak "discouragingly of the dynasty." People still lingered on the streets and in the public houses, only now they confined themselves to coded phrases and knowing nods. Storms were much discussed—when they would arrive, how much damage they would do. And so everyone waited.

Barrinalo's pen hovered above the parchment, a single drop of shiny black ink clinging to the tip. While he gazed unseeing at the veined marble wall in front of him, the ink drop fell, spattering on the cream-white page.

His fellow journeyman at Worlight's House of Letters, Golien, nudged Barrinalo in the ribs. "Hist!"

Pharon was dying.

"Eh?" said Barrinalo, shaking off the unthinkable.

"The copy," Golien said. He was a pudgy young man with a wispy black beard he'd grown in a desperate attempt to add age and sobriety to his childish face. "Look at your copy!"

Barrinalo looked down and saw the ink splash. Helped by the slant of the desk, the wayward droplet had run onto the colored uncial at the foot of the page.

"Blast," he growled, dabbing at the spill with his sleeve. Journeymen weren't supposed to drop ink on a finished copy like some raw apprentice.

Barrinalo slid off his high stool and picked up the candle from his desk. A shiny brass shield behind the flame reflected the golden light onto his face. The son and grandson of scribes, at nineteen he was the youngest journeyman in Worlight's stable of scriveners.

"I'll get pumice and white vinegar to clean it up," he muttered.

Shuffling away in his soft wicker sandals, Barrinalo heard Golien

4

whisper loudly, "If you pass the kitchen, bring me back a crust of bread, will you? And some cold bacon, if you find any."

Barrinalo walked on as if he hadn't heard, for his friend's own good. Master Worlight had already dressed down Golien twice for getting grease smears on his copies. Any more indiscretions and Golien would be cast out of the House of Letters.

It was late on a summer's eve, already dark. The age of ice still gripped the land, and the long corridor from the copy room was chilly; Barrinalo could see his breath. Was it the omnipresent cold that had weakened Pharon? Talk in the victual market said an ague had settled in his chest, but word in the Three Quills wine shop was, the old wizard had taken a fall and broken some ribs. Pleurisy set in after that. . . .

The supply closet was just off the main hall, where Worlight received clients high and low. Most of the House of Letters' work was copying books and documents. Barrinalo had learned much while making six copies of Pharon's famous treatise *On the Summoning of Invisible Entities*, the first work of magic he'd ever read. The experience left him wanting more, but since copying Pharon's text, all that crossed Barrinalo's desk were dry almanacs and legal amendments to the code of Kjeldor.

In the closet, Barrinalo set the candle on a shelf and poked around until he found a box of soft pumice and a bottle of white vinegar. He tucked a pebble and the red clay bottle into the waist pocket of his robe. On his way out, he heard voices in the hall. One of them was Master Worlight, speaking in an uncharacteristically hushed fashion.

He was about to slip away quietly so as not to disturb his master's business. Then Barrinalo heard the name "Pharon." On a moment's decision, he closed the closet door and stood in darkness.

". . . might last a week," an unknown voice said. "Or he might not live out the night. Our mistress is determined to wring out the old man's secrets before he dies!"

"Don't count Pharon out too quickly," Worlight replied. "He's lived more years than you or I together will ever see. Perish he might, but he won't go swiftly or silently!"

Barrinalo put his back against the cold stone wall and slid along until he reached the open passage into the hall. Worlight was seated at the marble table in the center of the room, his back to Barrinalo. Facing him was a tall, gaunt man in a fur-trimmed robe and cap. A tallow candle as thick as a man's wrist blazed between them. The tall man's face was screened by the candle flame, but Barrinalo had an impression of a long, hooked nose and dagger-sharp chin. Below the fur cap blazed a pair of the brightest blue eyes he'd ever seen. They seemed to glow from within in the semidarkness of the open hall. Though it was deathly cold in the hall, no misty breath bloomed from the visitor's mouth. Worlight was puffing like a teakettle.

"Pharon is a fool!" the gimlet-eyed visitor declared. "Thought he'd live forever, did he? That's why he didn't write anything down! What will become of his knowledge, his spells, when the grave claims him?"

"It's always wise to write down important information," Worlight said.

"Save the sales talk, scribe. You've got the job, never fear. How many copyists can you spare for the task?"

He saw the master's shoulders rise and fall. "Eight at the moment, including two journeymen."

"Make it ten. The Sorcerers' League is in no mood for half measures."

Worlight agreed. The gaunt stranger hefted a weighty suede sack onto the table. "Here is your fee. Have your men at Pharon's house by dawn," he said. "Finished scrolls are to be kept under close guard. Don't worry, we'll hire the guards. Someone from our order will inspect the documents and evaluate their worth."

"It shall be done, Master Cackluster."

"See that it is." He pointed a bony finger at Worlight. "We want everything Pharon says taken down, no matter how trivial it seems. There's four centuries of magical knowledge locked up in that ancient skull of his, and we want it! If we find anything is being held back—"

"Sir!" Worlight exclaimed, rising to his feet. "You impugn the integrity of the House of Letters, not to mention me!"

The wizard Cackluster folded his arms into his voluminous sleeves. "I impugn nothing. There are rogues in this town who would like to steal Pharon's legacy—freelancers not in our guild, and guild members who dream of taking the magus's place at court after he dies. Beware of them, Worlight."

Cackluster strode to the door. It opened at a wave of his hand, and a knife-sharp icy wind blasted into the hall. Worlight cupped his hands around his candle to protect it. By the feeble light Barrinalo glimpsed a monstrous form outside, waiting the sorcerer's return. It had four legs, like a horse, but the limbs were bulky with muscle, and the instead of hoofs, the beast had long white talons on each foot. It bowed its arched neck, showing horns and the suggestion of a beak, hooked like a falcon's but much larger.

"You have an honest reputation, scribe," Cackluster called over the gusting wind. "Be true to it! Remember, every word he says!"

With surprising agility, he vaulted onto the back of his monstrous mount. The beast bellowed like a bull and bounded away. Worlight left the dais and hurried to shut the flapping door. Snow swirled in around his feet, and the wind lifted the hem of his woolen robe, revealing his bowed legs. Then the candle on his desk toppled, completing the darkness in the hall.

Worlight shut the door and threw the heavy iron bolt. Sighing, he was resigned to groping his way back to his table in darkness when a flame flared in the corridor.

"Who's there?" he called.

"Barrinalo, Master. Wait, I'll bring light."

Bringing his candle from the closet, Barrinalo crossed to Worlight's table and held his flame to the still-smoking wick of Worlight's. The room brightened.

"Why are you here?" Worlight asked, once he was settled on his stool again. He did not thank Barrinalo for restoring his light.

"I've been to the supply closet, Master." He carefully avoided mention of his ink spill. Worlight was about to dismiss him when the younger man said, "Master, I heard what the wizard said."

"You were snooping?"

"I could not help it. Forgive me." Barrinalo bowed. It was a mild lie, told for a higher purpose. "Please Master, may I be sent to Pharon's house? It would be an honor, a great honor, to assist in preserving his wisdom for the ages."

Worlight's ruddy face assumed a sly expression. "It will not be an easy commission, and the pay will be half the usual copy rate."

Tight-fisted scoundrel. Cackluster gave you a fortune for the job!

"I care not, Master. I've always wanted to meet the great Pharon. This may be my only chance," Barrinalo replied.

"I see. I hope you don't have any ideas of turning the situation to your advantage, boy. Finished rolls are to be sent to the House of Letters under armed guard, so no pilfering will be possible." Insulted, Barrinalo bit his lip and said nothing. "Oh, very well," Worlight said. "I was going to send you anyway. Begone now, back to your work."

Barrinalo bowed again. "Thank you, Master. I will do honor to the House of Letters."

"See that you do. It is not I who will punish you if you try to cheat our clients. The Sorcerers' League is not to be trifled with.

I've seen their vengeance before."

Worlight visibly shuddered. He proceeded to relate an awful anecdote about a leather merchant who once tried to cheat a sorcerer named Eversson on the weight of some finished hides. Next time he bathed, his bath water was transformed into a tanning solution at full boil. The leather merchant was found the next morning, cured as hard and dry as an old goatskin.

The lesson delivered, Barrinalo bowed again and returned to the copy room. He found Golien asleep at his desk, his face pressed against the manuscript he'd been duplicating. A fine set of inked capitals on his cheek showed he had already turned his head once.

The blot on Barrinalo's page was too dry to remove with vinegar. He put the spoiled sheet aside, to be polished later with pumice, and started afresh. It took him most of the night to finish.

* * * * *

Day resumed hard and cold, with a sky as clear and brittle as glass. Three journeyman scribes, Barrinalo, Golien, and Ramanash, dressed in the frigid dormitory above the copyists' hall. They donned their heavy furs quickly and in silence. Worlight had them wakened well before sunup, then lectured them at length about the great task they'd been given. He put the eldest of the trio, Ramanash, in charge of the scribes being sent to Pharon's house.

Barrinalo and Golien went upstairs to the attic to roust out seven apprentices. Stumbling, grumbling and blinking in the chill light of dawn, the young scribes filed downstairs to the main hall, where Master Worlight and Ramanash had assembled supplies for the job—double rolls of foolscap, ten quills, and a thirty-dram inkpot for each. A servant wearing Pharon's livery waited while the scribes assembled, ashen-faced and trembling with cold.

"Boys, you're going on an important job, perhaps the most important in the history of this house," Worlight began. He stood behind the marble desk in the center of the room, hands clasped behind his back. The wizard's servant, looking quite wrung out, stood behind him.

"The stories we've all heard are sadly true. The great Pharon is dying. He hasn't much time left." Worlight and the servant exchanged meaningful looks. "It's vital every bit of the master's knowledge be taken down, for the benefit of future students of thaumaturgy—"

"And for the benefit of Worlight's purse," quipped someone in the crowd. The apprentices giggled.

"Silence! Show some respect!" Worlight snapped. "Ramanash, what kind of witlings are you training these days?"

"Idle, worthless ones, excellent master," Ramanash answered. He was a transplanted Fallaji, dark of mien and quick to use a corrective cane on his students. To stifle further quips, Ramanash struck the two nearest youths, neither of whom had made the sarcastic comment. The Fallaji's blows drove them to the bare flagstone floor. Standing over the fallen apprentices, he glared at the others, now cowering.

"Anyone else?" he demanded. The youths did not reply.

"Master, the time—" Barrinalo said quietly.

"Quite so," Worlight replied. "We've no time for foolishness. Get over to Pharon's estate and take down every word he says—be it spells, incantations, or ramblings about his youth. Take down everything! Every word the magus speaks has import, so don't miss a single one! Good luck."

Led by the pasty-faced servant in green and gold livery, the scriveners filed out. Wicker bags of writing supplies hung from straps around their necks.

Outside the cold was brutal, but the clarity of the new day's light made up for the icy temperature, at least in Barrinalo's mind. The narrow cobblestone lane in front of the House of Letters was free of snow—Worlight paid a sorcerer to keep the drifts away from his door. The pavement and the buildings around them glittered in the sun, gilded as they were with hoarfrost.

"Wonderful," Barrinalo said, smiling.

"Wonderful?" Golien groaned. "Worlight didn't even feed us breakfast!"

"Hide your face," Ramanash said sharply. "No complaining in front of the 'prentices."

The gray-faced servant doubled back a few steps and said, "Hot porridge and sourbark tea are waiting at my master's house. Come." That cheered the gloomy Golien.

They set out through the empty streets of Kjeld, down the cobbled lane to the thoroughfare called King's Way. A few early vendors were out there, trundling barrows over the slippery paving. The procession of fur-clad scribes, led by one of Pharon's uniformed servants, caused more than one vendor to stop and stare. Fresh grist for the gossip mills, Barrinalo mused.

It was a long way to the wizard's abode, and uphill too. By the time the scribes reached Palace Square, Golien was puffing hard, and Barrinalo was sweating inside his hood.

The residence of the kings of Kjeldor lined one face of the open square, rising to the highest pinnacles in the city. Behind the gray granite walls stood the turreted palace itself, looking as cold and forbidding as any natural peak. In contrast, the edifice facing the royal residence across the open square was built of snowy limestone, rising in terraced tiers to form a white step pyramid, not as lofty as the palace, but no less grand. This was the house of the wizard Pharon.

A squad of armed guards stopped the scribes at the entrance. The scribes were searched (much to Ramanash's displeasure), then passed inside. They traversed an ordinary, if opulent, series of rooms, heading deeper into the pyramid. The plastered walls were painted with vivid landscapes none of the scribes had never seen—sunny vistas overlooking broad green valleys, mighty forests, and blue-tinged mountains. Not a speck of ice or snow appeared in any view. These were images of the land before the ice came, twenty-five centuries ago.

Under foot, thick carpets softened their footfalls until they were no more than whispers. Deeper and deeper inside they went, the young apprentices craning their necks this way and that, taking in the rich surroundings. Colorful as the murals and furnishings were, they did nothing to prepare the scribes for what lay at the heart of the wizard's abode.

Following close behind Ramanash, Barrinalo got a whiff of something sweet. It was pleasant, not cloying, and he wondered what it could be. More aromas wafted down the corridor—complex smells of earth and growing things. He peered over the Fallaji's shoulder. There was a bright room ahead, as bright as day. He didn't understand it. The facade of the pyramid was solid stone, so where did all the light come from?

The servant leading them stopped.

"Wait here," he said haughtily.

Ramanash and Golien drew themselves up, with Barrinalo stopping just behind them. The apprentice scribes bunched up behind him, eager to see what wonders lay ahead. They jostled and whispered so much Ramanash had to rap a few skulls to quiet them.

The corridor gave way to a vast, open room, the dimensions of which Barrinalo could not guess, for it was filled with an astonishing array of living plants. Great, green, leafy trees scraped the corbeled roof, smoothly plastered and painted pale blue to resemble the sky. The trees were giants compared to the stunted specimens currently growing in Kjeldor. Ramanash's dark eyes widened when he spotted desert palms he hadn't seen since leaving his homeland, twenty-six years past.

"This is not the home of a man," he said solemnly. "It is the oasis of a god!"

Filling in between the trees were bushes, vines, and shrubs of many kinds, all exuberantly blossoming. The gaily colored flowers gave off the perfume Barrinalo had smelled. Their sweet, fecund odor hung in the air like a narcotic mist.

High above the garden, just below the peak of the vaulted roof, hung a blazing globe six feet across. The miniature sun was dazzlingly bright and threw off a fine, even heat. Between the painted sky and tiny sun, the illusion of being outdoors was very strong.

A new lackey, this one in a light, open robe, appeared on the gravel path through the foliage. He was leaning on a tall staff, topped by a small brass sistrum. It tinkled every time he let the butt of the staff strike the ground.

"Greetings, honored scriveners," he said. "I am Regitus, steward to the mighty Pharon. In his name, I welcome you to his house."

Ramanash seemed stricken dumb by their surroundings, so Barrinalo replied, "Thank you, Master Regitus. It is we who are honored to be here."

The white haired steward bowed his head slightly. "If you are ready, I will bring you into the master's presence at once."

Ramanash, now recovered, extended a brown arm. "Lead on."

"A moment," Golien said, swallowing loudly. "I am fainting . . . it's so warm in here! Might I leave off my furs?"

"Of course." Regitus clapped his hands together twice. There was a rustling in the dense undergrowth, followed by a high-pitched twittering. Nervously, the apprentices clustered together tightly behind their journeymen.

Fronds parted, and a small two-legged creature emerged. Bright green from head to toe, the creature stood about three spans high. At first Barrinalo thought it was wearing a close fitting suit of green, but he quickly realized the creature was naked. The frill around its neck and the 'skirt' around its waist were part of it, made of the same green skin on its face and limbs.

A second green being appeared, then a third and fourth. Three more joined in a moment later. They had pinched little faces, and when one yawned widely, everyone could see they had sharp, wooden-looking teeth.

"Take the visitors' wraps," Regitus said. The green creatures marched over and held out their arms—rather sullenly, Barrinalo thought. Weighted down with ten heavy fur cloaks, they staggered away into the underbrush chirruping and squeaking.

"What are they?" Golien blurted.

"Servants of the master," Regitus said. "They tend the garden."

He took them down the path, past towering palm trees and scent-laden vines. So intense were the surroundings, Barrinalo's head swam. The chattering, snickering apprentices fell quiet and followed single file through the lush greenery.

A bird erupted from branches of a magnolia, screeching loudly. The scribes flinched. In the next instant, scores of similar birds took to the air, rising in a noisy cloud. Their plumage was burnished metallic blue, set off by bright yellow beaks and breasts. The flock whirled away, alighting somewhere on the far side of the garden.

Regitus strode on, accustomed to the marvels around him. Barrinalo and Golien were squinting up at the false sun when suddenly Ramanash threw out both arms to halt them.

"What—?" Golien began. Barrinalo followed Ramanash's gaze and saw what alarmed the Fallaji.

Undulating across the path was an enormous serpent. Fully as thick as Barrinalo's thigh, the reptile's black scales had a purplish cast. The snake stopped and lifted its head. To the scribes' horror, the animal's face resembled a woman's. The skin was black and scaly, but the eyes, nose, and mouth were human-shaped.

"What lovely fellows," said the snake, in polished, clipped tones. "Been a long time since any young men came to see me."

None of the scribes said anything. The serpent coiled its long body and slithered closer. Golien stepped back. Fists clenched, Ramanash stood firm. Beside him, Barrinalo also held his ground, fascinated.

"What's the matter? Can't find your tongues?" asked the snake. She flicked her own tongue out to complete the quip. It was not forked, like a normal reptile's; it was long and pink, a travesty of a woman's tongue.

"Let them be, Kyram!" Regitus said sternly. "They're here on the master's business!"

"But they look so sweet!"

The steward struck the ground with his staff. Atop the shaft, the sistrum jangled. The snake-woman called Kyram shrank from the sound.

"All right, all right," she said. "I go, though how a lady's supposed to entertain callers with you around I can't imagine."

"You're not a lady," Regitus snapped. "And you're not to hamper these men in any way. They're scribes, come to record the master's wisdom."

Kyram's tail slid into the ferns. Her unnatural face popped back out, and she said, "The old coot is dying, you know. Soon he'll be gone, and you, my dear Regitus, will no longer be able to abuse his authority. On that day I shall embrace you, coil by coil, and surround

15

you with such affection you'll scarcely be able to breathe—"

"Begone!" thundered the steward, ringing the brass rattle again. With a flick of her tongue, Kyram vanished into the foliage.

Regitus waved them forward. "Pay her no heed. Kyram is not dangerous so long as I have the master's staff."

"Who—or what—is she?" Barrinalo asked.

"A sorceress from the southland who ran afoul of the master. She's been confined here in serpent form ever since."

The sun-globe was nearly over their heads now, signaling their nearness to the center of the pyramid. Over warbling bird calls, Worlight's men could hear falling water. Where the stony path came to an end, a curving wall of water three times a man's height rose up. It curved off in both directions, giving the clear impression of being a circular wall of water. What Barrinalo couldn't fathom was where the water came *from*; it simply appeared in midair and plunged into a circular stone trough on the ground.

Regitus held up his staff, and the wall of water parted. The ground where the water had been cascading an eye blink before was dry.

"Master Pharon," he said simply.

Within the water wall were a set of round stone platforms, each slightly smaller than the last, creating a rising set of steps. The scribes filed slowly in. Above, diaphanous white curtains wafted in a breeze no one felt. Regitus mounted the steps. At the top, he prostrated himself.

"Great Master, the scriveners are here."

There was no audible answer from within the waving curtains. Regitus rose, and with urgent gestures he signaled the men forward.

At the top of the platform (a fair dozen paces across) stood an enormous bed. Almost lost within the cloud-white cushions and quilts was the frail visage of an old man.

Barrinalo studied the aged face. This was the famous mage? He expected Pharon to resemble the wizards he saw on illuminated manuscripts and tavern murals—long white beard, a mane of snowy hair, and an air of ineffable wisdom. The man in bed was bald, and his hollow cheeks were clean shaven. Sunken deep beneath his brow, the old man's eyes were closed. He looked sick and weak, not the least bit powerful.

"You may position yourselves around the bed," Regitus said in a loud whisper. "Be sure to leave a clear path for the attendants to reach the master."

For a long time the only sound heard was the wall of falling water. Then the old man stirred. His liver-colored lips parted, showing yellow teeth, a bit of grayish tongue. He mumbled a few words Barrinalo could not make out. No one else could, either.

"Well?" Regitus said impatiently. "Are you scribes or curious pilgrims?"

Ramanash took charge. He ringed the massive bed with apprentices, who set their copy boards across their laps, sharpened their quills, and opened their ink pots. Each man was to write down what he heard. Later, the journeymen would collate the copies into one compilation. Before the last scribe was in place, Pharon began to speak. His eyes were still shut.

"I always hated Storgard," he said, quite clearly.

No one said anything, so Barrinalo prompted, "Why's that, Master?"

Regitus hissed for silence, but the ancient wizard turned his withered skull ever so slightly toward the sound of the young scribe's voice.

"You can't get good asafetida in Storgard. How was I supposed to make an effective Vapor of Banishment without asafetida?"

Despite the steward's angry glare, Barrinalo responded again.

17

"How do you make the Vapor of Banishment, Master?"

"Foolish question. Didn't the Sorcerers' League teach you how make it in your first term?"

"We're not magicians, Master. We're scribes, come to put your knowledge in writing."

Pharon's voice dropped in volume (but not in timbre), and he replied, "Of fresh asafetida, five scruples, of gum of blue cedar, five scruples, of Muort's Balm a full dram—"

On he went, faintly but clearly, listing the forty-six ingredients in the Vapor of Banishment. The scribes wrote quickly, hands darting from inkwell to scroll as the old man spoke. Sometimes the scratch of so many quills all but drowned out Pharon's voice, but with ten pairs of ears listening, they were able to get the entire recipe.

When he was done reciting the formula, Pharon fell into a light, uneasy sleep. He awoke a short time later and began to cough. Regitus clapped his hands, and two female healers approached from outside the billowing curtains. One pushed the mage upright by his shoulders while the other siphoned a pale green herbal decoction between Pharon's lips. His coughing fit faded.

The women withdrew. After securing Ramanash's permission with a raised eyebrow, Barrinalo followed them out.

"A moment, please!"

The yellow-haired healer paused. "Yes?"

"What can you tell me about the master's condition?"

"He's dying," she answered flatly.

Her bluntness took him aback. "Is there nothing you can do?"

"If the mighty Pharon can't save his own life, how do you expect me to?"

Barrinalo glanced back at the veiled pavilion. "What ails him?"

The healer rubbed her eyes. She had a strong face, sensitive and perceptive. "His principal ill is common ague," she said. "Compounded by fever, distemper, and dropsy." She looked up at the eager scribe. Her eyes were very dark blue. "What's truly killing him is melancholy. Master Pharon is four hundred years old. He's tired of living. When a man gets tired of life, he cares little what happens to him."

Barrinalo couldn't believe it. The most powerful mage in the world was dying because he didn't want to live? How could this be?

* * * * *

The vigil continued. It was a nerve-racking job. For hours the old man might lie motionless, hardly breathing and saying nothing. Then, acting on some internal whim, he would break into an lengthy discourse in mid-sentence, completely confusing his listeners. Ramanash and Golien tried prompting him, as Barrinalo had, but the aged wizard refused to answer anyone but Barrinalo. He acted as if he couldn't even hear the other two journeymen when they spoke.

"What makes you so special?" asked Golien, after Pharon finished describing how to defeat Arenson's Aura spell. "Why does he only answer you?"

"I don't know. Perhaps it's because I spoke to him first."

"Never mind," Ramanash said. He stood, rolling up a filled scroll. "As we shall have to eat in shifts, I'll go now with half of the apprentices."

"I'll dine after you," Golien said quickly.

Barrinalo shrugged. "Suits me."

In fact, Ramanash was gone so long Golien became weak with hunger and hurried away to find (he claimed), a crust of bread to stave off starvation. The remaining apprentices, told to follow

Golien to supper, trooped after him. Barrinalo was alone with Pharon, who'd been murmuring fitfully awhile but saying nothing intelligible.

"Kjeld, you wretch."

The old man's words were clear as crystal. Barrinalo leaned closer. "What was that?"

"Kjeld, you're a heartless wretch. Give me back my beloved."

He wrote the feeble man's words down and said carefully, "Do you mean Kjeld of the Ruby Clan?"

"Yes, yes. Greedy, selfish monster—"

King Kjeld was the greatest hero of the age, a peerless warrior of noble instincts who carved the kingdom of Kjeldor out of the ice-bound anarchy of eastern Terisiare. Barrinalo was startled to hear hostility directed toward so famous a figure.

"Why do you hate him?" he asked.

"He took Sirimiti from me. Sirimiti, the only woman I ever loved."

Pharon? Love? Barrinalo's pen flew. "Tell me of Sirimiti!"

When he was barely halfway through his first century, Pharon met a sorceress named Sirimiti. She was a master of crystalline magic, using natural and artificial stones as focal points for her spells. Ice being water turned to crystal, Sirimiti did well for herself during the age of ice.

She arrived from the north on an enormous sled made of lengths of feldspar, drawn by a team of pure white dire wolves. Having heard tales of the skilled wizards serving King Kjeld, she came south to test the mettle of these favored practitioners of the arcane arts. In short order she bested some of the best-know sorcerers in the land: Sparkfell, Ezni Orimander, Gund the Gemcutter, all tried their hands against her, and all succumbed.

In those days Pharon wasn't prominent at all, just one of many middle-of-the-pack wizards clustered around the font of royal bounty. When the most powerful sorcerers in Kjeld failed to defeat Sirimiti, Pharon saw his chance to advance himself in the eyes of the king.

"I challenged her," said the old wizard in a voice dry as the dust on King Kjeld's tomb. "We met on the Field of High Snow, outside the city wall. The whole city turned out to see us fight."

"And you won? How?"

"The other mages tried to overpower Sirimiti. They were proud men, confident of their power and strength. She had only to deflect their attacks until they were exhausted, then she countered with her own spells. I didn't attack her at all, not overtly. Touched by her handsome face and figure, I caused a rose to blossom at her feet.

"Puzzled, she stamped on it, without harm. Next she tried to pluck it out, but the thorns pricked her. Drops of bright blood stained the snow around the rose vine. When nothing else happened, Sirimiti laughed and prepared to smite me with a withering blast of ice. During the lengthy conjuration I stood patiently, not even preparing a counterspell. Before long, the rose had become a knee-high shrub. Diverted, she formed a block of ice around it, but the growing stems cracked through. Before she could finish her withering blast, the rose bush was waist high and beginning to tangle her legs. Sirimiti ordered her wolves at me, but I had studied animal spells under the great Olasson and tamed them with a word. By then, the thorny shrub had engulfed her up to her armpits."

"A very slow attack!" Barrinalo said, admiring.

"Slow and quiet. That's the way to fight braggarts."

Ramanash could be heard coming back from dinner with his cohort of apprentices. Barrinalo found himself wanting to hear the end of the story before his comrades arrived.

"After the duel, you became friends?" he asked hastily.

"We were lovers for one night." The emaciated old man sighed. When he didn't resume talking, Barrinalo feared he had given up his life, but the thick blue vein in his throat still pulsed feebly.

Ramanash didn't bother softening his voice. "Does he live?"

"Certainly." Barrinalo rose, coiling the scroll in his hand tightly.

"What's that?"

"Court gossip from the time of King Kjeld."

"Put it in the baskets with the others," the Fallaji said brusquely.

He did so, under Ramanash's tireless eye. Annoyed, Barrinalo stalked out of the garden. A liveried servant conducted him to a dining hall deep in the north side of the pyramid, and there he ate his fill of fresh fruit and tender lamb, victuals hard to come by in the cold climate of Kjeldor.

Melancholy, the healer had said. Pharon was tired of life, and it seemed as if everyone around him was eager to help him go. The Sorcerers' League, his peers, were ready to dispense with the man if they could preserve his valuable knowledge—and he, Barrinalo, was helping make it happen.

Something brushed the calf of his leg. Looking down, he saw Kyram's scaly hide go sliding by. Barrinalo jumped up, which made the snake-woman chuckle in a hissing, reptilian sort of way.

Her human-featured head popped up very suddenly across the stone table. "Hello."

He fought down an urge to move away from her. "Ah, Lady Kyram. Are you well?"

" 'Lady'—I like that! Yes, I am well, scribbler. What is in your mind?"

He choked a little. "Regitus told us you were a woman, transformed by one of Master Pharon's spells."

More of her heavy coils piled up on the table top. Kyram plainly enjoyed the young scribe's attention.

"It's true, I was once human," she said. "But I'm not Pharon's prisoner." She flicked her human tongue at him, and he could not suppress a shudder.

"Were you not bested in magical combat by the master?" he asked carefully.

"Long ago. I do not bear Pharon any ill will. He could have slain me, but didn't. I have this beautiful garden to live in, and all the rabbits and lambs I can eat—"

Barrinalo frowned. "Do you like being a serpent?"

"It has its diverting moments." Long eyelashes batted against black scales. "Why so many questions, my sweet?"

He shrugged, glancing around to see if anyone else was in earshot. "Just curious," he said. "The master told me a story about another sorceress whom he defeated but did not harm. He has a weakness for female magicians it seems."

"Not always. There is one he would gladly consign to the abyss—"

Before he could hear more, a servant appeared, bearing Ramanash's command to rejoin the scribes. Barrinalo said a hasty farewell and hurried away. Kyram watched him go wistfully.

"Seek me out again," she said. "Just call my name. I'm always about."

* * * * *

Three days passed. A weird cycle set in, a routine without regular hours. Under Pharon's artificial sun, there was no day or night. The unending light played havoc with the scribes' concentration. Some began falling asleep in mid-sentence, nodding off until their noses rubbed the fresh ink on the page.

Alone among his colleagues, Barrinalo remained immune to fatigue. The atmosphere in the pyramid garden seemed to invigorate him, and he worked longer hours and made better copies than anyone else. He began to look forward to the wee hours of the morning, when Golien was snoring at his board, and Ramanash muttered and twitched through dreams of his far-off desert homeland. When the others were asleep, Barrinalo asked Pharon to speak of his lost love, Sirimiti, and his centuries-old resentment of the great Kjeld.

"Why did the king force you to renounce Sirimiti?" Barrinalo asked.

"Hard to serve two masters," the fading mage said. "Liege lord or Love—whom did I serve? That's what he said to me."

"Sirimiti would not bow down to him?"

"She owed allegiance to no one."

"Then why didn't you go away with her?"

Pharon let out one of those disturbingly long, rattling sighs that sounded like the death-rattle of a lesser man.

"Stubborn. Stupid. Thought my place was here, at the king's side. Kjeld made me choose, and I made the wrong choice."

Curtained by falling water. Barrinalo looked around. No one else was awake.

"Why didn't you use your power to change Kjeld's mind?" he whispered.

"I couldn't. Wrong . . ."

"But you had the power, the knowledge—"

Pharon's eyes snapped open. All this time, through the spells, reminiscences, and gossip he'd related, his sunken eyes remained closed. Barrinalo had come to think of him as a blind man, sightless, perhaps eyeless.

He had eyes, of a sort.

Set in the old man's sockets were two orbs of polished black onyx, with stylized pupils inlaid in gold on them. The starkly false organs staring out of the wizard's blanched face horrified Barrinalo. Unthinking, he rose to his feet. His writing board fell to the stone floor with a loud clatter.

Ramanash grunted and stirred. "What it?" he said, forgetting proper Kjeldor speech in his sleepy state.

Golien likewise awoke. He scrubbed an ink-stained hand over his puffy face and opened his eyes. Seeing Pharon's eyelids raised, he let out a strangled cry.

"I had the power to destroy everything," Pharon intoned. "The great spell by which Urza destroyed Argoth, I found it! I speak of Obliteration. This is the Blare of Doom."

"W-What?" Golien stuttered.

For the first time Pharon acknowledged another voice. "A most powerful spell of destruction. It begins thus—with the blood of a black rooster, first describe a circle whose radius is exactly equal to the standing height of the operating sorcerer. Next—"

Ramanash recovered first, straightening his half-filled scroll and reaching for a quill. It was worn and dull, so he fell to sharpening it.

"Barrinalo! Golien! Don't just stand there, take down the master's words!" he cried.

"—inscribed with the names of the fifteen mighty elementals, Dalath, Sussurion, Penkiron Olubo, Myacanolor—"

"Did he say 'Sass-urion or Suss-surion'?" asked Golien, scribbling frantically.

"I heard 'Su-surion,' " said Barrinalo.

"Don't talk while transcribing! You'll only confuse yourselves. Write!" Ramanash snapped.

"—Tishanduras, Alalal Zati, Kufu, Hancoray—"

The commotion woke the apprentices. Upon seeing Pharon's

eyes, three of them fled, yelping for mercy. The rest were rooted where they stood, too paralyzed to move.

"What are you gawking at?" Ramanash thundered. "Get writing, or do you want to feel my cane?"

"The slightest error in placement of the hierarchy of elementals will incur the wrath of them all," the wizard went on mechanically. "Each mighty spirit has its own propitiating offering, which must be placed in the proper niche before the blood-ink name of the spirit. For Dalath, seven eyes of a yellow tree frog. For Sussurion, a puppet sewn of yellow silk, stuffed with acorns. For Penkiron, the skull of a man, painted with the sigils of his celestial realm. The sigils are drawn as follows . . ."

On and on the old man went, in stupefying detail. Hours passed, and the preparations for the terrible Blare of Doom were still not fully described. Morning arrived outside the pyramid—the scribes knew because Regitus returned and announced it. When he saw Pharon had his eyes open, the steward fell to his knees.

"May the gods preserve us!" he said, trembling. "The master hasn't opened his eyes in twenty-two years!"

"Can he see with those things?" Barrinalo asked.

"To the ends of the world! He searches for—her."

The young scribe didn't need to be told who Pharon was looking for. "Does she live?"

Regitus, all pomposity lost, prostrated himself on his face and moaned. "My great master is truly dying!" he said. "All is lost! What will become of this house, of me?" He started to weep.

"Please, I cannot hear!" Ramanash complained.

"Did he say 'worthless' or 'birthless?'" Golien asked frantically.

"*Still the sounds of grief!*"

The simple command, forcefully stated by the mage, quieted the room and struck Regitus instantly dumb.

Pharon turned his black orbs toward Barrinalo. Like a bard returning to a written text, he resumed his recitation of the obliterate spell.

"The offering for Omzatta is a ruby ring on a band of purest gold. The offering for Gahadron is a brazen knife in the Tocasian pattern, with a black leather-wrapped handle . . ."

Clutching his throat, Regitus fled.

The old man's description of the fantastically elaborate preparations continued. Scrolls were filled, cast aside, and new ones begun. Ramanash ordered one apprentice to do nothing but refill his colleagues' ink pots, so they could keep writing. A second youth was detailed to sharpen quills and distribute ready parchment to those writing.

In the midst of relating how the operating magician must purify himself, Pharon broke off the torrent of technical instructions to say with considerable anguish, "I am alone!"

All quills stopped scratching. Barrinalo said gently, "Your loyal scribes are here, Master."

"I cannot find her. She is gone."

"What does he mean?" Golien said feverishly.

The old man's chin rose, drawing the colorless skin of his throat taut. Black beads formed at the corners of Pharon's eyes. One fell to the floor at Barrinalo's feet. It was a tear—a tear of solid onyx.

Voice choked with grief, Pharon resumed, "The magus must bathe each morning for seven days in a purifying bath. Combine oil of roses, ten drams, oil of xissa, four drams, sea salt, six scruples, ambergris and musk, one scruple each . . ."

* * * * *

The scribes didn't know until later that Regitus had fled his master's house. Once outside, the injunction on his voice vanished, and he proclaimed his despair to everyone in earshot. Before long, armed guards appeared and took him away. They took him not to the palace but to a hall of the Sorcerers' League, where he was closeted with Dame Sikrid Veger, her secretary Cackluster, Harvald the Necromant, and other leaders of the order. When Regitus returned to Pharon's house a few hours later, a delegation of sorcerers came with him.

Barrinalo found them in the garden antechamber, where full scrolls were being stored. Dame Veger and Cackluster were rummaging through the curling parchment, perusing any documents that caught their eye.

"How goes it, journeyman?" Cackluster said.

"It goes. He is still dictating a very long spell."

"What spell is that?" Dame Veger said. She was a stout woman, shaped like a bell, with hair colored yellow by alchemical means.

"He calls it Obliterate, or the Blare of Doom."

A scroll fell from Cackluster's hand. "By all the gods," he breathed. "I never dared hope he would reveal *that* one!"

"Is it good?" asked Dame Veger.

"It is horrible." Ignoring the layman Barrinalo, he said, "The Blare of Doom creates a monstrous fireball that devours every living thing it touches. It's fed by the heat of life itself, so the more living souls it consumes, the stronger it is. The mighty Urza Planeswalker used the spell to defeat his brother Mishra and crack Argoth in twain!"

"Really, the very spell?" Dame Veger purred. "I didn't know old Pharon knew it."

"It's very dangerous! I wonder if Pharon has ever performed it himself?" Cackluster knitted his narrow white brows. "There was the thunderbolt that destroyed the armies of the rebel Kazontas, in the reign of Darien the First—"

"Is there any defense against it?"

"If there is one, only Pharon knows." Color came to Cackluster's dust-hued face. "The rest of the league must be told of this. If we can archive the Blare of Doom, it will change everything! We can negotiate with sovereigns as equals—superiors! We can claim a territory for our own!" The sorcerer's head swam with dreams of temporal power. "I will summon the membership!"

He hurried out. Barrinalo quietly resumed numbering the most recently filled scrolls. Dame Veger watched him.

"Scribe."

"Lady?"

"How many rolls have you filled so far?"

He told the truth. "About two hundred, lady."

"And how many sheets has the Blare of Doom taken up?"

"He hasn't finished yet, but so far, nine full scrolls," Barrinalo said.

She advanced until she stood over him, a perfumed mountain of velvet. "I want that spell," she said baldly.

"Lady, it would be worth my life."

"Don't be so hasty. I'm not asking you to die. As elected chief of the league, I'll have access to the complete manuscript, but those other dotards don't deserve such power. I want you to switch one of the sheets for a facsimile, one that leaves out a few vital details. Deliver the true page to me, and I will reward you greatly."

"I cannot, Dame Veger. My oath as a scribe—"

She turned away, switching the hem of her long skirt in vexation. "What is an oath compared to the largess I can bestow on you? Do you crave gold, scribe? I can give you double your weight of it. Do you dream of the admiration of women? With an amulet of my making, you can have your pick of lovers for the rest of your life. All for a single scrap of parchment!"

When he didn't answer, Dame Veger's black eyes narrowed,

and she smiled. "Power, too, can be yours. Would you like to take over Worlight's house? Or do you desire someone's death? Such things can be arranged so that no one suspects the true cause."

He knew a veiled threat when he heard one. Dame Veger was an accomplished magician, and he would not long survive her wrath. Being a humble journeyman, he had no means to hire a more powerful wizard to hold off her machinations. Still, he hated to see Pharon's power handed over to so unworthy a successor. And he had no assurance Dame Veger wouldn't kill him anyway, after he provided her with the key document.

There had to be a third way, to preserve his life and honor, and not betray Pharon. There had to be a way!

Not wishing to bring destruction on his master or comrades, he said carefully, "It could be done as you suggest. A single sheet, an altered line or two."

"Nothing an experienced sorcerer would notice, mind you!"

Barrinalo shook his head. "I understand what the lady wants. A page near the end, when most of the work is done, would be the easiest to alter—"

Just then Golien puffed in, followed by two sweating apprentices. "Barrinalo, where've you been? Ramanash is screaming for you. Scrolls are piling up around the magus's bed in drifts!"

"I'm just coming." Slipping past Dame Veger, they exchanged a significant look. Barrinalo nodded grimly and hurried on his way.

* * * * *

The great wizard stopped speaking just before midnight. His voice faded away into a sigh, and his eyelids closed over the black stone orbs in his sockets. A bit of down placed on his upper lip fluttered as he drew in slow, shallow breaths, but the end was near.

Like a guttering candle, the life in Pharon's body was about to depart forever.

Worlight had joined the crowd of magicians in the outer rooms of the pyramid, anxiously awaiting the end. He undertook an index of the scrolls gathered so far, culling out the historical and personal from those containing gems of Pharon's magical knowledge. Sorcerers from all over the kingdom stood over Worlight's shoulder, hoping to glean valuable tidbits from the dying master. They lounged in the halls of Pharon's home, drinking his wine and gobbling his food.

Barrinalo was disgusted. None of the wizard's colleagues showed the slightest sadness over the great man's imminent demise. Only Pharon's household servants were genuinely distressed, from Regitus and the human staff down to the green leaf-children in the garden.

"That's it, that's all," Worlight announced, tidying the last scroll on his lap. "Three hundred nineteen sheets in all."

"What about the Blare of Doom?" said Cackluster. His face looked waxen in the massed candlelight. "Did he finish it?"

"I think not," Worlight said. He scanned the last lines of the last foolscap sheet. "It just breaks off here."

"Blast it!"

"Filthy old mountebank!"

"Wretch—that's like him, to die without revealing his best secret!"

Barrinalo had to get out, get away from the scurrilous vultures. He stalked out of the room, ignoring Worlight, who tried to call him back.

He went straight to Pharon's bedside and slumped down, left arm propped up on the mattress. The shriveled old man under the sheets seemed already a corpse.

Barrinalo's head lolled. He was bone-weary after four days' work and little sleep. Once his eyes closed, he heard voices nearby— a female one, laughing lightly, and a solid, masculine one. Were

31

the callous sorcerers loitering in the master's very bedchamber now? Furious, he sought out the intruders.

He didn't have to look far. Just beyond the billowing gauze curtains, he spotted a voluptuous woman in an iridescent black robe, conversing with a tall man in white. He stormed over, ready to eject them, magic or no magic.

"Hello, young man," said the woman.

He paused in mid-stride, confused. Something about her was familiar, though he did not know her on sight. The man with her was . . . was . . .

"That's right," she said. "Meet Master Pharon as he once was."

It was him, with normal human eyes. Barrinalo stumbled forward a few steps then put his face to the garden floor. "Your Excellency!"

"Rise, good scribe. We've conversed long enough to be able to look each other in the eye, don't you think?"

The handsome lady helped him stand. "You are—?" asked Barrinalo.

"Kyram." She flicked her tongue out to remind him. "Remember?"

He nodded dumbly. "Has this all been a ruse, then? You seem well, Master!"

Pharon shook his head. He looked much like the figure in the bed, only fuller in the face. A closely trimmed beard covered his flat chin, and tightly curled white hair bloomed beneath a red silk skullcap.

"I am still the fading body in the bed. What you see now is my poor spirit, rendered visible before I depart forever," he said.

"And you, lady? Are you still a snake?"

"Not a bit." She looped his arm in hers and snuggled against him. "Pharon was kind enough to restore me to human shape before leaving. I am all woman again!" Her brow wrinkled a bit. "Though I still have a craving for live rats. . . ."

32

"Master," Barrinalo said, "if you have the power, don't die! Your fellow wizards are waiting outside, biding their time until you pass away. They care nothing about you—all they covet is your knowledge!"

Pharon laid a hand on the young man's shoulder. It felt solid and real, like anyone's hand. "I know. I foresaw this many years ago. I even saw you, Barrinalo. Why else do you think I spoke to you, of all your comrades?"

Bewildered, Barrinalo said, "What's going to happen?"

"We shall finish recording the Blare of Doom. Then you will deliver a portion of the text to Dame Veger, as promised."

"I cannot! She will use the obliteration spell to conquer the world!"

Pharon's shade smiled. "And how long have I ruled the world? The Blare of Doom does not make a god of its user. It can only be performed at great expense and terrible danger."

"Then why does the league value it so much?"

"They see it as a sword that can cleave through any armor. What they don't realize is how cold-hearted you must be to wield it. To ignite the soul-fire, there has to be a trigger, a living being who will be consumed first, as tinder lights a greater flame. If not performed properly, the Obliterate spell will consume the summoning magician as its first victim."

The mage's spirit bade Barrinalo get pen and parchment. The scribe sat down on the steps of the bed platform and waited for the final key to the Blare of Doom.

"I spoke to you for another reason," spirit-Pharon said. "You shall be my successor."

Kyram clapped her hands in delight.

"Who, me? I'm no wizard!" Barrinalo exclaimed.

"You have wit and talent, and you also have the power within you. I can see it clearly. You are marked for greatness, my boy."

"But I know nothing! The wizards of the league will have me for dinner if I try to claim your legacy!"

The hale figure of Pharon dimmed, like dyed cloth fading in strong sunlight. "You will have to start anew elsewhere and live modestly until you master the basic techniques of thaumaturgy. The league will forget you, and your master Worlight will scorn you as a failed scribe." Pharon dimmed further, extremities turning to wisps of vapor. "Your future lies far away in time and place, on an island in midst of the blue sea. . . ."

The specter vanished, and behind the curtains, the failing body of the great mage was tortured with fits of coughing.

"Stay out of sight!" he snapped at Kyram. For once she did not fling a double-meaning phrase back at him but slipped into the greenery with all the grace of her former serpentine self.

Worlight, Ramanash, Golien, all the apprentices, and a swarm of sorcerers burst onto the scene. Pharon was gasping words under his breath. Barrinalo climbed onto the broad bed beside the dying man and put his ear to Pharon's lips.

Worlight himself stood at Barrinalo's elbow. "He says, 'the operative sorcerer can be protected . . . from the soul-fire . . . by the following means.' " Worlight wrote with smooth efficiency, despite the pressure of the moment.

Barrinalo continued his translation, " 'On a disk of electrum, that is equal parts gold and silver, in the weight of forty-two drams, inscribe the following sigils. Obverse—the sign of Adarkar. On the reverse—' "

Worlight's pen went dry. He dipped it in the pot mounted on the lap table, and it came out empty.

"Ink!" he cried.

Ramanash and Golien scrambled around the breathless magicians, searching for a pot with ink in it. The apprentices joined in.

"There is no ink!" one of the youths shouted.

"Worlight, is this a joke?" Cackluster demanded.

"Certainly not! You, all of you!" He pointed to his scribes. "Fetch more ink! Try any shop in the city. Buy ink! Borrow ink! Steal ink! But hurry!"

The scribes boiled out of the garden. Worlight, brow sheened with sweat, turned to the sorcerers.

"Can any of you conjure up some ink?"

Harvald the Necromant fingered the sapphire stud in his earlobe. "I know a spell to impress words on stone but not to make common ink."

"You have a cantrip to make letters of fire, as I recall," Cackluster said to a red-bearded wizard clad in beaver fur robes.

"That's no good," Dame Veger said dryly. "Fiery letters would set the parchment alight."

The sorcerers fell to berating each other as worthless and ignorant for not having the means to conjure up a dram of ink. Some of them came to blows, others invoked warts and blemishes on the faces of their antagonists. Arkum Arenson, a master of snow calling, was winding up his hands to bring forth a blizzard on his colleagues when Dame Veger used her pendant of office to disperse the petty enchantments whizzing about the vast room.

"This is unseemly!" she scolded them. "Be quiet, if you can't be respectful!"

All through this hurly-burly, Pharon's lips never ceased to move. Barrinalo listened and did something no good scribe ever did: he committed what he heard to memory.

* * * * *

It was the longest half-hour anyone could ever remember. At last Golien appeared, flushed and panting, with a vial of red ink in his pudgy fist.

"I found it at the mapmaker's! No one else had a drop of black ink, not in all Kjeld!" he crowed.

"Shut up, and bring it here!" Worlight commanded.

"It doesn't matter," Barrinalo said calmly. "Master Pharon is dead."

"What? No!"

Cackluster and Worlight stood on either side, listening to the gaunt old man's chest and holding feathers under his nose, to no avail.

"Well, that's it." Worlight sagged to the floor. "Someone must go to the palace. The king must be told."

"You go," Dame Veger told Cackluster. "The king does not like my face."

The sorcerers filed slowly out. As they went, the sun-globe overhead dimmed from hot yellow to warm orange. Without Pharon to power it, it would soon fall to cherry red, then to final darkness.

"Harvald should summon old Pharon from the dead," said one of the wizards.

The necromancer replied, "Won't do any good. Even dead, he's too powerful for me to command. He wouldn't even show up when I call him, much less answer questions."

Last in the pack of dejected magicians was Dame Veger. She looked back at Worlight and Barrinalo, still at the bed. When the master scribe wasn't paying attention, she caught Barrinalo's eye. Raising her right hand, she tapped an index finger against her forehead.

Good thinking? or *I'll drive you mad?* Barrinalo wasn't sure of her meaning.

"Barrinalo."

Worlight was still sitting on the floor, surrounded by upset writing tables, broken quills, and dried-up inkpots.

"You're through, Barrinalo."

"Sir?"

The master of the House of Letters slowly stood. "You're no longer employed by my house!"

"But Master Worlight—"

He held up his hand, nostrils flaring. "No! That's it, you're done! I've never failed in a commission in all my life till now. To run out of ink at such a critical moment—it's an unforgivable disgrace!"

"Ramanash was in charge of supplies."

"Don't lay off blame elsewhere! I heard how the master favored you over the others. Well, that makes it your failure. Do not show your face at my house again!" He snatched the unfinished manuscript from Barrinalo's hand.

Being dismissed didn't hurt nearly as much as he once thought it might. Alone in the darkening garden, Barrinalo covered the dead wizard's face with the fine linen sheet. As he walked down the steps through the now-still curtains, he saw the denizens of the garden gathering to pay their last respects to their master. Besides the green-skinned little folk, he saw stumpy creatures covered with brown, warty bark, and slender gray bipeds the color and texture of mushrooms, with scarlet ruffs around their necks. In threes and fours, the strange little creatures climbed the steps and surrounded the body of their creator, saying nothing but demonstrating their respect with every bowed head and clasped hand, no matter what the color or texture.

Their grief was interrupted when Dame Veger appeared. She picked up one of Pharon's gardeners in each hand, lip curling with distaste.

"When I move in here, you insects will have to go," she sneered. She threw the squirming creatures to the ground.

"They can't live outside in the cold!" Kyram emerged from the greenery. Leaf-children clung to her legs, eyeing the mistress of the Sorcerers' League with evident fear.

"You're out too, snake-girl," Dame Veger said. She gestured, and a coating of frost engulfed Kyram and Pharon's creatures. A sorceress herself, Kyram shrugged off the spell, but the little hothouse denizens of the garden collapsed, stricken with cold.

Barrinalo ran down the steps and interposed himself between Dame Veger and Kyram.

"That's enough!" he said. The stout magician opened her fingers to make another esoteric gesture, and his heart raced.

"No," Dame Veger said. "I won't harm you. We have business to conduct, do we not?"

"Later," said Barrinalo. "I will see you later."

Laughing, Dame Veger turned away. As she walked away, she withered Pharon's flowers with cold spells, leaving a path of dying vegetation all the way out of the darkening pyramid garden.

"Thank you," Kyram said, "but beware. The lady is not to be trifled with."

With dead garden-sprites at his feet, Barrinalo knew the truth of it. "Come," he said. "I must leave Kjeldor, but before I go, I need your help."

"Anything for a brave young man," Kyram vowed.

* * * * *

Dressed in traveler's furs and leading a laden pack mule, Barrinalo tramped along the snowy street. A hundred paces in front of the city gate, two hulking figures barred his way. He took one look at their vacant eyes, bulging muscles, and protruding fangs, and he stopped without a fuss. One of the monsters extended a broad paw. Down a side lane, a coach stood waiting. Barrinalo went where he was bade.

Inside the warm interior, Dame Veger sat, her ample lap covered by a handsome fox-fur rug. A mug of cider steamed beside her.

When Barrinalo opened the coach door, she urged him to enter quickly and shut out the cold.

"Lady," he said, easing into the seat facing her.

"I summoned you from the House of Letters," she said. "Why did you not come?"

"I don't work there any more," Barrinalo replied.

"I believe you have something for me," she said, sipping her hot cider.

He reflected on the beasts outside and loosened the woolen scarf at his neck. From inside his coat he pulled out a flattened cylinder of white parchment.

"Is that it?"

"This is the end of the ritual," he said. "I wrote it from memory."

She smoothed out the document. "Lovely hand," she remarked. "Very legible." Barrinalo frowned. "Oh, your pardon!" she said insincerely. "I forgot, you're no longer a scribe."

Dame Veger read the twenty lines or so of text, nodded, then rolled up the parchment.

"About my payment," Barrinalo said. "Since my exile begins today, I'll take it in gold."

She tugged a suede purse from her bosom and tossed it carelessly in his lap. Like any tradesman, he opened the neck of the bag and counted the coins within.

"Twenty crowns? You mentioned twice my weight in gold."

"That was talk. This is coin of the realm. If you wish to haggle, my servants will be glad to listen." She gestured with one soft hand to the door where her creatures waited.

"No haggling," he said sourly. "I guess I should be grateful I'm not getting a knife in the ribs."

He stood, stooping under the coach's low roof. "Good-bye, lady. Perhaps one day we'll cross paths again."

"Unlikely," said Dame Veger. "Try to keep warm, won't you?"

He stepped out into a fresh snow flurry. Taking his pack mule's bridle from one of Veger's monsters, Barrinalo put his back to the wind and made for the open city gate.

He entered the guard's box. The soldier on duty, a white-haired oldster with a flowing mustache, hailed him kindly and asked him to sign his name to the day book.

"All folks leaving or entering must be recorded," said the guard. "If you can't write, just make a mark and tell me your name."

"I can write."

He dipped the dull, dirty quill in the inkpot and began his name: B-A-R-R-I-N—when he finished the 'n' the nib went dry. He dipped it again, but the pot was out of ink.

"Sorry, sir! I'll get some fresh for you!" the guard said.

"No need. I'm finished." So he had a new name to go with his new life.

* * * * *

One night, eight days out of Kjeld, he saw a bright glow light up the northern horizon, the way he'd come. Seeing the strange aurora, Barrin took a second roll of parchment from his left sleeve. Reading Pharon's true last words by the unnatural halo, he was impressed to discover that reversing the sigils on the protective amulet could produce such a dramatic effect.

The soul-fire needed tinder to start, the old master had said. Barrin hoped Dame Veger was enjoying the warmth.

Song for the Plague Rats
Philip Athans

She touched her mother on the shoulder, where there was a small patch of smooth, pale skin not twisted and puckered by one of the hideous sores. Her mother twitched and drew in a shuddering breath that hissed past rotting teeth and rattled into a throat choked with phlegm. The attempt at a deep breath made her cough, sending tendrils of infectious gray mucous whipping out of her mouth to slap down onto her sunken cheek. It glowed in the dwindling light of the hearthfire like a spiderweb. The girl knew not to wipe it away, not to touch it. She held her breath for fear that any of the spittle was in the air around her.

Her mother's coughing subsided, and the girl took her hand from the dying woman's shoulder. She reached into the little washbasin and folded her small, thin fingers around the rag she'd left soaking there. She could wipe the sweat from her mother's forehead, but would that carry the plague too? If it did, the infection would be in the basin water already.

Her mother hadn't looked at her in seven days. All she could do was lie in bed, sweating and coughing, her face occasionally twisting into a grimace of pain. She couldn't eat, but the girl and her father would force cups of tea and broth down her throat. They made her drink water, and they tried to keep her clean. Still, her mother, the bed, the room, the whole house, reeked of infection, bile, sweat, and hopelessness.

"I'll be right there," her mother whispered.

The girl looked up at the sunken ruin of her mother's face, but she already knew that the woman wasn't speaking to her. She would just say things sometimes, things that made no sense. She didn't respond to anything anyone else said. It was as if she was trapped somehow in her own disease-ravaged body, her mind locked in the shell of her skull, living a life all its own, in a world all its own, because what was left of her real life was too horrible to understand anymore.

At least, that's what the little girl hoped was true.

"There's seven of them," her mother muttered.

"Sleep, Mama," answered the girl.

One of her mother's eyelids flickered open, and the girl gasped. Her hand froze around the wet rag, and her skin crawled. Her mother looked up, and for the first time in so long their eyes actually met. Her mother's mouth opened, her lips seemed to tap together.

"Mama," the little girl whispered.

A tear traced a slow path along the side of her mother's face, and she managed to squeak out one single word. "Rats."

The word seemed to hang in the air between the girl and her

mother. It was spoken without the slightest inflection, without malice, anger, or fear. It was just the simple statement, the plain truth, the one word: rats.

The little girl nodded, then began to cry. Her mother was still looking at her when she died. Her eyes just went flat, and she emptied out somehow, right there in front of the little girl. Her last breath drifted out lazily, taking a long time, as if the air was leaking out. The little girl sat there crying, her hand still holding the wet rag, still soaking in the diseased water.

She heard a sound behind her. Thinking it must be her father, she turned around. In the far corner of the room, a rat as big as the little girl's head scurried along the wall, looking furtively around as if it was lost. The little girl's jaw tightened at the sight of it. They were in the house. They never came into the house, not while the fire was burning and people were there. The rats used to be afraid of people, but that was weeks ago, the rest of the lives of almost everyone in the village ago. No one knew how, but the rats had brought the plague. Maybe the plague had brought the rats, but everyone remembered seeing more rats, then more, then people started getting sick, and when they got sick, they died. Every one of them, every time.

The little girl threw the soaking wet rag at the big, black-gray rat. The rag hit the wall, missing the rat by nearly a foot. It looked up at her with pinpoint, dead black eyes, and it sniffed the air. The little girl shuddered at the thought that the rat was remembering what she smelled like, so it would know who to punish when it came back late in the night when she would be asleep no matter how hard she tried to stay awake.

The little girl swallowed, and that seemed to satisfy the rat. It turned away and scampered off, disappearing behind the old oak cabinet where they kept the flour.

Her father came in, and she looked up at him. His face was drawn and tired. His eyes were almost as dull as the corpse lying on her mother's bed. The little girl was crying, and he looked at her, then at his wife.

The little girl closed her eyes, certain her father would know what to do.

* * * * *

The girl looked up the hill at the castle. Framed against the blank gray overcast sky, it looked black. It was an ugly building, just a huge rectangle with straight sides. Battlements made the top look like an old man's teeth sunk into the sky. There were no windows until the top third of the structure. From the cemetery, the girl couldn't see the big arched doors that were the only way in or out of it. She could see a light in one window, maybe the baron's own bedchamber. He might have been sitting down to dinner as the sky darkened over the castle on the hill and the dying village beneath it he cared so little about.

She felt a hand on her shoulder and knew without looking up that it was her father. He pushed her gently in the direction of the winding gravel path that would take them back to the village. She shook her head and turned back to her mother's grave.

They had piled rocks over her. The soil all around the town was dry and rocky. Her father had explained to her that the farmers needed every bit of tillable land to keep them all fed. Land that was fit to bury someone on couldn't be wasted on a cemetery.

If she looked carefully, she could see her mother's right hand through spaces in the rocks. The long, thin fingers were the same gray color as the unhealthy sky.

Her father took his hand from her shoulder and turned away

from her. Tears streamed down her face as she listened to his footsteps join those of the other surviving villagers as they scuffled down the path, going home from the sixtieth funeral in fifty days.

She stared at that strip of her mother's flesh that was denied the privacy of the grave for a long time, long enough for the footsteps of the adults to fade away completely. All around her was the silence of the graveyard that had grown four times in size in the past month and a half. A scratching sound startled her, and she hugged her arms close around her body. Bumps broke out on her arms, and her teeth began to chatter.

The rats had waited for the adults to leave before coming. She could hear more of them than she could see, and she could see a lot of them, maybe a dozen. They were circling, sticking their pointed noses up into the air and twitching their tails. They could smell her mother, already rotting in her shallow grave. The little girl felt rooted to the spot, unable to go home for fear that her presence was the only thing keeping the rats away from her mother's hand.

She spared a glance back up the hill, and the castle seemed even blacker, the light in that lone window more mockingly warm. There was a man up there whom she had never seen, who never came out of his tomblike castle, but who was supposed to be taking care of them. The village, all the land around it, even the farm her father worked, belonged to the baron. The cemetery itself was on his land, and the entire village lived and worked at his sufferance. They planted and harvested his crops and traded his goods, but when the rats came, he did nothing. When the first signs of the plague made themselves known, he still did nothing. He stayed in his castle when more rats, then more and more came. He didn't seem to care when people started to die.

"Was she your mother?" a voice asked her, and she gasped at the sudden sound.

It was a little boy, sitting on the short stone wall at the edge of the cemetery. He was almost close enough that the girl could have reached out and touched him, but she hadn't seen or heard him approach. He was an odd-looking boy, if for no other reason than she had never seen him before. She knew everyone in the village, and everyone knew her.

"I'm sorry," the boy said. His voice was surprisingly deep for such a little boy. He was no taller and looked no older than her. "If that's your mother, I mean."

He was dressed all in black, in a coat and breeches the little girl had heard called a "suit." His clothes were remarkably clean, as were his face and his tiny little hands. His hair, which was a bright, healthy shade of brown, was flattened to his head and was very precisely combed. It looked like he might have put some kind of grease or oil in it. His eyes were almost black, and the sight of them made the little girl shiver. He was looking at her as if he was waiting for an answer.

"My . . . my mother," the girl said.

"I'm sorry," said the boy. His accent was as strange as his clothes. He seemed to speak words slowly, clearly, and one at a time, though his speech came as quickly as anyone else's. "Was it the rats?"

The little girl nodded.

"It's true then," the boy said, glancing around the ground under him, his eyes settling on the bloated gray rats that were succeeding in mustering their courage enough to either approach the grave or swarm over both of the children. "It's true that the village is overcome with plague rats."

The girl nodded again, standing her ground, trying valiantly to ignore the rats and concentrate on the strange boy.

"You're not from the village," she said, unsure why the mere presence of the boy was taking so much of the anxiety out of her.

The little boy chuckled lightly and said, "No, I'm not from the village, *per se*."

The little girl had no idea what "*per se*" meant, but she had come away with all the important information.

"Then what are you doing here?" the girl asked the strange boy. "How did you know my mother?"

The little boy stayed seated on the low wall. Behind him rose the utilitarian block of the baron's castle.

"I didn't know your mother, I'm afraid," the boy said. "What I'm doing here . . . well, I've never been to a funeral."

The little girl took a step closer to the boy. He reacted to her with a surprised, wide-eyed stare. She heard something and realized he was looking over her shoulder. Turning around, she watched as an enormous rat scrambled up behind her.

"They didn't used to bite," the boy said. "Are they biting?"

The girl shrugged. The rats were biting them but not too often.

"Don't you know the song?" the boy asked.

"The song?" the little girl asked. "A song about rats?"

The little boy smiled, and the girl almost had to turn her head away, his teeth were so bright.

"There's a song," he said. "It's a very old song, but not everyone can sing it. It's a simple tune, but the power it has over others—especially if those others are rats . . ."

"What do you mean?" she asked.

The little boy smiled again and said, "Do you believe in magic?"

Her mother had told her stories, as had some of the other children. She didn't remember if the stories were supposed to be true or not.

"The song is a magic song," the boy said, not waiting long

enough for her to answer. "If you sing it, the rats will do what you tell them to do."

"Will you teach it to me?" she asked, making the decision to ask at the same time she was actually asking the question.

The boy's smile widened. He held out a clean, soft hand, and said, "I can sing it for you, but I'll have to whisper it in your ear. Are you sure you want to hear it?"

As if on cue there was a clattering of falling stones. A big, black rat with open sores running along its left flank was standing on the little girl's mother's grave. She shuddered and went to the boy, taking his warm hand in hers and tipping her head, so her right ear was only inches from his lips.

* * * * *

She couldn't sleep the night after the funeral, but she couldn't leave her bed. She had nowhere to go and no one to talk to. Her father spent most of the night in the outhouse. At first she thought he was in there crying, so she wouldn't see him. She hoped that was true, anyway. She hoped he didn't have the stomach cramps and the loose stool, the sores under his arms and between his legs that meant she would be alone. He had been scratching under his arms and walking with his feet close together for a few days, though, so when she heard him groan loudly, and when the smell came all the way from the outhouse and through her bedroom window, she knew.

In the darkness of her tiny little bedroom, she kept her eyes closed tightly, hoping she would just fall asleep. She tried to ignore the sounds all around her. Sound traveled differently at night, and the noises were at once frightening and irresistible. She could hear her father in the outhouse. He was crying after all, but she couldn't be sure if he was crying for her mother or for himself.

She could hear the neighbors speaking in hushed tones about leaving town, leaving the plague far behind. The lady was afraid no other village would take them. The man was afraid he'd never find work.

She heard the dense, humid breeze push its way through the dry trees, and she listened to the rats.

They were outside the house, and in the woodpile. Rats surrounded the outhouse, and were wandering the narrow, deserted streets. They were on the roof, and in the cellar. They were in the walls, and they were in her room. She could hear at least two of them under her bed.

She opened her eyes when the sky flashed. The shutters were closed, and the moon was blocked by dense black clouds. The lightning was like the sun blinking open its eyes as it fought off sleep. The little girl sat up in her bed. The window was on the wall just next to her. She'd insisted on putting the bed up against the wall under the window even though she sometimes got rained on or caught a chill in the night. She flipped up the catch on the shutters and swung them open with a grinding squeak.

The massive black outline of the castle rose in the distance, with a tangle of twisted, dying trees ringing its base. The sky flashed brightly, making the girl blink, but the lightning was still far off. The thunder that came after it was a distant rumbling that seemed to come from the castle, as if the building were growling.

She didn't know what made her go outside, but she did. Even though there were rats under her bed, scurrying around her feet, and staring at her from the corners of her bedroom, she tiptoed across the little room and passed through the moth-eaten curtain that served as a door. She went outside into the cool breeze. She'd never been outside so late at night, and she marveled at how different the village looked, how different the air smelled. It was like the world changed altogether after midnight passed. The deep shadows held groups of rats that rolled over each other, and sometimes just sat there sniffing the air. One ran across the street as if it had someplace urgent to get to. She followed it with her eyes until it was lost in the shadows next to the neighbors' house. The neighbors had stopped the conversation about leaving town and had gone to sleep. Dozens of rats were around their house, looking for ways in.

She shivered a little when the first few raindrops made their presence known on her cool cheeks. Lightning flashed again, and she stepped out into the street. The thunder came more quickly, more loudly, and her blood ran cold. She walked into the middle of the street, and as the rain started coming harder, the little girl realized why she couldn't sleep. It hadn't been the sounds, even the sound of the rats under her bed, or the thought that her father had the plague. She couldn't sleep because of the song.

She had been singing it to herself, over and over since the strange boy had whispered it into her ear. All the sounds and the smells, the lightning and the thunder, didn't take the place of that song or what the boy told her the song could do if the right person sang it.

Lightning again, then thunder fast on its heels, and the rain was coming down hard enough to soak her. The rats hid under woodpiles and in the shelter of eaves. They cowered under carts, and dug their way into cellars. The street, the whole village, was full of them.

She sang the song.

The words felt like silk, like flower petals on her tongue, even though some of them were in a language she didn't even know. Her voice echoed in the confines of the narrow street, but it wasn't loud. There was a fluttering collection of lightning bolts and a crash of thunder that should have drowned out her voice but didn't.

Two rats came out of the shadows and stopped in the middle of the street, facing the girl and looking up at her. Their noses weren't twitching. She'd never seen a rat whose nose wasn't twitching. She kept on singing, and more rats came, all of them stopping in front of her. Some of them came around the girl, walking with tight, odd little steps to sit on the rain-soaked cobblestones and stare at her. Every flash of lightning revealed another dozen rats, another two dozen, another hundred.

A particularly bright flash of lightning hit just outside the village, not far from the cemetery. The jagged arch was like a crack in the sky itself. The brilliant light revealed a thousand rats arrayed in front of her like an audience at a grand opera, with the little girl the center of their perfect, still, black-eyed attention.

Her voice caught in her throat, and her skin crawled, almost bunched up, and the song stopped short. The only sound was the rain smashing against the cobblestones and pattering against the drenched fur of the thousand rats. Noses started to twitch, and the little girl turned and ran.

Houses swished past her. Lightning struck all around. Thunder boomed in her ears. Rain soaked her hair and blurred her eyes. She didn't go home. She wasn't sure where she was going, maybe she wasn't going anywhere at all. She was just running away from the staring eyes of a thousand rats.

When a flash of lightning revealed a human face she squeaked out a tortured scream and slid to a stop. A small, soft hand reached out to steady her, but she whirled—not to avoid the touch, but to look back behind her. She was sure she'd see a wave of ravenous, disease-ridden rats about to crash over her to rip her flesh off her bones in gore-soaked strips—but there were no rats. They hadn't followed her.

She turned back to face the boy and laughed, though tears burst from her eyes to mix with the rainwater on her face. The boy smiled, and she smiled back.

"I sang it," she said. "I sang the song."

"I heard you," said the boy. Lightning showed the delight on his face, and that pleased the little girl. "It was beautiful. You remembered it perfectly."

"I could feel it," she said, not even understanding the words that came to her then. "It just came out of me, and they listened. The rats stopped and listened."

The boy nodded, glanced over her shoulder, and said, "They didn't follow you, even though you stopped singing."

The little girl tipped her head to one side, and the boy smiled again. Lightning flashed, and the thunder didn't come as fast behind it this time. The rain was still coming down just as hard.

"They'll listen to the song as long as you sing it," the boy told her, his voice raised just enough so he could be heard over the storm. "They don't normally remain pliant when the singer is silenced. You sing it well."

"I don't understand," the girl said. The boy didn't talk like a child, but in a very real way she did understand him.

Over the noise of the thunderstorm, and the sound of her own voice, she heard the song in her head and knew the strange boy was right.

"Sing it," he said, "and they'll follow you, wherever you want them to go."

"I want them to go away," she said. "I want them to get out of the village."

The boy smiled, his perfect, straight, white teeth glowing in the less frequent lightning. "Then lead them out of the village," he said. "Lead them away."

She turned back to face the village and only then realized how far she'd run. They were standing against the low stone wall that encircled a fallow field. Behind the boy, some quarter mile up the steep hill, was the massive castle. The village was quiet, with only the sound of the rain and no more thunder.

She sang the song, and the rats came. It didn't take as long this time. They must have stayed close together after she'd run away from them. The boy remained quiet, leaving her to sing.

When she was satisfied with the number of rats that were standing gathered around her, she turned slowly away. She almost faltered in her singing when she saw that the boy was gone, but she continued the song. She put one foot in front of the other, ignoring the rain and the cold, and she walked away from the village. The rats followed her, every stinking, awful, plague-infested one of them.

* * * * *

It rained again the next night, but there was no thunder and lightning. The little girl went to bed early. She was exhausted from the night before. She had walked for miles—or what seemed like miles—before she let the rats scatter in the dark woods. When she came back to the house, her father was asleep, snoring loudly. The thunder was long gone, and the village was quieter than she'd ever remembered it, even before the rats had come. She cleaned up as best she could without waking her father and went to bed. She slept late, long into the morning, and when she finally awoke, she found that the whole village had done the same. Though the morning was cold and gray, it was peaceful.

People were commenting about how the rats were all gone. No one saw a single rat all day, and the girl beamed. She didn't tell anyone she was the one responsible for finally getting rid of the rats. There was little likelihood anyone would believe her anyway. She was content just knowing the rats were gone.

When she went to bed, her father tucked her in and kissed her lightly on the cheek.

"Things will start getting better," he whispered to her. "They're gone."

She smiled at him and managed not to cry. There were dark circles under his eyes, and his breath smelled bad. He itched under his arms, and when he looked at her, his eyes were sad. Even though the rats were gone, he had it. Maybe he would get better, though, with the rats gone.

When her father blew out the candle on her nightstand and passed through the curtain, the girl fell asleep. She had no way of knowing how long she'd slept before a noise woke her up. At first she rolled over, not opening her eyes. It was just a rat. There were always rats in her room at—

She came awake and sat up fast, her eyes open wide and her mouth open wider. She was going to scream but stopped herself. She saw a rat scurry along the baseboard and disappear under her bed. She could hear more in other parts of the house, and still more outside. They were back. All of them.

She gritted her teeth and clenched her fists and wanted to cry. She'd stopped singing in the woods, and when she stopped singing, the rats stopped listening. It took them all day, but they came back. They would always come back. She couldn't lead them far enough away, couldn't sing long enough to make a difference for more than a day.

Though there was no reason for her to believe that the boy would be at the cemetery, she slipped on her shoes, ignored the cold and the rain, and went there.

She didn't call for him because she didn't want to wake anyone, and she didn't know the boy's name anyway. She passed her mother's grave. The rats were swarming over the pile of stones. The little girl gagged, then screamed. She put her hands over her eyes and cried, forgetting that she could have at least driven the rats off her mother's grave with the song.

"That's your mother in there?" the boy asked from behind her, and she jumped and turned on him fast.

"They came back," she said, wiping the tears and rain from her face.

The boy nodded.

"How do I make them go away forever?" she asked. "Is there a song for that?"

"Have you ever heard of black magic?" the boy said.

She shook her head.

"The rats were brought here by an evil man," he said. "You know what evil is?"

She nodded, listening.

"They were brought here by my father," he said. He looked away, turning toward the dark castle looming in the distance. There was a light in a single high window that looked like a smudge on the night sky. "The baron brought them here."

"Why would he do that?" the girl asked.

"I don't know," the boy replied, and she believed him.

"I hate him," she said. "He should die of the plague he brought here."

She turned back to her mother's grave and began to sing. The rats stopped worrying at the spaces between the rain-soaked stones and turned to stare up at her. She let the song change in a way she wasn't sure how she knew how to do, and the rats stepped off the mound of stones that concealed her mother's body. A few dug their way out from under some of the stones, her mother's blood still ringing their filthy mouths.

She used the song to tell them to go away, and they did, without hesitation. When they were gone, she stopped singing and said, "You hate him too."

Though the boy was behind her, she could tell he nodded. "I can't kill him," he said.

"He should die of the plague," she said again, still not turning around. "He's the baron. He's supposed to be taking care of us. We're supposed to be his people. We thought he didn't care about us, and that was bad enough, but for him to bring the rats here, to bring the plague here . . ."

"There could be a new baron," the boy said. "There could be a baron who protects you all and who would never bring plague rats to the village."

"If you kill him," she said, "you become the new baron after he dies?"

She turned to look at him. He looked scared.

"If I kill him," he said, "I can't become the new baron. There are laws, and they would know. I would get nothing. The lands would be broken up and given to other estates. The village would die one way or another." He looked at her. "You have to do it."

The way he slipped that last sentence in took her off guard, and she actually giggled. He leaned in toward her, and his eyes were hard and glistened in the darkness. She shivered in the cold rain, and her flesh crawled.

"You can use the rats," he said. "You can control them long enough to kill him, then his spell will be broken. They won't be drawn here anymore, and when you tell them to go, they'll go, and they won't come back."

She shook her head but couldn't look away.

The Secrets of Magic

* * * * *

Before the rats came, when the sun used to shine, she was just a little girl. That was less than a year ago, so she was still a little girl, but then she used to play along the edges of the meadows, singing songs with her mother, laughing and exploring. She didn't sing songs to plague rats, she sang songs to her parents. She had friends, all of whom had died over the course of the last several weeks, and she never—not once—considered killing anyone. She was a child, how could she ever be in the position to kill someone—and not some other child, but an adult—and not some ordinary adult from the village, but the baron himself, the adult among the adults.

In her room, in her bed with the rats under it, she kept her eyes closed in the dark and tried to stop thinking about it. She could hear her father coughing in the room next door. Before the rats, people used to cough. Some people even got sick, and some people died. Since the rats came, everyone who coughed got sick, everyone who got sick died, and everyone who touched anyone who coughed, got sick, and died, coughed, got sick, and died. In a way, life in the village had gotten simpler—sadder, but simpler.

She tried again to stop thinking about it, and eventually she fell asleep.

* * * * *

She began bringing her father tea and started doing her best to take care of the house and kept doing that for six days. She made no effort during that time to sing the song or to make the rats go away or to find the baron's son. All she did was take care of her father and watch the plague overwhelm him.

On the seventh day, he died, and the little girl had no idea what to do. She wasn't sure who was left in the village who could help her. The neighbors next door had packed up their old cart and had driven their donkey out of town. Most of the rest of the people were dead.

She didn't cry when he died, or at all the whole time he was sick, except that time he told her he was going to be fine. The buboes were huge and scarlet under his arms, and his eyes were sunken and gray. When he told her he was going to get better, she wasn't sure if he was lying to her or if he really thought that. Either way, it disappointed her that he would say it.

She went to the front door of the house and looked out into the street. The sun had just gone down, and the gray sky was glowing softly, making all the shadows soft around the edges. The woman who lived across the street was sitting on the doorstep of her little brick house, staring off into the sky with dead eyes. She had her arms crossed tightly in front of her and was breathing loudly through her nose. The little girl used to play with some of the woman's five children, before they all died one by one from the plague. The little girl had seen her sitting there like that before and knew not to ask her for help. The woman wouldn't have heard her.

She went back to her father's room and grabbed him by the wrist. She pulled as hard as she could and moved his arms off the side of the bed before her hands slipped off his wrists. She took hold of his wrists again and pulled, but she couldn't move him. She grabbed the sheet he was laying on and pulled that, but all that did was make her hands hurt. She stomped her foot and wiped away tears. She needed to get him to the cemetery, but he was too heavy. She couldn't do it.

She hit her father on the chest, and her jaw clenched tight. She hit him again, and her eyes fogged over with tears. Her knees shook, and she almost slipped to the floor, but she stopped herself. She was still crying, and her jaw was still clenched tight, when she turned and ran out of her father's room.

She ran through the little house and out the front door without stopping to put her shoes on. By the time she got to the cemetery it was dark, the stars all hidden behind the clouds that never went away. She was breathing hard, her jaw had relaxed, and she was shuddering from cold, hunger, and sadness.

After passing through the gap in the short stone wall that led into the cemetery, the little girl turned around and around looking for the baron's son. In the distance, the huge black castle dominated the sky. She counted five windows with light coming from them, all high up on the flat wall. The cemetery was dark, and though there were rats around, the boy wasn't there.

She walked around the perimeter of the graveyard looking for him, but he wasn't there. She strained to look into the darkness of the trees but couldn't see anything. Finally she climbed over the little stone wall and sat in the wet grass, not caring that it was soaking into her thin nightgown. How could she expect the boy to just be standing in the cemetery all night, every night? She had stayed away for a long time, and now she'd changed her mind, but maybe it was too late. Maybe he had given up the idea of killing his father, deciding to let the black magic continue, the plague continue, deciding to let the village die.

She wanted to sing the song in hopes that maybe he would hear it and come, but she couldn't. All she could do was sit there and cry. She sat there and cried until she fell asleep, but she wasn't asleep long before someone shook her awake.

"It's time," the little boy said.

The girl blinked and looked up at him. "What do I have to do?" she asked.

"Just sing the song," he replied. "Gather the rats and have them follow you. I'll open the doors for you. Just sing the song, so the rats will swarm over him, make him fall down, and kill him. You know how to do that?"

The little girl nodded and said, "This is the right thing to do, right? He let a lot of people die."

"He's doing more than that," the boy said. "He's starting to study new black magic. He told me he's going to make himself immortal. Do you know what that means?"

The girl shook her head.

"It means he's going to change himself, so he won't get old—well, get any older anyway. He's going to make himself live forever. If that happens, the clouds will never go away, and there might even be worse things than the rats and the—"

"Stop it," the girl said.

The boy stepped back and let her stand up. She brushed off her wet nightgown and rubbed her arms.

"He's your father," she whispered. "Don't you love him?"

The boy's face drooped. He looked at the ground and said, "He sleeps in a coffin. He makes me sleep in one too."

"A coffin?" she asked. "What's that?"

The little boy looked at her, his eyes narrow with surprise. "All the funerals you've been to since he brought the rats here, and you don't know what a coffin is?"

She shook her head, confused. "What do you mean?"

"A coffin," he said, "is a box they bury dead people in."

"No," she said, "they bury dead people in the ground."

The boy laughed, and it made her skin crawl—with anger more than disgust. "They put dead people in coffins," he told her, "then they bury the coffin in the ground. They bury people in coffins."

The girl shook her head again and said, "They put people in a little hole, then cover them over with rocks."

This seemed to make the boy sad, but the little girl didn't know why.

"He makes me sleep in a coffin," the boy said, then turned to look off into the darkness beyond the little stone wall.

The girl looked down at the ground and started to sing the song. She sang it quietly at first, but the rats heard her.

As the rats gathered around her, the song gathered in volume and intensity. She didn't want to sing the song, didn't want any of what was happening, but she had to do it. Of course she had no reason to trust this strange boy who only told her that he was the baron's son. He might have been lying all along. He did teach her the song, though, but maybe all that meant was that he was the one who'd controlled the rats in the first place.

She had no reason to trust him, and she didn't really, but she had no choice. What else was she going to do? She was an orphan, with no one to take care of her and nowhere to go. She'd watched both her parents die of a plague brought by rats, and regardless of why the boy wanted to kill the man he called his father, the baron was supposed to protect them all, but he just ignored them as the whole village died.

The little girl was doing the only thing there was left to do, and she didn't even understand how to wonder if it was right or wrong anymore.

It took the better part of an hour of constant singing until no more rats started to join what had become a mass of writhing, wet, gray bodies. She couldn't stop singing to ask the boy where he wanted her to go, so she just looked at him.

His face was more pale than usual, and his mouth was hanging open just a little. He was looking at her the way she used to look at the stars in the sky, as if, even though he'd seen her before, he still didn't know exactly what she was.

"I never realized there were so many," he said, then took a step back.

He turned to go and waved her forward. The little girl followed him across the meadow and up the hill. The rats trailed behind her like the tail of a comet. They never came closer to her than a few feet and stayed in a fairly tight line. The little girl was breathing hard but kept singing. By the time they reached the top of the hill, she was barely able to continue the song.

The boy led her to the back of the castle. The building was the biggest thing the girl had ever seen. It seemed to rise up and up forever, filling the sky, almost swallowing her in its shadow. She could see bricks, moss on the wall, but no way in.

The boy glanced back at her when he came to within arm's reach of the wall. She tilted her head at him, hoping he would get on with it so she could stop singing.

He turned back to the wall and ran a finger along the space between two bricks. There was a grinding sound that echoed in the still, humid air, and a whole section of bricks sank into the wall, revealing a black space behind.

The boy turned to look at her and stepped in. He disappeared into the darkness, and she followed him.

She was singing softly, almost whispering, and the boy remained quiet. Though their hundreds of little clawed feet ticked across the stone floor, the mass of rats that followed them was quiet as well. The trip through the bowels of the castle seemed to take forever. The castle was the biggest building she'd ever seen from the outside. From the inside, it seemed even bigger. Hallways went on and on forever, and they passed one door after another. The boy seemed completely at home, and though she'd never know if he was just wandering aimlessly though a place he'd never been before, it looked like he knew where he was going.

After a while, they heard a voice. It was a man's voice, echoing all through the inside of the castle. He was chanting strange words over and over. Something odd happened to the boy's face when he heard the man's voice. Certain words would make him wince, the rest of the time his face was twisted into an angry grimace. The boy was either following the voice, or the voice happened to be where he was going, because with every turn in the maze of corridors, the voice grew a little louder. The girl realized that it must be the baron she heard.

The room they came into was huge—so big it could easily have held ten of the houses from the village. The ceiling seemed as tall as the sky, and the girl heard and saw something fluttering up in its farthest reaches. They were birds or maybe bats.

The room was lit by dozens and dozens of enormous candelabras. There were windows along one wall, but they were all firmly shuttered. The other walls were lined with shelf after shelf that contained more books than the girl could imagine existed in all the world.

At the far end of the room was a man, his back to the children as they came in. The girl was still singing, the rats trailing behind them. They were far from silent, the song and the *tap-tap-tap* of all those rats' feet, but the man didn't seem to hear them. If he did, he didn't turn around. He was hunched over something that might have been a table. His hands were in front of him, moving, working at something.

The little girl began to sing more quietly, the song fading from her tongue.

She couldn't do it.

"Father," the boy said. He didn't raise his voice, but it carried loudly through the enormous room, startling the flying things up above.

The man didn't turn around, but his voice echoed back at them. "You've brought me something, haven't you, Son?"

"A girl from the village," the boy answered, walking quickly across the huge room, fading in and out of the flickering shadows of all those candles. He stopped in the middle of the room.

"I don't need a girl from the village," the baron said.

The little girl walked more slowly than the boy, and though she was singing very softly, and her voice was almost gone, the rats followed her by the thousands—wave after wave of them, their eyes blazing in the candlelight.

Something dropped off the edge of the table the baron was standing in front of. It was a hand—a woman's hand—with strips of flesh peeled off it the way a rat would do if it was eating a dead body. The little girl crossed the room diagonally as the boy just stood there with his hands on his hips, staring at his father's back. When the girl came around she could see that it was a dead woman on the table. She was singing the song as if it had become a habit—an autonomic response like breathing. She didn't stop, even just long enough to gasp, when she realized that the dead woman on the table was her mother, and the baron had his hands in her chest up to his blood-drenched elbows.

She screamed out the words of the song as she sang, and both the baron and his son turned to look at her. She didn't really know how she sent the rats at the baron, she just did. It was just a change of inflection, a lift in timbre, and they were at him.

The baron was a tall, gaunt man, his head shaved, his eyes glistening in the candlelight. His robes were unlike anything the girl had ever seen. It was as if he was wearing a week's worth of clothes all at once, layered over each other. The material shimmered, and the color was a shade of deep blue like the sky just before you see the first evening star. He was just a man, but he looked like a creature from another world.

The rats poured at him like a storm cloud descending out of the west, their feet making a torrent of clicks on the marble floor, their nerve-shredding whistles and shrieks setting her ears to rattle.

The baron threw up a hand and started to sing the same song, but his was different somehow, in more ways than just the deepness of his voice. The rats pulled up short, less than one of the little girl's strides from the baron. They piled into each other and ended up a rolling mass of wet gray fur, sickly pink tails, and blinding white teeth.

In response, the girl sang more loudly, pushing her voice out of herself with a strength she never imagined she could possibly have. The rats, which were just about to turn around at her, didn't. They stopped and seemed confused. She could see the look on the baron's face. He was surprised by her and not in a good way. She couldn't see any fear in his face, though, and that frightened her.

The rats pooled around the middle of the room, fanning out to spill over the boy's feet. They almost tripped him. The noise in the room was incredible. Between the two of them loudly singing and the noise of the rats, the bats or whatever they were flapping around the ceiling, it was just a huge mass of noise that blended into one continuous sound.

The girl tried to set the rats on the baron, and the baron tried to set the rats on her, and that confused, even enraged the rats. They turned on the boy.

They were all around him, at first seemingly unaware that he was even standing there, then they were just on him—crawling and jumping up his body. The little girl could hear his scream take shape and rise against the background roar of everything else. There was blood splashing from him, rats being tossed off, and the girl felt a surge in the song. The baron had stopped singing.

She sang the rats off the boy, and they dived off him, falling into their own kind and starting to fight amongst themselves. Blood shot from the boy's throat and oozed from a hundred other places. His eyes rolled back in his head, and he slumped to the floor as his father screamed out what must have been a new song, a song that had nothing to do with the rats. The baron's song sent a wave of freezing air through the room. As the wave of cold passed over the girl, her jaw froze, and her voice caught. There was a palpable sense of confusion as the writhing mass of undirected rats tried to readjust to some modicum of free will.

The girl looked up at the baron, who was ignoring her. The man's face looked like her own father's face had looked the night her mother died. His eyes were fixed on his dead son.

She sang in a loud, clear voice, and the rats responded without a second's hesitation. They poured over the baron, who screamed in a way that was so monumentally disappointed it made tears burst from the girl's eyes even as she sang the rats at the man.

They ate him, rat-bite by rat-bite, and the girl closed her eyes and covered her ears, so all she could hear was her own song. It only took a few minutes for the baron to be reduced to shreds of bloody flesh falling over rat-gnawed bone.

She was sure he was dead, so she sent the rats away. She sang them out of the castle and sang them out into the meadows, and the fields, and into the woods, and away from the village forever.

When she stopped singing, she tried to cough, but all that

happened was her throat clenched tight, and her head throbbed. She opened her eyes but tried to ignore all the blood. There were a few dead rats on the floor. She crossed to where her mother was lying still on a cold steel table. The dead woman was drawn open, the flesh of her chest and stomach pinned down to the table. The girl turned away from the sight of her mother's entrails coiled in a pile.

She went to the windows and with some considerable effort managed to get one of them open. It was light outside already, and the girl drank in the fresh air like it was water. She breathed in dry, rasping, painful gasps. Along the horizon, the sun blazed, and the sky was a bright, even blue. She gasped at the sight of it, and if she had had any tears at all left in her eyes, she would have cried at the sight of the sun rising in a clear blue sky. She hadn't seen anything like that in a long—

The scream that came from behind her was shrill, and it sent her spine quivering in little spasms of terror.

The girl whirled around to see the boy scuttle sideways across the filthy floor, smearing his own blood. A shaft of light cut across the huge room from the open window and either the light or the boy's scream and sudden movement made the flying things flap around some more.

It took long enough for the girl to see all this before she understood that the boy was alive. She had seen the rats rip his throat out, but there was no wound there, just an angry pink scar that looked weeks old. He was holding his little white hands in front of his face.

"Close it," he groaned. "Please close it."

The girl turned and slammed the window shutter closed.

"Thank you," the boy whispered, rolling over onto his hands and knees. "The light . . . hurts me."

"They didn't kill you," she said, taking a few steps toward him. "I thought the rats killed you."

The boy touched the scar on his neck. It was white now, like it was even older. "He . . . did something to me."

The girl's heart sank for him, but she wasn't sure why.

"Is your mother here?" she asked him.

He looked up at her, a blank, dark look in his eyes. "I killed her being born," he said.

She nodded and said, "We're both alone now."

He nodded in response. "You're better than he was," he said. "It could be that you're better than he ever could have been. I hoped you would surprise him, but I never dared to imagine you'd ever overpower him—a child with nothing but raw talent. You could be a planeswalker."

The girl shook her head. She didn't know what that was.

"Where will you go?" he asked her.

She shrugged and said, "Home, I think."

The girl took a couple more steps toward him and stopped. The boy sat down, squinting at her from the deep shadows where the rats had knocked down a whole row of the massive candelabras.

"Will you be all right here?" asked the girl. "Are you the baron now?"

The boy nodded but didn't smile. "A baron who will likely serve you one day, if I am right about your talents."

"I don't want anyone to serve me," the girl replied.

The boy just nodded, looking at the floor.

"I think you're the only person in the world I know," she said, "but I don't even know your name."

He looked at her with his head tipped to one side. A sad smile drew his lips up, and a tear formed in the corner of his right eye.

"I don't know your name, either," he said.

"My name is Ravi," she said, returning both his sad smile and his tear.

The boy wiped the tear from his cheek and struggled to his feet. His knees were shaking as he took in the ruin of the room.

"I guess I am the baron now," he said. "The Baron Sengir, at your service, madam."

Part II:

Pre-invasion

In a time before
the greatest of evils . . .

A Nut By Any Other Name

Nate Levin

Kylor adjusted the straps on her light armor and slung her bow over her arm, wincing as the wood bit into her already chaffed skin. She sighed, thinking that she should talk to the village herbalist about a healing poultice for her raw shoulder. Perhaps if she rubbed more oil into her leather armor it would soften some, but she couldn't help longing for the supple fabric of her travelling tunic. She ran a hand through her short-cropped hair, still feeling the sting of the elder council's words. Certainly, the council's choice to send her to investigate the new human settlement reflected in part its intentions to teach her a lesson in humility. It was almost unheard of for a young woman to be granted the position of remote scout, but to be sent on a mission to a known settlement was a not-too-subtle insult.

"Stop it," she said to herself as she reached down to adjust the short sword hanging at her hip. "This is precisely the sort of self doubt the council wanted you to suffer."

Kylor looked around at the forest stretching, as far as her keen elven sight would reach, unchanged in every direction. She glanced up at the sunlight filtering down through the leaves and guessed it to be just past midday.

"I'm only three days from the village," she reassured herself and set off again for the forest edge on a trail that meandered away from the sun's falling arc.

* * * * *

Early evening was just beginning to blend the world with its inky shadows when Kylor neared the edge of the forest. The undergrowth was sparse, and the trees were becoming a bit thinner of girth. The forest gave way to the open plain as though it understood that it was nearing the edge of its domain and must yield to the open lands beyond. The elf slowed her pace as she approached the woodlands' end, her hand unconsciously reaching toward her bow. A vast plain opened before her eyes, a seemingly endless expanse of grassland, spoiled in its emptiness only by the human settlement a few hundred yards to the east at the bottom of a gentle slope. Kylor crouched low behind a nearby tree and settled in to study the outpost.

All around the site, men scurried about several half-built stone structures. Shoddily clothed humans were hauling large stones from horse-drawn wooden carts to the various piles that stood near each unfinished construction. Masons atop rickety scaffolds were placing the stones with an elaborate system of lines and pulleys. A lanky, bespectacled man stood near the largest structure glancing back and forth from the construction to a parchment he held in his hands. Armored knights rode horses amongst the workers, gesticulating wildly and shouting commands. Debris lay all about.

Three cloth tents stood just off from the main activity. They reminded Kylor of her own hut back in the village, although they were much larger than any elven shelter. A long central timber stood in the middle of each tent forming a point from which the canvas roof and walls were suspended. Stout ropes anchored with wooden stakes held the shafts in place. There was a small fenced pen with feeding troughs near the tents.

To her left, Kylor saw a tall man in flowing red robes emerge from the forest. He was standing on a path that was worn deep into the grass. Ridges of dislodged earth were pushed up on either side of the trail as if a giant claw had dragged itself from the forest to the camp below. Other men appeared, tugging on lengths of rope that were attached to a fallen tree, their bodies bent and straining against the weight of the immense oak log. As the men neared the robed figure, he stepped aside to let them pass, then lingered near the forest edge as though covering their retreat before rejoining them farther down the slope. Kylor watched the men struggle to drag the tree down the rise. At the far end of the trail, other fallen trees lay in an ordered row near one of the stone buildings. When the log was finally placed alongside the others, the robbed figure retreated toward the circular tents as the men collapsed with exhaustion.

"Those are ancient trees," Kylor whispered. "Older than most of your cities."

Kylor swept her gaze across the scene. Confident that she had not been spotted, she began scanning the forest canopy above for a suitable place to spend the night. A large and well-concealed branch drew her eye. Grabbing a low bough, she lifted herself from the ground and made her way quickly to the limb. She set her load down on the stout branch and removed her vine hammock from her pack. She looped a thick anchoring line around the trunk of the tree and began stringing her hammock about as a spider sets its web.

Small fires were twinkling to life in the plains below as Kylor settled back into her hammock. Her pack and bow were resting in the crook between the branch and the tree trunk, safely within arms reach. Fatigue from the day's long journey washed over the young elf, and she succumbed to her body's weariness.

* * * * *

Sound woke Kylor with a start.

She sat up, one hand grasping for her bow, the other grabbing for her quiver of arrows. The high pealing sound of a distress horn bleated through the air a second time. In a single fluid motion, Kylor shouldered her quiver and flipped herself over the edge of the hammock. Hanging above the forest floor she heard the horn blast a third time. She glanced down and let her hand slip from the vine. The young elf hit the ground silently—her bowstring pulled taut, the arrow she had drawn ready. She crept to the edge of the forest.

Two crumpled bodies lay near a small fire in the human encampment, broken limbs jutting out at odd angles from twisted torsos. Kylor watched as the remaining guard tossed aside his distress horn and drew his sword. He looked tiny in the presence of the silverback gorilla. The ape's swiftness caught the guard unaware as it grabbed his wrist and shook the sword from his grasp. The man's eyes widened in terror as the ape lifted him from the ground, his legs pumping frantically as though he could yet run away. The creature grabbed the man's midsection with its other arm and held him firm as it ripped his sword arm from its socket and tossed it aside. The hapless man's mouth opened to shriek, but no sound escaped. His eyes rolled back as his head slumped forward onto his chest. The ape tossed the body to the ground near the other two.

The outpost was in a state of chaos. Working men flew about the site in a panic, running around with no clear purpose save to flee the angered ape. They cowered under wooden carts and behind walls, some sought refuge among the circle of tents. Partially armed knights emerged from one of the tents, still fastening clips and buckles, to see why the alarm had been raised. One of the knights ran for the horses' pen to gather the mounts.

The gorilla stood near the fallen watch guards, scanning the outpost. Muscles bulged along its massive arms and legs. Its broad back shimmered silvery black in the early morning light. Its head turned from side to side atop its thick and corded neck which itself sat upon shoulders as broad as three men standing abreast. Suddenly, the beast sprang forward, lumbering across the ground on all fours. Great clods of earth flew up as the ape's immense knuckles churned ruts in the ground with each leap.

Screams from cowering workers mixed with the yelling of the knights. The gorilla charged one of the wooden carts as the men below it tried to press themselves farther into the ground beneath. With a great heave, the beast upended the cart, turning it over in a shower of splinters and falling stones. The men beneath sprang up to flee the ape's wrath. The ape swept two of the workers up in its arms. Ribs collapsed with a crack as the ape squeezed one of the men in a cruel hug. The other was hurled through the air to crash into a scaffold. The structure collapsed smothering the man in a pile of timber and planks.

Another man grabbed a plank and advanced on the gorilla. He swung the board in an arc before him as he stepped slowly toward the beast. Defiance and fear mingled on the man's face as he approached the ape. His look of daring became one of shock and defeat as the ape grabbed a nearby stone and threw it at him. The man turned quickly—but not quickly enough. The plank fell limply from his hands as the rock caught him in the side of the head, crushing his skull.

A group of knights had mounted their steeds and were charging the ape from across the camp. The ape turned to face them, crouching low to the ground. A battle cry broke the air as the fastest of the knights closed on the beast, his sword arm raised to strike. The ape dodged to the side as the horse was upon him, then shot up underneath the steed with its fist sending both horse and rider over. Man and mount fell back, the horse crushing the knight beneath as it fell to the ground.

The other knights circled around the ape, forgoing their swords for longer stabbing spears. Two archers closed on the beast as well, jockeying to get a shot at the ape from between the mounted soldiers.

Bowstrings hummed. Two arrows penetrated the ape's thick fur, piercing its flesh. As one, the knights lunged with their spears, their swiftness catching the ape by surprise. Sharp steel tips drove deep into soft tissue. The silverback staggered as crimson blood flowed from many wounds. The gorilla fell to its knees, and the knights pressed upon their spears with their weight. The archers let another volley of arrows fly.

Near the forest edge, a second ape appeared. Much smaller than the silverback, this gorilla was clothed in an elaborate cloak of multicolored feathers. Bone trinkets hung from the shaman's earlobes, and the fur on its chest was braided with small beads and jewels. It was clutching a stout wand in its hand, the top of the rod embellished with a series of tiny skulls. The creature lifted the artifact toward the sky and began shaking it vigorously.

Blue-pulsing light engulfed the silverback. Open streams of blood slowed to drips as the ape's wounds began closing around the embedded spears. With a howl the beast rose to its feet. Wooden shafts snapped as the knights struggled to keep the gorilla pinned down.

The red-robed mage emerged from one of the tents, scanning the forest edge intently. He nodded to himself as his eyes settled upon the gorilla shaman. The mage ducked back into the tent and came out again quickly with an armored knight in tow. The knight sprinted for the horse corral, quickly mounted up, and set off at a gallop for the shaman.

The knight urged his horse on with his spurs. The tiny skulls on the end of the shaman's wand ceased their wild flailing, and the gorilla turned to face the charging knight. Mere yards separated the two. Suddenly, the shaman swept the wand around in the knight's direction. Thorny vines blasted from the forest and struck the knight in the breastplate. Smaller sprouts erupted from the tips of the vines, digging themselves into the gaps between plates of steel. Leather straps strained against the force of the vines. With a tremendous pop, the straps gave, and the knight's armor slid away. Red stains fouled the knight's under-garb as the vines hardened, and woody thorns filled his upper body with countless holes. The knight fell from his horses, his life slipping away before his body hit the ground.

Enraged, the red-robed mage reached a grasping hand toward the distant shaman, his fingers tensed with rage. With a shout, the mage stretched his fingers. The shaman's body shot up and back into the trees as though it had been yanked by a massive, invisible hand. Arms flailed as the gorilla hurled toward the forest and slammed into the trunk of a broad tree. The shaman fell to the ground. A handful of colored feathers drifted slowly over the lifeless body.

In the camp below, the silverback sagged to the ground.

Kylor crept back from the forest's edge. She should return immediately to the village with news of the attack and of the humans' intentions for the forest. She shouldered her bow and turned to climb up the tree to retrieve her pack and hammock. The sound of an approaching voice stopped her cold. Someone was nearing the tree muttering to himself in what sounded like Elvish. Kylor scampered up to her hammock and pressed herself against the trunk of the tree. A figure appeared through the underbrush.

The creature was frail and short of stature. A huge mass of tangled gray hair sat atop his head, looking like a great mossy bird's nest, hiding his face from Kylor's view. His twiglike arms and legs were surprisingly lean and muscular, and he moved much too quickly for a person so apparently aged. A ragged and tattered green tunic, or what once would have been called such, draped the figure, tied about his waist with a length of vine. He appeared to be an elf, although Kylor wasn't certain.

Whoever he was, he was clearly perturbed. He was muttering to himself and swinging his arms about in wild agitation. As the figure drew closer, Kylor made out what were definitely Elvish words. The ramblings sounded like a stream of meaningless gibberish punctuated with an occasional reference to "shortsighted humans" or "angry gorillas." Or so she thought.

When the elf passed just below her arboreal perch, he stopped and said quite clearly, "I see you child." Turning his gaze up at her, he continued, "We are not safe here."

Kylor pushed herself against the trunk of the tree. One of the elf's eyes was looking directly at her as the other gazed, eerily off-angle, into the tangle of branches to her left.

"Come quickly," the aged elf admonished. "Come home, child."

80

He then turned and set off again at a frantic pace into the woods, his errant rambling starting anew. Kylor scrambled to gather her pack and hammock as the aged figure retreated into the forest interior without so much as a backward glance.

*   *   *   *   *

The old elf's pace kept Kylor half-running to keep up. She tailed a few hundred yards behind him, still uncertain if his pleas had been anything but more gibberish. He was heading back into the forest to the south, deeper into the woods but in the opposite direction from Kylor's village. Although not more than a few days' journey from the elven settlement, few elves ever ventured in this direction as it was well known that these were bordering on simian lands.

Around midday, the mumbling elf slowed his pace but continued as though he had a destination in mind. Kylor appreciated the more restful gait, and it afforded her the opportunity to take in more of their surroundings. The young elf was becoming more comfortable with the truly wild jungle around her, taking in the strange beauty of the forest untouched by eleven magic and hands.

They had been following a river for the past hour, the water's course becoming increasingly rough as they progressed. The forest was coming more alive with each step, echoing the river's growing turbulence. Small creatures scurried about underfoot, and the trees above were filled with a chorus of avian songs. Small twittering birds flew about the old elf's head in increasing numbers, and Kylor was certain that she saw a few of them disappear into his snarl of hair. Her guide's attitude seemed to be improving with each step as well. Although he still swung his arms about wildly at times, the gestures became less violent and his ramblings more subdued.

Kylor had become so enchanted with her new surroundings that she nearly walked over the old elf before she realized he had turned to face her. His immense mane flared out on either side of his face just barely betraying the points of his ears beneath. The old elf cracked what might have been a grin, although it was hard to tell, as he was still whispering to himself sporadically.

"Sit child," he said just above a whisper, as he himself sat down. Kylor settled herself on the ground and tried to look him in the eye, which she discovered was quite difficult with his eyes looking off in two different directions.

"Who are you?" she finally ventured to ask, breaking a long silence.

"I am unimportant, child," the elf said in a quiet and harmonious voice, "but I was once called Graddock, and you may call me that if you must." Graddock's speech was remarkably clear now, as it had been when he had first addressed her at the tree.

"The humans move, child, and soon they will come. No matter, though, they have been warned. The forest speaks to them of their folly, and we will react as we must." As if on cue a wild boar emerged from the trees behind Graddock and plopped itself down next to the old elf. Graddock reached down to scratch the beast behind its ear, sending the boar's curled tail into a fit of wagging.

Soon all manner of beasts and birds appeared from the forest around the seated elves. Tiny mice ran playfully around Graddock's bare feet. A number of deer emerged from the trees to graze on patches of bright green lichen. The branches above became filled with birds of all sizes, the smallest sitting amongst a number of larger owls and hawks. All about her, Kylor saw nature's pattern of predator and prey breaking down as evolution's mortal dance of survival was seemingly set aside in deference to this most bizarre old elf. It appeared as though all of the gathered creatures came to dote upon a long-lost friend. Even the most renowned of the village gamekeepers had not achieved such communion with the forest creatures. Trained falcons and domesticated elk seemed mere tomfoolery when compared with these creatures' outward display of affection.

"The apes were foolish to attack," Graddock said, more to address the gathered creatures than Kylor, "and we can learn from their failure the strength of the men who would despoil our home, my pets. We must not act so rashly again when they come to avenge their losses."

The creatures responded to Graddock's words with their silence, heads cocked aside as though they could understand his words.

"And you," he said, turning his good eye toward Kylor. "You my child must return to your village at first light. Your people must now come to the forest's aid." Graddock rose and ambled off, shouting back to Kylor over his shoulder, "But first we must eat."

Kylor remained seated as Graddock disappeared behind a large tree. Overhead, birds began to fly off into the forest, the smallest leaving first, the birds of prey waiting as if to give the smaller ones ample time to hide before they again became the hunted. Mice scurried off in all directions, disappearing into holes amid aged and tangled roots. Deer retreated from their mossy meals and faded into the undergrowth. The boar was comfortably curled up and snoring loudly at Kylor's feet. Graddock reappeared a few minutes later, his arms full of an assortment of nuts and berries, which he carried in a large, fleshy leaf. He placed the food next to Kylor and sat down, his mouth already full. Kylor grabbed a handful of berries, hesitantly.

She was soon stuffing herself with the forest's bounty.

* * * * *

Kylor awoke slowly, rubbing her eyes. It took her a few moments to piece together the events of the previous day. She sat up, sending a blanket of vines that had been covering her sliding down her body to land on the boar, which was still snoring loudly at her feet. The beast rolled over with a snort. Her pack and bow were resting on a root at her side. The old elf, Graddock, was nowhere to be seen. A large leaf full of nuts and berries sat a few feet away. Kylor rose and set about to examine the clearing more closely.

Unlike her village, which clearly showed signs of elven magic and work, the clearing just seemed to be naturally suited to habitation. A number of immense trees circled the area, standing like primeval sentinels over the scene. Smaller shrubs grew in the gaps between the ancient living columns, branches hanging low with purple and red berries. The ground was clear of twigs and fallen leaves, but Kylor saw no sign that anyone had bothered to sweep it. Even the roots grew as though they were intended for domestic use, rising from the ground in ways suggestive of a comfortable place to sit or rest.

Kylor followed a path that meandered off to a modest stream that rolled and gurgled among a number of small, deep pools. She knelt by the brook and splashed a handful of water onto her face. The icy liquid washed the last remnants of sleep from the young girl's mind. With cupped hands, she took a drink of the clear forest water. She was reaching down for another drink when a cold, wet nose pressed itself into her back. The boar nudged Kylor aside and dunked its snout deep into one of the pools. The beast pulled its head from the water, shaking and soaking the front of Kylor's tunic. It plopped itself down on its haunches and looked up at the young elf, its stubby tail wagging.

"So I'm just supposed to know what to do now?" she asked the boar. "Don't suppose you're going to tell me, are you?" The boar sat transfixed with the girl, the wiggling of its tail spreading slowly to its whole hind end as she spoke. She moved back to the clearing and began rummaging through her pack for some proper food. The boar was trailing behind her every step, its curious nose not the least bit shy of rummaging through her belongings too.

* * * * *

It was almost midday when Graddock returned. The old elf emerged from the forest silently, startling Kylor.

"You rise, child," he said, setting a long walking stick against a tree. "You slept so soundly, I wasn't sure you'd ever wake. The berries can have that effect on some." The boar brushed around Kylor's legs and rushed the old elf squealing, setting upon his ankles with its tongue. Graddock reached down to pat the creature's head with a grin. He ambled over to Kylor and sat down, pausing to grab a handful of nuts from the leaf. "I have convinced the apes not to attack again, although they were not too happy to assent," he said, popping a nut into his mouth as though for emphasis. "Stubborn lot those gorillas, as strong in their determination as they are of limb. Let us hope that the humans are not so set in mind."

"So you sent the apes?"

"No, child. The apes have acted of their own will. Listen to my council they might, but their course of action was chosen before I could stop them."

"But you were there with them," Kylor insisted. "And the creatures here, the birds and this boar, listen to you as though they understand."

Graddock chuckled. "No, young one, it is I who have been listening to them, an art that is being lost even among the elves. The small creatures act out of kindness and respect for me now, the apes still act of their own accord. They can see what these simpler creatures cannot. A small human outpost today will be a city tomorrow. The simians will not let this happen without a fight."

Graddock lifted his hand up toward the trees. A small yellow bird flew down to land on his open palm. The bird twittered nervously, its eyes darted about. Graddock stroked the bird gently with his other hand as he cooed softly. "Even this tiny bird feels that something is amiss.

"This forest has survived the ravages of many wars. Civilizations have risen and fallen. Races have come and gone, yet these woods have endured. The force of life weaves itself deep into the very fibers of these lands. From the trunk of the mightiest tree to the veins that run through the slightest leaf, that magic binds this forest together. The humans do not understand this complex web of life or the consequence of disrupting it. This is why the apes fight. This is why I must go to the humans and plead the forest's case."

Kylor rose to her feet. "You mustn't go Graddock. If you were spotted with the apes at the forest's edge, the humans will kill you. I will return to the village for help. I will bring the village archers. We will help you."

Kylor's excitement seemed to affect the old elf. His eyes rolled about in their sockets, wide with terror, and he looked at her as though he no longer recognized her. Incoherent mumbling sputtered from his lips. His head turned from side to side as though he was listening for something in the forest beyond. He jumped to his feet and began flailing his arms about, sending the bird skittering off for the trees. Kylor took a few steps back, unsure what to make of this sudden onset of rage.

After a few moments, Graddock sat back down. His ramblings became less frantic. "This will not do, this will not do," he was softly muttering to himself, rocking back and forth on his heels.

As quickly as it had come on, the storm of emotion passed.

"There is no time for this. Elven councils have never been known for their hasty decision making, unless things have changed dramatically since I left their world a few hundred years ago. Humans, on the other hand, have never been known for their level heads. Your people will get involved soon enough and warn them you must, but for now I must act."

"I will go with you then," Kylor said hesitantly. "You will need protection. I won't let you go to your own slaughter. If I act as an emissary from the village, maybe the humans will be more reasonable."

"No, child," Graddock shook his head. "I have been in touch with the treefolk, and they will send an escort. Even as we speak, a couple of stout old oaks are on their way here. They will accompany me."

"Even so," Kylor insisted, "I will come."

A familiar grin spread across Graddock's face. "Very well. It is not my way to choose another's path, young one, but I do not wish to see you come to harm." The grin on his face faded, and his eyes hardened. "Follow if you must, but if there is trouble . . ." His eyes became cloudy, and he began murmuring to himself again. "This will not do," he mumbled under his breath.

* * * * *

Two treefolk arrived at the clearing a few hours later. Kylor had never seen such wondrous creatures. They were vaguely humanoid in shape and stature. All similarity to any of the other races ended there, though. Thick and gnarled bark covered the creatures' bodies from head to foot. Their massive limbs looked like small tree trunks, their arms tapering down their length, ending in huge knots of wood from which sprouted three thick fingers and a slightly larger thumb. The treefolk's heads were tiny in comparison to the rest of their bodies and, like their hands, resembled knobby knots of wood. Tiny eyes looked out from deep-set sockets. The treefolk's eyes betrayed a depth of wisdom that Kylor had seen only in the most elderly of elves.

Graddock was obviously pleased when the great trees arrived and began at once to tell them of the recent events. He paced about the two purposefully, puffing himself to his full height when speaking of the silverback, then shaking his fist vigorously as the shaman had shaken its wand. He spoke of the red-robed mage and the piles of taken trees. The treefolk remained still as Graddock recreated the events of the previous morning. Through their stoic countenance, they gave no sign that they had heard the old elf, let alone understood him. His tales complete, Graddock settled himself down on a nearby root to await a reply.

Minutes passed in silence.

Kylor was beginning to loose her patience and began fidgeting with the fletching on an arrow when the huge trees finally moved. At first she was unsure whether they even had. Almost imperceptibly, they bent closer together as though intending to bump heads, and they each offered forth an arm. Their fingertips touched.

More time passed as the treefolk stood conferring. Then, as indiscernibly as it had begun, their consultation was finished, and they withdrew their arms and straightened to their full height. They turned to face Graddock.

"Yes, I am sure that the humans will come," Graddock said. "Although I don't think they know that it is me they will find. They will not let their losses go unanswered, and I feel the mage to be a particularly vengeful man." He paused. "I will reach the humans before they come looking. Although the apes have given me their word, I doubt they will sit passively if the humans come looking for trouble."

Again the treefolk bowed their heads. "Yes, it is a dangerous affair," the old elf continued, "but I am counting on the humans' love for ceremony and order to spare me until I can reach one of them with at least a shred of rationality." His lips curled into a grim smile. "Pray that we can avoid further bloodshed. We will leave tonight and reach the humans by morning, assuming that they are not so foolish as to travel these woods after dark."

"You, child," Graddock said turning to face Kylor. "As I said, you are free to join us if you must, but if danger should present itself, you must return to your village for help. I do not want you to sacrifice yourself to the humans as I do. Gather your things. We will leave shortly." Graddock's earlier fit and the presence of the eerily stoic treefolk made Kylor think better of raising an objection.

* * * * *

Kylor was arranging the last of her belongings in her pack, adding a handful of nuts at Graddock's insistence, as dusk was painting the clouds in its red glow. She selected her sharpest arrow to keep in hand before slinging her quiver over her arm. Her bow would not be chaffing her shoulder on this journey. Glancing over at the treefolk, she thought she saw their eyes widen slightly, although their woody faces made reading emotions all but impossible.

The night's journey proved uneventful. Kylor was surprised at her own level of alertness. Even considering her rest on the previous day, she was uncommonly energized at so late an hour. Although she was not a stranger to travel in the forest at night, she had never traveled this deep under the moon's light. Graddock's pace was not nearly as frantic as the previous day, and the young elf had no trouble keeping up. The treefolk traveled silently on either side of the elves, and at times Kylor forgot that the arboreal guards were even present. Trailing along at Kylor's heel, Graddock's attempt at leaving it behind having been wholly futile, the boar was uncommonly quiet, as though it somehow understood the gravity of the journey.

Rays of moonlight that filtered down through the treetops punctuated the darkness of the deep woods. Great hanging masses of moss cascaded from the trees like waterfalls, glowing in the dim light of the full moon. Luminous eyes peered at the travelers from the branches above, and small creatures moved skittishly across the trail.

Dawn was a few hours off when the travelers reached the edge of the forest. They had not encountered anyone along the trail, and if Graddock's judgment could be trusted, this meant that the humans had still not reacted to the apes' raid.

The treefolk stood silently at the edge of the woods. Small twigs and branches began to sprout from their stout limbs. As they raised their arms, the smallest of the twigs began to bud, and within moments they were covered in leaves. They became indistinguishable from the surrounding shrubbery.

Kylor and Graddock settled in behind one of them to view the outpost. A small fire blazed on the outskirts of the settlement, and a number of armed men stood warming themselves by its glow.

Activity began in the outpost below as the first hint of light was rising above the horizon. One of the guards walked around the camp rousing the workers from sleep. A number of guards emerged from one of the nearby tents, fully armed. The red-robed mage stepped out of the commander's tent clutching a tall staff in his hand. The staff, easily as tall as the mage, was topped with a dragon's head forged of steel.

The spectacled man hesitantly stuck his head out from behind the tent flap and gave a quick glance toward the forest before stepping out. He was wearing an ill-fitting set of chainmail armor with obvious discomfort. After conferring briefly with the mage, he retreated into the tent and emerged again with a short sword strapped awkwardly to his side. As the workers set about moving stones, the night watchmen assembled themselves with the other soldiers, all of them carrying large packs as though they were prepared for travelling. The mage joined the soldiers.

"I will go to the humans now," Graddock said reaching down to pet the boar. "Do not interfere. If there is trouble, you must go to your village and rouse the council, for war will not be far off. If I do not return by nightfall, assume I will not return at all. The treefolk will stay with you."

"This is madness Graddock, I will not watch you sacrifice yourself."

"Would that there was another way. The humans have chosen their course, and I must try to change it." Graddock scratched the boars ear. "Keep him safe for me, child."

He rose and strode from the edge of the woods into the open expanse of the great plain. He was half way to the camp before one of the soldiers spotted him and alerted the mage. The surprise on the mage's face slowly melted into a grim smile. With a quick word to the nearby soldiers, he started up the rise toward Graddock, two soldiers a step behind. Kylor drew back her bowstring instinctively.

Graddock stopped a few paces from the mage. The soldiers walked passed and roughly seized the old elf. Kylor watched with horror as the mage raised his staff, and Graddock's body slumped forward in the soldiers' arms. A squeal pierced the air as the boar shot from the forest and charged down the hill.

The boar lowered its head and slammed into one of the soldier's shins with a grunt. Shaking its head with a snort, the boar set about nipping at the man's feet. The soldier gave an annoyed kick, sending the boar airborne. The boar landed a few feet off but seemed unfazed by the soldier's kick. It charged the man with renewed fury rooting at his ankles with its tiny tusks. The mage stepped forward, holding the staff high above his head, preparing to silence the creature with the cruel weapon.

Kylor pressed herself against the treefolk, gritting her teeth. "Come on you silly bushes, do something!" she snapped. Her bowstring leaped forward sending an arrow whistling down the rise. The arrow struck the mage's wrist just below the palm and passed though, sinking the arrow, mid-shaft, in his forearm. The staff dropped to the ground as the mage grabbed the arrow with his uninjured hand. He snapped off the fletching and yanked the other half from his arm, tossing the bloody wood to the ground. The soldiers dropped Graddock, one turning on the boar with his sword as the other rushed to the mage's side.

Kylor felt a twig brush her face as the treefolk began to move. Branches and leaves rained down on her head as the treefolk shed their concealing foliage. The creatures moved away with a quickness that defied their woody forms, leaving Kylor open to view. The boar lay lifeless next to Graddock's body, the soldier wiping his freshly soiled blade nearby.

The mage stood to face the coming treefolk, leaning on a soldier with his good arm. With a quick word, he had the other soldier drop his sword and kneel. The treefolk stopped in front of Graddock's fallen body. A shout came up from the camp below as one of the workers raised a finger in Kylor's direction. The mage looked up at and then past the young elf, and just as she realized that he was not looking at her, she felt the tip of an arrow prick her back.

"Don't move Kylor," an elf's voice warned her, "you've caused enough trouble for today."

Kylor dropped her bow and let her arms fall to her side. She felt the arrow in her back ease up, and she craned her neck around to see who had sneaked up on her.

"It's alright Kylor, you can turn around," the now familiar female voice said. "You're not in custody. I just wanted to make sure you didn't send off another arrow or do anything else brash." The young elf turned toward the speaker. Her shoulders sagged with a sigh as she recognized Delva, captain of the village elite archers. "Those humans are going to be a bit upset with us and with your friend down there. As long as they don't act foolishly, the treefolk won't harm them. I don't know about the old elf, or us for that matter. From the looks of that red-robed sorcerer—" the captain paused, her brow furrowing—"I'd think he could slay with a single word." Kylor started to step toward Graddock's fallen body, but the captain's strong hand gripped her shoulder and held her back. "No, Kylor, we do this my way now."

Kylor turned back to the captain. "He's one of us," she hissed, the muscles in her jaw tensing as she spoke. "I won't abandon him to the humans."

Delva's eyes softened. "It's too late to ask the council for help. The humans are apparently more eager to start a war with us than we are with them, or they horribly underestimate the forest."

The workers were already getting back to their toil as though these minor battles were becoming a part of the day's routine. A number of guards had assembled themselves near Graddock's body. The sleeve of the mage's robe was stained black, his crimson blood mingling with the lighter red of his garments. The two soldiers who had accompanied the mage were helping him back down toward his tent, as two more were eyeing the elves.

"If I give myself up," Kylor began, "I can take responsibility for everything. They can take me, blame me."

Delva shook her head. "I'm hoping it won't have to come to that, Kylor. I'm no more fond of this new outpost than your friend down there, but maybe this mess is just what we need to get the rest of the village interested." Delva sighed. "Either way, someone's going to have to answer for sticking that wizard," she said, directing Kylor's gaze to the group of soldiers running up the hill.

Kylor reached back for another arrow, but Delva's hand caught her arm. Two more soldiers appeared in the forest behind them.

"Must have been ready for another ambush," Delva spat, dropping her bow. She put her arm on Kylor's shoulder. "Let them take us, Kylor. We can't beat these odds."

The soldiers seized the elves and led them down to the outpost. Kylor steeled herself for the walk and refused to let Graddock's fallen body affect her. Work came to a halt as the elves were led through the settlement. Kylor felt her ears redden as dozens of eyes looked her over.

They were led to the mage's tent, and the guards stepped aside as the elves were led through the flap. A number of small braziers were spaced around the interior, casting a soft light and throwing off thick black smoke. The smoke stung Kylor's eyes and nose, and the small tent left her feeling confined. The mage was seated behind a large, wooden desk. Large, well-armed guards stood to either side of the wizard. He sneered, brushing aside the man who was tending to his wound, and sprang to his feet.

"Fool elf," the mage spat, waving his injured arm. "Do you know what you've done?"

"I've simply given you what you deserved, mage," Kylor said through clenched teeth. "Did you expect your desecration of the forest to go unanswered?"

The mage stepped up to Kylor with his good hand raised. "Insolent imp." His arm swept through the air toward Kylor's face but was brought up short as Delva stepped forward to catch it.

"Don't do this, human," the captain of the archers said, gripping the mage's hand and then casting it aside. The guards drew their swords. "Neither of us wants war, and you know that the elves will now be forced to respond," Delva continued.

"Maybe so, elf, maybe so." The mage dropped his arm, his fist relaxed. "I should have known your kind would get involved," he continued. "Simple-minded fools you are. Change is upon the world, elf." The man leaned in to put his face right in front of Delva's. "A lesson your people never seem to grasp." He leaned away. "Time will not abide by your ancient customs and outdated morality. I assure you that this forest will fall, apes and elves with it." He smiled.

"Guards, bind these two and stick them in the supply tent, then bring the old one to me." The mage turned back toward his desk. "And, oh, yes," he added with a chuckle, "see to it that tonight's menu includes swine."

* * * * *

Kylor and Delva were placed in a much smaller tent that was filled with all manner of crates and barrels. Their arms were bound firmly behind their backs with thick, coarse rope. The tent was unlit and had no vents save the front flap, which Kylor guessed would be well guarded. The muffled voices of the workers and the sound of large stones being moved could be heard all around. Kylor was staring dejectedly at the hard dirt floor of the tent.

"Don't take it so hard Kylor," the older captain said. "I'm just glad that I showed up in time to stop you from causing any really big problems."

Kylor looked up. "You were following me the whole time weren't you, Delva?" She kicked at the dirt. "I guess that the council's distrust was well placed."

"Don't be so quick to dismiss yourself, Kylor. After all, the apes and that crazy old elf got this whole mess started." Delva shrugged.

"Anyway, it's about time that we elves started taking a more active interest in the developments of our human neighbors."

"There's something about that elf, Delva. Some kind of magic or some sort of link with the forest that we have lost. The animals adore him." Her face brightened as she remembered Graddock's clearing. "His home was wonderful. . . ." She trailed off. "All of the birds and animals . . ."

"Enchanted, I'd say," the captain said. "I lost your trail somewhere along the river. I looked all day for any sign of you but found nothing. It was really just a lucky guess for me to head back out here to look for you."

Late in the afternoon, the flap of the tent was brushed aside by two large men, and Graddock's limp body was brought in and dropped near them. His limbs were bound with the same rough rope that held Kylor and Delva. Kylor was heartened to see that Graddock was still breathing and that he had apparently suffered no physical harm, although he was only semiconscious. Even in this state, Graddock's mouth moved as though he was mumbling to himself. The young elf inched herself over to Graddock and softly called his name.

The old elf's eyes shot open, and his mutterings became immediately more clear. "No not yet, my pets. We must wait a bit longer," he rambled. "The treefolk will be here soon enough." His eyelids fluttered.

"Graddock," Kylor urged.

"Yes, more nuts," he went on, still oblivious to his surroundings.

Kylor nudged him with her foot. "Come on, old fool, wake up."

Graddock opened his eyes wide. "You should be careful who you call fool, young one," he said, looking now, at least with one eye, at the young girl. "Where is the sun, child," he asked.

Kylor shot Delva an alarmed look, wondering if perhaps the

mage hadn't knocked Graddock's skull with his staff once or twice for good measure.

"The sun is in the sky, Graddock, where it belongs," she assured him.

Graddock cracked a grin. "Yes, yes, that's all fine, child, the sun is in the sky. What time of day is it?"

Delva leaned toward the old elf. "A bit before sun fall I would guess, old one."

Graddock turned his head toward the archer. "Oh yes, you," he said. "Been sneaking around anyone's home lately have you?" Delva shrank back a bit.

"Well, it will be time soon enough," he said, to no one in particular. Graddock looked over at Kylor. "Do you have those nuts, my child?" he asked her. Kylor thought of her pack and bow sitting up at the forest clearing.

"No, I don't."

Graddock looked concerned. "We will hear about that."

Delva and Kylor looked at each other.

"Our human friends have decided that I am responsible for the ape's assault and that our young one here," he said motioning with his chin toward Kylor, "needs to face the consequences of putting an arrow through that wizard's wrist. We would all be killed tonight if the mage has his way. The spectacled one disagrees, of course. He thinks we should stand trial in Chalice. No less a death sentence than the mage's if you ask me."

Kylor sat up. "But the apes," she sputtered, "and the council. It would bring war!"

"Yes." Graddock nodded. "The apes and the council, not to mention the treefolk. I sent them away when I came to. That's how I ended up in here with you and not dead up in that field." He sighed. "That mage is determined to see us die, and I would be surprised if we survive the night." He turned toward Delva. "Will the village send help?"

Delva sighed. "No, old one, not for days. If we are to be rescued, we will have to do it ourselves."

Graddock nodded. "We will," he said, laying his head back down on the dirt floor, muttering to himself.

Kylor thought she saw him grin before a faint snore escaped his lips. Soon, he was fast asleep.

* * * * *

Time passed slowly. They had spoken little since Graddock had fallen asleep. Delva was resolved to make an escape and had been stewing for hours over how that might happen. Kylor had seen no way out and had succumbed to her exhaustion. She was sleeping as soundly as Graddock.

A rustling sound behind one of the nearby creates interrupted Delva's thoughts. She kicked her foot softly into Kylor's side. The young elf sat up startled but suppressed a cry when she saw Delva's look of alarm. The scratching sound continued, coming from several places at once.

Kylor felt a tugging on the ropes that bound her arms. Delva jerked with a start, and the scratching noise increased behind her. Kylor craned her neck, searching the darkness of the tent. Her restraints limited her view, but she could see a long bushy tail poking up from behind her hands.

Scanning the confined area, Kylor made out several of these small, bushy creatures climbing over Graddock, twittering excitedly.

The old elf woke with a giggle as one of the creatures nuzzled at his chin. "Ah, you've come my pets. Good." He sat up.

Kylor felt the binding on her wrists give way.

"Get ready now," Graddock said possibly to Delva and Kylor, possibly to the squirrels.

There was a loud snap, like a longbow being released. Then there were a few more pops. The pole at the center of the tent tottered hesitantly before falling to the side. Fabric came billowing down onto the elves as the tent collapsed. Kylor scooted over toward Delva and Graddock. Outside the tent, they heard the guards raise an alarm. Farther off, they could hear the frantic braying of spooked horses and more popping sounds as tent lines around the site gave way. The elves inched toward the edge of the fabric, and Delva poked her head out from under the tent.

Tents were collapsing all around. Guards were flailing about, swinging their arms in an attempt to rid themselves of the small, furry creatures nipping at them. A horse thundered by, the end of its tether frayed as though it had been chewed through by a tiny set of teeth, dozens of pointy eared squirrels biting at its legs. The mage's tent lay flat on the ground, although humps moved about underneath.

"Now, children," Graddock urged, poking Delva in the ribs with a bony finger, "to the forest." The three climbed out from under the fallen tent and made a dash for the tree line. Squirrels, by the dozens, ran about the outpost, nipping at heels and scratching at faces. Unarmored, woefully fleshy workers ran about screaming as the squirrels bit at their exposed skin. The supply tent guards writhed on the ground as a couple of squirrels had apparently made their way under the men's armor.

The elves made use of the chaos, dashing between carts and walls. They huddled behind a large unfinished building at the edge of the settlement.

"Now!" Graddock urged, his eyes wild with excitement as he broke in to a run, hordes of furry squirrels at his heels.

A shout drew Delva and Kylor up short. They spun around. The red-robed mage was clawing himself out from under the heavy canvas of his collapsed tent. The squirrels set upon him at once.

Blue sparks danced along the mage's fingertips as he tried to brush the creatures aside, to no avail.

"We end this here, wizard," Kylor whispered. Without hesitation, the young elf swept down to retrieve a sword from a fallen soldier smothered in a carpet of squirrels.

Kylor charged the mage. The squirrels' attack was faltering. Blood poured from the man's body, yet he stood up, shaking off the remnants of the attack. Tiny charred bodies littered the ground at his feet. His lips curled in a snarl, the mage lifted his arms in the air. Energies coalesced between his upraised hands.

Kylor lunged the last few feet, plunging the blade through the man's chest with a single thrust. His eyes rolled back in his head as the flames on his fingers slowly blinked into darkness. He fell to the ground, lifeless.

Kylor dropped the blade.

When she reached Delva, the two broke for the safety of the forest. Kylor could make out a line of treefolk waiting at the forest edge.

When they were safely among the hulking trees, they stopped. Graddock was waiting for them.

"Your pack, child," he urged, pointing down at one of the treefolk's roots.

Kylor and Delva gathered up their supplies. Only now that they had stopped did Kylor feel the furry body riding on her shoulder. A squirrel, the same one that had freed her from her bindings, was twittering in her ear. She reached into the side of her pack and produced a nut, which the creature set upon immediately.

As one, the three elves turned toward the elven village. "This is either the beginning or the end, my pets," Graddock offered. He paused to look back at the human outpost, then they headed deeper into the forest.

Goblin King
Jim Bishop

For the fifth time in as many days, Warmaster Jaxle Brey returned to camp red-faced and furious. His shield boys and squires saw him coming across the mud flats, and the talk froze on their faces. His big iron shield hit the mud, then his helm a second later.

"Wings!" he roared, his bushy moustache catching most of the spittle. "A month in the swamp, and they grow wings!" He unbuckled his sword belt and hurled it at the closest squire. The rest scattered toward the line of tents and knights' pavilions. They'd all felt Brey's hand since marching from King's Head.

Inside the council tent, the floor was carpeted in rich wool, now ruined by mud and the endless rain. Brey slogged into the smoky light of the oil lamps and brought a fist down on the map table.

"They're flying over us."

"The goblins, Lord?" The scribe Wolsey looked up in owlish surprise through his thick glasses. He hadn't heard Brey approach, and his hands were occupied with the toy army of tin soldiers laid out on the battlefield map. Brey's advisors were arrayed around the tent in folding campaign chairs: his captains of foot, horse, and archers in their full regalia, the siege master with one mailed foot resting on the table's edge, and Wolsey, the idiot professor. The tent smelled of wet wool and blood.

"Yes, Wolsey, the goblins. The army of goblins." He reached over his shoulder and pulled a black-fletched arrow from his cuirass with a grunt. "Out there."

"Wings, Lord?" Wolsey's bad eye winked at him. Brey found himself wishing he could throw out the old man's books again. That he could find some excuse to smash his glasses or toss him to the greenskins as a peace offering.

"They fly, Wolsey. We lost a dozen mounted and twice that in foot, because they flew. Over your wall." He slammed the scribe's brass spyglass on the table for emphasis. The stout earthen wall surrounding the camp had been Brey's idea, but none of the officers dared correct him. It had taken a week to build. A week they could have been riding, trying the goblins' defenses.

Brey turned to address the rest of the table, ignoring Wolsey's look of horror as the spyglass rocked on its bent frame. It was a present from his parents, both long dead, on earning his commission to the university.

"I want new plans drawn up in an hour. Contingencies, retreats, everything. Better plans. And build more siege wagons. I want cover for our next mission."

The warmaster turned to leave when Wolsey recovered his voice. "I'll need descriptions, Lord. Sketches would be better. Of the winged goblins." He indicated the ranks of tin figurines on the table: faithful miniatures of the king's army that faced ten times their number of tiny, leering goblins, each hardly more than a forge-drop. "For the simulations, Lord." He glanced around, finally realizing he'd said the wrong thing.

But Brey favored him with a smile, and a light shone in his dark, close-set eyes. "I think that can be arranged, Wolsey. You'll ride with the next scouting party into the mountains. You can sketch them all the better from close up." His teeth gleamed as he threw open the flap and strode out into the miserable rain, scattering squires like rats before a hound.

Inside the council tent, Wolsey rolled his spyglass in his hands and shook his head. The siege master touched his shoulder, but he barely noticed.

"Oh dear." He repeated, "Oh dear, oh dear."

Hours later, as his mule picked its way along the narrow trail behind the line of soldiers, Wolsey's mind wandered in thickets of language. Goblin, he thought. Strange that the word so closely resembled Go-blan, or "Many Kings" in the Sarpassian. The word was probably older than that, originally from the dwarves or first men. He'd have to check the university library when he returned to King's Head. If he returned, he thought with real regret.

The world of books and maps was far away from Gaslight Swamp, and he knew he wasn't prepared for the realities of war. The clatter of mail and plate around him reminded him that he was unarmored and unarmed but for the dagger the First Chair of History had pressed on him after the dinner in his honor.

"In case you're captured," he'd said. The bright steel of the blade was marked at the tip by a smear of blue alloy. Poison. Salts of cyanide and tincture of cobalt, he thought automatically. He was familiar with the metallurgy of it but had never seen one up close. He thought of finding a vein with that deep blue point and shuddered.

His mount was loaded down with leather map cases and surveying gear, and a wicker trunk held his small field furnace, ingots of tin and lead, and a dozen molds. Metals were his true love. He wished they'd listened to him when they ran down their list of "volunteers" for the king's army three months ago. He was no soldier.

The sergeant called a halt, and Wolsey found himself studying the man in profile, as a painter studies a landscape or a surgeon a wound. The helmet with its tall crest, the quiver of javelins, breastplate layered over mail and leather—all of it became bits of detail in his mind's eye, a future model to complete his human army. The sergeant ordered that camp be set and called out names for the watch. Wolsey only half listened. The soldiers cursed and laughed as they staked tents and dug latrines, but Wolsey barely saw, instead thinking back to the beginning.

* * * * *

The king's army, they called it. Wolsey remembered the day they'd ridden from King's Head, the whole city waving them on, a train of children in their wake. The Lord-Protector at the vanguard tipped back his helm and nodded gallantly, and ladies threw scarves and favors until his horse was festooned like a maypole. His warmasters rode behind him as an honor guard, grim and silent.

Wolsey had watched as Jaxle Brey dipped his lance to catch a scarlet favor that drifted from the pavilion seats like a drop of blood in water. Wolsey would have bet his books that the scarf was meant for another man—likely the younger captains who rode at Brey's side, tall and strong. Although Brey fancied himself a stirring figure in full plate atop his horse, the truth was his moustache covered a sneering mouth, and his pointed chin was more cruel than dashing.

It had been just three months, but it seemed a lifetime. He had ridden from King's Head with the field kitchens on a rickety carriage, his books and equipment crammed in with him and lashed to the roof. The plum trees were blooming, and their faint scent crept into the carriage and made him wish for his study with its patch of garden outside the high windows.

The other scribes hailed him as Brave Wolsey and Lion Wolsey, but he saw the relief and shame in their eyes. He was twice the age of Multon—why not a young man to play this game of war?

The king's army set out in spring to take the lands of Viscount Tardis. The nobleman refused to honor his king's apportion of iron and wheat, and spies reported a huge surplus piling up in his silos and swords being hammered in every furnace. It looked like a brewing rebellion, and Brey's force was sent south through the Gaslight Swamp to take the rear of Tardis's line. It had seemed like a good plan to Wolsey, indeed he had drawn it up. But they hadn't counted on the resourcefulness of the Half-moon goblins holding the pass.

The goblins' only frontal attack had come at dawn on the tenth day of what Brey called a siege and what Wolsey knew was a stalemate. It was the largest formation they'd seen—at least sixty green-skinned warriors in mismatched armor who marched down the mountain trail to the beat of hidden war drums. They took up a loose phalanx at the canyon wall and fixed their spears against a charge.

The warmaster was ecstatic. He gave cavalry sergeant Bronne the honor of the first charge, then he sat back in a folding canvas chair with a smirk on his narrow, impious face. The cavalry were saddled and mailed while the archers were still stringing their longbows. They rode to meet the goblin force with lances high, horses stamping and snorting clouds of mist.

Wolsey had watched the scene through his spyglass from his carriage, switching views from knights to goblins until they merged into one. Brey was already preparing his speech to the Lord-Protector, Wolsey felt quite sure.

From rocks and ravines all around the goblin position, more warriors flooded out. It seemed to be an ordinary flanking maneuver. But canny, he admitted to himself, these greenskins have read the Phorodotus. It was textbook execution. Then the flankers headed straight into the charging horses, leaving the phalanx far behind. They must have the Viema translation—it lacks the elegance of the original, he mused. He'd have to see about a new version when he returned. It would be a nice feather in his cap, a bit more gravitas than the metallurgy texts that were his staple. Then the first goblin runner exploded, and the shock wave knocked the spyglass into his eye.

Horses and knights rocketed into the air. The lead chargers reared up and spilled their riders, then were blown to bits a moment later. The swift legs of one goblin took him under the banner man's war-horse, and the blast that followed sent gobbets of horseflesh and smoking hide in a hundred-foot plume. Bitter permanganate, Wolsey's mind reeled off. Oil of the shale and yellow sulfur. He remembered long hot afternoons in the stone tower set aside for alchemists, his hair always singed and hands burnt pink from the explosive mixtures. But how had they isolated the yellow sulfur? A whole shelf was given over to treatises on extracting the mineral from coked ore—and these savages had it figured?

The rearmost riders turned to escape, and now, even with his ears ringing, Wolsey could hear the screams of dying men and the frantic whinnying of crippled horses. Still more goblins surged into the line of knights—barrels of the explosive strapped to their scrawny backs—and exploded one by one like a string of midwinter firecrackers, flinging full-grown men into the air like dolls. A fresh line of goblins herded the remaining men into a circle; some threw their swords to the ground and begged for mercy. Wolsey heard a high, wavering scream from somewhere behind the crowd. It was the young sergeant pleading for mercy, his foot turned completely around on his leg, the ground around him soaked in blood. Then the goblins tightened their ring in a deafening thunderclap that rocked Wolsey's carriage on its axles, and smoke filled the battlefield.

When the cloud cleared, nothing was left on the field but a circle of burnt ground pocked with bits of armor and blackened flesh. The tail end of the goblin phalanx disappeared back up their trail into the mountains. Their war drums picked up then stopped at a stroke. In the quiet, Wolsey heard loud cursing that could only be the warmaster. He collapsed his spyglass and stepped out of the carriage to see what he could do and was rewarded with Brey's full fury and blame and a dressing-down that ended with Brey hurling his books—his heirloom strategy primers and handwritten histories—out the window of the carriage, where they lay in the gray mud like dead birds, their pages flapping in the wind.

Looking back, he couldn't imagine their confidence on that ride from King's Head. The other warmasters had chaffed Brey for his plum orders. The rest of them would face men, Tardis' men, trained by the king's own sergeants when the two realms were at peace. It was all bluff—in truth they must have felt sorry for poor, bullying Brey who always got the worst assignments. Only the best of the armies' officers ever earned the rank of warmaster, and only one would become Lord-Protector when Highsmith finally passed. There was no glory in butchering goblins, and his orders meant the end of Brey's dreams for that high post. But Jaxle had confided to Wolsey that he meant to take the pass in a week and be ready to seize Tardis' banners before fighting broke out on the plains of Tormuk. He had asked Wolsey for a plan, and the scribe had brought him the chapter straight from Eduard's excellent *On Fighteyinge in the Fielde*. The fool hadn't read it in school, and he thanked Wolsey as though he'd handed him the Protector's crown on a platter.

A month into the campaign, they were still three leagues from the pass, and every move east brought more attacks. The ingenuity of the goblins seemed bottomless. On the first night, Brey had ordered the camp set against the rocky side of the canyon and had posted sentries to watch for an approach across the plain. Their first night of sleep had been interrupted by the crash and rumble of falling rocks and screams of pain. Wolsey had dashed from his pavilion in time to watch a dozen goblins rocketing down the steep canyon wall on what seemed to be ice sleds, preceded by a tumbling avalanche of rock. The sentries had been a hundred yards away, facing the wrong direction.

The sleds and rocks had crashed through the footmen's tents with a sound like melons falling onto flagstones. The goblin pilots had leaped to safety and had run through camp slashing at anything that moved. The horses had panicked and broken free from their pen to gallop through the crowds of panicked men. A page had stumbled into an oil lamp and become a shrieking firebrand when the heavy tank upended on his head. Men with crushed arms and legs, with bits of rock embedded in their chests and bellies, had lain strewn across the scene. It was pure carnage, pure chaos. And still the goblins had come, wave after wave of sleds and rocks, until the warmaster's whole force, three thousand men and a thousand horses, had raced like whipped children for the safety of the plain. That night as they bound their wounded and sent riders for fresh reinforcements, Wolsey found he had gained a whole new level of respect for their enemy.

Brey's force was under constant attack from that night on. The goblins fought in small units, no more than a dozen warriors, but the units were everywhere and didn't seem to need supplies or orders. They put sharpshooters in every cave, and skirmishers waited in the swamp to slit the throats of scouts who wandered too near. They darted in to strike at the army's flank and rear but never stayed to fight. They set fire to supply wagons and killed horses in the night.

They dug pit traps and strung game snares across pathways. It sounded comical, but horses in full barding tipped into those holes, breaking all their legs and smashing their riders to bloody paste. Brey never heard about the snares, the snipers, or the dozen other reasons why a steady trickle of casualties bled away his main force night and day. He'd taken to whipping pages that brought him reports, and by the tenth day they flatly refused to enter his tent. He sat atop his white horse, now tarred with black mud, or on his canvas chair, and contented himself that the greenskins were finally on the run. Meanwhile, the cavalry had no targets to tilt at, the archers no mass of troops to punish with flights of arrows. The foot soldiers slogged knee-deep in brackish water, growing tired and falling ill, losing their taste for war by the hour.

As if to punctuate the situation, as if this wasn't bad enough, just yesterday the gliders had appeared. They swept in from the cliff tops and dropped stones, captured weapons, even bones and garbage on Brey's army. For every one that fell to an archer, another ten took flight, until Brey ordered the whole force deeper into the swamp, where the camp now sat ankle-deep in mud.

Our second retreat, Wolsey had thought, from an enemy Brey boasted he'd clear out in a week. From an enemy he'd called "little green whelps" in his farewell toast to the court. Again Wolsey had found himself feeling something like fondness for his enemies. They knew more about fighting wars—winning wars—than any commander he'd encountered. And they were humiliating Jaxle Brey, he had admitted to himself, and that put them high on his list.

One night, as the officers ate in silence, Wolsey caught himself humming the tune to *Lord Chaster's Last Ride* (the comic favorite of enlisted men, featuring a fool of an officer and his many losses in the field) and looked up into shocked silence to see that he hadn't caught himself quickly enough. Brey sat at the head of the table, his shoulder bandaged where an arrow had stuck him. His eyes were glazed with anger, but he didn't say a word, and they all resumed eating. But when Wolsey returned to his carriage, he found most of the furniture ripped out and a crowd of apprentice carpenters hammering it apart on the muddy ground not twenty feet away. The hammering continued through most of the night, and at dawn a gallows stood tall by his gutted quarters.

I get the message, Warmaster, Wolsey had thought. I get it just fine.

But even with the constant stresses of his little war with Brey and the real war outside their tents, Wolsey found time for his true love. The night his carriage had been gutted, he had set up his foundry on the bare floor and poured a dozen mini tin foot soldiers, lining them up in ranks on his valise and leaving tiny spatters of silvery metal where he worked. He sculpted during the days, sneaking time while the warmaster busied himself with reviewing his officers and men, a tiresome, morale-sapping task that Brey alone relished. He shined his ridiculous swagger stick and strode up and down the line, smacking in guts and smacking up chins, holding to absurd formalities while their food ran low, and the goblins killed them slowly, like lampreys on a fish.

As much as he hated those pompous exercises, Wolsey appreciated the time they freed up. During Brey's parading, Wolsey had made miniatures for the goblin sleds and a working model of a snare trap.

* * * * *

That night, as the soldiers made camp in the mountains and Wolsey stretched out on his bedroll over hard rock, he worked from sketches he'd made from a pair of wings. The armatures and delicate stretched wings were taking shape in a lump of wax and clay, and his thumb smoothed the contours of the grinning goblin face in the flicker of candlelight. If he worked through the night, he thought, he'd have a first cast by morning.

* * * * *

High in the mountains over Gaslight Swamp, King Jugrut was dying. This was the third challenge to his rule, and the smart money said it would be his last. He and his challenger faced each other across the sandy floor of the arena. Above them were the screaming masses of the Half-moon tribe. In the dim light cast by the cooking fire in the center of the arena, only the teeth and eyes of the spectators could be seen. The king and the upstart circled the fire, and the cauldron suspended above it bubbled and spat. They moved slowly on short wooden stilts, perched like seabirds on their roosts as they maneuvered for position. The challenger held a tin cup in one hand, Jugrut his scepter, a brittle wolf bone topped with a chunk of amber. The rules were firm on the stilts and the weapons. The arena measured fifty paces across, and the pot of grease had reached the roiling boil as prescribed. The forms had been obeyed.

The young buck—his name was Baglag—circled Jugrut with sure movements, stilts crunching on bones and twigs as he crept around the field of firelight. Jugrut had a bad scald over one eye, and another on his foot. The ripe white blisters chafed against the stilt's leather strap as he strained to keep the younger goblin in view.

Baglag stomped in close to the fire and dipped his cup full of boiling oil. He grimaced with the pain but kept a brave face, his snaggleteeth pointing out of his mouth like the needles of a compass rose. He took a few tentative steps and then rushed in, battered cup held out like a hawk's pinion. The shouts and cheers were deafening. Baglag's supporters were stacked four deep around the pit. Jugrut saw just a few friendly faces: Liklik and Picknose, Dagdug and Wibbles, and a few others. They flinched when Baglag struck, feinting to the left and rocking his weight back to the right, splattering the full cup of boiling fat across the king's chest. Money changed hands, the clatter of silvers drowned out by Jugrut's yips of pain.

He staggered forward holding his chest, and strips of cooked skin oozed out between his fingers. He took three steps and fell from his stilts to one knee, his face a mask of pain. As he tried to raise himself, the scepter snapped under his weight, and he dropped facedown in the sand. The crowd erupted in screams, and someone pelted him with the coins he'd lost.

Baglag stretched his hands to the spectators in triumph, his mess of teeth and gums doing a bad impression of a smile. He made a circle of the pit, the ends of his stilts stamping little half-moons in the sand, and dipped his cup deep in the cauldron. He raised it high, and the crowd howled when they saw the sheen of grease running clear down to his elbow. He was flush with victory, too caught up in the glory of his coronation to notice the pain. He made another circuit of the arena to soak up the cheers, then made a show of setting up for the coup de grace.

The king got to his feet and mounted his stilts, swaying a little a few yards from the kettle. Lines of blood and oil ran from his chest and brow. He reached out with the stump of his scepter and took a drunken step forward, away from Baglag. The crowd booed and tossed coins and trash.

His challenger lifted the cup to his lips and mimed taking a sip to general laughter. Then he screwed up his face, set one leg of the stilts against the rock wall, and pushed off at a dead run. Jugrut never saw it coming.

The king swayed forward and stopped his fall at the last moment, jerking back in reflex. His reaction toppled him back, and he fell hard on Baglag's outstretched stilt. The stilt dropped like the arm of a lever, and Baglag took flight, catapulting headfirst into the black iron kettle. His head and neck snapped forward into the boiling grease with a sound like a suddenly extinguished candle. The chants and hollers from the crowd died to a worried murmur. In the sudden hush, Baglag's head splashed up for air, his eyes already cooked egg-white, lips turned back at their corners like fried rashers.

The king found his feet and planted the splintered end of his scepter into the base of Baglag's skinny back. There was a grinding snap and a warm rush of blood that soaked his arms up to the shoulders. King Jugrut pushed until the jagged bone sprouted from Baglag's chest. The challenger shook once more and was still.

Jugrut tossed the stump up to the roaring crowd and staggered to the gate. It was good to be alive. His stomach fluttered, and he steadied himself against the stones, seeing black spots as he shook his head. The jailer hurried to the portcullis jangling keys, with a look of terror on his face.

This one bet against me, Jugrut thought as the gate rose. He would have his green head by nightfall. It was good to be alive but even better to be king.

*   *   *   *   *

The next morning Jugrut sat high above the pass to observe his troops. It was still cool, and the black flies were just beginning to come off the swamp. He had spent the night in painful consultation with the Half-moon's chirugeon, a blind, old greenskin called "Wack Eye" for his wild strokes with the needle and knife. Wack Eye had patched him up good. The wound to his head was caked in a poultice of pigeon droppings, and his chest was newly furry where a wolf's pelt had been stitched.

His foot was the real marvel—an enormous pink appendage rested beside its smaller green brother on the warm stone.

"Five toes!" he said to himself. The knight who'd donated it was on the menu for supper. He wiggled the pink nubs again and laughed. What did the pink-men need with such a luxury of toes? Six inches of splotchy skin was stitched to the green stump with catgut and twine, the whole leg smeared with shiny grease. The brains of a challenger are a sovereign cure, but after his victory Jugrut had shouted that Baglag had no brains at all and had called for the oil he'd cooked in instead. His subjects howled to hear him boast, and the elders reassured themselves that he was a fine king, a born king. He wore his crown again, with its spikes of wolf teeth, and bore a new scepter carved from Baglag's arm bone.

Far below the goblin position, a line of footmen advanced in slow, yard-by-yard fashion across the muddy flats. They formed a wedge behind a slowly trundling siege wagon, and they walked with shields raised, not taking any chances, no longer surprised to be under attack. The wagon's big wooden wheels were studded with hobnails for traction in the slime. Even so, the barded dray horses struggled to pull it forward under the weight of a layer of hammered tin that covered the slate roof. Brey had cannibalized half their cook pots for this armor, and his vanguard walked on in moody silence, only their stomachs protesting aloud. A plume-helmed captain rode alongside on a tall courser.

From Jugrut's vantage, the commander was no larger than a wasp. A glittering wasp with a spear in its tail, he thought. He brought his stumpy fingers up to his eye and mimed a swat. Only a wasp, he thought. A nuisance.

Ten dozen of his brothers were around him on the high mountain perch, the scouts flat on their bellies along the edge. The day was bright and clear. A storm crow settled on the arm of a dead maple and *rook-rooked* at their backs. When he gave the command, and the sappers dug out their tunnel posts, and the ground swallowed the line of men like a dog taking a snap of meat, there was hardly a sound.

* * * * *

At dawn Wolsey wearily folded away his lead apron and gloves, and went to cool the mold halves in the stream that cut through camp. Gold light poured over the canyon walls and filled the little ravine with a luminance, an ethereal importance that Wolsey couldn't begin to guess at. He finished and sat down by his bedroll with the cold cast-iron halves, inspecting the mold channels for hints of rust or burnout. Satisfied, he packed them into a canvas sack, rolled it up, and was tying it with twine and looking for the cook fire when he noticed the first goblin.

It was a little one, no bigger than a small dog. It looked so harmless that he forgot all about being frightened. Only its head was visible, a squinty green head that seemed to have sprung up overnight like a misshapen cabbage, square in the center of camp. It turned slightly, and Wolsey saw that the head belonged to a neck, and the neck protruded from a tunnel. Its beady eyes rolled at the sun. Its nose twitched, rabbitlike. Then it dropped back into its hole and was replaced by another, a larger head that popped into place like a children's atog-in-the-box.

Wolsey gathered his newest miniatures with one numb hand and crept toward his mule, moving to keep a creosote bush between him and the goblins. He didn't dare make a noise. He mounted and got the bundle stashed in the growing light, and when he turned back, the camp seemed to explode with green-skinned goblins like an instant spring, the ground giving up its secrets in a flash. Dozens of them burst from the ground with their curved knives and set upon the sleeping men with a wild, ululating cry.

The sentries went first, as Wolsey watched, fascinated, like a spectator at an especially bloody lecture. School was in session, and the goblins had much to teach on the subject of war. They were among the men before the first soldier rose, slashing at necks and ankles of sleeping figures. Some carried torches, and as they ran, they set fire to tents, bedrolls, and wagons. Within a minute, the camp was blanketed in dense gray smoke, orange flames licking from every tent and banner-pole. The panicking coursers broke their reins and galloped through the camp, some trailing entrails where a long, curved knife had done its work.

As the men rose and began to retaliate, short, black-fletched arrows peppered their ranks. They screamed as the arrows pierced them, and it only made the killing easier for the goblins in melee, who closed with their wicked knives as wounded men begged for mercy.

Wolsey watched, still half-dreaming, still shocked, as the sergeant appeared at the door of his tent, roaring, blood soaking his cuirass and spattered across his face. He cut down two goblins blocking his way, then a third. He raised his banner and called for his men to rally, and an instant later, his head was shot full of black arrows from a dozen hidden sharpshooters. His banner man threw down his sword and instructed his guard to do the same; they showed their empty hands to the goblins and fell to their knees to surrender, and the leering goblins slit their throats with no more thought than a butcher wringing chickens.

Wolsey drew his dagger and was feeling for the pulse at his elbow when his mule reared and dumped him hard on the rocky ground. His wicker trunk slid off the mule's flanks like a toboggan, smashing into his chest and knocking the wind out of him.

He lay there for minutes, maybe hours, his breath harsh and gasping and legs flapping around spinelessly. Finally he pushed the trunk to the side, and it fell open with a crash, spilling ingots and finished models on the ground. Still his breath wouldn't come. I'm a fish, he thought, remembering summers from his youth, sunfish and pickerel that flapped their lives out on the pier. They've turned me into a fish.

Finally his breath returned, and he dimly realized that there were no survivors. Even the squires had been rounded up and slaughtered. His poisoned dagger was just out of reach, and as he stretched for it, he saw that he was covered in drops of bright metal. No, not drops—tin soldiers. His eye settled on a goblin glider that still drooped lines of flash from the mold. He'd pressed a dozen that morning and was proud of how they'd come out. The tiny metal face peeked up from where it had fallen in the rocks, stretched wings no larger than a moth's. He picked it up.

As he admired the work, he felt rough hands on him, jerking his torso upright. A dozen beady black eyes were focused on his.

"There are many more hill over that men," he squeaked, throat closing up tight. "Men over that hill," he corrected. As he gestured toward the ravine's lip, a single tin goblin fell from his shoulder and landed face-up in his lap. There was a pause, and he realized they weren't listening to his bluff. He closed his eyes and tried to remember the Goblinese he'd studied in secondary school.

"My men," he began in the tongue-thick tones of their language, "are full of horses. She has one thousand apologies for urinating, so you see. I'll never return yesterday and do it repeatedly."

He checked his throat to make sure it wasn't running blood, and continued, "Your king is my first wife and has bedded us all before. Celebration!"

He peeked out to see how it was going. Dozens more goblins had gathered around him. They hadn't heard a word of it. Instead, they were picking through his collection of soldiers and fighting over loose pieces on the ground.

Slowly, carefully, Wolsey extended his arm and opened his fist to reveal the tiny glider inside. They gaped. Their eyes literally bulged—something he'd have to note if he lived to write a monograph on this trip. The spears at his neck fell back a little as his captors watched him execute a barrel roll with the tin model. Then, in a stroke of inspiration, he snatched up a pinch of gravel and sent the glider on a bombing run against a collection of tin foot soldiers. He'd never enjoyed such a rapt audience. When the rocks struck home, the goblins hooted and clapped their hands. He began to feel that maybe they were the captives, that he'd captured them somehow with his picayune magic.

"I am making these all in twenty minutes," he said, once more swooping in for the kill against a mounted knight. "Never have I eaten a batch. They are yours to take, because you are my ugly, husband-less daughters. Let me live, yes!"

They lifted the trunk with surprising care and gathered the soldiers scattered on the canyon floor. Wolsey guided them to his best work: the proud sergeant-at-arms, the stealthy sharpshooter and skirmisher, the outriders on their tall horses. They beamed at each new goblin face that appeared and snarled at the men. Wolsey felt like a primitive shaman, doling out miracles to his obedient tribe.

When the trunk was emptied, he arranged them in careful ranks, and as he had done at the map table when no one was looking, he walked the tiny soldiers forward, issuing orders in a faraway voice, his eyes detached and content. There were no longer any spears on him. As the campsite burned in pillars of oily smoke and the bodies of fifty men grew cold and white, Wolsey and his audience played toy soldiers like a pack of innocent schoolboys.

* * * * *

King Jugrut was having a day. He was almost ready to give up his crown and go back to being a humble knife sharpener for the digging corps, if it meant an end to days like this. There was a problem with the latest batch of powder, and to everyone's misfortune, he was in a foul temper: his chest itched abominably where the wolf pelt was stitched to his natural skin. The powder was bad, according to the artisans in charge of its manufacture. It was banging goblins before they left the caves—banging, apparently, at the least jostling. A loud fart had set off a cask this afternoon.

Jugrut took two heads in his displeasure and would have taken more, but his scouts interrupted with news of the pink-men. He looked from the scouts down to the prostrate Mukel—Mukel had bet against Jugrut at the last arena. Not heavily, but he'd bet. He reached down, took hold of the artisan's left ear, and sawed it free with two strokes. He held it up to his lips.

"I have your ear, Mukel. I tell you here—" he pantomimed a stage whisper— "and you hear wherever you are. You obey your king. Throw the junk powder to the pink-men, and make a new batch, or I'll find a new goblin for your job."

To Mukel's credit, he did not cry out but backed from the throne room in silence like a beaten dog. Jugrut rounded on his scouts and motioned for seats with his curved knife, spattering blood on the faces of his advisors.

"Sit and tell King Jugrut." Blood soaked the steps leading up to the throne, the throne itself, and Jugrut's robes of office.

The scouts had good news, which was lucky for them. The itching had grown worse as the day passed, and now at midday, it felt as though worms were crawling under his chest. As they talked he scratched the stitches with the point of his knife, but the rounded tip was too dull to get at the deep itch. He scratched anyway, grunting in pleasure even as blood ran down his side.

They had surprised a pink-men scouting party in the foothills and slaughtered them all, with few goblin casualties. Jugrut grinned, and his advisors grinned. The Half-moon goblins agreed on this much: they liked fighting the pink-men. Fighting other goblins was work. In last year's war against the Blood Fang, both sides lost whole generations in just a few weeks of fighting. They struck a peace to avoid the extinction of both tribes. But pink-men—

pink-men stood in line out in the open, they wore noisy armor and rode noisy horses, and by the wisdom of their pink-gods, they couldn't even see in the dark. Yes, pink-men did what they could to make goblin life easy.

But, the scouts reluctantly added, there was something else. Jugrut sat up and cleaned the point of his knife on his check. The scouts admitted that they'd taken a prisoner.

Jugrut frowned at that, and the little runts edged back in their chairs. A special prisoner, they insisted. He made magic dolls that would guarantee the king's victory. Jugrut was dubious, but he motioned for them to bring in this captive.

The pink-man was ancient and stooped, so feeble the scouts hadn't thought to bind his hands. He shuffled in so slowly that Jugrut laughed out loud.

"Woman!" he called in his native tongue. "Pink-man is old woman!" His court laughed and pointed.

To Jugrut's surprise, the pink-man answered in broken Goblin. "The king is a double old woman to you, sire. You must be twice as happy to meet me, I am more famous even than you." He made a stiff bow from the waist.

Jugrut's itch deepened to a burn. He flashed his long curved knife and rose to answer the insult. He shook his head in mock sadness. It was bad enough that they'd disobeyed his orders against taking prisoners, but this old pink-man had insulted him in his own throne room. First the prisoner, he thought, then the scouts who'd brought him. He might saddle them with the bad powder and kick them off the cliff. Or make them fight worgs in the pit. It was shaping up to be a busy day.

But as he approached the pink-man, he looked over to make sure the scouts understood they were next, and quick as a shot, the prisoner took the dagger from his hand. Before Jugrut could call for his guard, the old man knelt and offered a long, bright-steel dagger in return. The pommel was tipped by a clear stone the size of his thumb, and the blade ended in a bluish tint—the same color the Half-moons called their own; exactly the same shade as his kingly robes.

Jugrut was too shocked to be angry. Why does this prisoner have a weapon? his mind thundered. But look at the weapon, his eyes said. He reached out and took the outstretched blade in one hand. His guard came running in, and he stopped them with a look. The balance was perfect, the blade light and strong. One thing the pink-men did well, they made wonderful steel. He had always wanted a fine steel blade for his own, not a plain battle weapon but something polished for court. And it was just the right length to find that itch—he dug into the line of sutures on his chest with the blue tip and sighed happily as the raw flesh seemed to go numb where it touched. A fine gift.

"My shield-brother!" he called to the court. "My pink-man brother!" He had already decided to kill the old man later, but for now, Jugrut was content to watch as the pink-man paraded a fabulous army of tiny soldiers before his eyes. And they were impressive. The toy goblins were so detailed, the king had to remind himself they weren't living creatures.

Still, he had more pressing matters to attend to. Jugrut sat back and scratched all around the pelt line and nodded distractedly at each new miracle the pink-man set before him. Even as his head went light, he smiled and scratched.

* * * * *

They came running with curing draughts, but the poison did its work quickly—his breathing was shallow and labored, and after a few seconds, he never breathed again.

As the court gathered around their stricken king, Wolsey packed his toys back into their trunk, a smile across his thin lips, already sizing up the king's robes against his own stooped frame. In the end, they had to cut three fingers before the dead king's hand would release that perfect, blue-tipped blade.

Two days later, King Wolsey tipped his crown forward and winced at the pain in his hand. The entire arm from elbow to fingertip was scalded red, and where the blisters popped, a clear fluid leaked onto his deep blue robes of office. He hadn't trusted old Wack Eye to touch the wound. When that pretender Picknose was dead—Wolsey's stilt rammed clear through his chest—he'd wrapped the burn himself after soaking it in any icy underground pool. It wasn't quite right to leave the challenger's brains untouched, but Wolsey made it clear that a lot would be different under his rule, beginning with this business with the brains.

The pain aside, he was enjoying his first morning of court immensely. After instructing the artisans on how to derive a stable form of yellow sulfur from ore, he turned his attention to foreign relations. This morning his scouts brought word that the last of the human force was breaking camp, headed east. He had suspected they'd leave without him, but he was still surprised at the depth of his anger—they were leaving without him, leaving him for dead! He got over it quickly: he didn't plan to return in any case.

"King Wol-zhee?" his advisor prompted. It was the closest they got to a proper pronunciation, but it would come in time. His own Goblinese had progressed in leaps. He smiled at the busy goblins—his subjects, he reminded himself—who thronged his throne room, cheerily hammering away at the work tables he'd put in.

Molten metal ran down a stone channel into a series of grooves that distributed the alloy into a dozen identical molds. Today it was horses. Tomorrow they'd tackle foot soldiers and archers. Perched on the arm of his throne was a tiny tin model of a bearded man, bent with age, who carried a spyglass and a sheaf of paper. A tiny crown topped its hairless head.

An enormous battlefield map filled the floor around his throne, with every detail of the canyon and swamp laid out to scale. Wolsey motioned the scouts and advisors around the map and began placing soldiers: Brey's force in regular ranks, his own in a labyrinthine web around the canyon's largest dogleg, where the swamp widened to a morass of knee-deep slime.

As he talked, the soldiers took on a life of their own, now charging straight into the canyon's throat, now feinting north or south. The battle lines advanced and retreated like waves on a beach. The sharpshooters plucked their tiny short bows, skirmishers screened the advance of grenade troops, gliders in the vanguard shattered the siege wagons and heavy horse and led the wild hand-fighters into melee. It ended in ten moves, and even the goblin elders—the old greenskins who'd seen a hundred battles— even the chief advisors looked on in respectful silence. Brey's army was shattered in six pieces, like a remote archipelago surrounded by endless green seas. Each island was cut off, isolated, surrounded. Doomed.

It had elements of Eduarde, and the spirit was all Phorodotus and Wells, but this plan, the finest of his life, worthy of a First Chair, worthy of statues and portraits, this plan would never have seen paper in the city. It was a mountain plan, a thing of the goblins themselves. He set his blistered red hand on the map, finger hovering above a single mounted figure. They'd done the cast just last night, and it was good work. You could almost make out the aristocratic sneer on that narrow face, the swagger stick tucked under the arm.

"Kill all the rest, but bring this one to me."

They understood. They never questioned, never feared or doubted.

"The one who captures him will be shaped in metal. That goblin will be a soldier of the Half-moons forever." He touched the crest on the warmaster's helm and smiled as his army howled around him. It was good to be king.

* * * * *

Warmaster Jaxle Brey groaned in agony as he sat up. His stomach leaked blood from a long, jagged cut that refused to close. The wrappings soaked through as quickly as he bound them, and he had given up, content to feel the blood growing sticky, clotting to his shirt. If he had a light he could try to burn the edges, maybe staunch the bleeding. But it was dark, pitch black, and the only sound was the blood pumping in his ears and his own uneven breathing.

He couldn't understand what had happened. Even when he had been in it, even now as he remembered every scene, he couldn't make sense of what had happened. They had packed up the camp at dawn and marched east behind siege wagons and heavy horse. He had his archers in the very center of the formation, protected on all sides. Outriders scoured the canyon ahead to a half mile, and trumpeted back the all-clear every five minutes. They were taking the canyon, by god, and the greenskins be damned. He felt good. He felt like a conqueror.

The gliders came first, but they had been ready. A hundred archers had taken aim at the skies, and a hundred long shafts had sped to meet the swarming attack. A few had dropped, and the rest had passed overhead without loosing their cargo.

Easy as kicking a dog, Brey had mused to himself. Easy as putting on a crown. His officers muttered that they had been just scouts, but he had waved them away.

An hour later, the front line of siege wagons had dropped into a long trench that had opened up as they stepped onto it, and he had winced to hear the screams of the broken animals. Somehow the trench had been rigged to hold the weight of a single light horse— the outriders had crossed it without a hitch. But even for this, they had been ready. Carpenters had raced to the vanguard with their lumber and set about building bridges. It had been slow work. Brey had looked around at his gleaming force in the afternoon sun. They had sparkled like cut stones, like new-minted coins. He had heard a whistling noise then and turned in time to see the next wave of gliders come sweeping around the canyon's dogleg. Only then had he noticed that his outriders were late with their signal.

The gliders had come in low, barely thirty feet off the ground, each pilot clutching a heavy rock in his arms for ballast. Brey had called for archers, who were bunched behind the formation of foot soldiers, too far back to see the low-flying targets. They had fired anyway, and the deadly missiles had zipped through the ranks of his knights before he could scream for them to stop. Brey had watched, helpless, as the gliders dove onto his siege wagons and his heavy vanguard like falcons. When they had released their lethal stones, the sudden buoyancy seemed to rocket them into the air, and they had disappeared above the canyon walls.

The horses and wagons were decimated. Each attack had found its costly mark in the roof of a wagon or the back of a barded courser. When it was over, rocks had staved in all but two of the wagon roofs, and the cavalry had lost half their number. The rest had been too spooked to advance, and Brey had been forced to order the heavy foot soldiers to take the vanguard as they crossed their makeshift bridges across the trench.

That was not the worst. It had gotten much worse after that. In the middle of the dogleg, where the swamp narrowed his advance to twenty across, grenadiers had come out of hiding and boomed into his right flank, while at the same instant, hidden sharpshooters on both cliff walls had let loose with a fusillade of their cursed black shafts. Brey had boomed orders in a rush of excitement—now this was battle, this was what he trained for! But he quickly found that the grenadiers were only a bluff, and the men he had sent to them had been separated from the main force by skirmishers and cut to ribbons. Rock sleds had slammed down into his rear, and panicked horses and men had rushed forward, turning his disciplined formation into a milling crowd.

Everywhere he turned, a new assault had opened up. More goblins than he dreamed were in this world had poured from their caves and hiding places, and lit into the left flank wailing horrible nonsense. The gliders had returned, this time sweeping in from the rear and raking his archers with grapeshot. The sharpshooters kept up their pace, and it had seemed the sky rained black arrows. His men had screamed and died, and with their screams in his ears, Jaxle Brey had turned his big courser westward, toward King's Head and safety, and he had ridden for home as if all the demons of Hell were on his tail. He had cleared the first line of foot soldiers, their eyes widening in sudden realization and surprise even as the greenskins ripped into them. He had covered only ten more feet, and a tripwire had tightened at his horse's knees. His last thought, as the ground came up to meet him, had been his relief that he wouldn't have to explain all this to the Lord-Protector.

He had no memories of his wound or of being taken prisoner. No idea where he was or for how long he'd been here. He guessed that the jagged tear in his belly was from the fall. When he woke in this darkness, it was already festering. Without a healer, he would die of sepsis in days.

Even now his whole chest felt hot and feverish. With rising dread he pulled the wrappings away from the wound, and his fingers met a slick rope of intestine poking into the air. He breathed deeply and made to push it back inside, but it was too much. He gagged, and his vision went white, and he slumped back into darkness. Some time later, he woke to the sound of keys in a cell door.

"Spare me please . . . a ransom for my return. They'll give you whatever you want." His own voice shocked him with its frank cowardice, its pleading. He had heard that voice before, from captured officers up to their knees in their own guts, as he laughed and asked his questions. The light that poured through the open door was blinding. A small figure stood in silhouette—a single goblin. Brey's tongue felt like a slab of hard leather as he strained to wrap it around the creature's unfamiliar language.

"I . . . see all your . . . bigs . . . ?" He managed. He cursed himself for not studying harder. The language was on the curriculum at the Lord's Academy, but by his second year, Jaxle had bullied a younger boy into writing his assignments for him. He'd never learned any Goblinese but the curse words.

"Escape me . . . yesterbody . . . one at a time . . . dog-waste?" He tried. The goblin did not speak. It stepped into the gloom, and the warmaster saw it was carrying something—a sword? He cringed back against the wall, crying out with the pain of his wound. But the goblin only chuckled at his fear and stepped closer. Brey was dimly aware of the sound of many voices outside his cell, the smell of a fire, of cooking oil.

"King Wol-zhee," it began, better than he'd expected with the human words, "begs a moment of your time." It dropped the objects it was carrying at his feet and stepped back. It grinned a wide, toothy grin. On the floor was a pair of short wooden stilts and a metal cup. Jaxle Brey sobbed and began strapping the stilts to his feet, his middle weeping blood. Outside he heard a mob of goblins, cheering and shouting, and Wolsey's voice in Goblinese, urging them on, shouting above the din like a conqueror.

"Don't be sad," the goblin told Jaxle Brey. "Today you may be king." And it turned back for the door.

Burning Vengeance
Chris Pramas

The Suq'Atan merchant ship never had a chance. Traveling without escort while laden down with trade goods, it practically invited assault. Onboard his ship *Burning Vengeance*, the pirate captain Murad could smell the kill on the salt air.

"Aziz!" he bellowed, "take the wind out of their sails!"

Aziz, a wild-haired man festooned with talismans, snarled his assent and began whispering words of power. He worked furiously, tracing patterns in the air with his talismans while his whisper built into a scream. With a roar, Aziz released an arcing lance of fire that pierced the sails of the merchant ship. In seconds, flame raced across the canvas, destroying the Suq'Atan's only chance of escape.

Murad, shaved head glistening with sea spray, approached the mage with a smile on his face. Aziz returned the grin, pleased with his own handiwork. He didn't even see the backhand that dropped him to the deck.

"I said take the wind out their sails, Aziz, not burn them to the water line!" shouted Murad. "Now we're going to have minutes to plunder that ship instead of hours."

Aziz tried to get up, but Murad knocked him back down.

"Next time," the captain said fiercely, "you do what I say, or I feed you to the sharks."

"Yes, Captain," muttered the mage, blood in his mouth. For just a moment, the mage considered unleashing a spell on Murad, but he kept his hands away from his talismans.

Murad turned his attention to the matter at hand, shouting a stream of orders to his crew. Pirates young and old grabbed up cutlasses, boarding pikes, and belaying pins in anticipation of the imminent boarding action. Murad's cabin boy dashed in and out of the crowd, scattering sand on the deck to soak up the blood. By the time *Burning Vengeance* reached the crippled merchantman, the whole bloodthirsty crew was ready. They waited for only one word.

"Attack!" shouted Murad, as the two ships came side by side.

Grappling hooks shot out from *Burning Vengeance*, grabbing the enemy ship and pulling it into a deathly embrace. Suq'Atan guards tried desperately to cut the lines, but a hail of missiles from the rigging drove them back. The two ships shuddered as they locked together, throwing sailors on both ships to the deck.

"Follow me, me hearties," bellowed Murad, as he launched himself onto the blazing Suq'Atan ship. He landed scant feet from a dazed guard and quickly broke the man's jaw with the bell-shaped guard of his cutlass. To his left, another guard stared dumbly at the shaft of the boarding pike stuck in his belly.

Murad pushed the broken-jawed man out of the way and made for the aftcastle. The Suq'Atan captain was there, and he and his mate were putting up a spirited defense. Two of the pirate crew were down already, and Murad's other men were hesitating. This was supposed to be an easy kill, and the captain's skill had taken them by surprise.

Both ships were now choked with smoke. The merchantman's sails were blazing, and the fire had spread to the mast. Murad silently cursed Aziz as he pulled a dagger from the bandoleer across his chest. He flipped the dagger into the air and grabbed it by its blade. He drew a bead on the Suq'Atan mate who was standing at the top of the stairs fending off several pirates with a spear. The pirate captain hurled the dagger with a practiced flick of his wrist.

It was not Murad's best toss, but it was enough. The dagger winged the mate's right arm, and the man's hand jerked open, causing the spear to dip momentarily. That was all the other pirates needed. Nesir, one of Murad's old hands, dashed up the stairs and buried his cutlass in the mate's guts. Murad bounded up the stairs next to face the Suq'Atan captain.

"The battle is over," Murad snarled. "Surrender, and you won't be harmed."

"I am to take the word of a pirate?" the captain retorted. "I think not. I may have lost my ship, but I will not lose my honor."

Murad sized up his opponent. The man's clothes were finely cut, but his saber was no ornament. From his stance and the practiced ease with which he held his blade, the man also appeared to have some training. Murad, however, was mindful of the spreading flame and smoke. He had not boarded this ship to hone his fencing skills, but to win booty.

"I salute your bravery," Murad announced with a flourish of his cutlass, "but I have no time for your honor today." The pirate captain turned to his assembled crew, who had by this time ended all opposition on the Suq'Atan ship. "Take him, boys."

A half dozen pirates rushed the Suq'Atan captain. He flailed about with his saber, trying to keep them all back, but to no avail. Two men grabbed his arms while Nesir thwacked the back of his head with a belaying pin. The captain slumped into unconsciousness.

* * * * *

Twenty minutes later, the flaming hulk of the merchant ship slid under the waves. Murad's crew had worked fast, but at least half of the cargo remained in the hold. Murad now surveyed the deck of the *Burning Vengeance*. Despite Aziz's impetuousness, it had been a good haul. Crates of spices and other trade goods were scattered where the crew had tossed them. The ship's doctor treated the wounded, of whom there were few. The only casualty had been the cabin boy, felled by a random arrow as he raced about the *Burning Vengeance* distributing ammunition.

The survivors of the Suq'Atan ship were huddled in the prow. They totaled seven, including the captain. Murad, noticing that the captain had awoken, approached the prisoners.

"I'm glad to see you survived Nesir's attentions." Murad smiled.

The merchant rubbed his temples and tested his neck. "I don't see why. Am I now to provide sport for your crew? If you plan to kill us, I ask you to do so quickly."

"Please, Captain, enough with the dramatics. We'd only kill you if you were a slaver." Murad leaned closer, looking the Suq'Atan captain up and down. "Are you a slaver, Captain?"

The captain stiffened. "No, of course not."

"Then you have nothing to worry about," said Murad with a grin.

The prisoners looked dubious. They had heard plenty of pirate tales, and none of them ended well. And even if the pirate captain had a glib tongue, his crew looked like as murderous a bunch as ever sailed the seas.

Murad could see their distrust. "Let me tell you how it's going to be," he announced. "We were able to salvage your ship's boat. We'll be putting six of you into it with three days' food and water. The seas are busy hereabouts, and you should be picked up soon."

"And the seventh?" asked the Suq'Atan captain.

"So good of you to ask, Captain. The seventh is, of course, you. If the ring Nesir took off your pinky is any guide, you come from a wealthy family. You, we are holding for ransom."

The captain looked down at his right hand; he hadn't realized the ring was gone. Murad grinned again as the Suq'Atan captain buried his head in his hands.

* * * * *

The night was quiet and the seas calm. The *Burning Vengeance* bobbed gently in the water as the crew enjoyed the spoils of victory. There had been rum aplenty, and many of the men were already asleep on the deck. Others gambled or swapped stories. In his cabin, Murad reclined with a cup of wine and a hookah. His first mate, Yousef, was with him.

"We put the prisoners in the boat as you ordered, Cap'n," Yousef said, taking a sip of wine. "One of them tried to sign on with us, but I sent him off."

"You know," Murad scratched his chin, "we could use an extra man while the wounded regain their strength."

Yousef laughed. "A man, indeed, but not a boy. This one's face was as smooth as a baby's ass. He couldn't have been more than eleven."

"Well, let's hope those Suq'Atans don't have a penchant for buggery. You may not have done the boy any favors!" Both men laughed, and more wine flowed. Murad blew smoke rings as Yousef gave a detailed report on the captured booty.

"And what of our precious merchant captain?" queried Murad.

"He's locked down in the brig. There'll be no escape for him."

* * * * *

Topside, two shadows huddled in the ship's prow, their hushed voices drowned out by the splashing water.

"What's with all the skullduggery?" asked Nesir. This close Aziz could smell the rum on his breath. The man's golden earrings twinkled in the lantern light like a distant constellation.

So much for discretion, thought Aziz. "I wanted to talk to you in private, but I didn't want the captain to get the wrong idea," he replied.

Nesir looked amused. "If the captain were to find us out here, don't you think he'd be even more suspicious?"

Aziz was so fed up with pirates that he was tempted to unleash a djinn right then. It would only take one push to knock Nesir over the side and less than a minute for the djinn to hold the smart-mouthed old salt under the waves until the briny water shut him up for good. But no, this was not the time.

Aziz forced a smile. "Indeed," he said, fingers reflexively grasping the talismans that hung about his neck. "Let me get to the point then."

"A fine idea," agree Nesir. "I still have half a bottle of rum to finish tonight."

"I've heard some of the men talking about the last mage to serve Murad," Aziz began. "I get the sense he met a terrible fate, but none of the men will talk about it. Can you tell me what happened?"

"Simple. He broke the code."

"What code?" Aziz asked. He had been sailing on the *Burning Vengeance* for three months, and this was the first he had heard of any code.

The old salt whistled in disbelief. "You're more of a lubber than I thought."

Aziz felt his ire rise once again. Was the man trying to provoke him?

"Look," said Nesir matter of factly, "the sea is a dangerous place for a single ship. How do you think we've survived out here for so long?"

The mage considered the question, his anger forgotten for the moment. "Murad is a good captain and lucky, and his ship is fast," Aziz concluded.

"All true," replied Nesir, "but it's the code that gives us the edge." The exasperation the mage felt must have been plain on his face because Nesir continued on. "Out here it's us against the world, warlock. The code is simple. You are my brother and I yours. While we sail together, we share a blood bond. We fight together, whore together, and loot together, and we never, ever, betray our own. That's what it means to be a pirate, and that's why we've never been caught."

"And this other mage, how did he break the code?" asked Aziz quietly.

Nesir spat. "That bugger sailed with us for a year, and we all trusted him with our lives. Then one day he led us into a trap. Turned out he was working for Zhalfir the whole time."

Aziz could believe it. The nation of Zhalfir had a huge price on Captain Murad's head. The captain's disregard for the order the Zhalfirans prized so highly offended them deeply. Even worse, his continued successes made their navy look foolish. After all, Murad was only one man and the *Burning Vengeance* only one ship, but somehow the pirates continued to elude them.

"Luckily," Nesir asserted, "the captain has a nose for trouble. The Zhalfirans tried to box us in and board us, but we broke out and left their slow boats behind. It was then that the mage tried to fry the captain."

Aziz was intrigued. "How did Murad survive?"

"As you said," Nesir replied with a smile, "the captain is lucky. The ship hit a swell just as the mage finished the spell, and it threw his aim off. The bolt of fire meant for Murad sailed right over his head."

No wonder the crew didn't talk about this mage, Aziz realized. Not only had he tried to kill their captain, but also, if he had had any skill at all, he must have bloodied the crew before making his escape.

"Have you ever seen that mage again?" Aziz asked.

The old salt chuckled. "Not since we killed him."

"You . . . killed . . . a mage. . . ." The words trailed off; Aziz was dumbstruck.

"Yep, he's dead all right. I whacked him upside the head with a belaying pin before he could cast another spell. The captain did the rest." Nesir paused. "It was . . . unpleasant."

At first Aziz thought that maybe he didn't really want to know. But he had to ask. "What did Captain Murad do to him?"

"I knew you wouldn't let it lie," Nesir said, shaking his head. He spoke so quietly that Aziz had to strain to hear him. "The captain took the ship to a spot northeast of the Burning Isles. The water is nice and warm there, but it's infested with sharks.

"Murad cut him up with a dagger. Nothing too deep, mind you, just enough to get the blood flowing. We rolled him off the back of the ship and pulled him through those waters for several hours. The sharks took care of the traitor, piece by piece."

Nesir fell silent. He looked as if he needed more rum. Aziz was about to say as much when he caught a flash of movement out of the corner of his eye. He turned to see a shadowy figure flitting across the deck.

His hands instinctively leaped to his talismans, and words of magic came unbidden to his lips. The night was suddenly illuminated by tendrils of energy that formed into a crackling net of magical power. The shadow form was caught up inside the lattice and held fast.

Nesir padded over to the trapped figure, belaying pin in hand. Aziz was walking up to join him when the old salt exclaimed, "It's the boy!"

"What boy?" asked the mage.

"The one from the Suq'Atan merchant ship. The one who tried to sign on with us this afternoon."

Aziz peered through his netting and saw that Nesir was right. Trapped by his spell was a small boy with nut brown skin and close cropped hair. His wide pantaloons and homespun shirt were both wet.

"I thought we sent you packing, boy," barked Nesir. "What are you doing on the *Burning Vengeance?*"

The boy was clearly frightened but controlled it well. "I swam away from that other boat as soon as I could." His voice was high pitched but steady. "I want to join your crew."

"It's *my* crew, boy!" boomed Murad, drawn out of his cabin by the commotion on the deck. "And what makes you think we've got a place on this crew for a beardless boy?" Murad now loomed over the bedraggled adolescent, a giant shadow in the dark of the night.

The boy remained defiant despite the magical netting that still entrapped him. "Your cabin boy was killed today. I saw his body this afternoon."

Murad turned to Aziz. Before he could speak, a shout rang out from below decks.

"Fire! Fire in the hold!"

Murad's head whipped around to see a plume of smoke bellowing out of the stairway.

"Nesir!" he shouted, "bucket detail now! Aziz, you're with me!"

Wrapping scarves around their mouths, they plunged down into the hold. Crewmen stumbled about in the smoke, coughing and spluttering.

Murad grabbed Aziz by the arm. "What can you do about this smoke, warlock?"

The mage reached under his shirt and pulled out an amulet of onyx. Clasping it in both hands, Aziz intoned, "By ancient pact, by blood and fire, I summon thee, djinn, in the name of my sire."

In the midst of the smoke and the chaos, a blue-skinned djinn appeared from nowhere. Floating in the air, the djinn bowed to Aziz, making its ample earrings jingle like wind chimes.

"How may I serve you?" the djinn asked in a booming voice.

Aziz bowed in return. "Get rid of this smoke and quickly."

"As you wish," the creature replied. The floating djinn began to spin. Its legs disappeared from view, turning into a whirlwind as it twisted and turned. The djinn was now moving so fast that it looked like a living cyclone. The smoke, so thick mere moments before, began to pour into the funnel the spinning djinn had created. The air cleared enough for the bewildered crew to sprint for safety and Captain Murad to spy the source of the fire.

"It's coming from the brig!" he shouted to Aziz.

The two men ran down the hall to the brig, where the merchant captain had been imprisoned earlier in the day. The door hung open, and a fire raged inside. It was still confined to the brig, but licks of flame darted into the hallway.

"Where is Nesir with those buckets?" griped the captain.

Aziz ran his fingers over his talismans, mentally ticking through his spells. He had no water spells for a situation like this, and his djinn was busy. Then it came to him. Laughing like a jackal, the mage reached into one of his pouches and pulled out a handful of sand. His time in the desert, it seemed, had not been a waste after all.

Shouting out the incantation, Aziz hurled the sand into the brig. A sandstorm, ripped straight from the bowels of the desert, whipped up in the brig in an instant. As Murad stared in disbelief, the room filled up with sand, smothering the flame. By the time Nesir had arrived with the first bucket of water, the threat was over.

* * * * *

The next morning Murad and Yousef were sweating below deck, watching as the deckhands disposed of the accumulated sand. A chain of sailors passed buckets up the stairs to be dumped into the heaving sea. Murad paced restlessly, eager to examine the burned out brig. It was already clear that there'd be no ransom money, but Murad hoped to at least learn how the fire started.

Yousef walked the line, offering water to the shirtless sailors. The men were tired, having already hauled out of the ship what had seemed to be an entire desert, so they could only grunt in appreciation as Yousef passed around the water. When he reached the brig itself, Yousef paused to look at the ruined room. As he scanned the scorched wood and remaining sand, he glimpsed a glint of metal on the floor. He bent over and brushed the sand away, revealing the burnt out remnants of a leather pouch. Inside were flint and steel.

"Captain!" Yousef yelled, brandishing the pouch, "you must see this."

Murad made it to the brig in three long strides. He seized the pouch and examined the flint and steel. "It seems the merchant-man used this to start the fire, but why?"

Yousef scratched his head. "Maybe he thought the fire would force us to release him from the brig. He may have planned to escape."

"Yes." Murad wrinkled his brow. "At night, with a fire raging, he would have had a good chance to get himself overboard. Don't know what he had planned once he was in the drink though."

"It does seem quite risky, sir," agreed Yousef. "He knew we wanted him alive for ransom, why did he risk his life to escape?"

"I know why!" piped a small voice.

Murad and Yousef turned around to see the would-be cabin boy standing by the doorway. Yousef scowled at the boy, but the lad stood his ground.

"I know why," he repeated.

"If you want to join my crew, lad, you'd best start calling me sir," growled Murad.

"Sorry, sir!" the boy shouted, puffing his chest out.

Murad sighed. "All right, boy, why don't you tell us what you know about the dear captain."

"Sir, the merchant captain wanted to escape before you found out that he was a slaver."

"What?" roared Murad. "That bucket of beetle dung was a slaver?" Blood was rushing to his face, and anger rose within him.

Yousef looked dubious. "That was no slave ship," he pointed out.

The boy stepped back from Murad. He could see the captain clenching and unclenching his fists.

"Sir, the Suq'Atan captain only took one or two slaves at a time. If you knew the right people and paid the asking price, he would get you young girls. Very young girls . . ."

All eyes turned to Murad, whose face was twisted with rage. The captain turned to the bucket brigade and said, "You lot, dig out his body. Yousef, get Aziz down here now."

Yousef nodded curtly and hustled up the stairs. The crew set to on the remaining sand. Within minutes they unearthed the charred corpse of the Suq'Atan captain. He lay on his back, his burnt clawlike hands thrust toward the sky. His rictus grin made it clear that he had died in agony.

Aziz arrived shortly, talismans jingling as he sprinted to the brig. He found Murad standing above the merchantman's corpse.

"Captain," Aziz ventured, "is there a problem?"

Murad spun about. "Yes," he hollered, "there is a problem. The problem is this—" he spat on the corpse— "son of a whore!"

The mage was bewildered. "Sir," he said quietly, "the man is dead. What would you have me do?"

"I have heard of magic," said Murad, "that can bring a man back from the dead and trap him in his broken body." Aziz paled as the captain continued. "I have heard of spells that can tear a spirit back from the afterlife and torment it for decades on end. If you have it in your power, I want you to make this man pay!"

Aziz licked his lips nervously. "Sir, such magic twists the soul. It is the stuff of black mana, the very essence of death. I know many spells and charms, but I leave black magic to necromancers and their ilk." The mage bowed his head. "I'm afraid I cannot help you."

Yousef grabbed the mage's arm and motioned him above deck.

As he turned to go, the captain barked, "Aziz!"

The mage stopped. "Yes, sir?"

"You did the crew proud last night. I'm honored to have you aboard."

* * * * *

"Ship to port!"

The lookout's cry galvanized the sailors of the *Burning Vengeance*. A pirate crew knew that any ship could be a victim or an executioner, and they had to be ready for either possibility. As the buccaneers secured lines and checked weapons, Murad emerged from his cabin cutlass in hand.

"Yousef, what have we got?" the captain queried.

The mate lowered his spyglass and grinned ear to ear. "Fat merchant ship, Captain, dead in the water."

Murad chuckled. "Booty, what a way to start the day. Where's Aziz?"

"Here, sir," replied the mage, bounding up the stairs.

Murad grabbed his mate's spyglass and threw it to Aziz. "What do you make of our morning find?" the captain asked.

Aziz put the spyglass to his eye and scanned to port. He saw the merchant ship immediately. It was heavy in the water and still. Perhaps a dozen sailors were at work on board, and none of them had noticed the *Burning Vengeance*.

The mage leaned back on the rail and considered the mark. "I don't like it, sir. It seems too easy."

Murad slapped Yousef on the back. "You see that, Yousef, he's cautious. I like that." The captain joined Aziz on the rail. "Some days," he said to the mage, "the sea smells like dead fish, but today the air is clean."

The captain stood up. "Ship to port," he bellowed. "We're going in!"

The crew cheered, brandishing their weapons aloft. The sailors set to work immediately, changing course to bring the *Burning Vengeance* on an intercept course with the stranded merchant ship. The pirates had been spotted now, and the merchant crew began frantic preparations of its own.

Murad made a circuit of his ship, encouraging his crew and making sure all was ready for the assault. He stopped when his eyes came to rest on his would-be cabin boy. The youth was crouched on a barrel, cradling a belaying pin in his small hands.

"What do you think you're doing, lad?"

"Getting ready to fight, sir!" said the boy.

Murad grabbed him by the scruff of the neck and dragged him toward his cabin. "My last cabin boy was killed in an action like this. I can't very well train you if you get it today. Now," he said, throwing the boy into his quarters, "stay in there until the battle is over."

The boy leaped to the doorway. "Does this mean I'm joining the crew, sir," he said excitedly.

"That's right," Murad said, repressing a smile. "Now do as I say, and keep yourself safe."

"Thank you, sir, you won't regret it!"

Murad wasn't sure of that, but he put the boy out of his mind as he finished his inspection of the crew. His men crowded the decks, boarding pikes and cutlasses gripped in sweaty hands. They were ready.

The *Burning Vengeance* slid alongside the stationary merchant ship. Grappling hooks shot out, and sailors heaved to lock the ships together. The merchant sailors had already retreated to the other side of their ship, leaving the pirates an uncontested crossing.

"There's no fire in their bellies, boys!" shouted Murad. "Disarm them, and seize the cargo."

Murad and his crew vaulted across to the stricken ship. The merchant sailors huddled in a mass, weapons raised halfheartedly.

Yousef approached them with half a dozen pirates at his back. "You don't need to die today, lads. Let us take your cargo, and we'll be on our way."

The sailors said nothing. Several cast nervous glances at the hold. Yousef followed their stare and saw the glint of metal below.

"Captain!" he yelled, "Look out!"

Doors flew open fore and aft, and feet pounded up from the hold. With a roar, dozens of scale-mailed Zhalfiran marines poured from below decks.

Captain Murad, scant feet from the hold, met the Zhalfirans' charge with one of his own. His cutlass slashed across the eyes of the first marine. The blinded man tried to stop, but he was trampled by the weight of men behind him.

"Back to the *Vengeance*, me hearties!" shouted Murad. "Cut lines and push away!"

Yousef and his gang formed a wedge and tried to fight their way back to the ship. They thrust their boarding pikes forward, trying to clear a path. A short Zhalfiran ducked under one of the pikes and sliced open a pirate's belly with his curved scimitar. His toothless grin turned sour when Yousef caught him in the side of the head with a hatchet.

Meanwhile, Murad had fallen back to the railing with three of his men. His cutlass lashed out again and again, trying to keep the marines at bay. He felt a scalding heat behind him, then arcing bolts of fire seared into the Zhalfirans in front of him. The marines screamed as the fire punched through their armor and roasted them from the inside out. Murad stole a glance behind him to see Aziz already preparing another spell.

"Fall back!" Murad shouted, and his men seized the opportunity to do just that. The captain, however, charged into the Zhalfirans, determined to keep them off balance. He pulled a dirk from the sheath of a dead man and attacked the scorched Zhalfirans with cutlass and dirk flailing.

The marines fell back from this fearsome foe, but the Zhalfiran captain stood his ground. He was a huge man, with a long, oiled mustache and beard. He gripped an enormous scimitar in both hands, barring Murad's path.

"Your pirating days end now," he said simply.

While Murad and the Zhalfiran captain circled, pirates cut the lines. Aziz unleashed raining hammers of magma onto the surviving marines, pounding them to the ground with fiery force. The mage laughed like a man possessed as he pummeled the air with his fists. The magma weapons followed his every move, crushing the life from Zhalfirans with brutal efficiency.

The Zhalfiran captain, enraged to see his men die, charged Murad with scimitar held high. The giant weapon came down, and Murad was barely able to parry it with his off-hand dirk. The pirate captain deflected the blow, but the Zhalfiran managed to knock the dirk from Murad's numbed hand.

Murad hoped that Aziz's next spell would take care of the angry giant, but a marine arrow caught the mage in the shoulder and knocked him to the ground. Cursing, Murad attacked. His point found the Zhalfiran's thigh, but the man punched Murad in the jaw with the hilt of his scimitar. The pirate captain was knocked into the railing, and his cutlass went flying across the bloodstained deck. The Zhalfiran captain stood over him, scimitar held ready for execution.

"The punishment for piracy is death!" he shouted. He raised his blade high.

And the huge weapon fell from his hands.

The Zhalfiran pitched forward, revealing Murad's cabin boy, bloody dirk held in both hands.

Murad could feel the two ships starting to drift apart.

"Let's go!" he shouted to the boy. The lad stooped over the body of the dead Zhalfiran. "Now, boy, now!" Murad screamed.

Captain and cabin boy leaped from the Zhalfiran ship back onto their own boat. Although they had left behind too many comrades, they had escaped the Zhalfiran trap.

When they reached the safe deck of the *Burning Vengeance*, Murad grabbed the boy by the shoulders. "I should beat you for disobeying my orders, but instead I'm going to thank you for saving my life. Well done, lad."

The boy smiled. "All in a day's work, sir."

Murad struggled to his feet. "You know, I don't even know your name."

"My name is Sisay."

"Sisay?" said Murad. "That's no name for a boy."

"No, sir, it isn't—and I'm not, a boy that is. But I'll be your cabin boy just the same."

Murad sat down again, rubbing his jaw where the Zhalfiran had punched him. "So you will, Sisay, so you will. Now, why don't you tell me what you were doing at the Zhalfiran's belt."

"I didn't want us to leave without some booty," Sisay said, holding up a leather pouch, "so I took this."

Yousef, Nesir, and Aziz stumbled over to where Murad took his rest. All of them were bruised and bloody, but they laughed when Sisay produced the pouch.

"Why don't you take the first choice, Sisay. You earned it," said Captain Murad.

Sisay opened up the pouch. Her fingers ran over a purse of coins and a gold necklace but did not tarry there. She grabbed a set of flint and steel and held it aloft.

"I'll take this as my prize," Sisay asserted. "I lost my last set in a fire."

Like Spider's Silk

Cory J. Herndon

She stood before the tranquil pool at the edge of the clearing and gazed down at her reflection for the fifth time in as many minutes. Absently, she tucked a lock of scarlet hair behind one ear and examined the image before her from top to bottom.

High cheekbones had been made up with subtle face paint that enhanced her natural beauty, and jeweled rings—a gift from the king of Caeliyan—hung from her ears and jangled as she turned her head. A string of multicolored wildflowers hung suspended in the radiant hair that fell between her shoulders. The green silk dress—not a gown, it's a dress, she told herself—gleamed in the light of the spring sun. The dress was cut in the Veshayn style, meaning it balanced elegance with functionality—the prettiest hunting garb I've ever worn, she reassured herself.

Ornate armbands, also silver, circled her upper arms, the same armbands that her mother had worn to her own wedding. A simple jeweled pendant adorned her neck, and as the sun struck it, the red gem flashed with brilliant fire. The ceremonial longsword that hung from her simple leather belt lent an aura of nobility and strength. She supposed she was a vision. Good thing, since the joyous, long-promised day had finally arrived.

Teyna Vesh couldn't remember the last time she'd felt so utterly ridiculous.

She started as the band of her father's favorite balladeers launched into yet another song of love, honor, and spring. She remembered immediately that she was being watched.

The elf girl knelt and took a gulp of cold water to settle her stomach. A moment later she stood and took a deep breath, exhaling with a quiet sigh. Teyna made a brief show of adjusting one of the myriad ribbons that seemed to be tied to everything she wore, shifted the sword on her hip, and set her face in an enthusiastic, albeit dishonest, smile.

The sword's weight was reassuring, at least. Though she wore this particular weapon for ceremony, it was quite functional. She had fenced with her brother using this very blade on several occasions. Sparing one last glance down at the pond, Teyna whirled on one booted heel to face her nightmares.

The nightmares met her gaze as one. There had to be at least two hundred of them. Teyna recognized only half of them—the groom had a guest list too. The assembly filled the natural amphitheater known as Rima's Green.

As she moved toward the crowd, they continued to gaze at her with expectation, slight impatience, and no small sense of awe. Most of the ones she knew were elves like her, although a few stoic guests from the nearby dwarven enclave of Battavorn stood near. The other half of the assembled crowd was made up of humans—merchants, nobles from the surrounding areas, and more children than she'd seen in one place in her entire life. This would no doubt be Beric's friends and family, along with a few trading partners that had also accepted her father's invitation.

The soft, expensive silk somehow began to itch. She fought the urge to tear it from her body and run pell-mell for the water that still wasn't too far behind her. The bands around her arms felt like iron manacles, the pendant around her neck a noose.

She hadn't spoken—hadn't been allowed to speak, in fact—to Beric Rycaelin since he arrived with his entourage over a fortnight before. Servants, a horse-drawn carriage, a half-dozen priests and advisors, and of course the people who would soon be her in-laws—the king and queen of Caeliyan City—had rolled into Veshaynya, her village. She'd told her brother she was surprised he hadn't bought a fleet of carriages and brought the entire city along for the trip.

Typical of humans. Spoiled fop.

Now the young human to whom she was about to promise the rest of her life stood nervous and distant. And a bit twitchy, from the look of him, she thought. He, too, wore silk and finery—black, with silver trim—although Beric looked far more comfortable in the formal attire than she would ever feel. The humans of Caeliyan City were not as martial as her own people, the Veshayn, but he still wore a ceremonial weapon on a wide black belt: an bejeweled dagger with a predatory animal head on the hilt.

Beric caught her gaze. He smiled, and for a moment she thought she caught a hint of sympathy in his look.

No, that wasn't sympathy, she corrected herself bitterly, that was condescension. Look at the pretty princess.

The humans did not treasure the forest as her people did. They were traders and merchants who had built a city of luxury off of lucrative trade and land holdings. Humans valued the pursuit of material wealth more than any elf, save perhaps her father. Farom Vesh was unusual in this respect, and Teyna had never really understood his humanlike values. She could not believe that she was about to spend the rest of her life among these people.

While a formal marriage between a human and an elf was rare, such joinings were not unheard of. This was the first such wedding between human and *Veshayn*, however.

Necessity in this case motivated the union. The wealthy humans of Caeliyan had long traded with the Veshayn, but a recent population boom among the elves meant the forest-dwelling people had to trade more and more for medicines and basic foodstuffs that they simply couldn't produce in great quantity. The elves were expert hunters and masters of the forest, but they were not farmers, and their shamans practiced magic, not chemistry. As the once-temporary settlement of Veshaynya continued to evolve into a permanent home, a hunting economy was simply not enough to sustain the population.

No, if Veshaynya was going to survive, it was going to be Teyna's doing. This union between human and elf would result not only in increased trade between the Veshayn and the Caeliyan, but the human King Derc Rycaelin had also granted her people farmlands to the northwest of Veshay Wood. Without those farmlands, her father told her, Teyna's people would likely starve.

Farom Vesh, chieftain of the Veshayn, stood on the raised platform at the fore of the amphitheater, his bearing solemn, the picture of warrior nobility in his ceremonial battle armor and flowing red cloak, a heavy bow decorated with the crest of Vesh slung across his back. A bow that hadn't been pulled in decades, by

Teyna's estimation. Farom stole a brief look of impatience at his daughter, then once again was the picture of paternal pride.

Yes, father, she thought, I'm here. The cow is ready to go to market.

Kolo stood to her father's right. Kolo would soon receive the reins of power from her father, and despite the connection she felt with her older brother, he was practical and would not object to this travesty on her behalf. The fourth figure on the wooden platform was Ezzik, the respected high shaman of the Veshayn. His laughing eyes met hers, and she tried with little success to draw strength from his reassuring presence. But he would conduct the ceremony, how much assurance could he offer?

Teyna set her jaw and stepped onto the platform to meet her fate.

* * * * *

"Report."

"The perimeter's clear, Captain," the young scout replied.

Dewer Runnda, first captain of the Veshayn Sky Guard, sighed. Playing nursemaid to Vesh's daughter held little appeal for this veteran of countless border skirmishes with the goblins, orcs, and worse. He stood twenty-five feet in the air on a particularly large limb of one of the Veshay Wood's many gurna pines. This is no job for a soldier, he thought. Still, Runnda respected the chain of command, and if the chieftain wanted his daughter's wedding guarded by a contingent of his finest troops (plus their captain), then those scouts would do their jobs, and by Lewela's beard, he would see to it that they did those jobs with expert precision.

True, the *finest* troops had been granted a short leave, but odds were that "Farom the Forgetful" wouldn't notice that Runnda had gathered a collection of his most promising younger soldiers to do the job. They needed a little practice in a real tactical deployment operation, he reckoned, and it wasn't like goblins would attack this far into Veshay Wood.

"Thank you, Lieutenant," he told the scout, a well-disciplined thirty-three-year-old named . . . Corbin, Corwin? Something like that. Practically an infant, anyway. Another youth looking for adventure and action, and a talented one at that—still, the captain could hardly keep track of the names anymore. He chided his memory, which had begun to fail him more often than he liked to admit when it came to little details.

Where had all of his contemporaries gone? Farming, most of them. Or dead. And yet Runnda stayed on.

"Return to your lookout post, and report back in one hour." He spared the scout a reassuring smile. "With any luck, we'll be heading back to the border by sundown. Dismissed."

Corbin/Corwin turned and scrambled up the nearest pine, setting off into the thick forest canopy. In seconds, he had disappeared.

That boy could use a sense of mortality, Runnda mused. They all could. The border with the goblins had been disturbingly quiet lately, and the orcs had virtually disappeared. The youngsters weren't getting the experience they needed to stay sharp. Besides, orcs just didn't *disappear*. They were probably up to something. Unless something else, some enemy he didn't know about, had been attacking the orcs on another front. He would have to look into the latest intelligence when this grand spectacle of a wedding was over.

Of course, the Sky Guard had to stay well clear of the ceremony itself. Vesh seemed obsessed with impressing his "city cousins," as he called them, and wanted nothing to upset his wealthy guests. It made the job a little more complicated, but Runnda's men were more than up to it. Those who hadn't encircled Rima's Green in the treetops stood watch at the open end of the clearing, near the water.

The most dangerous foe the Sky Guard would face was the monotony of the next few hours, Runnda was certain. The Veshay Wood—the lower territory of the Northern Forest claimed by the Veshayn—had been cleared of dangerous predators decades ago, not long after the once-nomadic tribe had settled here. The bandits who had initially plagued the village were soon killed or sent packing. These days, a soldier would be lucky to find a hungry wolf or self-styled highwayman within twenty miles of the village. Perhaps that, more than the need for farmland, was behind the recent push to expand the borders of Vesh's fiefdom. It's hard to build a peaceable kingdom when you have combat-ready troops in every tree, and the chieftain knew it. Better those troops have plenty to do outside of the kingdom, allowing the citizens to remain peaceful, but defended.

Runnda leaned on his bladespear as he turned back to peer down through the boughs. Lute music wafted in from the gathering at Rima's Green. Through the trees, he could just make out the shapes of dancers.

Of course, there's something to be said for village life. Runnda had been serving the Sky Guard for over four decades. Watching the performers, he began to think that as he approached his seventieth year, maybe it was time for him to finally settle down. Why shouldn't he, too, find a woman, raise a family? Leave the business of fighting goblins and orcs to the young. They certainly seemed ready.

Dewer Runnda smiled and picked a handful of needles from the tree. They fell from his grasp as a lightning-fast blow came from behind his right shoulder, cleanly separating his head from his neck. It landed on the wide branch with a splat.

* * * * *

I really should have insisted on a pair of gloves, Teyna thought, *his hands are even sweatier than mine.*

Her right hand had been bound to Beric's by a long strip of silk ribbon, according to custom. The clammy feeling did nothing to improve her attitude toward her betrothed. He looked as uncomfortable as she in the midday sun, only warmer.

She had never trusted humans. As a child, she had too often seen their disrespect for the forest firsthand—the very farmlands that were to be deeded to the Veshayn were once untouched woodland, and the humans had ruthlessly stripped the land bare to make room for their fields and crops. It had frustrated her to see the forest laid low, and angered her further that her father had never objected.

Intellectually, she knew that not all humans were responsible, but as she met Beric's gaze, she had difficulty seeing anything more than a forest-killer.

This was going to be a long marriage.

Antlers dangling from the shaman's staff clacked together as he waved a spell of some sort over the couple's clasped hands. The old elf rattled a bit as he spoke the ceremonial words that would bind Teyna to the human prince, and he often had to pause for brief but vehement coughing fits.

"Vashayn ka, Caeliyan ka, kanira potundi. Teyna akat Beric, kaniri tomol. Kaniri tonol."

So there it was. "Teyna and Beric, forever bound." Wonderful.

Technically, she was now married, but before their bond was formally declared, Ezzik launched into a long chant of blessing for the newlyweds. Teyna found her mind beginning to wander as Ezzik continued his chant. It shouldn't be too much longer.

She glanced up at the trees that ringed Rima's Green. They

were mostly centuries-old gurna pines, although here and there stood the enormous silhouettes of the old giants of the Northern Forest—the ancient pinnacle cedars that had stood for millennia. After decades of living here, the Veshayn had still not explored the upper reaches of the magnificent mile-high trees.

She saw movement and tried to catch a glimpse of the Sky Guardsman who had allowed himself be seen infringing on the festivities. She knew they were on watch but forbidden to make their presence overtly known.

Father's going to have Runnda send that one to the goblin border.

Even as that thought formed in her mind, she realized it was completely wrong. Whatever was moving through the giant gurna boughs was *much* bigger than a Sky Guardsman. And faster. It took her a split second to wrap her brain around what she saw darting from branch to branch straight for Rima's Green. As her jaw dropped, she wished she'd had taken that second to scream a warning. She tried to shout, *It's a spider! A gigantic spider!* But no sound escaped her mouth.

A colossal arachnid leaped with unnatural agility onto Farom Vesh and opened a set of chelicerae as long as Teyna's arm. Foot-long fangs sunk into her father's abdomen, and in a heartbeat he was bundled into a webbed cocoon.

Most of the crowd panicked. A cacophony of screams and shouts of horrified disbelief shattered whatever peace remained in the clearing.

"*Vesh t'kayl!*" Ezzik bellowed, which caused the beast to drop Farom Vesh and turn toward him. The shaman's staff glowed with crackling blue energy that suddenly lanced out at the spider's abdomen. The acrid smell of scorched chitin filled the air for a moment as the creature burned in magical lightning, but the victory was short-lived.

So was Ezzik. The spider's forelegs slashed like knives, and the shaman's remains fell to the ground in several grisly pieces.

Teyna immediately jerked her hand free of the ribbon that bound her to Beric, causing the human to lose his balance and fall over backward off of the platform onto the ground below.

He should be safer there, she thought grimly. She drew her sword and ran to her father's side, gaping at the menacing giant that had been momentarily stunned by Ezzik's energy blast. That thing's got to be as big as Ezzik's hut. Glancing down at what was left of the old elf, she fought back a cry and fell to her knees at Farom's side. As she tried to calm her shaking hand—it would do her father no good if she freed him while simultaneously cutting his throat—Teyna slid the razor-sharp sword blade under the thick, ropy webbing that encircled his torso. She gently but firmly pulled up on the blade.

The stuff would not give. If she forced it, the pressure could drive the end of the sword into her father's chest. Maybe if she tried another angle. . . .

But Teyna didn't have time to waste. She spared a glance over her shoulder to check on the spider's location.

She saw Kolo was fighting for his life, and help looked to be nowhere in sight. Her brother hacked and slashed, dancing just out of reach of the monster's grasping forelimbs.

"Teyna, get out of here!" he called, returning his attention to his horrifying foe.

Teyna dropped an ear to her father's chest—he still breathed. There had to be poison in his system, but she didn't have time to worry about that. She blinked as her brother's blade flashed in the sun. Dodging and jabbing, Kolo tried to drive the beast back in the direction of the wood. Unbelievably, the beast actually retreated from Kolo's sword—but not far.

She worked to pull her blade gently from under the strands of webbing. Kolo couldn't be more than sixty feet away. She'd be there in plenty of time to help him. She brightened as she heard the pounding of heavy-booted feet. Three very angry dwarves had come to join the fight.

Two of the warriors from Battavorn moved to help Kolo, while a third flanked the spider. The desperate fighters managed to force the beast back up onto the wedding platform.

One of the dwarves—a commander in the Battavorn militia named Urutor—scored the first real blow against the monster. The commander sank his axe into the thick, hairy chitin that covered the spider's abdomen. The dwarf bellowed a triumphant battle cry, but it was cut short as his mouth filled with webbing from the gargantuan arachnid's spinnerets. Within seconds, Urutor was imprisoned in a silk tomb, suffocated.

With one swipe of his battle axe, another burly fighter managed to sever the end of one of the spider's forelegs. The creature emitted a high-pitched shriek as its limb plopped to the stage. Kolo and the dwarves involuntarily clutched their ears in pain.

Teyna's sword was nearly free. "Hold on, Kolo! Hold on!" she shouted. "Hey, eight-legs! Over here! Come and get *me!*" Teyna waved one arm madly. Perhaps she could distract the monster, give Kolo and the others and opening.

The spider swung its uninjured forelimb and knocked the two remaining dwarves off of the stage with a wide sweep. Then it turned to focus on Teyna's brother. With a bound, the spider flexed its legs and leaped straight up into the air. Kolo took to his feet and whirled to face the monster as it dropped behind him, but the spider didn't oblige.

"Above you!" Teyna screamed as she jumped into a run, but she was too late. The spider landed *over* Kolo on the tips of its footpads, forming an enormous birdcage over her brother's body. Fangs dripping with venom punctured Kolo's leg as he scrambled to get out from under the creature, and her brother began to spasm uncontrollably.

Teyna charged the gargantuan arachnid with no thought but to hurt the cruel, mindless thing, and hurt it badly. She would hack into the creature's brain and pull out the venom sacs. Give it to the shamans, they'd come up with an antidote. She would save them and destroy this horror herself.

As she neared the beast, the dwarves managed to regain their footing. One raised a hand, trying to motion Teyna back.

"Get back, Princess," the warrior—Teyna thought his name was Gorta—bellowed, "we'll handle this."

Those would be Gorta's last words. As Teyna tried to move around the dwarf to reach Kolo, the spider struck again with its remaining blade-leg. The dwarf's body was severed at the waist, just under his breastplate. Gore and blood exploded into the air, covering Teyna and Kolo with Gorta's innards.

The last dwarf roared in fury and charged the spider again. The monster simply flicked a leg forward, and the second dwarf was instantly impaled. With another twitch, the spider flung the heavy corpse into the air, where it flew in a slow arc before dropping with a crunching thud on the ground of the amphitheater. The creature hissed as it turned again to Kolo and Teyna. Satisfied that her brother still lived, the girl let loose a keening battle cry and maneuvered to strike the beast, trying desperately to turn its attention from her brother.

At that, at least, she succeeded. She locked eyes with the alien gaze of the spider. The monster swiveled and moved toward her. With speed born of years dashing through the treetops of Veshay Wood, she dodged and feinted, drawing the monster farther and farther away from her brother's inert form.

As the spider swung at her with its slashing foreleg, she ducked to the side and stabbed at the spider's pulsating abdomen with all her might. She felt a moment of elation when the longsword sank deep into the thick chitin. That elation was short-lived, however, as the monster spun again, and Teyna felt the hilt of the sword yanked from her gore-splattered hands. The beast was wounded, to be sure, but she apparently had not scored a killing blow.

Weaponless, she could only try to get away, preferably with Kolo. She danced back to her brother's body, intending to knock him off of the platform and reach the dwarven battle axe that rested in a pool of blood next to Kolo.

So focused was the elf princess on the deadly foreleg of the monster, she forgot for a moment to watch out for its tree trunk-sized hind legs. She did manage to dodge most of the blow at the last second, but it felt like being kicked by a horse. She rolled uncontrollably back over the creaking, broken stage. She saw a flash of black move in front of her eyes just before she rolled off the platform, and her head struck something solid on the ground. Blackness took her as consciousness fled.

* * * * *

Dim orange light greeted Teyna's squinting eyes. The light disappeared as a wave of pain washed through her entire body. She cried out softly, and her face contorted with agony. The pain centered in the back of her head, but she had no idea what could have caused it. Her chest felt horribly bruised, she might even have a broken rib or two. Where was she? Wasn't she supposed to be getting married today?

The pain in her head was nothing compared to the torment that now erupted in her heart. There had been a wedding, or most of one. Then . . .

It all came back in a rush, and she stifled an involuntary cry.

She forced her eyelids open and slowly turned to take in her surroundings. She was in what looked like a small, low-ceilinged cave, but as she looked closer over her head, she could have sworn that the stone was veined, like wood. Could she be inside a tree?

The tang of cedar filled her nostrils, and she realized that was definitely the case. She'd heard that the humans and other elf tribes would sometimes cut into the gargantuan trunk of a pinnacle cedar to build such structures, but no Veshayn would ever do such a thing—it was completely against their belief system. Was she in the spider's nest? Did it even *have* a nest?

She could feel that she rested on a thick blanket of some kind, so that seemed unlikely. She sat up to take in her surroundings. A small fire burned nearby. Definitely not a spider's nest

Her hand moved instinctively to her waist. She felt the soft leather of her belt and the top of an empty scabbard. She stood on wobbly legs and conducted a quick search of the immediate area but could find no trace of her sword.

A scuffled footstep echoed down the darkened passageway. She dropped to one knee and reached inside her footwear. The hunting knife Kolo had given Teyna slid easily from the top of her boot, and she crouched into a defensive position. She clutched the knife with white knuckles, wondering frantically if spiders had any weak spots she might exploit with such a tiny weapon. Judging from its reaction to her sword, probably not, but she figured she'd aim for the head. Teyna sidestepped to the wall at the right side of the entrance and waited for her moment. Closer . . . closer . . .

Teyna leaped forward and turned in midair. She slashed the knife blade down, hoping to separate the giant spider's head from its abdomen with one blow.

As it was, Beric managed to duck out of the way just in time.

* * * * *

"What in the name of holy Haynya is going on, Beric?" Teyna demanded through mouthfuls of radafruit. The two sat cross-legged on the floor, the fire between them as they conversed in hushed tones.

"What does it look like? I've brought you back some food," the young human replied. "No need to thank me." He raised a hand to his head, where he had a new bump resulting from a recent collision between his temple and the rock-solid cedar wall. Teyna's blade hadn't hurt him, but his last-minute dodge to avoid it was going to leave a mark. "If memory serves, I just saved your life, too." He smirked, an expression she immediately found both infuriating and somewhat disarming.

"Thank you," she shot back, "There, that make you happy?" She tossed the radafruit core over her shoulder and stood. "We shouldn't even be wasting our time here. My father and brother might still be alive. What happened? Where are they?"

"I think the spider took them," Beric offered. "But it was hard to see. I was mostly concerned with carrying you out of there."

"Why didn't you fight? What's that hanging from your waste, a toothpick?"

"I wasn't afraid to fight. Last I saw, more dwarves were having at the thing. I didn't know how badly you were hurt or if you were even alive." His expression darkened as he stared at the coals, adding, "I refuse to apologize for trying to save my wife."

"I'm not your wife," Teyna said and immediately regretted it—

he looked as if she had struck him with a hammer.

She spared another look at Beric, this human she had only met on her wedding day. He was actually rather handsome for a human, she decided. His stiff formal wear was ripped and stained with blood—possibly her own—and the odd thought struck her that it lent him the appearance of a rakish rogue.

She was determined not to be charmed. Still, he *had* saved her. "Let's worry about that later. I do appreciate you saving me. Thanks. Now, please," she continued, "help me. I have to do something to save my father and Kolo."

She stood and backed away to a more comfortable distance. She straightened and sat back down, working into another piece of fruit. Teyna looked around the inside of the cedar.

"So where are we?"

Beric appeared gratified to learn that his new wife didn't know *everything* about the forest. "It's a sentry outpost," he said. "And I think it's pretty old."

"Sentry outposts in the Veshay Wood? Who built them? Why?"

"They haven't been manned for centuries. My ancestors hollowed these things out long before the Veshayn ever showed up," he replied. "I've been camping out in these things since I was a kid. Spent an entire summer in this one, in fact. It seemed like a safe place to take you."

She *had* underestimated Beric. Perhaps he was more than a spoiled rich brat. "That's pretty smart thinking," she said.

"What now?" he asked with a thoughtful frown. "It's only been maybe an hour. Maybe the dwarves—"

"Maybe, maybe not." She found herself assessing the situation like a general. "We won't find out in here. I hope you know how to use that dagger."

"Actually, I thought we could use these," he said with a grin as he unwrapped the bundle on the floor. He had dropped the bundle when Teyna had nearly taken his head off, but she hadn't yet thought to ask what had been wrapped in the cloth.

As he unfolded the ragged material, her heart jumped. Beric revealed a blood-stained sword and a battered axe. "I didn't think the owners would need them as much as we would," he said.

She gratefully took her brother's longsword into her hand, and slashed the air with a few practice strokes.

"Beric," she replied, "I could grow to like you yet."

*   *   *   *   *

The soft moss that covered the forest floor hid the sounds of the pair as they crept with as much speed as they dared back to Rima's Green.

"We've got to act fast," Teyna whispered. "That poison doesn't seem to kill right away, at least, my father was still breathing when I last saw him. I think Kolo was, too. If that thing's gone, maybe we can find a trail."

He shot a glance over his shoulder at their recent shelter. "I didn't take us too far from the Green."

She skidded to a halt as Beric froze and held up a hand. They had reached the edge of the clearing. Except for a few birds shouting calls of warning at their approach, the air was silent and smelled of blood.

As they crept out from the tree line, she saw why. The dead were everywhere, most of them, anyway. The monstrous spider had cut the dwarf warriors into pieces, and it was impossible to tell from the mess if any had survived. Here and there, other bodies were scattered and torn amongst overturned benches and broken weapons. No living person was in sight.

The platform upon which she and Beric had so recently stood was a shambles. The poles that had held the colorful celebration banners lay on the ground, snapped like twigs in several places and tangled with ropes and large sheets of red and green cloth. She felt a surge of nausea as she drew closer and saw the twisted, shattered bodies of people she knew.

Of her father and Kolo there was no sign. Desperately she ran through the amphitheater, looking at every severed head and snapped limb. No, they were not among the dead. In fact, at a rough count, she reckoned only thirty to forty of the guests had met their demise here, the others must have escaped, or . . .

"It must have taken them," she told Beric.

"Or it ate them," he replied.

"Spiders wrap up their food and string it up on a web. That's what spiders do," she said more harshly than she meant to. She added, "They're alive. I can feel it."

"You didn't happen to see any of . . . see my parents? I can't find any sign of them." Beric looked as if he was about to be sick as he asked the question.

That caught Teyna off guard. She'd been utterly selfish. Of course Beric was concerned about his own family and friends. "No, I didn't see them." She forced a grim smile. "Maybe they made it back to the village. Maybe they're raising an army."

"Right," Beric said.

Beric's eyes widened in surprise as something over her shoulder caught his eye. Fearing the worst, she whirled, ready to fight.

What she saw shocked her to her core, not with fear or horror, but overjoyed awe. With calm, deliberate steps, Ezzik, high shaman of the Veshayn, strode across the scene of carnage toward them.

"Takes a little more than a bug to slay a high shaman of the Veshayn, children," the wizened old elf cackled as he stopped before Teyna and Beric and leaned on his staff.

As Teyna's shock faded, she leaped forward and embraced the shaman. Before she knew what was happening, she had burst into tears.

Once Beric and Teyna had both regained their composure, the trio walked cautiously toward the edge of the bowl that formed Rima's Green. Though none of them said it, Teyna could feel they all wanted to get away from the corpses and wreckage.

"What I don't understand is how you could even be here," Beric said to Ezzik. "We saw—"

"You saw a simple illusion, my boy. The lightning was real enough, though. But I'm not such a fool that I intended to just stand there and let the beast take me apart. I summoned forth a golem—an artificial construct made in my image—to stand in my place." The high shaman peered into the trees around their heads, searching for a sign that would show him where the spider had gone. "Then it's as simple as a minor cantrip of invisibility, and I live to fight another day." He added, "It's not something I do often, then, it's not often called for. But it's a nice trick."

"Nice trick," Teyna agreed, and then added bitterly, "So you ran."

Ezzik met her steely glare with his own. "You need to learn respect for your elders, Princess." He coughed, and for a moment, every one of his advanced years showed in his stance. Then he took a deep breath and stood tall once more. "I saved as many as I could, but I'm afraid many more were taken by the beast." Turning to Beric, he added, "I'm afraid your parents were among them, Beric. Farom and Kolo, too. I am profoundly sorry."

Beric merely stared at the ground, but Teyna could see that he had just received an invisible blow.

Chastened, she softened her tone as she asked, "Can you make out any kind of trail, Ezzik?"

"With these old eyes? Not at all. Let me try a little something I picked up from a ranger friend of mine. . . ." He muttered a few strangely accented words in Elvish, and his staff danced a geometric pattern in the air.

After two minutes had passed in silence, Ezzik suddenly froze and turned as if guided by the staff in his hands. With agonizing slowness, he lifted the staff like a pointer and aimed it into the upper forest canopy.

"So they went that way?" Teyna asked impatiently, breaking the calm.

"Sshhh," Ezzik admonished as he slowly opened his eyes and looked intently down the length of the staff in the direction it pointed. "Give it a moment. . . . There. Think you can follow that?"

Teyna gasped as a string of blue lights began to glow softly on the branches above. The tracks extended as far into the wood as she could see. The jagged line they formed pointed straight to the base of a particularly enormous pinnacle cedar that Teyna guessed stood two miles distant. A thought struck her, and she turned on her heel and stalked back toward the poles that lay tangled with corpses and tattered banners. Drawing her knife, she cut loose as long a piece of rope as she could find.

She quickly began to coil it as Beric caught up to her. "Teyna? You have a plan?"

"We're going to climb a tree," she replied.

*   *   *   *   *

"You know, I'm not a complete idiot," Beric said.

"Who said you were?" Teyna asked. They had paused to rest for a moment. Teyna guessed they had been climbing and running through the canopy of the Veshay Wood for nearly two hours.

Beric took a long pull on his waterskin and offered it to Teyna, who took it gratefully. "Not me." She added, "An idiot would forget to bring water."

He grinned. "Thanks. But really, you weren't too impressed with me. Admit it."

"I didn't think you were an idiot, exactly," she explained, "but yes, I wasn't too impressed with you. I never wanted to get married." She looked at him with skepticism. "You didn't know that, did you?"

"How would I? It's not as if we ever had a chance to talk about it," Beric said. "And you don't say no to Derc Rycaelin. Not if you're part of the 'royal brood,' anyway." He sighed. "I guess I might be all that's left of the royal brood now."

"We'll find them, Beric," Teyna said. Seeing his despondent expression, she tried to change the subject. "At least we're getting some use out of these wedding clothes."

Beric laughed, and Teyna found herself giggling almost hysterically. "Well, I certainly didn't intend to put this getup back on anytime soon," Beric said as he struck an overtly foppish pose. He looked so ridiculous in his tattered silk, axe hanging from his waist, that Teyna collapsed again with giddy laughter, and Beric joined her.

"At least you didn't have to deal with the ribbons. And flowers. Here, have some," Teyna said, pulling a few crumpled blossoms from her hair and tossing them into the air like confetti. They fluttered down into the darkness below like snow. For some reason, that suddenly struck her as very sad. Despite her resolve not to show weakness to Beric, she hung her head.

"Hey, Princess. Sorry, *Teyna*," Beric said softly, crouching beside her. "We're going to find them, just like you said." Now it was

Beric's turn to change the subject. "I've never seen a princess fight like that. Have you trained in Caeliyan?"

She shot him an incredulous look. "Why would I do that? Kolo trained me. He's a commander in the Sky Guard. I wanted to join, too, but father would have none of it. He was too interested in making me an attractive sale."

"That's what you think this was?" Beric asked.

"Wasn't it?" she replied in kind.

"I never thought of it that way," he said. "I never felt like *I* was for sale. I felt coerced, and I felt like my free will was being taken away from me, but—"

"You were being sold just like me, but you didn't realize it," she said. At that, Teyna stood and offered Beric a hand up. "Come on, it's going to be dark in a couple of hours."

"It's already dark," he said.

"There's dark, Beric, and there's *dark*. Just wait until the sun sets."

Teyna stopped for a moment to check that they were headed in the right direction. Satisfied, she began to move forward, following the glowing tracks.

Suddenly, Beric tapped her on the shoulder, and she stopped short.

"What is it?" she whispered.

Beric didn't speak, only brought one finger over his lips. He then pointed ahead and to the left, in an area Teyna hadn't looked. She immediately saw what had brought him to a halt.

Gorillas. A pair, from the look of it. One silverback appeared to be eating a piece of radafruit, while its companion, a female, groomed the fruit-eater's back. Both apes seemed preoccupied. Fortunately, Teyna and Beric were downwind.

This was going to be tricky. Of all the dangerous creatures that

lurked in the Veshay Wood, the gorillas had been the most difficult for the Veshayn to clear out. It was well-known that many
still lurked in the trees, and all but the Sky Guard simply did
their best to avoid the creatures if they encountered them more
than a few miles from Veshaynya. The apes didn't seem interested in attacking the village, but they reacted to strangers with
aggression.

The powerful primates were easily the equal of a Veshayn when
it came to traversing the treetops. And although they didn't eat
elves—as far as Teyna knew—they were quite territorial and very
strong.

Teyna communicated to Beric through gestures and simple
hand signals that their best bet was to sneak by and avoid the
apes entirely. Even if they lost the trail, they were sure to pick it
up again. It was glowing, after all. Beric nodded in agreement.
Teyna in the lead, they proceeded as quietly as they could, each
endeavoring to keep one eye on the gorillas without losing their
footing.

The going was slow, but Teyna thought they might actually
make it. The trail was clearly evident not a hundred feet off, which
she estimated would get them clear of the apes. She glanced back
over her shoulder, checking that Beric remained with her. Her eyes
then flicked over to the gorillas to confirm that they had not
moved.

The gorillas were gone.

She turned back to point this out to Beric, just in time to see
the silverback leap on him from above. The ape—a small male—
roared as it came down, slamming the human prince into the thick
gurna branch. It pinned Beric between its powerful legs and
pounded its chest in triumph.

Teyna backed away and drew Kolo's sword. She scanned the

boughs above for some sign of the second ape while keeping an eye on the silverback. Beric wasn't moving.

She didn't have to wait long. The second ape dropped onto Teyna from directly above, mighty arms extended. But the elf girl was prepared, and with a well-timed thrust she impaled the gorilla, and the beast's own weight drove it down to the hilt. The female's roar was cut off immediately as her heart was skewered, and the primate's body landed on Teyna, pinning her to the broad branch.

Teyna struggled to free herself from the massive weight of the dead gorilla. The first ape roared again. She could hear it scuffling toward her.

With all her strength, she pushed herself out from under the corpse, which rolled off the branch and disappeared. She staggered to her feet to face the remaining gorilla and realized with dismay that Kolo's sword had still been in the ape—today was not her day for keeping weapons. Glancing at her feet, she saw she was about to run out of tree limb.

The gorilla was almost upon her. Out of options, she prepared to jump, hoping she could catch herself on a branch. It was her only chance. Yellow canines flashed as the ape bellowed and pounded its chest. It dropped to its knuckles and charged. Teyna steeled herself and dropped into a crouch, preparing to leap with everything she had left.

The gorilla screamed then, a scream not of rage but, Teyna soon saw, of pain. Beric howled—sounding a bit like a gorilla himself— as he drove the dwarven battle axe into the ape's back.

The next few seconds would play out in Teyna's mind over and over again in the next few hours. The wounded ape whirled, yanking the axe from Beric's hands and flinging it in a bloody arc into the air. Teyna had to drop again to avoid having her head taken off by the whirling blade, then it was gone, clattering through the gurna branches. The maddened gorilla leaped at Beric and tackled him in a mighty death hug.

A half-second later, the tangle of ape and man plummeted into the shadows far, far below. Teyna could only stand and stare.

* * * * *

Tears streamed freely down Teyna's eyes as she dashed from branch to branch, following the glowing blue trail.

Beric was dead. He could not possibly have survived the fall. And he had died saving her life. Saving her life again. She hadn't realized how close she had begun to feel to him in the last couple of hours, yet there it was.

And she was alone.

Why hadn't she sent him back to the village to get the Sky Guard? Or to Caeliyan City, or anywhere but into these damned treetops? She wasn't sure he even would have listened, but she should have tried, *she should have tried*.

Teyna forced herself to bury thoughts of Beric. Right now, his was just another death to be avenged. There might still be people alive, depending on her whether they knew it or not. She *would* save the spider's captives, even if she had to do it alone, with nothing but a knife to protect her.

She almost ran right past the bend in the trail.

The faintly glowing blue markers ran right up the trunk of a colossal pinnacle cedar tree. Staring up, she began to curse the setting sun, wherever it was, as the dim light faded. She couldn't tell if the trail ended a few hundred yards up, or if that was simply the point at which they became too small to see. There was only one way to find out.

While the Veshayn elves had never scaled one of the mighty

pinnacle cedar trees all the way to the top, she saw that the climb would be possible. Pinnacle cedars were heavily branched, and like the relatively smaller gurna pines, they had branches easily wide enough to stand upon. She swung the heavy end of the rope over her head and with a grunt of exertion set off up the side of the biggest tree she had ever seen.

After half an hour, Teyna still hadn't reached the end of the trail, and the canopy of gurna pines was several hundred feet below her. She paused on a wide bowing cedar branch and caught her breath. She could see the entire world spreading around her in all directions but couldn't bring herself to enjoy the wondrous view.

Out of the corner of her eye, she thought she saw movement above. When she turned to look, whatever had moved had disappeared in the increasing darkness. She drew her hunting knife, gripped it in her teeth, and resolutely continued her climb.

She'd gotten another hundred feet when she very nearly climbed right into the spider's web. She was barely able to see the gigantic web against the darkened gray-blue sky, but there it was, and it was *huge*. It spread between her tree and another massive cedar almost a quarter mile away. Skeletal husks clung here and there to the thick lines of webbing, and at first she feared all her efforts had been in vain. Upon more careful inspection, though, she saw these could not possibly be the wedding guests—the skulls bore the distinctive shape of goblinoids. The orcs. Runnda had said the border had gone quiet, she thought.

If not for the day's events, she might even have found it quite beautiful. Under the circumstances, the predator's web simply filled her with cold dread.

Just a spiderweb, she told herself. You've seen those. Sure, the spider's big enough to swallow you whole, and this web could cover the whole of Rima's Green—

Her musings were cut off by another flash of movement. Knife in hand, she whirled around on the wide branch. She noted absently that her rope slipped away at that moment, but she didn't dare try to catch it.

She had only a moment to scream before the giant spider seized her and sank its fangs into her neck.

* * * * *

This time, she awoke in darkness. Not just the darkness of night but the darkness of an enclosed space. She felt hot breath against her face and realized it was her own. The tug of gravity told her that she was in an upright position but not standing—there was no weight on her feet. She tried to move her arms, but they were pinned to her sides. She tried to swing her legs, but they too were bound.

Great Haynya, she thought, I've been cocooned.

The sting of the bite in her neck pounded along with her pulse, but she fought back panic. Actually, she didn't seem much the worse for wear. Her muscles ached, but the venom seemed to have left her body. Was it this easy for everyone to recover from the poison? She felt a glimmer of hope.

That glimmer burned into a flame as she struggled within her bonds and realized she still gripped her hunting knife. Could it possibly cut through this stuff? She hadn't been able to cut her father free with her sword, but if she could somehow move her arms, she might be able to exert enough force from inside the webbing to at least make a hole large enough to see. Wriggling with as little movement as possible, she pulled her fist up along her body. After several agonizing minutes, she had worked both hands up in front of her face. Carefully, for the blade was only a hair's breadth from her chin, she turned the knife outward, then pushed with all her might.

The blade slid through the webbing. More accurately, it slid between the fibers.

Her heart pounded. She turned the blade at neck level and twisted her wrist to cut horizontally, with the "grain" of the webbing. The knife began to slide through the stuff more easily, and soon she found herself wearing a sort of spider-web hood.

She hung suspended in the enormous web. It was a very long drop to the bottom of the forest. She suddenly thought again of Beric's death and fought back bitter tears.

Teyna's entire body swayed gently in the breeze as the web caught the wind. Squinting, she tried to see if her activities had drawn any attention. As far as she could see, they had not. In fact, the spider was nowhere in sight. So far, so good. She cautiously pulled the knife back down to shoulder level, and this time managed to cut a hole through which she could push first one arm, then another. With her arms free, she went to work on her legs. She slid the blade around her waist, trying to cut the cocoon in half. After some contortion, she succeeded

She spared another glance up. Still no spider. She swiveled from side to side, and realized that she had only been attached to the web at leg level. Her upper torso seemed able to move freely. Reaching above her head, she managed to grasp at a rope-thick line of webbing. Calling on all her reserves of energy, she achingly pulled herself up from the lower half of her cocoon.

She had half expected the thick webbing to be sticky—that's how they caught flies, wasn't it?—but the cable felt smooth to the touch and did not cling to her hands. Once her legs were free, Teyna pulled herself up a few "rungs" and tried to catch some glimpse of other captured prey.

It didn't take long. The moonlight reflected on the bundle of cocoons with a white glow. Several dozen victims had apparently been bound together with another length of webbing and hung from the far side of the web, a quarter mile from the tree she had used to get this far. Still wearing part of her cocoon like a tunic, she set off across the web, trying not to look down.

Within a hundred feet of the cocoon bundle, she caught sight of the spiders. None of these was the arachnid that had abruptly ended her wedding ceremony, she realized. There were at least a dozen of them, all with glinting greenish abdomens and thick black legs, but they looked like toys compared to the monster that had caused so much death and horror at the ceremony. Each one looked about the size of a dog. Must be the babies, she figured. Where was their mother?

The spider's young began to swarm out along the web as she approached. Grasping the web in her left hand and planting her left foot firmly in the junction of two web strands, she prepared to meet the onslaught.

The first spider didn't even reach her. As it skittered along, Teyna hit it squarely with a well-aimed orc skull. The impact knocked the young arachnid from sight, and she readied to meet the next one.

Can't cut all the strands away, and I can't reach any more orc skulls, she realized. I need something to stand on. The second spider received an upward slash from a long knife blade, and it too dropped like a stone to the forest floor.

Perhaps they can't even spin a web line at this age, she thought. Lucky me.

Three, four, five, a half dozen dog-sized arachnids plummeted to the ground before one finally made it past Teyna's defenses. The young spider boldly leaped from a strand above her head and dropped onto her back. There it clung, all eight legs digging into her between the shoulder blades. A second spider slammed into Teyna from the side, nearly knocking her into the air to her certain death. Spider after spider leaped upon her. Blinded, her balance completely thrown, she gave up trying to hit her attackers with the knife. Teyna simply did the best she could to hang on.

Teyna's stomach leaped into her throat as she dropped straight down. Still unable to see through the arachnid that was clutching her face, she scissored her legs—the only part of her body that could still freely move—wildly.

Her actions were immediately rewarded with a jarring pain that wracked her lower body as first one, then another leg caught on heavy strands of webbing. Her fall jerked to a halt. Her vision returned as the spiders' inertia caused them all to continue to plummet.

Teyna struggled to right herself as fire shot through her right leg. She hung upside-down, her legs forming a crude **V** shape, but one limb was bent at an unnatural angle just below the knee. Probably broken. Suddenly, her upper body was yanked downward. Three of the spiders still hung from her upper body by long strands of webbing.

The arachnids swung lazily in the wind as they climbed back up their safety lines. The nearest one might be 200 feet away, although it was difficult for Teyna to gauge the distance upside down with a broken leg and blood rushing to her brain.

The swaying motion of the spiders on the wind reminded her of something. A game she'd played with her brother, long before the Sky Guard and the hunting trips. Children holding hands in a line, one big kid at the end cracking the whip. . . .

Struggling to stay calm, she stretched her arms out wide,

taking all three web lines in her hands. With relatively small movements, she slowly began to swing the long strands in a pendulum motion.

All three of the spiders continued to climb the webs, but their own weight began to work against their efforts. Teyna continued to crack the whip back and forth, each swing bringing new agony from her broken leg. Now it was the arachnids' turn to instinctively hold on for dear life as their arc swung wider and wider.

Teyna heard three satisfying thuds as the young spiders collided explosively with the side of the pinnacle cedar. Most of the corpses peeled free of the rough bark and swung back into the air.

Somehow, Teyna retrieved her knife, and with great effort and a howl of pain, she brought herself upright. Extricating her legs from the tangled webbing nearly made her to black out, and she ground her teeth as she cut herself free with one hand, hanging from the other. Her useless leg swinging free, she managed to use her good leg to keep stable. She swung hand-over-hand toward the bundled cocoons.

Teyna silently cursed the loud winds at this altitude. But at least she was on solid wood, not a web.

By pressing her ear against the cocoons, she could just barely hear whether the person inside still had a heartbeat. Fortunately, the lightweight but sturdy spider's silk was an excellent sound conductor. She didn't know how many of the cocoons she could carry back by herself and grimly realized that any cocoons without heartbeats would have to stay, for now. The important thing was to get the survivors to safety.

Out of thirty-two cocoons here, she'd detected heartbeats in only five. She cut off several lengths of webbing and managed to tie the five cocoons together at the top, forming a very heavy bundle that caused the web to sag. She then fashioned a thick loop that she could hang over one shoulder, allowing her two free hands to climb. With a soft groan, she looped the makeshift web-strap over her shoulder and slowly began to crawl across the spider's web.

Every swing brought new agony to her shoulders and back. Her good leg afforded a bit of support when she could find a web to stand on, but it was all she could do to keep the pain of the broken leg from overwhelming her. Teyna was not a small girl, but she had five adults slung over her back, and the strain just to keep her grip soon became a battle. With painfully labored slowness, she crossed the great divide by moonlight.

She had to stop after progressing only a third of the way—otherwise, she was going to fall. She needed a better way to get back to the other side, to the stability of the tree.

Teyna searched the giant web for a line that would serve her purposes. Despite its enormous size, the web looked like almost any ordinary spider's web in design—concentric circles of webbing, strung around a starburst of web lines radiating from the center. The top anchor points of the giant web actually disappeared into the dark on either side above her head. She needed to find exactly the right anchor line . . . there.

Teyna stabilized herself on the web, then proceeded to wrap her left forearm around the anchor line she had chosen. Making sure her precious cargo was securely attached, she raised the knife in her right hand.

Suddenly, the entire web began to bounce. Teyna's broken leg slammed into a thick rope of webbing, and she screamed, but held on. She soon saw what had caused the sudden bounce.

Mother was home, and she was dashing across the web toward Teyna at astonishing speed.

This had better work, Teyna thought, and brought her arm down in a sweeping blow that severed the anchor line. The wind blasted her face as her weight and the weight of the bundled cocoons pulled her down in an arc toward the trunk of the pinnacle cedar and away from the monstrosity bearing down on her.

Teyna missed the actual trunk by mere inches.

She would have slammed directly into the thick cedar bark had her "rope swing" not been slowed and tangled by the upper branches of the cedar. Those branches brought her to a jarring halt, and again she thought she might pass out from the pain.

Teyna opened her eyes, and saw she was dangling only a few feet above the wide branch upon which she had stood just before setting out across the web. The cocoons hanging from her body felt like the weight of the world. She shrugged the bundle from her shoulder and lowered it as gently as she could manage. Then, with a flick of her wrist, she dropped to the natural wooden platform below.

She landed on her good left leg, though the impact still made her see stars. She hobbled onto her one good foot and looked back the way she had come. The giant was still headed toward her, and Teyna was all that stood between the spider and its victims. Somehow, she raised her knife and prepared to finish this, one way or the other.

"Teyna!" It was Beric.

"Beric? Is that you? How did you—?" Teyna shouted, keeping her eyes on the approaching doom. She couldn't believe her ears.

Teyna had done, and was still doing, quite a bit of damage to the web, so the beast was forced to take a circuitous route to reach her. A small comfort.

"Where are you?" she called.

"Maybe a hundred feet below you! Teyna, the spider—"

"I see it! Beric, I've got five survivors up here. I'll try to fight this thing, but . . ." She couldn't continue.

"I'm coming, hold on!"

"Make it quick, or you might as well not come at all," was all Teyna could manage before she swung painfully out on the web toward the spider.

Teyna wasn't going to survive this time, she was certain, but that thought gave her a strange sense of calm.

Beric was alive, and that filled her with unexpected joy. And here he was again, coming to her rescue. Sorry to disappoint you this time, husband, she thought.

Teyna intended to stop the spider if she had to cut every line of the web, taking herself with it. As she and the spider continued on a collision course, she swiped left and right with the knife, cutting web line after web line. Soon, she would cut the line from which she hung, and the beast would die with her. Sparing a last glance behind her, she saw Beric climbing onto the wide branch that held the cocoons.

The time was now. She had severed all of the lines around the spider, and it was headed toward her on the same rope of webbing she held in her left hand. Reaching behind her head, she swung the knife—and dropped like a stone.

The next few seconds seemed dreamlike. As she fell feet first, Teyna looked up, hoping to catch a glimpse of the monster falling alongside her.

It still hung from the webbing. A little farther down than it had been, but there it was.

"No!" Teyna screamed. She flailed her arms. By blind luck, she caught one of the few remaining anchor lines low on the web. She held it in a death grip. Teyna's momentum carried her farther down, and for a split second she feared the line might snap under her weight.

Instead, it turned into a giant bowstring, with Teyna as the arrow. Once she had reached the nadir of her descent, the line snapped her back upward, and she found herself flying aloft. The remaining blade-leg of the spider just missed her as she flashed by, and the elf princess hung from the web once more, this time well above the monstrous arachnid.

"Teyna, I'm coming to get you! Hold on!" Beric shouted from far away.

"Stay where you are, Beric," she replied. The giant, now directly beneath her, turned and scrambled energetically up the web straight for her. With one hand, she clutched the tiny knife. One more try, she reckoned. If she could time her leap just right, she could tackle the thing and take it with her. She turned back to Beric, and her eyes locked with his. She smiled and mouthed the words good-bye. With that, she jumped away from the web and half-fell, half-dived directly for the spider below.

She missed the creature's eyes—where she had truly hoped to strike—but managed to stab her knife into the spider's abdomen, right where it attached to the monster's head. The hilt slipped from her fingers, and she clutched instinctively at the coarse hairs that covered the spider. She had to grab it, pull it down with her, destroy it.

To her utter disbelief, Teyna felt her hand close around a familiar sword hilt. The same sword she had worn to the wedding and thought lost forever. The spider hadn't taken it out—it remained deep inside the monster's guts.

Teyna held onto the hilt of the sword with both hands, hanging like a child pulling an enormous lever. The longsword slid through the spider's exoskeleton like it was paper. The steel blade ripped open a huge gash that sprayed guts in all directions. The spider let loose a keening hiss of pain and fell backward into the open sky.

Teyna released her sword and caught herself on the webbing once more. A wet, splattering thud echoed through the canopy as the creature's carcass collided violently with the forest floor. The young elf crawled hand-over-hand back to the branch where the five rescued cocoons still waited and collapsed in a heap.

*　*　*　*　*

Teyna's eyes blinked open. She looked up into the smiling face of Beric. As he she coughed and struggled to sit up, he reached down and helped her up, and the smile turned into a laugh.

"But how did you . . . ? I thought you . . ."

Beric smiled. "When I went over the edge with the gorilla, we bounced from branch to branch. We came to rest only a few hundred feet below. The gorilla's body cushioned my fall, but the impact had knocked me unconscious. When I came to, Sky Guardsmen were climbing the cedar." His smile grew. "I reached you first."

Maybe her new husband had a little Veshayn in him after all.

Ezzik had come with the rescuers, waiting to help the victims when they reached the bottom. He had managed to revive all five of the victims she had personally saved, including Beric's mother, a young Sky Guardsman named Cowan, and three Veshayn villagers. He also magically mended Teyna's broken bones and nearly dislocated shoulder as good as new.

As the Sky Guard set up a perimeter and retrieved the remaining cocoons from the web, Teyna and Beric received alarming but happy news: these victims, too, were alive! Ezzik believed that the spider's venom had put them into such deep comas that Teyna had simply been unable to hear their hearts beating. One by one, he resuscitated the captives, who were still extremely weak.

As he worked, Teyna told Ezzik about her experience and how she had so easily shaken the effects of the poison. The old shaman's eyes gleamed.

"Those chants did *mean* something, you know," he cackled. "I do more than golems and lightning. There was a spell of health, purity, and fortune—and a good one, if I do say so myself—on you and this fellow. One of the most ancient wedding spells in my repertoire, in fact."

"That explains how I killed the spider—good fortune," Teyna said.

Ezzik considered for a moment. "I doubt it," he finally said, "There's only so much power in one of those spells, and I'd guess you used it up pretty quickly."

"That was all you, Princess," Beric said.

As soon as Ezzik declared Kolo and Farom Vesh fit, Teyna gingerly embraced her father and brother. They were enraptured by her tale. And although there was joy at the rescue, there was great sadness—many good people had died today. Farom Vesh swore that the Sky Guard would clear the pinnacle cedars, and despite his condition, he was soon immersed in plans with Kolo, Derc Rycaelin, the remaining Guard Captains, and several Battavorn dwarves. Teyna and Beric, exhausted beyond belief, quietly slipped away in the commotion.

As they walked hand-in-hand back to Veshaynya, Teyna realized she still wore much of the cocoon that had saved her from the bite of the young spiders. She shrugged, and laughed.

"You know, I'm not even sure I can get this stuff off. Besides, it's kind of comfortable."

"We'll see about that," Beric said.

"Oh, *please*," Teyna retorted, but she did so with a grin. Suddenly, she took his face in her hands, and kissed him. "We need to work on your sense of humor, husband," she added. "But thanks for coming back for me."

Drawing on each other's strength, the pair continued down the road in comfortable silence, happy to be alive, happier to be together. For the first time in years, Teyna looked to the future without bitterness, only hope.

Part III:

Invasion Era

The darkest hour . . .

Behold, the Fish
J. Robert King

Let me tell you about a fish—the smartest fish in a smart room.

Here's how smart the room was: While every other merman and merwoman and merkid fought in a foreign war against a foreign species that didn't even breathe water, this room of folks had spent two years talking philosophy and making music and having the kind of visions you can get only from licking a blowfish. While every other Vodalian was making war with air suckers, we Eliterates were making love with water suckers. It wasn't that we were cowards. We'd been fighting Vodalia for fifty years. As far as we were concerned, the Phyrexians were just more Vodalians. Their biggest crime wasn't their kill-'em-all attitude, but the fact that they were ugly and did ugly things and made the world ugly. We knew how to fight ugliness—by making beauty. That was our war, and we had formed a secret artists' colony to wage it. When ships fell from the sky, and spinal centipedes ran people through, and plagues swept across the tides, we were ready with satire and parody and farce.

No genocidal dictatorship can stand against farce.

So, now you know how smart the room was, or at least how smart everybody in the Rift Café thought we were.

As to the fish, he was a genius. He had a head like a coral reef—big, oblong, colorful, and swimming with amazing things. He had a voice like a lone whale calling out across a thousand leagues of ocean to his lost pod. He had a presence that was more than the iridescent scales that ran from belly to tail, or the cocky cant of his back as he read his poetry, or even the insolent snap of his fingers not in a rhythm but in a kind of spastic fury. You listened to him. I was his best friend and the second smartest fish in the room, and even I listened to him.

The merman's name was Destry.

That day, the Rift Café was jam-packed. Damsel fish crowded the front and drank their tube-worm delicacies. They rarely listened to the recitations, preferring to burble in eddies of vapid conversation. Behind them drifted artists and poets, coiling about the kelp stalks that were planted in the floor. Even they usually lent only half an ear. The Rift had an open niche: Anybody could swim up to recite, and most folks were lousy.

Destry wasn't just anybody. He cruised slowly up there—he had a kind of snarling charm that made you thank him for inconveniencing you—and even the urchins and fries in the back shut up and listened.

Destry fixed us with a sultry stare, and his narrow purplish lips curved in a smile. He looked like a barracuda with a sense of humor:

"The man . . ."

The words had exactly the *snick-whoosh* of a harpoon gun.

> "You've heard 'bout the man,
> 'bout how he snares fish in tin buckets
> and makes tides run red and black
> and kills anything he can't suck. It's
> a shame for our world. It's a smack
> in the face to get faced by the man."

He stopped and pointed to someone significantly. We all turned to see a fish reclining in the center of the crowd. He had a weird black hat and hairlike curls and a tail fin that seemed like black boots crossed over each other. That was the most we glimpsed of him, though, because Destry jetted some red anemone spores from his gills, and we looked back.

The cloud floated like blood around him and deepened his aura:

> "The man . . .
> You've heard 'bout the man
> but you don't know him.
> Point him out, if you can.
> You say Vodalians swim
> all around us and net us and
> prod us, so they're the man.
> Or for killers on land
> there only one Man: Phy-re-xi-an.
> No. . . ."

He clucked and shook his head. A smile began like the flash of teeth before a great white bites. He bit.

"You're the man!" Destry growled, jabbing his finger at a coral sculptor. Snarling, Destry pointed his nose at a mermaid. "You're the man!" Then all around the crowd: "You're the man! You're the man! You're the man!" Last, to himself, over and over: " I'm the man! I'm the man! I'm the man!"

The crowd chanted with him. "I'm the man. . . . I'm the man. . . . I'm the man. . . ." They kept up this counterpoint while Destry swam on:

> "If the world is ugly, it is ugly in my perception,
> and if my perception is ugly, it is ugly in my mind,
> and if my mind is ugly, it is ugly in my soul,
> and if my soul is ugly, I am doomed and damned,
> I am Vo-da-li-an.
> I am Phy-re-xi-an.
> *I am the man!*"

The chant stopped. The fingers started: a swimming ovation.

I was snapping with the rest of them. I was a poet myself, the second best in the room, but still there wasn't a shred of jealousy in me. Destry got what he deserved—praise. Unadulterated praise.

I glanced over at the fish with the hat and saw him snapping too. Strange thing was, he uncrossed his tail into a pair of legs. Stranger still, he tipped his hat to me and vanished.

Well, not exactly vanished.

"Behold, the man!" Destry cried, pointing toward the sky.

We all looked up.

There was a skylight in the grotto, leading to shallow waters that cast a wavering light across the crowd. Through that wide circle we saw him. Above the sea, in the midst of a cerulean sky, hung the strange man with the hat. He looked weird up there, distorted by air. I was so dazzled by him, I almost didn't notice when Destry swam up. Almost.

I flicked a fat finger skyward. (I was a fat fish next to Destry. Couldn't help it. The food in the Rift was great.) "Who's the guy?"

Destry smiled. It made everything else in the room seem dim. "Friend of mine. A planeswalker. Ancient. Goes by the name of Bo Levar."

I squinted. The guy had his arms spread wide and cast a giant shadow across us all. "What's he up to?"

Destry shrugged. "Said he had something big planned. Said he was going to thumb his nose at Yawgmoth."

"This I've got to see."

I did. I, and Destry, and every artist and poet and freeloading love minnow in the Rift. We all saw that one crazy man thumb his nose at a god.

Suddenly, there was blackness in the West. No, the West *was* blackness. It was as if the world was disappearing. Sky. Sea. Silt. Stone. All of it dissolved. I'd seen hurricanes that came like a wall and tore the air and churned the water. I'd seen warring leviathans lift a fathom of silt from the seabed, but I'd seen nothing as impenetrable and absolute as this. With any natural storm, there was noise—vitality. With this cloud, there was only silence.

Somebody said the word *"beautiful,"* and I guess it was, the same way that rushing blood is beautiful before it spreads through the water and brings the sharks.

Half the sky was gone. Bo Levar hung in the bright wedge that remained. His arms were flung wide as if to embrace the darkness. It struck him. He didn't move. He only flared brilliantly. The darkness had a hard time eating him away. It had to go tissue by tissue and cell by cell. Each one gave up the ghost grudgingly. This Bo Levar hadn't a single soul in him, but a hundred thousand, a million, and every last one poured from dissolving pores. Auras traced out his veins and nerves, the lines of memory imprinted over eons of life. Energy gathered in fingertips and toes and shot outward. From the man spread a great web of power that reached out around us all.

I don't mean just around the Rift Café or just around our secret colony. I mean that the globe of magical protection spread from that one man with the million souls to engulf sky and sea and silt and stone in a sphere that was a league in diameter. The man spent his souls for those of us who'd already hawked ours three times over.

It was quite a thing. Even Destry stood there gulping like a yokel, and he never did anything like a yokel.

Energy encircled the trench and everyone living in it. Darkness encircled the energy. Our sole sun was the man Bo Levar, who even then flamed away to nothing. Suddenly everything was black and silent.

I floated there, cringing. I heard the ragged rush of water through my gills, and through Destry's, and through a thousand other fish's as they struggled to breathe.

Somebody had called that darkness "beautiful," and it had been beautiful, until it filled the water all around us. Now it was ugly. There aren't words for that darkness. Caliginosity, adumbration, tenebrosity—all are too luminous. Opacity, crepusculence. No. This was the blackness of the innermost chamber of a dead heart buried beneath ten thousand leagues of monstrous machines.

This was the heart of Yawgmoth.

Everybody churned in terror. We didn't bump into each other. Merfolk have pressure points along both flanks to let us swim in schools. But we schooled nowhere. We circled within the Rift Café through water that reeked with fear.

194

The bartender pulled out a jar of trench fish, glowing beasts bottled at extreme depths. In the eerie light of those frantic fish, we saw ourselves—frantic fish. We had kin in them. We both had been bottled under enormous pressure.

Even Destry was scared. I'd never seen him scared.

I said, "What do we do now?"

He shook his head, a black mass in all that darkness. Then a little light came on in his eyes.

"What are you going to do?"

He shrugged. "What good is art if it can't break a crisis?"

"How could art . . . ?" I began, but didn't know what to say. I stumbled on. "Don't you see what just happened? The world is gone. We're krill caught in the baleen of Yawgmoth! What are you smiling at, you crazy fish?"

"The best ones are crazy," he said. He waggled his way across the Rift.

We all watched. We didn't so much see him move as felt him in those pressure points. His motion brought the rest of us to a standstill. Some folks were thinking he was heading up to the niche to tell us what to do, but not Destry. No.

He was more likely to tell us where to go.

"Oh, shut up," he began, a preamble that silenced the last worried whining in the room. He poked a finger at one of the damsel fish who had been most hysterical, cocked his hips, and said, "You think this is bleak? You ain't seen bleak."

As soon as he started, I knew he was riffing, making up the lines with each snap of his fingers and lips.

"Bleak is when you reach into your purse and find sharks' eggs."

We all laughed, but especially the damsel fish. It was a great one for her. A shark's egg sack is called a mermaid's purse.

Destry pointed at another jittery fish, a fellow with the rep of a heartbreaker. "Bleak is when you serve your girl a worm with a hook." More laughter came. Destry turned his gaze on the woman whose heart had been most recently broken by the fellow. "Bleak is when your blind date turns out to be a randy whale."

She laughed. We all laughed. There is no better sound in the middle of dark desperation. Destry was saving us, no less than that. That's why he was great. He was riffing and saving us all the while.

Destry dived out of the niche and snatched a clam shell from a nearby table. It was filled with green goo—a delicacy. He held it up and made a gagging motion.

"Bleak is when your fish jelly turns out to be jellyfish." He dragged long tendrils from the stuff.

Amid the laughter, someone else shouted, "Bleak is when you meet a cephalid pickpocket."

Destry applauded. We were all into it now. Here's how we'd been fighting Yawgmoth all along.

Somebody said, "Bleak is biting into an eel before you know it's electric."

Over the hilarity, I jumped in with my own: "Bleak is finding out your greatest foe has just been killed by a greater one."

The room went quiet. Dead quiet. Like I said, I wasn't any Destry.

"Off you go to your caves, now," he said placidly. "What hardship is darkness to so many philosophers and poets, anyway? You'll come up with deeper philosophies and better poems—or at least you'd better. I'm sick of the rot you've been bringing here. Bunch of hacks! These are the hours when poets are born, folks," and then behind his hand, "or at least when they're conceived. So get home!"

He abused us, and we thanked him. That's because we all knew he'd saved us. Through the preternatural darkness, we flocked home. There, we holed up and waited for the sun to rise again.

* * * * *

Next morning, the sun didn't rise. Two more tides came, which told us it should have been light, but it wasn't. All remained black. Then there weren't even tides. It was as if Yawgmoth had reached up to the heavens and ripped down the very moon. And if he had taken the moon, what had he done with the sun?

We all lingered in our caves, watching our glowworms die and not having the courage to go collect more.

This was bleak. We didn't know bleak before this, but this was bleaker than an urchin suppository. That's one I thought up after my flop the night before. Somehow, though, farce was no match for Yawgmoth. He was the one genocidal tyrant who was immune.

Finally, on what was probably the third day but seemed like the third month, the darkness was done. It fled away faster than the murk that flees the dawn. It was as though every octopus in the ocean had sucked its ink back in, leaving the waters clear once more.

I floated beside Destry, and the two of us stared out, stunned.

The darkness had been a mercy. Though the entire colony had been saved—tidal gardens, tiered flats, coral caves, kelp forests, the Grotto, the Rift Café, and every other hot spot—everything beyond Bo Levar's sphere was decimated. Every weed and stalk, every coral and barnacle was dead. All plants had turned to gray mush, as lifeless as bleached silt. The animals were worse. Some lay on the bottom, half-skeletal. Others floated on the surface, great bladders of trapped gas. Most, though, were in the process of rising or sinking. It was a steady rain of bodies, and no sharks remained to clean them up. The sharks were among the dead. As far as the eye could see in any direction, the ocean floor was the color of dead fish, and the water was charged with them.

I tried my suppository line on Destry. He was unimpressed.

"We're going to have to go out there," he said quietly.

I nodded. "We'll send a scouting party—"

"We're going too."

"We?" I spread my fat fingers innocently across my chest.

"Where's your poet's heart?"

"Inside, where I hope to keep it."

He shook his head. "This is too big a moment. The Vodalians will use this catastrophe to claim the whole ocean."

"So, let's send soldiers," I said.

"We can't possibly fight them with soldiers—even if we had any. They'll take over everything and write the histories of this hour. That's where we fight. We battle their propaganda with truth. We poets need to become historians."

"What makes you so sure we won't die the moment we leave the sphere?"

"Yawgmoth wouldn't dare," he joked. "I'm Destry."

Before the sun had reached midday, Destry had gathered the strongest, bravest, heartiest souls he could find in the colony. I now think we were also the stupidest. Philosophers and poets don't survive in the wild. They only eloquently observe their own deaths.

We were even provisioned like idiots. Sacks of brine bass and jerked squid hung off our backs. Each of us had a ten-day supply of food, if we were cautious. An assortment of sponges would keep unwholesome waters out of our mouths and gills. We also wore tridents, though none of us knew how to use them. We did know how to use the puffer quills and octopus ink and ray-skin rolls—for writing observations and history . . . and doodles, most likely doodles. A few of the younger fish took along conch armor and swordfish blades, fearing close-range combat with Vodalians or Homarids. I tried to tell them that armor and weapons would only slow our swimming away, which was our only hope of survival. They laughed and said that an old manatee such as myself should leave the strategy to younger heads.

Younger, emptier heads.

We swam. It's work to swim when you're a fat fish, but I wasn't about to let the young minnows realize how hard I worked. Nor did I want Destry to know. The truth was, we all worked hard. None of us were patrollers or fighters. We were artists. The hardest work we were used to was cracking crab legs and forking out the meat. Our rations of brine bass and jerked squid made awful fare, and in too small portions.

But really, the worst burden of the journey was what we saw. The water was brown and clear. The krill that once had scintillated through it were purged. We could see for a horrid hundred leagues. The kelp forests were leveled. Coral reefs that had survived Argoth didn't survive Yawgmoth. Every creature in that vast and complex symbiosis had gone down together. The bottom was a deathbed. Fish in their anonymous billions, sharks, rays, eels, seals, snakes, whales, and, yes, merfolk.

The first band of Vodalians lay only a league from our canyon. Damned scouts. And we'd thought our secret secure. Four of them crouched together in the mouth of a small cave. They had apparently used it for some time; weapons and stores were crammed at the back. The scouts surrounded a slab of stone where they had spread a ray skin. As if frozen in time, the four figures crimped their fingers on the skin, seeming to study it. They were not rotten, these four, but petrified by the presence of Yawgmoth. His very touch had calcified them, locked them in utter stillness.

Destry looked down solemnly and disturbed the stillness. One flick of his tail cleared the ray skin, and we saw a detailed map of our colony. Every cave, every canyon, every home and meeting place appeared. The strategic points had been marked with **X**s. One such mark obliterated the grotto where Destry lived. His name, and my name, and many other names were written full beneath.

"So, they knew about us," I said.

"Damned Vodalians," Destry replied eloquently.

I flicked a nervous glance at the others gathered around. They returned my gaze with their own concern. These young fish were more shaken than I. We all had believed that our colony was beyond the notice (let alone reach) of our oppressors. It was nerve-racking to realize we'd been in their dirty claws all along. We were alive only because they hadn't squeezed.

I spoke for all of us. "How long did they know, and why didn't they bring an army to destroy us?"

A philosophical look crossed Destry's face. "The second question answers the first. They didn't destroy us because they were busy fighting Phyrexians. If they were busy fighting Phyrexians, they could not have known about us until after the war began."

"Two years," I said bleakly. "And now that Yawgmoth is gone— if he truly is gone—how long before they pay us a call?"

Destry stared off into the dim brown waters. "I'd wager that they're on their way even now. Unless . . ."

"Unless what?"

A rueful gleam showed in the fish's eyes. "You've heard, 'the enemy of my enemy is my friend'? It may be that Yawgmoth himself has reached down his black and pestilent hand and done us a great favor."

I smiled, though a chill ran through me. My flop of a joke came back to me, and it seemed no joke. "No. It would be just like Yawgmoth to slay every good thing in the sea and leave the one rampant evil."

"I Caught Me a Dogfish," said Destry, announcing one of his old standards. The words were so familiar, I joined him, and the rest of the party did too.

> I caught me a dogfish as mean as can be,
> With serrated teeth and a black eye to see
> Through my soul. I took that old dogfish to chase up three
> Catfish, but gods damn that dogfish, he bit me instead.
> I grabbed him and punched him alongside his head.
> I told him 'Catch catfish, or you'll end up dead.'
> He said, 'Boss man, know that I'd eat up a catfish,
> But mer-meat is really where my taste is at. Dish?'
> I killed him and ate him and then got my wish.
> He'd swallowed a litter before he was caught.
> I ate them with liver. A lesson was taught:
> Hunt where you're told, or you'll die on the spot.

The chant wasn't about dogfish and catfish, of course, but about Vodalians and us. They should have gobbled us up before Yawgmoth gobbled them up.

Yeah, we felt like sly catfish, our barbed whiskers gleaming. Still, we hadn't much of a domain to prowl anymore. Yawgmoth had left us with nothing. Silt and rot and bones. It wasn't much fun to preside over a nonexistent food chain.

"What are we going to do for food?" I asked as we swam on.

Destry jabbed a thumb over his shoulder. "We've got our rations."

"No, I mean the colony. If the ocean's dead, if there's no one to trade with, what do we do for food?"

His gills flared, but he said nothing. He'd not thought about that.

I shrugged. "Maybe there are more like those scouts—I don't mean merfolk, of course, but fish that were mummified, that would be all right to scavenge. Or maybe the seasonal migrations will continue, and we can harvest the whales that come through. Or maybe there are creatures like us, safe in hollows here and there, and they'll come out, and we can set traps."

With each suggestion I offered, Destry's lips grew tighter. By the time I was done, he looked like he had no mouth at all. "We've never had to think about food. It was always abundant."

"Yes, but we have to think about it now."

"Food!" he continued, as if I'd said nothing. "Paltry, measly food. How can we think about beauty if we're scrabbling for food? How can we care about truth when we're grubbing among corpses in search of some hunk of meat?"

"Well, in the long run, things will work out," I said. "If some of those corpses are rotting, they have parasites, bacteria—the lowest levels of life. The food pyramid is beginning again. We just need to hope the next thing in line comes along, and the next, until the one just below us has eaten."

"Listen to yourself! Sometimes you act like a scurvy little crab, plucking dead skin and jabbing sea monkeys into your mouth—"

"I'm just trying to think in terms of beauty, of Nature reasserting herself."

"Yes, and how long will that take? Ten years? One year? Even one month is longer than we can last. What if Nature reasserts herself and we're gone?"

"So you agree—we need to think about food," I said.

"Scurvy little crab!"

There was no answer to that. Destry liked to have the last word.

He was damned clever, but the problem was there was nothing left to be clever about. How do you parody a mass extinction? How do you play a room when nobody's left in it? Destry was an artist, and an artist is an apex predator—rare and impressive but dependent upon all the creatures that lie below. When a society is decimated, artists become beggars. Sculptors learn to quarry stone. Poets learn to write histories. Dancers learn to lift and stack. Every beautiful thing waits while we tend to every needful thing.

I sensed resistance and resentment in Destry. There was nothing he would ever do as well as write and recite and snap his fingers, but those were no longer needful things.

We swam on. Vodalia lay hundreds of leagues east by southeast. I insisted we orient off the sun. The magnetic poles had been flip-flopping since the night of the blackness, and even now, the fields fluctuated and shifted. We all could sense it, and it was a nauseous feeling. When we were in the colony, surrounded by other directional cues, we could ignore the whirling giros in our heads, but here, in this desolation, the sun alone would tell the truth.

"What are you doing?" Destry asked, exasperated as I bumped him eastward. "You're curving south."

"No," I replied. "Look at the sun. You've been curving north all day."

"It doesn't feel like east. East is that way. It tugs your breastbone—the place of beginnings, the place of history . . ."

"Not anymore. You can't go by how it feels," I said. "You have to go by how it *is*. Nothing feels right anymore."

It was true, perhaps too true for Destry. I was telling him to live at odds with his internal compass, his heart. "You're sure Yawgmoth didn't screw up the sun too?" Destry was a smart guy, the smartest guy in a smart room, but Nature doesn't care about genius, only about survival.

"I'm sure. Now move over." We had our hands full with survival.

"Scurvy crab."

We'd swum sixty leagues by nightfall, reaching a deep chasm that was slowly disgorging heavy, cold water from its depths. We continued on, well out over the grim blackness of it, and waited for the moon to rise. There had been no tides, so we should have guessed there would be no moon. It made me unutterably sad. I would miss that glimmering thing most of all. I had half a hundred poems in my head with the moon in them, and every last one seemed suddenly precious.

The stars rose, dancing pinpricks. I could do a little with them. We kept on our tack, directly toward distant Vodalia. It was eerie to swim in that cold, deep place, watching the stars trace lines down our backs. What if something lurked below, something that had escaped the death-touch of Yawgmoth and hoped, as we did, to eat a passerby? There was nothing any of us could do about it.

That's when Destry came into his own. Art thrives when everything is working beautifully or when nothing is working at all. Either way, nothing else remains to be done, so you have time to listen and think. Destry made up some art to help us across that black space. He used the rhythm of our stroking tails instead of snaps, and he spoke the words in a soft lullaby:

> When through the darksome deeps you swim,
> be mindful I am watching you,
> but not with eyes that blink and dim
> in distance, no. With vision true
> I watch. With heart and hope, I watch.
>
> And should some beast arise to slay
> and do you battle more than you
> can bear, then die. But know I lay

your head beside my heart, and too
I die. With dread despair I die.

For why am I above the brutes,
the hungry mouths of nature's plan?
Because I love. Because my roots
lie in your heart. Oh, frightened man,
believe! With dread and hope, believe!

He sang the song but once, and all was quiet except the vital pulse of tails through water. Still, that song remained in us. It was a light—the single hope of a benighted race. We weren't alone. As long as we were capable of compassion, we weren't alone.

* * * * *

We *were* alone. The next day told it unmistakably. We had made another sixty leagues past the nighttime trench when we found them. Row on row they lay, as if in a decorous graveyard. Aside from a thin layer of silt, though, the Vodalian army had not been buried. They rested in such order because they had swum so when Yawgmoth had struck them. And if he had not struck them, they already would have struck us.

We floated there above the rows—three legions, with fin-soldiers and mounted warriors and even contingents of siege sharks. The Vodalians had planned to overwhelm us, subdue us, enslave us—perhaps even slay us. It was hard to stop sharks once blood was in the water.

Lucky for us, it had not been blood but Yawgmoth.

"We have to go down for a look," I said, watching my shadow drift over the bodies below. After three days of uncertainty and two more days of hard swimming and iron rations, my shadow was noticeably thinner.

So was Destry's, except that he had already been lank before this ordeal. "Why go down there? They're dead."

"There might be salvage. There might be battle plans. If we knew who ordered this and what the intention was, we could use that knowledge to prepare for . . ."

Destry had stopped listening and was drifting down toward the fields of the dead. While my mind raced among tactical matters, Destry wallowed in all things metaphysic.

"Shall we mourn?" he called up to me and the others.

We followed him down; we were so used to it. The scent of dead flesh was sharp in the brown waters, and it grew stronger as we went.

Destry seemed oblivious. "These are our brothers, lying in this mass gave. Shall we mourn? Or shall we laugh? These are our foes, laid out dead at our feet. Here is the death of oppression and greed, of tyranny and murder. Shouldn't we eulogize these wretched dead with a laugh?" He had reached a soldier. The merman's tail arched back, and his hands clutched his heart as if in the final spasm of death. His eyes were as white as spermaceti. "Can I laugh at you, brother? Dead brother? Brother who wished to kill me?"

"Get away from there!" I shouted. "There's bound to be disease."

"Where is your poet's heart?" he asked, cradling the dead merman and kissing his forehead.

"It's not on my sleeve, like yours," I responded. "Do you want to die with them?"

"They were headed to our colony to destroy us, but they were destroyed instead," Destry replied. "Is it tragic or comic? Is it meaningful or absurd? Does it do anything for you at all?"

"Yes, it makes me thankful."

"To whom?"

"To Fate. To Fortune."

"To Yawgmoth?"

Destry had had the last word.

I understood what was happening. The world had changed, but Destry couldn't change with it. He thought that if he banged his head hard enough against it, he could put it back the way it was. Either that, or he would dash out his brains. One way or the other, he and the world would soon be rectified.

"Get away from that fish!" I shouted. "It's leaching rot into the water!"

Destry wouldn't listen. He lamented like a hired mourner over the fallen army. At the time, I thought he was weeping for the Vodalians. Now I realize he was weeping for himself.

* * * * *

It was five days of hard swimming later before we reached Vodalia. The distance had taken Yawgmoth a mere moment to cross. In the second moment, he had struck with a vengeance.

The old empire was gone. It had been utterly destroyed. The buildings remained, of course. I marked the stonework Temple of Valshee, the Coral Coliseum, the Diluvian Opera House, the Seat of State, the canyon marketplaces, the palaces, the guildhalls, the slums—but all were draped in bodies and silt. Not a creature moved. No scavengers remained to worry the dead. The citizens had perished under the iron hand of Yawgmoth.

It was one thing to see an enemy army slain in their ranks. It was quite another to discover decimated civilians in our onetime homeland. We artists had spent our lives hiding from and fighting the Vodalians, believing them to be the Great Foe. Yawgmoth could not possibly justify our ire, but Vodalia could.

You don't rail against those you hate. You rail against those you love.

Vodalia was gone. It was unbelievable. I stared, openmouthed. I did not see tyranny lying dead in the streets—or greed or oppression or murder. I saw kin. I saw myself there, dead. I could not bear it and turned away.

The faces of the young poets among us were more horrible to behold than the ruined city. In their eyes, I saw all the wreckage reflected. The carnage was overlaid with astonishment, terror, nausea, despair. Those young fish would never be young again.

"They're dead," one of them said. "They're all dead."

I shook my head slowly. I wasn't sure what I would say until I said it. I guess I was riffing. "No. They're not all dead. We—you and I—are Vodalians. Despite everything we've said, despite the battles we've fought, we are and have always been Vodalians. Our secret artist colony existed only in its radical rejection of Vodalia, and now that Vodalia has ceased to be, we have ceased to be as well. We have inherited all its history, all its art, all its culture. We are Vodalians."

Hope gleamed, small and fragile, in their eyes. I needed better words to convince them, the words of a better man. *The* man—the smartest fish in a smart room.

"The man," I said. "You've heard 'bout the man, but you don't know him. Point him out, if you can. You say Vodalians swim all around us and net us and prod us, so they're the man. No. . . ." I pointed to the first fish in the squad. "You're the man!" I jabbed my finger at another. "You're the man!" And at each of them: "You're the man! You're the man! You're the man! I'm the man!

"If the world is ugly, it is ugly in my perception, and if my perception is ugly, it is ugly in my mind, and if my mind is ugly, it is ugly in my soul, and if my soul is ugly, I am doomed and damned. But if I can save myself, it is beautiful in my soul, and if my soul is beautiful, it is beautiful in my mind, and if my mind is beautiful, it is beautiful in my perception, and if my perception is beautiful, it is beautiful in the world. I am the man!"

The words were hitting them like the pulses of their own hearts. They were hitting me the same way. So this was how it felt to be Destry.

"Yawgmoth has given us the end of Vodalia. I reject it out of hand. Vodalia does not end with Yawgmoth. It begins with us."

They were smiling. In the horrid gray light of that decimated city, they were smiling. I was smiling too. I felt proud, like I had blindly led them to the truth. What is an artist but a blind man who is willing to risk all and grope and stagger and crawl until he finds the truth? I felt like I had said what Destry would have said if he had . . .

"Where is Destry?" I wondered. He was not among the platoon. Had he gone down to soliloquize above a dead child? I turned. My eyes traced out the tortured streets, the domes, the columns, the bodies. "Where is he?"

The others knew whom I sought. They sought him too.

One of them pointed and shouted, "There!"

We spun and saw—not Destry but the one thing we had both hoped and feared to see: living Vodalians.

A mismatched platoon of them rose with inescapable speed toward us. They outnumbered us three to one, and they looked like they knew how to use their polearms.

I flipped over and shouted, "Swim! Swim for your lives!"

I got no argument. The others whirled and rushed along beside me. Instead of letting out a war cry, we just plain cried. Our armor and weapons slowed us—empty heads!—and the pressure points at my tail told me the Vodalians were closing. Glancing back, I realized we didn't even know how to run away; we were swimming deeper into the city.

Everything I had said suddenly seemed false. We weren't Vodalians. Vodalians were the brutal bastards who were chasing us. Vodalians were going to kill us. Brainless bullies, imperialist pigs, they dominated smaller nations and lived off the spoils. We Eliterates had specifically chosen not to be Vodalians. If we had taken their history as ours, their city, their name, we would have become them—a fate worse than death.

Just now, though, death didn't seem all too attractive either.

With flashing scales of azure, the Vodalian platoon swarmed us. A sphere of blades bloomed to every side. We slowed to a stop. None of us even reached for our weapons, knowing we would die. The younger fish stared all around with wide, terrified eyes. Beyond the stingray points and the pearlescent shafts lurked strong, battered, angry faces. These Vodalians were merfolk, yes, but the darkness in their eyes and their habitual scowls made them seem a different species.

The bulkiest warrior—a mere sergeant with a head like a bullfrog, wore the deepest scowl of all. He approached among the shafts, entering the deadly sphere.

Stowing his own trident at his waist, he said, "What have we here? Civilian survivors? Perhaps. But in the new order, you'll make good slaves."

I hardened my gaze. "We aren't Vodalians, and we certainly aren't slaves."

"What are you, then?"

"We've come to aid your rescue attempts," I lied, trying to keep the tremors out of my voice, "and to negotiate alliance."

The sergeant laughed, a brutal blast of water. "You mean, you wish to offer your unconditional surrender." He snuffed. "I know slaves when I smell them."

"What right do you have to negotiate anything, Sergeant . . . ?"

"Sergeant Blatik," the man supplied angrily. His jowls puffed, and his froggy eyes became slits. He clutched the sergeant's pin on his armor. "I am the highest ranking survivor of the Vodalian empire, and as such I am the new emperor. My will is law throughout the sea." Here we go again, I thought. "If I say that you are slaves, these folk will make you slaves. If I say that you are dead, these folk will make you dead."

"And if I say you are a liar?" blurted a new voice.

I craned to see beyond the sergeant, where iridescent scales gleamed across his canted back. Another merman approached, a slender fish wearing the uniform of the Vodalian army. He moved with absolute confidence, his fingers snapping.

Blatik's green face flamed to red. "A liar! Who dares?"

His soldiers kept their tridents trained on us even as they turned to see who approached.

"I dare, Sergeant. I—Captain Omen. And yes, you are a liar, sir. If you're not careful, I shall call you a murderer as well!" The newcomer swam at last into the light, and all of us could see him. Destry wore the cloak of a Vodalian captain, torn but unmistakable. In one hand, he absently twirled a trident as he made his way toward Blatik. The fingers of Destry's other hand snapped with sharp, insistent reports. "I've been calling and pounding for nearly a week, trapped alone in the barracks cellar." He leveled the trident and his baleful eye. "Did you think to check the cellar?"

The sergeant's color was fading, but his teeth still flashed sharply between bulbous lips. "We *did* check the cellars. All the food was rotten."

"You didn't check *all* the cellars!" Destry roared back indignantly. "You conveniently missed checking the one cellar where I was trapped! The food survived, and I survived on it—much to your chagrin, I see, Sergeant Blatik! Perhaps you intended to let old Captain Omen die, so that you could be emperor!"

"Captain Omen! I didn't even know you were in that cellar!"

"Your words betray you, Sergeant!" Destry snarled, jagging his finger at the man. "*That* cellar, you say. *That* cellar! Why else would it be *that* cellar unless you knew I was in it?"

"What?"

Destry turned, pinning a private with his gaze. "Did Blatik here forbid access to certain areas of the base?"

Gaping, the man said, "Yes, Captain. To the restricted areas."

"Ah, hah!" Destry said triumphantly. He had slipped into the performance groove. No one could best Destry there. "Sergeant Blatik denied access because the area was restricted, and the area was restricted because he denied access!"

"Nonsense!" Blatik exclaimed.

"Nonsense, indeed!" Destry said. "And if you used this sort of nonsense as a cover story, what horrendous sort of nonsense were you covering up! I'll tell you what sort—nothing less than the negligent murder of the man who by rights would be emperor! Regicide!"

I almost began to laugh but was too afraid to.

"I'm innocent. Since when is it regicide to forget to open a cellar?"

"He admits it! He willfully forgot the cellar that held his only rival!"

The sergeant trembled, whether from fury or fear, I couldn't tell.

Destry *could* tell. "As ranking officer, I'm taking over this unit. Our first order of business will be an investigation into these heinous happenings. Do any of you have complaints about the conduct of the sergeant?"

All around, hands rose eagerly. This man had been a tyrant, and he was meeting a tyrant's end. I saw in those hopeful young faces reflections of my own face. Perhaps we weren't Vodalians, but we were their brothers.

"You four, take hold of Sergeant Blatik!" Destry ordered.

With alacrity, four of the man's underlings rushed in to grab his arms and strip his weapons.

"Conduct him back to the brig and lock him up. We'll not have more bullying. That was the way of Old Vodalia. This is the way of New Vodalia. I am ad-hoc emperor, Emperor Omen, until safety can be restored. We'll have no more nasty bastards while I'm in charge."

I had to laugh then, but the sound was covered by the relieved laughter of the Vodalian troops. They were only following orders, both when they obeyed the brutal sergeant and when they arrested him. Perhaps some soldiers suspected Captain Omen, the living parody, but still, they wanted to be free. Even a joke emperor was better than a brutal sergeant.

No genocidal dictatorship can stand against farce.

Strutting among the remaining troops, Destry whirled his trident indolently, nodded toward us, and said, "What's the story with these scurvy crabs?"

The other soldiers traded glances, unsure who had the right to speak. One young fish said, "Strangers, Emperor Omen. We found them scavenging."

I broke in. "We are from the secret colony code named the Eliterates."

"Eliterates!" crowed Destry. "I'm a great fan of your poet Destry. Is the genius still alive and well?"

213

"Still flapping."

Destry nodded gravely and barked, "Well, what do you want?"

"Alliance," I said simply. "We've fifty times your population and have avoided the worst of the devastation. We have plenty of food and the desire to help you plant new crops and raise new schools of fish, hunt pods of whales and do all the many things that both of our societies need if we will survive."

The eyes of the Vodalian soldiers grew wide with hungry hope.

"Preposterous!" spouted Destry. "Why would Eliterates want to help Vodalians?"

I smiled, realizing it only then. "Because without Vodalia, we don't know who we are."

* * * * *

That was the beginning of the Vodalian-Eliterates alliance, created when a smart fish started a smart riff. The whole thing was based on a farce, a lie—the sort of secret that can save whole nations.

It was hard going at first. We had to worry about food and every other measly particular. Emperor Omen commanded us all to scour the ruins. We found many sealed cellars, with other survivors and enough food to support all the Vodalians and Eliterates for a few months. We also found unspoiled seeds for potables of all kinds. Vodalians and Eliterates worked side by side, burying the dead and planting new life.

While civilians cleared the city, Emperor Omen did the same to the military. He promoted the best and brightest in the platoon, establishing a hierarchy that was strong but democratic. He even let his upper echelons in on his masquerade. It was a good sign that they all found it funny. Destry warned them to keep the secret, not allowing it to creep into the Vodalian histories of the age. (Of course, we Eliterates weren't so tight-lipped in our tales.) He also made them promise to go easy on the belligerent sergeant—once all of us Eliterates were gone.

We all planned to swim back to our not-so-secret colony. Emperor Omen, meanwhile, planned to die.

He arranged the whole thing beautifully. During our send-off ceremony, Emperor Omen delivered an impassioned speech about renewed brotherhood. At the height of his oration, a great white came out of nowhere and snatched him up. It was quite a realistic shark, and the blood was so thick that Destry was long gone before the crowd could follow. His accomplice—a stage-magician and illusionist from our hearty band—had done his work flawlessly.

I shook my head in grief. Vodalia had never had a greater ruler. Still, Emperor Omen had had to die if the poet Destry would ever live again.

I felt no small relief when Destry, unharmed, joined us later as we returned to the Eliterates.

A year has passed, and I led an expedition to see how New Vodalia fares.

The city thrives. Every day, more merfolk arrive, refugees seeking a fresh start in a new city. The more the merrier. The fields around are verdant, the herds graze in safety, and there's even enough time for art.

I sit just now in the Antediluvian Theater, the old opera house. Tonight, it has become a realm of poets. The famous Destry is here, along with me and a few other Eliterates. Destry has made sure to alter his appearance from his days as emperor, for we are performing before a packed crowd.

"The man . . . You've heard 'bout the man. . . ."

J. Robert King

As I listen, I have to laugh. Destry's gotten a lot a use out of that poem.

Once again inspired by him, I turn over the evening's program, pull out a urchin quill, and start writing a history of my own. It's the story of Vodalia's fall and a new alliance. First, a title:

"Behold, the Fish."

Journey Home

Will McDermott

Carnage. The field was awash in red and black at a time of year
when it should have sported shades of green and gold. Death. Oil
and blood intermingled, soaking the trampled grains and the trampled bodies in a sick ochre that would take months to wash away
in the coming rains. Decay. The vultures circling above the bodies
would have a hard time determining who had won this war—if
they even cared—for this was a war with no victors, only survivors.

Even the vultures could not win this day, for they would not eat
well due to the stench of the phyrexian machinery and the slick, dirty
oil that pervaded the field and spoiled the meat of the dead and dying.
In a few days, even the vultures would be dead from the phyrexian
poisons—poisons that had nearly destroyed an entire world.

There were other scavengers on the field, though. Scavengers who had lost at least part of their life, part of their spirit, during the war. For even the survivors of this apocalypse would return home partly dead inside. In the middle of the battlefield, a lone dwarf picked his way through the maze of dead bodies, twisted metal, decaying phyrexian hulks, and blasted war machines looking for something, anything, of value that he could take away from this awful scene.

"Damn vultures!" yelled Balthor as he swatted at one of the ugly black birds that kept diving down at him from the hazy, smoke-filled sky. "Ye can have yours when I'm done with 'em. For now, bugger off!"

Balthor Rockfist was a typical rough-hewn boulder of a dwarf. In fact, all of the dwarves on Dominaria had a certain look about them; a look as if they had all been carved from the rocks of the same mountain. Balthor's ash-gray face was mostly covered by a short-cropped red beard and long, thick strands of his red hair, which also cascaded down over his shoulders. Though still quite young for a dwarf, having seen only forty-five winters come and go, his face was already etched like a weathered stone from a lifetime of battles.

As Balthor moved through the dead, swearing and swatting at the vultures, he scanned the bodies and wreckage looking for the glint of steel, the sparkle of gems and jewelry, or a decent pair of boots. The scavenging dwarf had already replaced his leather armor and metal helm, two items he had lost in the claws and jaws of a phyrexian warhound he'd fought earlier. At the tough dwarf's side jangled a pouch full of coins, semiprecious stones, and gold rings he'd also appropriated.

"Ye can't eat this, and he won't be needing it where he's gone," called Balthor up at the circling vultures as he pulled a silver bracelet off another fallen warrior. "What are ye looking at? I gotta eat and pay me way back across the sea to me home, don't I? Bah! Leave me alone, ye buzzards!"

Just then, a flash of sunlight reflected into Balthor's eyes from a piece of metal jutting out of the chest of a massive phyrexian beast. The dwarf had mistaken the mighty bulk for a war machine until he saw the beast's legs stretching out behind its barrel-shaped torso.

Ever attracted to shiny objects, Balthor climbed atop the oily, black creature to get a better look at the silvery object.

"Bah! It's just the butt of a sword," said the dwarf as he stood on the great beast's stomach and looked down at the cylindrical object poking out of its chest. "Still, I could use a backup weapon in case I lose me battle axe."

Balthor spit on his hands, rubbed them together, then leaned down to grasp the protruding handle. As he heaved the weapon out of the dead phyrexian beast, he let out a low whistle, for this was no embedded sword. It was a seven-foot-long staff made of the brightest, most reflective metal the dwarf had ever seen.

"Fiers's blood!" said Balthor, looking at the flawless, straight, silver shaft. "You're a mighty fine hunk of steel. It's a good thing I came along, or ye might have rotted inside that poisonous belly. I'll give ye a new home just as soon as I get back to me bellows and forge ye into something more useful."

With that, Balthor stowed the staff on his back and jumped down from the phyrexian beast, looking like a flag bearer who'd lost his flag. The lone figure on the battlefield moved on to look for some new boots to wear on his long trek home, while a vulture landed behind him and began pecking at the eyes of a dead warrior.

Days passed, and Balthor saw nothing but carnage, death, and buzzards as he trekked south toward the sea. The roads were barren except for an occasional wrecked war machine, but the fields were still mired with the dead. Balthor's coin purse jangled heavy and full, but his belly growled constantly from emptiness.

"At least I got new boots to pad me aching feet," he told his only friends late one afternoon. The vultures that followed him, hoping for a meal, didn't respond. "Still, a few more days without food, and ye'll finally get your chance to dine on the finest dwarf cuisine." Balthor tried to chuckle, but his mouth was too dry, and all he could manage was a dry, rasping wheeze.

Just then, Balthor heard the unmistakable sounds of battle. Metal rang out against metal from somewhere around a bend in the road, and Balthor heard an unholy howl that sounded like a saw blade being scraped across a slate floor. Warhounds! Swallowing a small bit of spittle that his wheeze had brought up from his throat, Balthor dropped his coin purse and the hunk of precious metal strapped to his back into the ditch, then trotted up the hillock to get a view of the battle.

Just as the dwarf had thought, several warhounds had surrounded a warrior on the road. The hounds circled and snapped at the besieged man with their massive jaws, howling every time the fighter connected with his large, two-handed sword.

But this was no ordinary warrior. He faced the circling hounds with stoic courage, the remnants of two other beasts lying at his feet. Balthor recognized the warrior's race. He was a barbarian from the Pardic Mountains of Otaria—Balthor's own homeland. The barbarian stood nearly seven feet tall and was as broad as a brass boiler in a dwarven forge.

Tired, hungry, and half-dead, Balthor didn't hesitate to join the fight. Dying in battle was far more preferable to the slow agonizing death awaiting him down the road. Besides, the dwarf could see a water skin strapped to the barbarian's back, and he couldn't take a chance it might get punctured when the warhounds pounced on the lone warrior.

Hooking the twin blades of his battle axe between the heels of his new boots, the dwarf crouched down into a ball and pitched himself forward into a rolling, bladed, somersault down the hill. As he reached top speed near the bottom of the hill, the dwarven ball of death rolled right through the legs of a warhound, gouging out a large chunk of its stomach before emerging on the other side.

Jumping up from his roll and twisting around in the air to land back to back with the besieged barbarian, his battle axe still in hand, Balthor said, "Cut 'em in the belly, lad. It's their only weak point."

"I noticed," said the barbarian as he swung his large sword at the hound in front of him. The blade rang out loudly as it glanced off the beast's snapping jaws. "But, thanks!"

Oil and sludge oozed from the belly of the hound that Balthor had wounded, but the fire in its eyes had not dimmed as it reared up and tried to swat the dwarf with its massive paw. Seizing his opening, Balthor dropped into a crouch to dodge the attack, then brought his axe up over his head and lunged forward driving both blades up into the beast's bleeding stomach.

As the warhound struggled to get a paw on its attacker or release itself from the barbed points of the axe blades imbedded in its guts, Balthor twisted his torso to the side and ripped the axe free, tearing the huge beast in two as oil, gears, and intestines rained down on the ground at the feet of the dwarf.

"Your problem," said Balthor over his shoulder, "is that you're too tall. Ye can't get that big blade up underneath the beasts from way up there."

"I'm doing fine," said the barbarian, glancing back at the

carnage behind him. "But thanks for the help." When the warrior's head turned, the beast in front him pressed its attack, lunging toward the large man's exposed neck. The warrior swung his five-foot blade up and across in front of him, catching the beast between the ribs, just behind its forelegs.

With strength that only the mightiest barbarians possess, the fighter plunged his sword into the hound, snapping ribs and slicing organs until it lodged in the beast's spine. Bringing the sword down through the remainder of the blade's arc, the barbarian slammed the warhound into the ground, driving the beast's metal snout up into fleshy brain.

As the beast's body crumpled to the ground beside the barbarian, the warrior said to his newfound fighting companion, "They seem to have two weak points!"

The final hound, seeing the bloody remains of its four companions piled up around the mighty warriors, turned and loped back down the road. Before the beast could round the bend, both Balthor and the barbarian heaved their weapons at it. The sword hit first, piercing the beast's skull and driving deep into its brain. But before the hound could fall, Balthor's axe slammed into the pommel of the sword, pushing the blade out through the creature's eye and down into the ground, pinning the limp body to the road.

"Nice shot," said Balthor, grudgingly. "How do ye toss a weapon that big?"

"Practice," said the barbarian as he turned to face his fighting companion for the first time. "Yours was a mighty throw as well."

"Thank ye, but I was aiming for the beast's neck," admitted Balthor. "The kill is yours, as are the spoils of the battle."

"Spoils?" asked the barbarian.

"Aye, that's right," sighed Balthor. "These beasts have no meat, nor do they carry anything valuable, unless you're a phyrexian looking for spare parts."

"I am no phyrexian," protested the confused barbarian.

"No, of course you're not," replied Balthor, walking over to pick up his axe. "You are a barbarian. I've never met one of you before, but me and me clan see your tribes roaming the foothills of the Pardic Mountains all the time."

The barbarian warrior placed his foot on the neck of the dead warhound and yanked his sword out of its skull. "You are of Otaria?" he asked.

"Aye, that I am," replied Balthor as he guided the other warrior around the bend toward his hastily stashed treasure. "Me name's Balthor. Balthor Rockfist of the Rock clan. I came up here to fight in Urza's war, and now that it's over, I'm on me way back home."

"As am I," said the barbarian. "My name is Matoc. I am the champion of Auror village, and I too fought beside the great planeswalkers in the phyrexian war."

As Balthor tied his pouch around his waist and slung the staff back over his head, Matoc continued. "If you intend to return to Otaria, we should travel together. The roads are not yet safe."

"Aye," agreed Balthor. "I've noticed. Well, let's be off then."

As the two veterans of the great war headed down the road together, the vultures heard their former companion and potential meal say, "Ye wouldn't happen to have anything to drink in that wineskin, would ye?"

Although there were pockets of phyrexian resistance left after the final cataclysmic battles of the apocalypse, nothing between the battlefields and the southern coast could stand up to the power of the two Otarian warriors. Eventually, Balthor and Matoc found towns and villages populated by fellow survivors of the war where they could bed down in safety and barter for provisions.

Balthor found that his recovered gold and jewels were less useful in such barter than his strong arm and sharp axe. Matoc never asked about the pouch or the staff, but he rarely discussed much of anything other than battle tactics and the splendor of the Pardic Mountains. Such was the way of the barbarians. But Balthor did worry about his possessions. He always kept his money pouch safe and hidden in the towns, and he wrapped the staff in leather after the gleaming metal drew stares in the first town.

Eventually, the two warriors found themselves in a port town that had survived the worst of the devastation, and they were able to book passage to Otaria. Balthor paid his way with half the contents of his pouch, while Matoc pledged to work as a deckhand and aid in the protection of the ship during the voyage.

"I should have worked the voyage as well," grumbled Balthor one evening while the two ate hard bread and washed it down with weak ale. "Not only do I have to share me quarters with ye, but the food's not even fit for rats. I should have saved me gold."

It was the same argument that Matoc had heard for weeks, but this time, instead of letting the dwarf vent his frustrations and let it go at that, he asked, "Why do you worry about your treasures so? Do all dwarves covet gold so much?"

"Nah!" replied Balthor. "Most dwarves don't care a whit about gold and jewels. All they care about are rocks. We move rocks here, and then we move them there." To illustrate his point, Balthor broke up the rock-hard bread into several boulders and moved the pieces slowly and carefully, one at time, from one end of the table to the other, then repeated the process in reverse until all the bread was back where it started. "It's called 'tending the mountains in the Lady's name,' and it's almost as exciting as it sounds."

Matoc picked up one of the bread boulders, considered it for a moment, then popped it in his mouth and chomped down on it. "Then why have you carried that pouch with you all these miles, if not to impress your kinsmen or pay the dowry on a wife?"

"Because I'm not going back to the clans," snapped the dwarf. "Dwarves may not covet gold, but men sure do. I'll be needing this booty to pay me way in the world of humans because I can't go back to moving rocks. Not after this war."

"I don't understand, Balthor," said Matoc. "We've talked about the Pardic Mountains—the splendor of the green foothills in the morning dew, the majesty of the russet peaks at sunset. I know you want to return to the mountains. You've said so yourself"

"Aye, you're right," said Balthor. "Ye don't understand." Balthor took a long draught of ale before continuing. "I wasn't made for that stone druidical life. From me earliest days I was trained to be a warrior. Ye see, the dwarves have a long term relationship with Dominaria—only the elves have been here longer—and we take our role in the world very seriously. We tend to the mountains as the elves tend to the forests, and we protect the spine of the world at all costs, for without it, the land would sink into the oceans."

"I'm sure they would, Balthor," said Matoc reassuringly as he rose from his seat. "Let's get you to bed, so you can sleep this one off."

"Sit down, ye daft barbarian!" snapped Balthor. "I ain't drunk. It'd take casks of this watery swill to just cloud me vision. Now let me finish while I got me nerve up. I don't tell this tale lightly."

Matoc dropped back into his chair and stared hard at his normally inscrutable companion.

"Now, we dwarves have a certain kinship to the mountains and a duty to protect them, so clan elders watch for signs and portents of coming dangers. We knew this trouble was coming long, long ago, and the elders decided to raise an army, to prepare for war before the war ever started. Thus, a generation of warriors was born to the clans across Dominaria. Born, raised, and trained to be the toughest, the strongest, and the fiercest warriors in the history of the clans to help fend off the coming darkness."

Balthor poured himself another flagon of ale, downed it without even swallowing, and continued. "I've spent me whole life making me body strong, learning to defend meself, and preparing to fight and die if need be in the name of Fiers and his daughter, the Lady of the Mountain. The only problem is that I didn't die, and now I can't return to a peaceful life of moving boulders. Not after what I've seen. Not after what I've done."

"Balthor," said Matoc after a long silence, "perhaps it won't be as bad as you think. The clan will still need protection. I bet there's even goblins still living in the mountains."

"Goblins? Bah! Any dwarf can best a hundred goblins!" snorted Balthor. "Nah. Ye still don't get it. I crave the excitement of the heat of battle. I'm not alive except when I'm tearing the throat out of some beast. I'm more of a barbarian than ye are. There's no place for me in dwarven society anymore. I'll have to live with humans. I still won't fit in, but at least it won't be because I'm too savage."

Matoc slammed his fist down on the table, toppling the flagons and sending the bread flying. "That's it!" he roared. "Balthor, I have the answer. . . ."

Before the barbarian could finish, shouts were heard from outside the cabin. "Pirate ship to port. All hands on deck! Pirate ship to port. All hands on deck. Prepare to repel boarders."

Matoc jumped to his feet, grabbed his great sword and headed for the door. As he pulled the latch, he looked back at Balthor, who was kicking his treasure pouch under the bunk.

"Are you coming? Could be your last fight for a while."

"When ye put it that way, how can I resist?" said Balthor, smiling for the first time in weeks. "I knew I should have signed on for this voyage. Would have saved me a lot of gold."

The first part of the naval battle was fairly boring for the two veterans of the great war. The crew worked frantically hoisting all the sails, while the captain tried to round the pirate ship to gain the wind. But the pirate vessel cut inside the captain's course and stole the wind from their sails. At that point, the captain turned the ship to try to ram the smaller vessel.

But as the ships drew closer, a new danger presented itself. Fireballs began to reign down around the sailors, igniting the sails and forcing several men to jump overboard rather than burn to death.

"They've got a mage on board," yelled Balthor as a bolt of lightning ripped through the railing next to him. "We need to stop him before he sinks us! Any ideas, barbarian?"

"Only one," said Matoc, "but it's a bit crazy."

"My kind of plan," yelled Balthor as he dodged another lightning bolt. "What do ye have in mind?"

"This!" grunted Matoc as he grabbed Balthor in both hands, hoisted him over his head, and heaved him over the railing. The screaming dwarf flew high up in the air toward the pirate ship.

As he began his descent, Balthor could see the deck of the pirate ship approaching. He stopped screaming and rolled himself into a ball, his axe hooked between his heels. Ducking his head as he hit, Balthor rolled down the deck, knocking two pirates overboard and gutting a third who couldn't get out of the way of the spinning, bladed dwarf.

With his momentum slowed by the pirates, Balthor slammed his feet into the deck on his next revolution, sending him flying back into the air. Flipping his axe back up into his hands, Balthor landed again and quickly spun around, swinging his blades out to their full extension to cut down three more pirates who had closed on him.

Just then, a bolt of lightning slammed the dwarf back into the rail, scorching his armor and burning away several strands of his thick, red hair.

"Ah, there ye are," said Balthor as he spied the pirate mage up by the ship's wheel. "Is that the best ye got?"

The smoldering dwarf patted his charred hair and leather armor. "C'mon, ye weak dock rat. Try that one again." But as the next lightning bolt shot toward Balthor, the dwarf dove to the side and heaved his axe up at the mage while in midair. The spinning axe flew right past the incoming lightning bolt, hitting the mage in the chest with one blade, which crushed his ribcage. It ripped through his heart and continued spinning, slicing through the spellcaster's left lung and severing his spine with the other blade.

As Balthor rolled back to his feet, untouched by the second bolt, the mage toppled to the deck beside the captain, cut nearly in half by the dwarf's mighty attack.

"Get him!" yelled the pirate captain to his crew.

The pirates hesitated after seeing their mage so brutally slain, but several realized that Balthor no longer had a weapon and rushed him with their knives and cutlasses. Balthor moved methodically toward the ladder that would take him to the captain and his axe, grabbing the sword arm of the first pirate to attack him, breaking his wrist with one quick jerk and grabbing the man's cutlass before it hit the deck.

The next pirate lunged at Balthor from behind with his knife, but Balthor spun around and slammed his elbow into the back of the man's hand to deflect the attack and continued on around, swinging the cutlass high up over his head right through the pirate's neck.

As blood spilled onto the deck, Balthor jumped for the ladder and scampered up to the bridge faster than most seasoned sailors.

Advancing on the captain, who now held Balthor's battle axe, the dwarf said, "Ye picked the wrong ship to attack today, Captain. I suggest ye turn about while ye still can."

"Not while I can still do this!" yelled the captain as he raised his hand, palm out, and shot a ball of goo at the advancing dwarf, which exploded into large, sticky net upon impact.

The explosion knocked Balthor off his feet, and the goo quickly hardened into thick strands of rope that held the dwarf immobile on the deck. The captain advanced on Balthor, spinning the dwarf's axe in his hands.

"Did you ever think you'd die on the blade of your own axe?" asked the captain, smiling as he raised Balthor's blade up over his head in both hands.

The captain's smile turned to a look of horror and pain as a large, two-handed sword suddenly emerged from his chest. Even that look was short-lived however, as the impact of the thrown weapon slammed the captain into the railing beside the dwarf, jarring Balthor's axe free from his grip before he toppled over the edge to the frothy sea below.

Moments later, Matoc jumped across from the other ship and freed Balthor from the magical net. Seeing the two warriors in command of the bridge, the rest of the pirates dropped their weapons.

"Thanks, Matoc," said Balthor as he picked up his battle axe, and looked over the railing at the spot where the captain's body sunk. "I'm sorry ye lost your sword, though."

"It's just a weapon," replied Matoc. "I can get another. But where would I ever find another Balthor?"

"I am one of a kind," said Balthor while the two friends made their way back to their ship, "as I was telling ye just a little while ago—a barbarian dwarf."

"Exactly," said Matoc, putting his arm around the dwarf. "Which is why you should come live with my tribe."

"Bah! Live with a bunch of barbarians?"

"We fight all the time. It's who we are," said Matoc as they reached their cabin. "Fiers's blood! I'll fight you every day if it will keep you happy."

"All right then," agreed Balthor. "I'll try it."

"There's just one problem," said Matoc.

"You'd better not need me to move any rocks."

"No. You have to pass the chief's initiation trial to be admitted to the tribe."

"That shouldn't be too hard," said Balthor. "What do I have to do?"

"I can't tell you," said Matoc.

"Great. Just great."

The rest of the voyage was uneventful for the Balthor and Matoc. The two warriors often sparred on the deck to keep their skills honed and to help pass the long, boring days for Balthor. They arrived on Otaria several weeks later, landing in the northern port town of Landshome. There was no hero's welcome for the two veterans, but neither man expected or even wanted one.

Landshome bore few lasting marks of the long war. There were far fewer people roaming the docks than when Balthor had left, but the town itself had not been touched by battle as had all the towns and villages in the northern continents.

As the two warriors traveled south toward the Pardic Mountains, they could see that the war had not come to Otaria. There were no battlefields, no dead bodies rotting in the fields, no scorched and still burning forests, and no oily, smoky haze choking the sky and filling their lungs. But they also saw very few people. While the battles of the phyrexian war may not have made it this far south, the awful phyrexian plague spores certainly did. It would be generations before the population of Otaria returned to normal.

The warriors traveled in silence for most of the trip, lost in their own thoughts about the well being of loved ones. The days grew longer and longer as they plodded south through desolate towns and silent forests. But once Balthor and Matoc rounded the southern edge of the Krosan forest and could finally see the Pardic Mountains in all their glory, their spirits brightened, and the rest of the trip to the village of Auror went all too fast.

Not stopping to sleep the last two nights of the trip, in anticipation of once again seeing his home, Matoc forced the grumbling dwarf to continue on through the nights. By dawn of the third day, the two friends could see Auror below them as they crested a ridge and looked down into a lush, green mountain vale.

As the warriors entered the village, news spread of Matoc's return, and the two veterans were quickly surrounded by a throng of barbarians, all happy to see the returning heroes. A hardy race of people, this tribe was not hit as hard by the plague as were the people of the plains or the coast, and the entire town gathered in front of the chieftain's home to cheer for Matoc, slap him on the back, and hear tales of the evil phyrexian hordes he had faced.

Most of the barbarians were just as happy to greet Balthor, especially after Matoc told them that the dwarf was a fellow veteran of the great war. However, one stern-looking, gray-haired barbarian eyed Balthor suspiciously.

"Why have you brought this dwarf into the village?" asked the stern barbarian. "He is not of our tribe. He should return to his clan and not taint us with his presence."

Matoc pulled himself away from his friends and family to face the barbarian, who, though much older than Matoc, still appeared to be a match for the young, strong warrior. Taller and broader than Matoc, the gray-haired barbarian's muscles still rippled beneath his tunic, and Balthor could see the head of a huge two-handed axe over the man's shoulder.

Matoc bowed low and said, "Forgive me, Galdan, my chieftain. Balthor is my friend, a fellow veteran of the great phyrexian war, and the mightiest warrior I have ever met next to you. He is truly a barbarian at heart and wishes to join the tribe. I would sponsor him as my brother."

Galdan turned to face Balthor, stared hard at the dwarf for a moment who neither flinched nor blinked under the icy gaze, and then turned back to Matoc.

"To become a barbarian, he must face the challenge and pledge himself fully to the tribe. Is he ready to face the challenge?"

"Yes, Galdan. He has not slept in two days and has eaten nothing but the fruits of the mountain."

"I knew there was more to that forced march than your eagerness to get home," grumbled Balthor. Matoc smiled at his friend.

"What do you pledge to the tribe, dwarf?" asked Galdan.

Balthor looked to Matoc for help.

"You must pledge your life to the greater good of the tribe," whispered the barbarian to his friend, "and give up your most prized possession as a token of that pledge."

Balthor glared at Matoc, obviously not happy that his friend had not told him about this part of the ritual. Turning back to the chieftain, the dwarf bowed low and said, "I, Balthor Rockfist, swear in Fiers's name that I will lay down my life in the defense of the tribe, that I will tirelessly fight the enemies of the barbarians, whoever they may be, and that I will not allow any harm to befall this village so long as I draw breath."

Pulling his battle axe from its sheath, Balthor dropped to one knee and laid the weapon at the feet of the chieftain. "I give to the tribe my most prized possession, the battle axe given to me by my father, said to be forged in the fires of Mount Fiers by my ancestor, the legendary Balthor Stoneface, thousands of winters ago, I have wielded this axe my entire life, defending the spine of the world in the name of the great Fiers and the Lady of the Mountain. I give it to you, Galdan, as a token of my pledge."

Galdan picked up the axe, weighed it in his hand, flipped it once in the air, catching it by the handle, and then nodded at the dwarf in front of him. "I accept your pledge and your gift in the name of the tribe," he said. "Now, follow me to the arena for the challenge."

As Balthor rose to his feet and followed the chieftain, he looked quizzically at Matoc. "Challenge?" he asked. "Arena?"

"You must fight Galdan to be accepted into the tribe," Matoc replied.

"Great. Any suggestions?"

"Don't kill him."

The arena was nothing more than a flat, barren, outcropping of rock outside the village, with a low stone wall built around the edges where the villagers gathered to sit and watch the challenge battles.

"The rules of a challenge battle are simple," said Galdan as he faced Balthor in the arena. "Two warriors enter the arena and battle until one wins. I will use your battle axe. What weapon do you choose, dwarf?"

Balthor looked at his mighty two-handed axe—held easily in the barbarian's large right hand—sighed, and pulled the leather-wrapped staff off his back.

"I will use my staff," he called out to Galdan. "At least it will give me more reach," he grumbled to himself.

The two warriors began the battle by testing out their unfamiliar weapons. Galdan swung the well-balanced axe back and forth in front of him as he paced around the arena, while Balthor twirled the staff over his head, getting a feel for the weapon that was nearly twice his height.

Unable to use his rolling blade attack, Balthor waited for Galdan to make the first move. He didn't have to wait long, as the older barbarian rushed in, almost too recklessly as Balthor was still getting used to his new weapon. Rather than take advantage of the out-of-control barbarian, Balthor dove to his right, rolling over his staff and using his momentum to pop back to his feet yards from where he had been. Looking back at Galdan as he rolled, Balthor saw the barbarian halt his headlong rush several strides from where Balthor had been in perfect position to strike down the dwarf had he lunged forward with his staff.

"Hmm. Nice feint," mumbled Balthor. "So that's how you like to play it."

The next time Galdan rushed Balthor, the dwarf tried a more aggressive tactic. Standing his ground and waiting for the feint, Balthor bent low at the last moment and swung the staff at the barbarian's feet.

Galdan halted and slashed down at the dwarf with his axe, but Balthor was no longer there. Having followed the staff down onto the ground, Balthor flung his legs into the air, pushed off the ground with both hands, and slammed his feet into Galdan's stomach.

The seven-foot-tall barbarian fell to the ground a little dazed and completely out of breath from the blow. As Balthor continued over and came to his feet, he set the staff hard against his back, held fast behind his elbows, and twirled his body around hard, smacking Galdan in the back of the head with the spinning staff.

Galdan's head and chest flew forward and bounced off his legs. As his torso rebounded backward, the large barbarian arched his back, threw his arms up over his head, grabbed the ground behind him, and catapulted himself up and over backward into the air, landing on his feet a few yards from the dwarf.

"That hurt," said Galdan. "What's that staff made of, metal?"

"Come take it and see," goaded the dwarf.

"Have it your way, dwarf," replied Galdan as he strode toward the dwarf, hand out.

As the large barbarian approached and tried to grab the staff, Balthor swung with all his might, trying to knock the hand away and find an opening. But Galdan was even stronger than he looked, and caught the staff with his palm, stopping it in mid-swing.

The barbarian lifted the dwarf off the ground by the staff, as Balthor held on tight, unwilling to give up his only other weapon. Seeing the dwarf flail at the end of the staff, Galdan held it out at arm's length and pulled his other arm back for a mighty blow with the axe.

Seeing his own weapon coming toward him once again, Balthor swung his legs up and caught the axe head in between his heels as he had done so many times before. He stiffened his arms against the staff and kicked his legs toward Galdan, releasing and spinning the axe head with his feet, so the flat of the blade slammed into the barbarian's face.

Knocked backward from the blow, Galdan released his grip on the staff, and Balthor dropped to the ground with a groan. The barbarian crowd gasped as they saw blood on Galdan's face, his nose broken from the blow. But there was blood on the axe head as well, and Balthor fell to his knees as the gash in his calf had severed tendons and muscle, rendering the leg useless.

Dazed but still standing, Galdan advanced once more on Balthor,

235

pointed the axe down at the dwarf and asked, "Do you yield the field, barbarian?"

No one in the arena missed the meaning behind Galdan's request, not even Balthor. "I yield, my chieftain."

As cheers erupted from the gathered tribesmen, Galdan reached down to Balthor and helped the limping dwarf to his feet. "Rise, Balthor Rockfist, barbarian of the Auror tribe," he said. "Let us retire to my home to mend our wounds and drink together as brothers."

* * * * *

Several months later, Matoc visited his dwarf brother, who had been busy building a forge outside the village and working on a project that he had kept secret even from Matoc.

"Almost done re-forging that staff?" asked the barbarian as he came up behind Balthor.

Balthor's finishing hammer stopped above his head, and he turned around to face Matoc. "How did you know what I was working on?"

"Balthor, I know about the staff. I could tell from the beginning it was valuable, and it looked familiar to me, but it wasn't until you hit Galdan during the challenge battle that I realized."

"Realized what?" asked Balthor, looking at his feet as he kicked at a loose stone.

"I told you that I fought with the planeswalkers during the war."

"Yes?"

"I actually fought in one of the units assigned to Urza," said Matoc as he grabbed Balthor's shoulders and leaned down to look his friend in the eyes. "I heard the low thrum of that staff many times as it smashed phyrexian beasts on the battlefield. That was Urza's staff, wasn't it?"

"I believe so," replied Balthor. "I found it imbedded in the chest of a phyrexian juggernaut after the final battle. Once I pulled it from the wound, I realized immediately that it was thran metal, and I know of only one being on Dominaria who wielded a thran metal staff."

"You lied to Galdan. That staff was your most prized possession," accused Matoc.

"I didn't lie about the axe," said Balthor, looking his friend in the eyes for the first time since he arrived. "It was my father's weapon. It is thousands of winters old, and I do believe it was forged in Mount Fiers by the great Balthor Stoneface, the first dwarf of legend. But, yes, Urza's staff far surpasses even that mighty weapon. What will you do, Matoc? Should I pack my belongings and head into the plains?"

"No, brother," replied Matoc. "Your secret is safe with me. I still believe your pledge even if you did not seal it with your most prized possession. I understand. Who could give up such a prize as the staff of Urza?"

Balthor finally smiled at the large barbarian. "Funny you should ask," he said. "Perhaps you should take a look at what I have been working on for the past few months.

As Balthor moved aside from the forge, Matoc saw not a dwarf-sized battle axe but a barbarian-sized great sword lying in the white-hot coals. Fully six feet long and five inches wide along its full length, the sword gleamed brighter than the surrounding coals in the noon sun.

"You see," said Balthor. "I do plan to give my most prized possession to the tribe. This is for you, brother, for saving my life—twice. Use it well to protect the tribe—and the spine of the world—from harm. And when you grow old, pass it along to another worthy member of the tribe. It shall stay with a barbarian of the Auror tribe for all eternity."

"Thank you, Balthor," said Matoc, still staring at the incredible blade. "But what of your battle axe? What will you use in battle?"

"I can always find another weapon," said Balthor, "but where will I ever find a treasure so great as a barbarian brother?"

Part IV:
Post Invasion

In the aftermath . . .

Stolen Harvest

Vance Moore

The fish swam toward the cooler depths of the shallow sea, its brilliant scales dimming as the water cut the strength of the sun. Its eyes looked down to the coral mounds in the depths below. Seaweed and soft coral waved in the currents as a school of fish swirled around the submerged reefs. The fish came closer to the coral, the piles becoming buildings, portals and windows emerging from the shadows. The seafloor was a city, and it stretched out in all directions. This, however, was not a cluster of dead stone and wood. This city was alive; each building pulsed with vitality. Kelp and living fans served as curtains over the smaller openings, hiding what happened inside. Huge valves opened suddenly to let inhabitants pass through, only to snap shut against any intruder who dared to enter.

The citizens of the city moved in a complex flow of traffic, the direction of movement varying with their height above the seafloor. The path of swimmers might dip into a building only to be rerouted as the valves allowing entry closed. Most of the swimmers were mermen and their servants. Predatory fish and eels circled, bodyguards for their noble masters. A group of mer and barracuda passed by a low hump of coral that released several frenzied clownfish.

The fish swam on to the center of the city.

The main building had several towers that erupted from the massive foundation of the palace below. The upper stories abounded with ledges and cubbyholes for those who desired light and perhaps the suggestion of heat from the sun. The living structure also stretched out roots through the sand and debris to lock into the bedrock below. It was rumored that hidden rooms and dungeons lay deep in the bowels of the structure.

The lone swimmer passing by the more colorful towers could see down into a spacious room. The roof was open in several places, the skylight valves quivering as they admitted the sunlight from above. The room below thronged with mermen and a few other denizens of the sea. The mermen wore fine jewelry, and their fins were elaborately cut and frilled, living capes and fans to show their status. A gigantic lobster stood near the doors, its blue and green carapace highlighted with gold. Its claws were encrusted with jewels, but the mermen ignored it, showing their disdain for its pincers. The Berbous merman ruled the seas in this part of Dominaria, and none were allowed to forget it.

A group of cephalids crowded against the wall. The humanoids were a fusion of merman and octopus, having tentacles and skin instead of the scales and flukes of their betters. Their skin flickered with color. The cephalids communicated emotion through skin color, and all of the diplomats curbed their anger at their treatment, leaving their skin a dull gray-green through iron control. A minor race, they waited at the pleasure of the emperor who called them together. The solitary fish watching all of this arced toward the roof, only to be devoured by an eel guard hiding in the ceiling who watched over the throne room with his fellows.

"We accept the congratulations of the cephalids on our approaching rebirth," the leader of the Otarian seas said grandly from his throne. "Where is King Aboshan of the cephalids, our brother ruler of the sea?"

Guards shifted from their positions at the entrance, pushing the soft-bodied ambassadors through the crowd toward the throne. The noble mermen did not move, and the cephalids were forced to squeeze between the courtiers to reach the emperor.

Tajaras, monarch of the mermen, reclined in a throne of coral and soft anemones, the tiny branches working at the merman's skin. Each delicate touch fed a dollop of power to the monarch from the living walls of the palace. The royal merman was a riot of brilliant color. Most of his fine scales were a rich blue, like the depths of a tropical sea. Brighter hues glinted and seemed to flow as living decorations slowly painted new patterns on his skin. These symbols of authority faded in and out of view as the coral redrew tattoos.

The cephalids drew up before the throne, their anger at their treatment muted by the general contempt of the court for them. They swayed in the current as the ambassador lowered himself to the sandy floor in homage.

"I bring greetings and good wishes from our king to your court," the noble said as he rose, his skin flickering between neutral and angry colors. "He regrets that he could not attend, but affairs of state precluded his attendance."

Tajaras glowered, his lip curling in a sneer. "Nothing outweighs his responsibilities to this court."

The cephalids cowered, but flashes of defiance still played on their hides.

"Aboshan will bend his will to the throne and renew his allegiance. The seas themselves must flow in harmony with the Coral Throne," the emperor said and concentrated, drawing on the power pulsing in the palace walls to create a flickering shaft of light. The room glowed in soft pastels as the structure and the colonies of bioluminescent creatures cast light rays.

The magical light was almost languorous as it followed the emperor's directions. The empire's noble mermen communed with their sovereign, their wills moving in concert with his own as they followed the tired ritual.

This spell was a test, demanding not power but control. The spell was unstable and flawed, easy to disrupt. Only by surrendering control to the emperor could the spell succeed. Tajaras tested his court frequently, asking for a humbling show of obedience from each person in the room whenever the desire struck him.

The cephalids and the other subject people did not surrender their will, and the light flickered. The circuit of power was incomplete, and the emperor received no power from his court. The giant lobster in the back of the chamber shuffled impatiently.

Every thirty years, the mermen swarmed together over the sandy reaches off the southern Otarian coast. There the mermen raised power to renew the empire. Primal magic flowed over the seabed and drained into the millions of eggs produced for those thirty years. Tough leathery shells protected the nation's unborn from decay and predators. It took an extraordinary event to release the waiting generation.

The bulk of the sea nation would die on the final day. They

would sacrifice their lives to fuel the glorious rebirth—the rebirth of their nation. An elaborate ritual would collect the sacrificed energies and channel them into the new citizens of the merfolk nation. The eggs would hatch, and the death of thousands of mermen would magically drive the young ones' growth. In moments, an entire nation would roam the seas. Not all the mermen would die in the final spasm that powered the spell. A few surviving mermen would become nobles, a remnant of the ceremony's power and glory draining into them.

The emperor and his key courtiers would direct the sacrifice spell and the new subjects' birth. The newborn would be completely loyal to the ruler, cementing noble and royal authority. Meanwhile, Tajaras regarded the court narrowly, marking out those mermen who did not now freely bow to his will—those who did not pass his magical test.

The merman reclining in the throne ruled the empire, but there were others that might direct the ceremony. By law and ancient decree, the emperor could not act against possible contenders to the throne without proof of treason. The Festival of Rebirth must have a leader. The danger of a coup increased as the ceremony approached. The ambitious often took a last chance to seize power before the cycle turned. The masses of the reborn nation would unite behind the festival leader. If someone were capable of dispatching the emperor and placing himself at the head of the festival, the usurper would have a ready-made army and a loyal empire in one short swoop. Tajaras tested his court to avoid just that occurrence.

The shaft of light, embodying the court's unity, suddenly dipped and wrenched free. The aristocrats were aghast, nobles doing their best to seem as if others must be at fault. The light dimmed, and it wandered through the throne room as if lost. The apparent unity of the court was broken. The cephalids withdrew, hoping to avoid royal notice as the emperor split his attention between the spell and finding the person who disrupted it. The last soft-bodied retainer sneered toward the rest of the court as he and the ambassador headed for the door.

The spell showing the will of the Coral Throne writhed as the will of the majority fought a single dissenting voice in the chorus of power. One practitioner's chaos was enough to destroy the light's integrity. The manifestation vanished, the light curling into a barbed coil before evaporating, leaving a globe of hot water. The emperor's eyes stabbed to the left to regard hotly one particular subject.

Laquatus smiled serenely as the other courtiers turned toward him. The aristocrat was thinner than his ruler, still young and freshly risen to the nobility through the practice of ambition. The fins on his arms and tail were understated and his scales a pale blue. He lacked the living displays that adorned his sovereign, but his eyes held the rest of the court in disdain. His manner claimed a royal precedence even if his blood and position did not warrant it.

Laquatus found this exercise pointless. Performing tricks for the lesser nations of the seas was beneath his dignity. The day had been so promising in the beginning. The rebirth was nearly upon them, and the aristocrat believed that he would be one of its key figures. The merman remembered swimming over the sands after the Festival of Rebirth. He thought of his stupid reverence for the emperor in the moments after coming into existence. It would be at least ten years before any of the newly sprung subjects could think of anything except absolute obedience. It took time to instill treachery and ambition.

There lay Laquatus's problem. The nation would be monolithic in the days after the spell, and he had no wish to submit again to the whims of another. He thought of his unquestioning obedience and felt sick at the memory. The emperor's failure to override Laquatus's disturbance in this little test of light seemed proof positive that Tajaras did not deserve his obedience or his respect. The merman knew that there were pretenders to the throne that lacked the courage to disregard the royal will. The young merman's disloyal train of thought was broken as the emperor called out.

"Laquatus, isn't it?" Tajaras said, his voice sure and even as he asked the question. The emperor carefully tracked those nobles whose loyalty might be questioned. Laquatus had served Tajaras in earlier days by spying and acting against those who might lead the Festival of Rebirth. Though law and custom made the royal rivals safe from harm, the noble lured several rivals into indiscretion, allowing the Coral Throne to act against possible treachery. Laquatus had alienated most of the court in return for probable royal favor. He had not been rewarded. "Do you know who disrupted my spell?"

"Your Imperial Eminence," Laquatus said with only a touch of oily insincerity, "I must admit my own failings. Distracted by the beautiful complexity of the spell, I let my attention wander. I myself might have disrupted your direction, lost as I was in awe of your abilities."

"Perhaps I was too subtle for those of limited ability," Tajaras said cuttingly, drawing an amused murmur from the other nobles. The rivals that might lead the ceremony did not draw attention to themselves, he thought. "A simpler, cruder exercise of power might teach the dull-witted."

* * * * *

The underwater cavern was outside the capital, a tunnel into a rocky hill rising up from the sandy bottom of the sea. The guards the emperor had sent ahead left as Laquatus and the court approached. The column of mermen entered the opening and swam down the incline into the inner cave. The cavern was a place for illicit duels and posturing commoners, far enough from the city that it was not patrolled. It was close enough for duelist to come and parody the pomp and majesty of their betters.

Laquatus knew Tajaras was mocking him, for no noble or worthy fighter ever used this cavern once he had been accepted to the court. The emperor's choice of venue implied that Laquatus was unworthy of the capital's official practice caverns and lagoons.

The first nobles inside the cave concentrated and drew magic. Their spells went forth and sought old channels in the rock. The walls began to glow, but it was a dim and sickly glow compared to that of the palace. The cavern ceiling rose more than a hundred feet into the murky darkness. A thick layer of silt covered the floor. Each flick of a merman's tail sent up an obscuring plume of filth.

"Clear the area, Laquatus," Tajaras called as he and his courtiers swam to one side of the cavern. No one even looked at the irate aristocrat as they hurried to curry favor with their ruler.

"At once your majesty," Laquatus said, spreading his arms wide and sweeping over the floor. Each beat of his powerful flukes propelled him inches above the buried floor. The noble clenched his teeth and drew power, his grimace of distaste mistaken for effort by the rest of the court. Some of those trying hardest to impress the emperor openly laughed at the sight.

"Am I a common servant to cleanse a room?" he burbled silently as he directed his disgust at the silt. His spell spread from his arms and a current swept mud up in a roiling wave. The muck roiled and obscured the light as more sand and debris was sucked up from the floor. Nobles eager to please redoubled their spells to light the rocky chamber.

Laquatus accelerated, his muscles surging to keep up with the spell that was forming before him. The silt gathered itself into the form of a great manta, the mouth gulping down the loose material. Currents surged from the apparent gills as the spell moved over the floor. The summoned manta came close to the court. The faint of heart swam back as a current sucked away the sand and mud from beneath their flukes. Laquatus turned the beast and sent it toward the cavern opening. The great sea creature left the cave, and the noble let the magic drain away from his creation, leaving only the filth from inside behind. Guards and servants waiting outside were unprepared for the dirty eruption, and Laquatus heard them gasping as the dark cloud clotted up gills. The light from the surface faded away as he moved back in the cavern, the floor now bare, swept clean by the strength of his spell.

Tajaras laughed and waved as if congratulating Laquatus on the quality of his job. To nobles of the empire, the only thing worse than doing a menial job was being praised for it. Despite his style in completing the task, it was still beneath his dignity. He was no slow-witted sturgeon to find the completion of a simple task cause for celebration. Tajaras mocked him, and Laquatus's honor burned at the insult.

The emperor had as little respect for Laquatus as the indignant noble felt for his sovereign. Tajaras could have dismissed Laquatus to oblivion but instead seemed intent on drawing out the spectacle for the rest of the court.

"Ready?" called the emperor, his voice thick with false concern. "Perhaps you need more time to prepare for our little game."

Laquatus gritted his teeth, turning to hover over the clean floor. He had no companions, abandoned by the other courtiers for the emperor's circle of friends.

"Always ready, sire," Laquatus called, and he summoned his fighter.

The fish that shimmered into sight was so small that it was lost in the immensity of the cavern. "Control and subtly," muttered the aristocrat, seeing the other nobles enhancing their sight to spot the insignificant creature. Let the emperor taste mockery. This exercise was to show delicacy, not power. The young grandee enhanced his own vision to look at his opponent.

Tajaras smiled, his face indulgent as if the creature were expected. The circle of nobles moved back as the muscles in his shoulder twitched in agitation. The emperor strained as if summoning great energy, but Laquatus detected no significant flow of magic. The court looked anxiously about for some mighty summoning though the contemptuous noble knew no mighty beast would swim into existence. The emperor's spell was so insignificant that many of the supporters surrounding the sovereign missed it until their more gifted fellows pointed it out. A tiny shrimp swam into view, dim and drab even against the bare rocks of the cave. It was so tiny that Laquatus's fish seemed a whale beside it. Laughter exploded at the joke, the equivalent of a rude noise at a banquet. Laquatus was the object of ridicule, and he snarled before changing his expression. But the court knew his anger, and the laughter grew more frenzied as they sought favor from the emperor with their loud mirth.

Laquatus could feel the energy pouring from the royal merman to his creature. The crowd might see it as ridiculous, but the flow of energy to the diminutive champion increased. The shrimp snapped its claws, and the burst of noise echoed in the cavern. Claps of thunder reverberated with each snap as the crustacean swam toward Laquatus's creature. The assault pained the ears of the spectators far from the tiny fighters. Through his enhanced vision, the dueling noble could see his fish spasm with each attack. The assault stripped away scales and ruptured organs. The tiny fish floated belly up toward the cave roof as the crowd laughed and acted out the battle. Several mermen floated on their backs as their fellows issued clicks like demented dolphins. Laquatus summoned a more powerful creation, eager to provide fresh spectacle and stop the attack on his dignity.

An octopus flowed into being in response to the noble's spell. Its flexible body followed the contours of the underwater cave, eddying in the small crevices exposed by the earlier cleaning. Its color changed to the red of anger. Laquatus fed more power to the beast, and his emotions fueled the color and increasing frenzy of the animal's movement. The octopus jetted several times, its pulsing hide hard to see until the courtiers providing the light increased the brightness of their spells in the cave. The favor seekers surrounding the emperor muttered as they saw his display. The dueling aristocrat commanded the creature to show more neutral colors as it made for the shrimp.

The tentacles spread in a net as the octopus swooped over the ruler's diminutive fighter. Its enemy's soft body muffled the shrimp's thunderous attacks. Laquatus's creature cycled through colors, flashes of anger, then pleasure as it devoured its foe. The dueling noble smiled briefly in triumph only to be answered by a new spell from Tajaras.

A shark shimmered into being. Long and dusky, it was lost against the cave walls. Though it was no giant, the courtiers stirred uneasily. Mermen had as little to do with sharks as possible. The summoned creature spiraled up toward the cave ceiling as it tasted the water for its prey.

Laquatus felt a command spring from the emperor to the predator. It surged toward the octopus, the quick action startling spectators as it whipped by them. The octopus changed color and jetted away, leaving a cloud of ink to mislead the deadly fish. Laquatus sent commands to his creature, its color altering until it was completely lost from sight.

The toothy mouth opened as the shark accelerated, its eyes rolling back. The fish could sense the play of life within the octopus and altered course, homing in on its invisible opponent. The jaws snapped shut, and the long body whipped in a brief frenzy to tear apart its prey. The octopus reappeared. Pain and disorientation colored its hide as it swam away. It left a trail of blood as it escaped the jaws. Only the cephalopod's jet propulsion saved it from a wholesale devouring. It left a tentacle, sheared off by the fearsome teeth.

The octopus began to pulse with new power, Laquatus feeding it energy until it shone like a crazed star. The shark's eyes rolled back again, relying on its other senses to direct it once more.

The seven-tentacled beast came toward the crowd of courtiers. Ink spewed out, mingling with blood from the octopus's stump. The emperor laughed, able to see the creature and direct his living projectile. The cloud spread as power from Laquatus poured into his wounded fighter. Now the thin streams of ichor filled the ink cloud with pulsing life. The shark dived into the darkness, its senses confused by the growing spell. The octopus jetted toward the courtiers and disappeared from view as it reached the surprised nobles.

The shark came through the cloud blind, its mouth opening to tear into its prey. But the emperor had no view of the octopus, and the great fish snapped blindly, sinking its jaws into the spectators. The predator was not much bigger than the mermen, but its jaws cut away chunks of flesh as it ate. Those avoiding the teeth still suffered as the fish's rough hide tore away skin as it thrashed. Laquatus chuckled at the emperor's clumsiness and lack of control.

Emperor Tajaras breathed faster, his gills pulsing in agitation at having been fooled. This combat had been meant as a joke, but the tides had turned, and now the joke was on the emperor. A foolish courtier tittered, too stupid to realize the ruler's anger. The shark completed a sweeping turn, its rough hide scraping the laughing merman's flesh down to the bone. Laquatus doubted the injury was an accident.

The monarch was frozen in thought, and the predatory fish came at the injured nobles. The courtiers drew power, preparing themselves to kill the beast. Tajaras broke from his thoughts and frowned at his supporters who would dare to interrupt his battle. Afraid to act against the emperor's shark, most froze in sick fear as the sea beast came at a bleeding merman. A few, too fearful, sent power crackling over their scales to armor their flesh against the teeth, but the shark faded away as the emperor cancelled his spell.

The aristocrats wondered if the contest was at an end. Laquatus smiled at the apparent victory, savoring the moment of superiority. He could see some of the ruler's supporters smiling emptily while slowly moving away from the emperor, avoiding his notice.

However, the emperor was not finished, and other creatures flowed into existence. Long somber eels twisted though the water, their undulating bodies creating knots that dispersed as they separated. The spectators tried to crowd around the emperor, recognizing the beasts. The ruler would have none of their timid company and more eels swam into existence around him.

Bolts of magical power arced back and forth between the creatures. Courtiers shuddered as the energy played over their scales. The blood in their veins boiled and foamed under the attack. The emperor continued to chastise those who strayed too far from his good graces.

Laquatus sent his octopus into the cloud of ink and mystical camouflage in the center of the cave. Perhaps his fighter could hide. The new beasts were becoming more powerful as the school of eels grew in response to the emperor's will. The ruler's proxies tied themselves together in a shimmering web of power. They moved as a group into the center of the cave.

The ink cloud shrank, the magical lightning tearing away at the obscuring liquid. Laquatus's octopus was losing its hiding space as more eels appeared and tied themselves into the destructive network. Should he summon more creatures? There were monsters immune to the power playing through the water. It was only a temporary setback, but Laquatus could see the hungry look on the emperor's face and knew that the ruler would never let him win. He could attack his opponent directly rather than fighting only Tajaras's creatures, but there were legions of soldiers waiting outside, and while the courtiers were contemptible there were enough of them to overpower Laquatus alone.

The realization of his own weakness was bitter on his tongue. He watched stoically as streams of power teased his summoning from its inky cover. The octopus was dim with despair as it was torn apart by electrical strikes. The emperor laughed in delight as Laquatus gritted his teeth and dipped his head in defeat, swearing to revenge this humiliation. He would find allies, he vowed, but not amongst the cowardly mermen of the court.

* * * * *

"Get them," the cephalid soldier cried out as he watched the battle, acting like a fan at a sporting event. The spectator jetted up into the air, and Laquatus could see the tentacles flapping through the disturbed window of the water's surface. The soldier's body was a mass of writhing arms, the skin flashing bursts of excitement as he left his familiar environs. His iron trident led the way as the jumper crashed back into the cold southern water. The weapon dragged him to the rocky bottom before another set of contractions sent the soldier back to his cheering fellows. Laquatus shouted with the rest but cared little for the real outcome.

The noble had left the scene of his defeat as quickly as possible. The tidal wave of congratulations to the emperor on winning the duel was more than Laquatus could bear. A duel? More like a farce. He left, derided by those that bothered to notice him. As soon as he left the cave he swam away from the capital to visit a different court.

The cephalids ruled a tiny portion of the southern Otarian Sea. The mermen considered them to be gross parodies of the their own masterful forms. Instead of a tail and flukes, the cephalids were a combination of merman and octopus. The more powerful empire kept them at the borders of the continental shelf. The southern seas swept across many a rocky island in stormy waves, far from more congenial waters. Laquatus found the court off such a dreary point.

The cephalids were entertaining themselves, proving the superiority of the sea over the land. The bay bottom just off the surf line was teaming with massive crabs, their claws clacking open and shut as they advanced up the volcanic rock to the beach. The crustaceans were giants, many weighing hundreds of pounds and covered with parasites and camouflage as they went forward. Laquatus popped his head above water. On the shore was a large herd of elephant seals. The gigantic males with their short trunks reared up, their loud cries reverberating over the surf as they struck at the invaders. Each step of the sea fighters brought them closer to the bull seals' territories and provoked charges as six-thousand-pound animals humped their way over the rock into the surf. The mammals' massive jaws could only break through the armor of the smaller crabs, so the larger crustaceans continued on.

The seals' blubbery bodies smashed down on shells as the bulls and cows tried to crush the enemy. Leg joints gave way, and the cracking of chitin shells assaulted the aristocrat's ears. He ducked his head under the surface, but now the sea tasted of blood. He broke into the air to look once more.

The crabs scuttled in a relentless wave, their claws shearing into mammalian flesh. The wounds gaped open as the undersea creatures cut through the protective blubber. The elephant seals' charges pumped rushes of blood streaming over the rock, ignoring the wounds as they protected their territory. A red froth blossomed at the surf line. Both forces died in great numbers as the aristocrat watched.

The merman dived down and back toward the cephalid court drifting in the tide. The tentacled king, Aboshan, was the largest cephalid, his skin covered with designs proclaiming his sovereignty. His aristocrats jetted from place to place, never still though obviously keeping their attention on the king.

Aboshan continued to send commands to the crabs. His tentacles gestured and sent messages swirling out in coils of magic to drive the crustaceans on. The entire court moved closer, the bloody water coursing through their gills and filling their bodies as they jetted toward the beach. Aboshan paused, lest he expose himself to the upper world.

The soft-bodied ruler hated those who needed air and took every opportunity to cleanse air breathers from the sea. Sentries tracked the merman's progress as he approached the king. The soldiers were on guard not against sea monsters but against messengers from the queen. Aboshan's wife had close allies among the air-breathing peoples of the sea. Such slaughter as the king now directed would offend the selkies or were-seals that served as servants in the cephalid court.

The merman swam slowly forward, giving the attendants time to announce his presence to the king. Mermen ruled the seas, and as a noble of the empire he was due prompt recognition. The guards held their weapons tightly, turning from the slaughter on shore to look at the interloper. The cephalid king's colors turned to a dark brown as he ceased exhorting his creatures to attack. The royal hide stayed dark as he drifted into deeper water. The magical commands and driving spells stopped as the attention of the court now focused on the merman.

On shore, the crabs scrambled back into the water, surrendering the beach to the seals that bellowed in triumph over the defense of their territory. The surviving sea fighters fled along the surf line. The large crustaceans the king commanded were smart enough to leave. The crabs had no wish to be used as shock troops in further attacks. Their smaller unintelligent relatives continued to scuttle through the bloody water, snatching scraps of flesh that rolled in the waves. The angry seal colony pushed crushed bodies back into the surf, and the small scavengers lost themselves in an orgy of cannibalism.

"What brings a friend from our cousin to us?" Aboshan asked, schooling his features to be as unreadable as his hide. The court was spreading out, and the merman regretted that he had no one to watch his back.

"I would have words with you in private," Laquatus said grandly, his eyes flicking to the surrounding warriors in disdain. "The message I bear is for the prince of the cephalids alone."

The ruler's skin swirled in angry colors at the slight on his rank and the suggestion he could not control his court. But the power of the mermen was such that he could only acquiesce with ill grace. Even a king must bow to those far stronger than he. His tentacles spread and waved his retainers away. The nobles and guards swam toward the shore. The surviving seals were fighting. Now that the invaders were gone, the survivors were taking the territory from the dead. The corpses of bulls and cows were pushed into the sea as every animal tried to expand its holdings. The remaining crabs attacked the blubbery bodies, snipping off flesh that the cephalid guards and nobles grabbed. The feasting was in full swing as Laquatus and the king withdrew.

"I await the will of my brother," Aboshan said stiffly, letting displeasure sour his voice. With no witnesses, a little anger shone through. Laquatus said nothing, raising magical power as he swam away toward privacy, up the coast. The sea ruler stiffened and followed with care, the cephalid raising his own energy to counter a possible attack. Laquatus wove a net of magic to prevent others from hearing what he would say. The king was familiar with such charms, and Aboshan let the merman finish with visible impatience.

"Are you tired of being a subject of the emperor?" Laquatus asked suddenly. The cephalid froze in surprise, wondering what trap the merman set. He looked nervously to see if enemy soldiers waited to spring from ambush. There was only volcanic rock, washed by a cold sea around him. The noise of the surf along a set of cliffs on shore covered the sounds of the feasting court down the coast. He could see nothing, but treachery was a dish often served by the mermen.

"The Mer Empire has restrained the rightful destiny of the cephalid race for long enough. It is long past time that you rose to the rightful place you deserve," Laquatus continued, turning in the water to regard the frozen ruler. He smiled and tried to cajole when he wanted to command. The noble was pouring power into the water, surrounding the pair of them with pounding waves. The water rolled up to smash into the cliffs, the sound preventing anyone from hearing them, even through magic. Only inside a pocket of calm around the noble and the king could anything be heard.

"Such words are treason, and those who speak them risk death," Aboshan replied, though he did not call out for the guards. His skin's colors reflected thoughtfulness rather than fear. "Those who act on them risk far worse," the king said, though his tones invited further conversation.

Laquatus continued to pour flattery, trying to puff up the cephalid's ego. Like waves against the shore, he tried to batter down the king's resistance and gain an open declaration. Finally, Aboshan spoke bluntly.

"Why should you come to me?" The cephalid's hands playing with his scepter of office. The gold and bronze mace was thick with jewels and pearls. The glint of light from many of the stone hinted that the scepter embodied more that moral authority. The ruler continued talking, pushing for an answer.

"My wife and her allies have more links to the mer," Aboshan stated, his jealousy showing. The ongoing feud between the king and queen was a source of constant gossip in the ocean. "She even has allies with air-breathers and monsters from the abyss. Why come to me, whose power and influence is limited to my own people?"

The monarch's candor and accurate self-appraisal was deeply distressing to Laquatus. The last thing he needed to deal with was a thoughtful ruler. He had already discounted many candidates for being too smart to control.

"There was no choice between you!" he stated emphatically, as if the idea were preposterous. The merman tried to sooth Aboshan. "The connections that you speak of limit her actions rather than increase her power. More importantly, they limit her vision." Laquatus bowed to the cephalid, paying homage even as he wished to issue commands.

"Only those of royal blood with the courage to seize opportunity are of interest to me," the noble said expansively, reinforcing the spell of silence that enfolded the pair. "And in all the sea, only you can take the actions necessary to change the course of history."

"And how can I do that?" Aboshan stated coldly, the set of his tentacles on the scepter telling Laquatus that his time had run out.

"By replacing the king during the Ceremony of Rebirth," the merman answered blandly, ignoring the ruler's gaping expression of surprise.

* * * * *

The capital's population swelled as schools of mermen closed on the city. The scales of the arriving soldiers glinted as they came, eager to die for the empire. From the beginning, the Berbous tribe of mermen gathered and died to fuel the birth of a renewed nation. Born of the spell, they were compelled to experience it again lest they sicken and die. The ambition that fueled all mermen drove them to the crucible of the ceremony. The arriving citizens of the empire knew that death waited for most of them but for a lucky or powerful few. The nobility awaited a chance to gain power in the new nation. The ceremony began as nobles curried favor with the emperor by sending out the call. With every moment, a wave of power spread out from the rebirthing grounds. The command echoed deep in the bones of the nation, dragging all citizens to the capital. Only allies and the lesser races protected the borders as the soldiers swam to the ceremony. For a short time the emperor's hand would lay lightly on the seas.

Laquatus swam in a group of mermen, setting his will against the call that tried to compel him. He was no dolphin or whale to come at a call. He, alone, decided his course. The others in his party slowed as they reached the beginning of the birthing grounds. In the far distance, he could see the rocky enclosure that protected the emperor's stand. Tajaras and his chosen retainers would spend as much of the ceremony as possible protected on three sides by walls drawn from the bedrock.

The land sloped up, and the sandy bottom was close enough to the surface to be disturbed by storms and waves. The current eddied over the land, slowly uncovering the eggs awaiting to be awakened below.

Laquatus wondered if he should have convinced Aboshan to attack the skeleton forces protecting the borders. However, within a few days the empire would be more powerful than ever, its ranks swollen with loyal minions formed during the rebirthing. No, he had a much better chance going to the ceremony.

The noble waved to the retainers following him and joined the trailing edge of the massive school. For better or worse, he was committed now. Light shone in a blinding array as it reflected off the scales of the mermen. A steady rain of jewelry and weapons began to fall to the sands below as each swimmer surrendered to the ceremony. Here and there a few retained their possessions, and Laquatus noted them. Those who could hold on to their individuality were likely candidates for the nobility.

The mermen converged in a swirling whirlpool over the birthing grounds. The magic call of the Rebirth Ceremony surged from the emperor. His attendants grew stronger. The waters grew crowded with the circling bodies.

The emperor poured more magic into the ceremony spell. Laquatus could feel the call of generations pouring through him and into the sands below. The energy reverberated and reflected back up to the skies above. Like crashing waves on rocks, it pounded into his body and mind. The light from above dimmed.

Laquatus leaped into the air and looked around before he splashed back into the water. The mermen of the empire formed a great circle whose edges stretched beyond his vision. The sky was darkening as clouds converged from every direction. The ceremony clashed with time and nature. The weather changed as the power overloaded the seas and the skies as well. He felt a burst of pride in his race. Other mermen in other seas might let time and nature direct their course, but the Berbous sprang full formed into the world. The Ceremony of Rebirth was already overturning the natural order of things.

The sandy bottom began to flow up toward the surface as a current sucked away the sand. Silt and seaweed flowed away, exposing countless eggs. The spheres gleamed with a pearly luster that began to fade with the dimming light. The eggs had been laid by the efforts of hundreds of merfolk. Those hard workers had been rewarded with treasure, but in the end, it was the emperor and his nobles that served as true parents to the nation.

The mermen circling below were in a trance. The swimmers jostled each other as the magic flowed through their bodies and soaked into the eggs below.

Laquatus and his companions neared the center of the birthing grounds. They swam across the circle, the other merfolk whipping by in their blind paths. His companions formed a barrier that shook as dazed citizens impacted the stationary figures. Bones broke as a steady stream of ceremony-crazed fish-men rammed the group. The broken merfolk bodies piled up, blocking the path of others. A barrier of mangled citizens protected Laquatus and his companions now.

A deeper note sounded through the water, like the call of a great whale. The nobility and those gifted with power could feel the flow of magic changing as the emperor moved on to the next phase of the spell. The last vestiges of the call faded as the nobles ceased their magic and converged on their ruler. The exhausted masses slowed, and Laquatus and his companions surged for their destination. In the distance Laquatus could see the final streams of mermen entering the circle of bodies. The Berbous were over the sands, and the swirling crowd slowed as the Tajaras's voice shook the ocean.

"It is time!" the ruler cried. Above the surface, winds howled, and it began to rain. The water turned dark, and a few of the emperor's nobles used magic to light the now murky sea. Laquatus could not see the emperor, but he knew his sovereign and the other courtiers would be drawn into a tight defensive position.

The magic came forth again, this time exploding in the minds of the mermen over the exposed birthing grounds. Soldiers and citizens collided, driven insane by the energy raging in their skulls. In moments, tens of thousands were swimming at each other. The magic seemed to jump free of its temporary hosts. Long streamers of ethereal energy connected the closing citizens. Bands of energy crisscrossed the huge school. Each connection grew more brilliant as spells and instinct fueled the fights. Power poured from the emperor, and even Laquatus found himself lending some energy to the conflagration over the eggs. The magic seemed to echo among the huge mass of swimmers, growing stronger instead of weaker.

Few of the combatants were ever able to touch. Laquatus could see the bones inside soldiers. The closer they came to their targets, the more energy seemed to pour through and from them. As hands reached for each other, the maddened, lustful merfolk began to explode. The concussions came furiously, deafening Laquatus even with his distance from the fighting.

The strands of energy reformed as the weaker merfolk dissolved under the power of the spell. A continuing torrent of blood and flesh wafted down to the exposed eggs. Magic from the emperor merged with that drawn from the dying to vanish into the pearly spheres. The ocean grew too red to see anything, and the fighting paused as the ground below attracted the currents of life and death to play over the eggs. The clearing water revealed many mermen yet alive, and a great cheer echoed through the ocean. The survivors had completed the first steps of the ceremony, and all felt magic surging through their veins, drawing them closer to nobility and power in a reborn empire.

Drunk with power and ambition, the crowds began to call to each other. "Think you are worthy . . . ? I can kill any three of you. . . . I can out-swim anyone."

The boasting continued as Tajaras recovered and prepared for fresh efforts. The crowds cleared enough that Laquatus could catch glimpses of the sovereign. The treacherous aristocrat could feel the pull of ambition and started forward only to be restrained by his companions. The others in his group were unaffected, and he wondered why—then his mind cleared. His nod of thanks was ignored as the merman looked to those over the eggs.

The emperor said nothing that Laquatus could hear, but new spells roared into existence. The drunkenness became more intense, and the nobleman exerted more energy to protect himself. Power began to radiate from the sands, and a school of boisterous merman entered the energy cloud. Their boastful cries became screams as the forces raising up from below scoured power from their bones and flesh. The draw became furious, drawing life away to the eggs below. Citizens faded and vanished, every drop of their existence feeding the spell and the eggs on the sands below. A few survivors cried out in renewed vigor as the flow of energy reversed for a second, filling them with power. A new school of merfolk surged forth, each member sure they would survive. Again many died, and the few survivors drank from the flow of power.

Laquatus stayed at the edge of the birthing grounds. His own magical efforts shielding him even as the emperor and his noble cronies protected themselves. The magic was surging unpredictably; the call of the birthing grounds seemed like a living thing. Those who retreated to the periphery were drawn in, their minds vanishing as they swam in suicidal rushes toward the center of the ceremony. Survivors drunk with luck and destiny dragged mermen to the life-sucking sands.

The mad rush pulled all but the strongest back over the sands. Laquatus's companions fought off individuals trying to drag them in, ignoring the spell. Only the aristocrat in the center struggled to control himself.

The crowds vanished over the sands as each group charged and died, their lives extinguished to feed the magic. Thousands faded away, but a few survived and devoured the power rebounding from the eggs and sands below. The final seconds of the mad rush saw many evaporate, and the side effects of their disappearance sent waves of power spreading out in all directions. Even far from the center of the storm, Laquatus felt renewed energy.

Not everyone died in the schools expiring over the sands. Thousands still lived, each now encased in a writhing ball of energy. The first wave took the weak of spirit and flesh. Now only the strong remained. The cloud's power was immense, filling the sea and each of the living mermen in the bloody mix. But despite the overwhelming magic, the eggs were not hatching. Each sphere gleamed with reflected power but showed no signs of breaking. The resilience that allowed the eggs to survive decades in the sea locked them closed. More energy was required to open them.

Rage and disappointment shook the seas as the empowered

commoners roared their displeasure. The skies above echoed and punctuated the emotion with a storm of lighting that arced from the seafloor to the black clouds. The two groups at the edge of the sands, centered on Tajaras and Laquatus, did nothing. The spell seemed to spring from the eggs themselves.

"More!" they cried, and the survivors gave them more. Like turgid whales, the surviving merman closed, swollen with energy and in a drunken rage. Bolts of pure power flew between them. There was no style, no technique in the attacks. Raw might drove waves of emotion and energy against enemies until one lost and was instantly consumed. The last remnants of the old order except for the emperor's circle vanished.

Streams of lightning played over the eggs below as the victors tried to force the eggs to hatch. The massive amounts of power, so jealously won by the mermen, flowed to bring forth a new nation. The emperor was moving closer, leaving his enclosure for the climax of the ceremony. But Laquatus, though on the opposite side of the ceremony, was far closer to the center.

The treacherous noble and his party moved over the eggs, separating and swimming hard. A survivor of the battles sent power leaping toward the aristocrat. Laquatus was skilled in the use of magic, but the bolt still shook him, and his protection shredded under the primal attack. The warriors over the eggs had an empire's magic flowing through them. From these remnants would flow the future nobles and magic practitioners. However, right now they drew as much raw power as they ever would. Laquatus wondered if he could survive as another merman swollen with energy approached. One opponent was barely manageable, two would surely kill him. He sighed in relief as the two embodiments of mer power fell upon each other. The pair and all the other surviving fighters collided with shattering force.

The tide of battle ebbed as Laquatus tried to reconstruct his protective spells. The emperor directed the last stage of the spell, losing himself in the moment. The remaining mer listened to Tajaras's silent commands echoing through the energy cloud. Drunken rage ebbed as the emperor tried to direct the final moments of the spell.

"It is time," Laquatus called, sending the shout through the waters. The cry was not loud, but it cut through the noise. The combat was over, but there were still flares of power from below. As the noble's companions spread out, they fell prey to the flows of magic.

What appeared to be mermen shimmered like images in a rippled pool. Blue and gray scales were replaced with constantly shifting colors. Fins separated and became tentacles, the freed soldiers rolling and stretching. The cephalids' magical camouflage was no longer needed, and they ceased their spells. Laquatus laughed as he saw the cephalid court hovering in the water. The imposters could not have invaded these sacred grounds except today. The ceremony overloaded magical senses. The guards that might pierce the veil of deception were dead or floating stunned over the sands. The merfolk still alive converged on the invaders. The residual magic from the ceremony rebounding from the eggs below filled the cephalid's with power. For a few seconds, the soft-bodied warriors brightened as might thundered through their veins.

The trespassers swelled, growing larger as they soaked up energy. The mermen reached out to tear apart the intruders. The cephalids hovered and released clouds of ink. The dark liquid did not float but instead fell. The largest cephalid bellowed and drew power. The emperor swam toward the center of the once swirling mass—the center of the Rebirth Ceremony—but King Aboshan occupied the space, and he began casting his own spell. The few cephalid guards with their ruler could only release more dye into the water. Like dark waterfalls, the cephalids' juices fell over the eggs, concealing them from view. The invaders drew on the cloud of magic, swelling their bodies even more. The soldiers began to explode in showers of ink that smothered the ground, obscuring everything.

Tajaras swooped over the sands, trying to rally the survivors and dispatch the cephalid invaders. He tried desperately to finish the ceremony, to hatch the eggs that claimed so many lives. The invading king's spell continued as Laquatus directed his own magic to aid the cephalid monarch.

Aboshan's soldiers emptied pouches of opaque, tubular bulbs to the ocean floor—cephalid eggs that would nest among those of the merman. The last few enraged Berbous merfolk charged at the trespassers. But before they could strike, they were sucked into Aboshan's dark spell. Scales and muscle dissolved. The merfolks' bodies fell as bloody clouds to the ground, mixing with the unholy brew below. The magic rebounding from the eggs to the mermen stopped. Laquatus could feel the spell strengthening, trapped in the ink.

"Traitor!" screamed a gasping voice, the exclamation clipped as if the speaker could barely talk. The emperor and his retainers approached the treacherous merman. Tajaras looked at the birthing grounds in horror. The ink continued to roll around the sand and rock, covering everything. Geysers and waterspouts flared up, wiping away some of the ceremony's survivors. The inky mass was blasphemy to the merman court. The emperor and his aristocrats trembled in fear and rage.

A soundless concussion shook the sea as the first eggs hatched. The last traces of blood and gore vanished into the inky obscurity. The few cephalid guardsmen remaining to protect their king vanished into the dark. Aboshan's body was splayed out like a star as he floated lower over the birthing grounds. The storm overhead thundered a last time, and lightning connected the sea and sky. The few cephalids remaining tried to flee but were set upon by furious mermen, torn apart by scaled hands.

The remains of one soldier lay half immersed in the ink, and his color vanished as if sucked dry by something below. Cephalids diving to escape died the moment they touched the darkness. However, so did the mermen following them. The dark liquid erupted in a dozen places, forcing the ceremony's survivors to flee the field. The emperor and the nobles followed Laquatus in a dash for safety. Only Aboshan remained behind, the ink fountains rising above him.

The Emperor Tajaras tried to draw power, shaking in a seizure. He had exhausted every resource, and even with his courtiers helping, no magic was raised. The ink began to subside and flow away, but it was Aboshan who commanded the waters. The eggs hatched, and at last all could see the birth of a nation.

More eggs sundered in ethereal explosions, the tiny forms struggling into the sea to writhe and expand. The tempo increased until those watching lost all sight against the magic's glare. The mermen blinked and wept oily tears as the forms below came into focus. The seafloor was covered with cephalids. The waving tentacles of fully grown warriors spread out, the creatures jet-black. The teeming hordes overflowed the birthing grounds. A steady stream of newborn soldiers started toward the empty capital. Aboshan rose, his pride and triumph proudly displayed on his skin for the world to see. Eggs still hatched, but even though merfolk eggs broke open, the tiny forms became cephalids. The Festival of Rebirth had ended.

"Only one of royal blood can perform the ceremony," Laquatus said smugly to Tajaras and his courtiers. Soldiers passed the treacherous noble, moving to capture the former ocean ruler. The defeated aristocrats were too stunned to act. "So I found royalty with which I could deal."

"Aboshan will reward me for helping him usurp the ceremony," Laquatus continued, patting a newly hatched warrior fondly. He looked toward Aboshan, the new emperor. The merman bowed low before turning back to his former sovereign. The traitor's face was serene. "It took only a few cephalid eggs and courage to take the empire."

"Murderer," the old emperor burbled, his supporters withdrawing as Aboshan drew nearer. The ceremony survivors fled as the seafloor continued to vomit up the new master race. "You've killed your people."

"Why ever should I care," Laquatus chuckled, waving to the capital being reoccupied. "I am the only surviving retainer in a new empire. With you, the best I could hope for was survival. The choice was obvious."

The mermen trying to withdraw were halted as cephalids in hundreds of thousands filled the sea.

Family Man

Scott McGough

"And just who are you supposed to be?"

The tall man smiled as he closed the door behind him. He faced three men across the bare wooden room, casually noting their various bodyguards waiting in the shadows. He knew all three by name and reputation, each a powerful witch from a powerful family. He stifled a derisive snort.

"You may call me Virot," he said. "I am here to represent the Maglan family's interest in the port."

He wore a form-fitting tunic of hardened leather and a luxurious black cloak, a long saber at his hip. His proud, bald head and sharp features loomed high above the other men's. Though he was slightly older than they, his shoulders were broader than theirs, his eyes clearer, and his skin smoother.

The man who questioned Virot was squat and hairy like a boar. He wore a coarse hemp shirt with the Ilyssa family crest embroidered on the shoulder. His thick, black beard covered the upper half of his chest, and his piggish eyes glared suspiciously at the newcomer. The men flanking him stood silent, one with an eye patch, and one whose features were hidden behind a grinning silver harlequin mask. Both looked back and forth between the bearded man and the new arrival.

"This is a private meeting," the bearded man growled, "and you are not welcome. Get out while you still can."

Virot's smile remained unchanged. "The port is ours and always has been. The likes of you aren't even allowed to think about it without our permission."

"Watch your tongue, filth," the bearded man said. He snapped his fingers, and in response, three shadowy figures shambled forward from the darkened depths of the room. "I am the second-born son of the Ilyssa house. I will not be insulted by a Maglan errand boy."

Virot Maglan laughed. " 'Filth?' You come fresh from the cemetery, caked in graveyard dirt and reeking of corpses, and you call me filth?" He shook his head. "Only the Ilyssa could maintain such pride in the face of reality."

The bearded man snarled, and the shambling figures advanced on Virot. Two human zombies and a reanimated wolf stepped into the light, grasping and moaning.

"This will be a short meeting, Maglan. I'll send your still-living head back to that viper you call a mother as fair warning. She should choose her envoys more carefully in the future."

The one-eyed witch put a hand on the zombie maker's shoulder. Sweat had broken out on his brow, and he daubed at it with a silk handkerchief.

"A moment," he hissed. "This meeting was supposed to be secret, yet the Maglan are here. He may not be alone." His voice never rose above a hoarse whisper, and Virot wondered if he had lost a lung as well as an eye. "My family is not willing to antagonize the Maglan. Not openly. Not yet."

The Ilyssa witch sneered, and his zombies hesitated, lost without his continued direction. "The Maglans are in decline," he said. "That's why we're here. Killing him will make it even easier to achieve our goals."

The harlequin giggled, whinnying through his nose. His voice was high-pitched, and it echoed behind the metal on his face. "I agree with Ilyssa. If they knew about us meeting, they would have come out in force." He whinnied again. "I think he is all the force they have."

Virot smiled. "I see the Ilyssa have not lost their touch for choosing the best and bravest to conspire with. But how did such clever folk make the catastrophic mistake of allying with such common gravediggers?" Virot's saber slid out of its sheath, and he pointed it at the bearded man. "As for you, corpse-grinder, I assure you that mother chose very carefully when she sent me." He ran his palm across the back of his blade and shook his own blood onto the floor, first to his left and then to his right. Wisps of smoke rose off the spatters of blood as Virot spoke a few guttural syllables, clapped his hands together, and said, "Rise."

A small bat-winged humanoid rose from each spattered line of Virot's blood. Each was covered in coarse black hair, and their eyes glowed orange. The feral imps bared their fangs in unison, then spread their wings and began circling the room.

The one-eyed witch took a step back, hissing in alarm. The zombie maker and his masked cohort both jeered.

"Is that all?" said the face behind the mask. "A dandy with a sword and a pair of homunculi?" He whinnied. "Nine hells, you Maglan are arrogant. Here. Let me show you a real witch's body-guards." The man puffed air through the pursed lips of his mask, creating a high-pitched whistle. There was a flash, and the room was suddenly crowded with a seven-foot-tall ogre, a two-headed goblin, and a small buzzing firefly that spat sparking embers around the room. The goblin bore a jagged rock tied to a stick, and the ogre carried a heavy wooden club spiked with shards of bone. It crouched as it rolled the club over in its hands.

The zombie maker said, "Well, Maglan. You said you were here to represent your house. In fact, your only chance of getting out of this room alive is to carry this news back to your mother: Withdraw your claims on the port. It now belongs to the Ilyssa and our allies." He indicated his partners on either side of him. "All three of our noble houses stand together against you. If we see any of you curse-merchants on the docks, we won't leave any pieces big enough to bury."

Virot's smile hardened. "I have a counteroffer. Stretch out your necks, fools. Close your eyes, and die quietly. The alternative is much, much worse."

"Enough," the bearded man said. "He dies now. Agreed?" The harlequin nodded, whistling laughter through his nose. The one-eyed man dabbed his brow but did not reply.

Virot shrugged. "So be it."

The room's occupants exploded into action. Virot clicked his tongue against the roof of his mouth, and the imps came screaming from the rafters. One of them slashed the firefly from the air as it flew past, and the volatile insect exploded on contact. The ogre leaped forward with a wild swing of its club, and the goblin let out a war whoop as it followed behind. The zombie wolf crept around Virot to attack from the rear, but the human zombies remained at their master's side.

The first imp darted past the undead humans and grabbed two handfuls of the zombie maker's beard. It jerked him into the one-eyed witch while the other imp tore silver and flesh alike from the harlequin's face.

Virot hopped back from the oncoming ogre, smoothly reversing his saber, so that the tip stuck out behind him. He felt the point drive home into the wolf's body. It wouldn't kill the undead animal, but it would protect his hamstrings while he fought the others.

The ogre's first wild swing fell short and took out a chunk of the floor. Virot rolled over the ogre's weapon and slung the wolf off the end of his saber, into the oncoming goblin. Neither creature was intelligent enough to determine friend from foe in these close quarters, and they fell into a tangled heap, snapping and tearing at each other. The ogre realized that Virot was now straddling its club and tried to reverse its swing to crush him against the ceiling.

Virot was far quicker than the muscle-bound brute, however. Positioned as he was, he had only to extend his arm to bring his hand close to the ogre's face. He spoke a clipped series of guttural sounds, kissed his bleeding palm, then clamped his hand across the ogre's nose and eyes. There was a soft implosion and a foul odor.

Immediately the ogre howled and clapped both hands to its face, dropping its weapon in mid-arc. With a precise, powerful swing, Virot embedded the long edge of his saber in both the ogre's wrists, cutting into but not through the bones. He gave the blade a vicious twist as he pulled it free, and the ogre's half-severed hands flopped grotesquely back and forth on its ruined arms.

Its face was no better off. Virot's spell had flooded the brute's head with noxious black magic designed to cripple an opponent's senses. The ogre's eyes were melting into slime, its tongue swelled to bursting, and blood poured from its nose and ears. It gagged and choked as it tried to draw air, and sank to its knees as the life ran out of its arms.

The Ilyssa witch had broken the wing of the imp in his beard, and he cursed Virot as he grappled with it. "Kill him!" he roared to the human zombies, and they dully shambled forward.

Virot stepped behind the ogre and placed his bleeding hand on the back of its skull. He growled out another series of syllables, and the ogre turned its sightless eyes upward as its mouth opened in a silent scream of agony.

The spell took effect, and the ogre's body deflated like a punctured skin of water. As its muscles wasted and shrank, Virot's swelled and expanded. In moments, the ogre was a spindly sack of bones held together by tough red flesh. Virot had grown accordingly taller, wider, and heavier as the ogre's might coursed through his body. He cast his cloak back, his muscles rippling with stolen strength. He stomped down with his right foot, squashing both of the goblin's heads into the hardwood floor. The wolf snapped as he pulled his foot free.

"Let's put the Ilyssa zombies to the test." Virot tucked his sword back into its sheath. "Are they truly undead or just reanimated corpses?"

He waited until all three zombies were closer and then smiled his most charming smile at the bearded witch. Then, in a blur of motion, he plowed through them all like a barbed arrow through clay. One moment he was crouched and facing the zombies, and the next he was on the far side of the room covered with necrotic gore. A trail of rotting flesh, broken limbs, and other sundered flesh lay strewn in his wake.

Before the ogre's borrowed bulk faded, Virot struck again. He streaked across the room behind the three witches with his saber at calf level. The bearded Ilyssa and his cronies screamed as the muscles and tendons in their lower legs split beneath the blade. They fell painfully to the floor, crippled and immobile.

Virot's body started to shrink back to his normal size. The ogre itself remained emaciated, however, its fabled strength gone forever. Virot prodded one of the severed, decomposing arms with his boot.

"Just as I thought. If this were a true zombie instead of a cheap Ilyssa knock-off, these pieces would still be after me." He sauntered back toward the ogre, casually clicking another command to his imps. The vicious little creatures were crippled and bloody, but they had enjoyed their messy work. The one-eyed man was now a no-eyed man, and both the bearded Ilyssa and the harlequin had been savagely mauled about the neck and face.

"You're dead, Maglan," the Ilyssa husked. "I am the second-born son of the Ilyssa. My family will—"

"Almost done," Virot called pleasantly. He stood behind the ogre once more, raised his saber, and plunged the length of it down into the top of the wasted brute's head. The ogre barely twitched as it died.

"This is something new that I've been eager to try," he said. He spoke in the harsh language of his family spellcraft once more, and he absorbed the ogre's death as he had its mass. A whirling halo of smoke and sparks formed around his head, and he held his bleeding hand out toward the imps.

"Return," he said. The winged monsters scrabbled and flew across the room in unison, disappearing headfirst into the slash on Virot's palm.

"Mercy," wailed the now-blind witch. "Forgive me, Maglan. I am your servant. Mercy."

"Oh, please," Virot said. "Have some pride." With one hand on his sword and the other extended, he went from witch to witch, touching each on the forehead and inscribing in blood the same complicated character. When the Ilyssa resisted, Virot stabbed him lightly in the ribs.

"If it were up to me," Virot said, "I would keep you three around. It seems so wasteful to cast conquered enemies aside when they could be put to work instead. But mother was quite clear on this issue."

"Mercy!"

Virot smiled. "Not tonight." He paused, bringing the precise words out of his memory. "Hear me, marked ones. On behalf of the Maglan, and especially myself, I offer your most valuable treasure to the Wealthy One. Your lives are forfeit to Kuberr."

The bearded witch coughed and spat his final defiance at Virot. The masked witch struggled to produce another whistle through his torn lips and shattered mask. The blind witch simply groveled. Virot waited until their efforts were spent, then spoke clearly in the silence as they gathered their breath.

"In his name, I bid you—Suffer."

All three of the crippled witches suddenly stiffened, convulsing in pain and choking on agony.

"Wither."

The skin on their bones hardened and cracked, growing blacker and blacker as their blood became a desiccating poison and their veins spread it throughout their bodies.

"Die."

Three separate rattles groaned out of three separate throats. The Ilyssa and his co-conspirators slumped heavily to the floor and shuddered, never to rise again.

Virot Maglan surveyed the carnage in the silent room. He smiled, his dark eyes fairly twinkling in the gloom.

"Goodnight, gentlemen. It's been a pleasure, in the truest sense of the word."

The Secrets of Magic

* * * * *

The Maglan family manor dominated the west end of the city. It was a huge building, three stories high surrounded by a full acre of swampy ground. The manor was enclosed inside spiked gates and stone walls and was warded with the most fearsome spells imaginable. Virot strolled through the secret entrance he had created in the northwest corner of the wall without announcing himself and without fear. As a member of the family, the manor's magical defenses were his to command.

As the third son of the house, he had also been raised to be more terrible than anything he might encounter inside or outside of the manor walls. He heard the heavy tread of the guard beasts in the distance and saw the indistinct shapes of life-sucking shades flitting through the trees. He paid them no more mind than he did the carnivorous grass beneath his feet. All of the resident monsters recognized him by sight, smell, or aura, and all found somewhere else to lurk or else cowered fearfully as he passed.

He found two of his older siblings, Valdim and Vinyata, waiting for him on the front steps. They were complimentary twins, mirror images of each other. Valdim had been born first, with one blue eye, one green eye, and half a head of sharp white hair. Vinyata was the same, but her eyes were switched and her half-tresses sprouted from the opposite side of her scalp. Mother was especially proud of the twins, for she had performed many painful and complicated rituals while they gestated to grant them their special gifts. Neither was as powerful a witch as Virot, but together they were capable of unparalleled feats of clairvoyance.

"Hello, little brother," Vinyata called. She was the more outgoing of the two.

"Vinya," Virot said. "Val." He gestured to the skein of silver thread that his brother held looped around his hands and his sister was rolling into a ball. "Are you working or playing?"

"We are waiting," Vinya said. She turned to face Virot and winked her green eye. In unison, she and her twin said, "We know what you did."

Virot's jaw tightened slightly, but he maintained a cheerful expression. He didn't like the idea of the twins monitoring him for their own amusement. He liked it even less if they did it on mother's orders.

"I did as I was asked," he said. "I broke up the Ilyssa conspiracy to take over the docks before it could even get started. I killed the Ilyssa's chief negotiator and sent a strong message to the other noble houses. And I did it with my usual flair and efficiency."

"You did it with a spell that no one in the family has ever heard of," Vinya said. "And you did it to the second son of the Ilyssa. His father is very upset."

"So is our older brother," Val droned. Vinya bounced the ball of thread lightly off of her twin's forehead.

"Hush, now." Vinya smoothly caught the ball and resumed adding string to it. "That was the secret part."

Virot relaxed. "I see." He bowed to the twins, then stepped forward. They remained as they were, facing each other and coiling string, without looking up. "Excuse me," he said evenly.

"No, little brother. Mother made herself clear, and we promised. Sit and talk with us awhile. Val's arms must be getting tired." She patted the stone stair beside her. "Come on now. Obey your elders."

"Look into your own future," Virot said quietly. "And see what will happen if you don't get out of my way."

Vinya laughed merrily. "You can't hurt us. We're family."

Virot feigned shock. "Who said anything about hurt? I'm merely pointing out that we all have secrets." Val started to moan, but Vinya shushed him. "Since you told mother about my new spell, it's only right that I tell her about the entrails you've been using for your predictions lately. You've been warned about taking children from the neighborhood, haven't you? Several times, if I'm not mistaken."

Val wailed softly and dropped the rest of the string. Vinya took his hand and squeezed it, crooning softly until her twin settled down.

"Oh, Virot," she said. "Cruel Virot." She pulled her moaning brother closer and held him tight. "Go on," she said, her voice muffled by Val's long hair. "But at least tell mother that we tried to stop you."

Virot smiled wide. "I'll do better than that. Blood has spilled tonight. The feud between Maglan, Ilyssa, and their allies will most likely resume in earnest. Even our brother cannot complain if you use the children of our enemies, no matter what part of the city they come from." He casually inspected the hilt of his saber. "It would be very easy for you to collect your specimens if I made a point of driving them toward the manor, wouldn't it?"

Vinya caught his meaning and returned his smile. "Yes, little brother. Yes it would."

"Consider it done."

Val looked confused, but as Virot passed them, Vinya was whispering excitedly in her twin's ear. As he entered the family manor, Virot heard his older brother give an exultant cry and clap his hands together.

* * * * *

Virot's mother sat high on a thronelike chair in her luxurious private chamber. The gems and precious metals that decorated the walls were worth more than the rest of the manor combined. Her chair had been carved from a dragon's skull by master craftsmen.

She carried the symbol of her supreme power, the Maglan family scepter, tightly in her right hand.

Lady Maglan was over seventy years old, her limbs thin, and her skin stretched tight across her face. She had yellow cat's eyes, complete with vertical pupils, and her hair was a shining cascade of copper strands that had been enchanted onto her head. She was not an overly vain woman, but she understood the importance of appearances. Upon the death of the children's father thirty years ago, she had adopted the copper hair as an accessory to the family scepter.

Currently, she and her eldest son Vozama were receiving a visitor. Vozama was a stern, pinched, white-haired man with long arms and sharp nails. A man with the Ilyssa crest on his shirt was glowering in front of the two eldest Maglans.

"Virot, my boy. Come sit by my side." His mother's voice was calm but hard, her innate sharpness hidden like a dagger in a sheath. Virot always likened her style to a slow stab rather than a brutal thrust.

Virot hesitated. He did not routinely participate in this kind of meeting. "Mother. Brother. I wasn't sure you'd be pleased to see me. The twins—"

"Sit," she commanded, and Virot lowered himself to the steps next to his mother's feet. "I think I may need you after all." To the Ilyssa envoy, she said, "You were saying?"

The messenger looked suspiciously at Virot then continued. "Simply put, your position is indefensible." Virot noted that he spoke in a slow, official tone, reciting a message he had been made to memorize. "You do not have the resources to control the docks, and you do not have the power to conquer Ilyssa. Maybe twenty years ago but not today."

Vozama flushed and angrily flexed his fingers. Virot hid a smile. Mother didn't react at all.

"And your message?"

"It is a demand, Lady Maglan, not a message. The savage who murdered the second-born son of Ilyssa will be given over to me. If I return to the Ilyssa manor alone, then you may consider the truce at an end." He paused and dropped his formal tone. "My master will destroy you all. His minions will overrun the city. We have seen the portents, and the time of zombies is almost upon us. Within a generation, everything dead will rise again. The Machine God will repair and revive anything that has ever fallen, and those of us who have perfected this art will be rewarded. It has been foretold. Check with your own augurs if you do not believe. Be wise, Lady Maglan. Submit to us now, that we might spare you when the Age of the Undead begins."

"I see. If you return alone, it means violence and conflict. And if you do not return at all?" She gestured to Virot. "Bring him up, my boy."

The messenger yelped as Virot sprang on him, twisting his arms behind his back. He forced the man up three steps to the chair, then onto his knees.

"You will be my reply," she said. She rose, drawing a long metal spike from her sleeve as she stood. Though old and thin, her arm flashed downward into the messenger's face with the speed and force of a guillotine blade. She nodded to Virot, who let the twitching body drop.

"Deliver him to his master," she returned to her seat, her breath easy and unlabored. "The feud is on."

"But mother," Vozama said.

The old woman raised her hand. "I know what you are going to say. 'We are overmatched. We should negotiate. It's better to have a small slice of the pie than to be dead.' But there is only one way to deal with these grave-robbing vermin."

"Hear! Hear!" Virot said.

"Hold your tongue," Vozama said. Then, to his mother, "I would have said those things, mother, yes. And I would have been right."

She shook her head. "They have been testing our resolve, squeezing our territory, and whittling away at our influence for the past five years while this damnable truce was in place. They are brutes, and brutes only understand a sharp blow to the face."

Vozama crossed his arms, but Virot could still hear him picking at his own fingernails in frustration. "And when the zombies break through the main gate? When Ilyssa cutthroats murder us in our beds?"

Lady Maglan sighed and looked to Virot. "This is why I can never retire, my son. Your older brother knows how to use power but not how to keep it."

"He is a worrier, Mother. It is his nature."

"And you are an animal," Vozama said. "All you need do is kill. It's up to me to make sure that we live."

"Hush, my children. Virot understands the use of force, Vozama. You would be wise to listen to him." Virot smirked, and she added, "And you, Virot, should be more respectful to your elders. If Vozama worries, it is because he has the family's long-term interests in mind. Glory belongs to the Maglans as a whole, not its individual members. We have survived, prospered, and dominated in this city for generations because we have never strayed from that belief. A Maglan has wealth, power, and most importantly, purpose. What more could anyone possibly want?"

Virot bowed his head. "Yes, Mother."

To the still-furious Vozama, she said, "And the Ilyssa can't simply kill us all in our beds. We have maintained the flow of commerce to and from the city for generations. The slavers and the smugglers and the pirate kings are used to dealing with us. If we disappeared overnight, it would take years to reestablish the level of security and trust that we provide. Each family would try to make its own arrangements, and full-scale war would break out in a matter of weeks. The Ilyssa know this. It's one of the reasons they're so angry all the time."

"I think we are overestimating the Ilyssa's grasp of the situation and underestimating their greed."

"No, my son. The Ilyssa will bluster and perhaps even bloody our noses, but they will not storm the manor. If we don't make a stand now and match them blow for blow, we will never revive our prestige. And our prestige has suffered lately." She coughed dramatically into her fist. "I am not as young as I once was. What kind of mother would I be if I were to turn over the family business to you with our power at its lowest point in a hundred years?"

"So," Virot said, "we will fight."

"You will fight," mother said, "and, I hope, with a little less relish than you exhibited tonight. We," she motioned to Vozama, "will take up the other front. The subtler battlefields of negotiation and influence. If we all play our parts, the entire family will benefit. Which is as it should be."

Both Maglan sons answered in unison, "Yes, Mother."

Though he could see the wisdom of his mother's words, Virot couldn't stop turning over her rhetorical question in his mind. He had wealth. He had power. He had purpose.

What else *could* he want?

* * * * *

That night, in a dream, Virot stood alone on a vast expanse of polished black stone. The wind whipped past his ears, filling his head with an endless, droning roar. Far in the distance loomed a huge

285

mountain that shimmered with reflected moonlight. Something vital was at its peak, something old and vast and valuable beyond measure. He started toward it.

He marched for an eternity toward the mountain, but the pyramid-shaped mass came no closer. He realized that was because as he moved toward the mountain, it moved away.

"You are the one." The booming voice replaced the wind in his ears. Like the wind, it seemed to come from every direction. For the first time in his adult life, Virot Maglan dropped to his knees before someone other than his mother.

Virot squinted upward. "I am Virot Maglan." His voice was half-defiant, half-questioning.

The booming voice chuckled. "For now."

The mountain was looming larger but not because he was approaching it. Instead, it was bowing at its middle like a gentleman, the peak rushing downward at a frightening speed. He could see the pyramid for what it was—a giant pile of gold coins. A huge crowned figure sat on a lavish throne at the very top. The figure bent forward in its chair to get a better look at Virot, and the mountain bent forward to accommodate its king.

Virot started. This was suddenly familiar to him, the mountain, the coins, the throne and its occupant. He read about such a scene in the ancient text that gave him the spell he used to finish off the Ilyssa conspirators.

"Kuberr?" he said, and the wind died, leaving an eerily calm silence. "Are you the Wealthy One?"

"Once," the voice said. "Perhaps someday again." Virot saw the figure's outline clearly now, but its features were lost in the shadows of moonlight.

"You are the one," the voice said. "The one who called me. The one who offered treasure to the god of wealth."

"I am."

"Your offer was accepted. What do you seek?"

Virot was never intended to be a politician, but he recognized the opening of negotiations.

"Position," Virot said. "Power. Dominion over all who come before me. I want their fear. Their respect. Their awe."

The mountain stooped even lower, and Virot saw the figure on the throne clearly for the first time. It was a gargantuan, organic humanoid, almost featureless in the dim light. It seemed to be dressed in a high-collared robe, but the garment was the same pitch-black as the figure, and Virot could not see where the body ended and the robe began. On its head was a crown with spear-long spikes.

A huge crescent smile revealed row upon row of the figure's razored teeth. Above the smile was a row of eyes, evenly spaced around the entire head. Kuberr opened his mouth wide, his grin expanding to fill Virot's field of vision, his eyes in constant motion, searching the horizon in every direction as he spoke.

"Fear, respect, and awe. These things can be yours. For a price."

"Name it."

Kuberr laughed, shaking Virot and the ground around him. "Slowly, slowly. Let us test each other with a small bargain. I will give you what you have asked for. In return, you will enter my service."

Virot started, fresh panic rising. "Kuberr is kind to offer such treasures as a 'small bargain.' But I cannot accept. I am already pledged to serve another."

"No matter. I do not ask you to break from your filial duty. I only ask that you do as you have already done. In my name, and with my methods, continue to serve your family. That is how you will serve me."

Virot pondered.

"Before you answer," Kuberr said, "understand. In my service, you will learn what true wealth is. All that you treasure now will become hollow and drab, and when you finally understand the greater gifts I offer, you will do anything to possess them. This is no game or confidence trick, Virot Maglan. I will give you what you want, and when I am done, you will beg me for more and thank me when I give it to you. For indeed, the prize is worth the price."

Virot Maglan smiled. "Show me, then. For power as you describe it, I will serve you, Kuberr."

"Then serve you shall." In the distance there was a crack of thunder that sounded like Kuberr's laughter. Kuberr's arm swung forward, and he extended an index finger, taller than Virot, to touch the Maglan enforcer on the forehead. Virot shuddered, fell, and kept falling.

The wind whipped up once more, and the mountain began to straighten. The laughing figure of Kuberr was carried up and away.

* * * * *

Virot awoke with a painful jerk. The sun was slowly rising outside his window, and he could feel the electric hum on his forehead where Kuberr touched him. He rushed to the mirror at his bedside but found no marks on his face. For a split second, he wondered if the dream was a curse sent by the Ilyssa or a playful fancy sent by the twins. But when he looked down at his hands, he could see the ghost of the character he had inscribed on his victims' foreheads earlier. He steadied his trembling hands, clenched them into tight fists, then jerked the bell cord. After a short while, a graying servant shuffled in.

"Yes, Master Virot?"

"Take my hand."

"Master?"

"You heard me." The servant tentatively reached out, and Virot grabbed on with his fingers and palm. The servant moaned, and when Virot let him go, he staggered back, rubbing his hand.

"Will there be anything else, sir?"

"Yes," Virot said, wishing he could remember the old man's name, "in fact, there is.

"Servant," he declared. "Suffer, wither, and die."

The old man gurgled, convulsed, and collapsed into a pile of black shards and leathery debris. Virot stifled a roar of delight.

He could kill with a touch and three simple words. By way of an introduction, Kuberr had made him the most powerful witch in the city, and all he had to do in return was employ that power. From this would flow the recognition and respect he had requested.

"If these are your lessons," Virot said out loud, "then I am ready for more."

Outside, as if in response, a chill wind kicked up and a soft peal of thunder rattled like the laughter of a god.

* * * * *

Over the next few weeks Virot was busier than he had been in years. Threats and angry exchanges flew between the Maglan and Ilyssa manors, and an escalating series of assaults rocked both families and their retainers. A squadron of zombies forced their way into a Maglan moneylender's office, murdered the staff, and burned the building to the ground. An Ilyssa grave-robbing team was eaten alive when they cracked open a mausoleum and found Virot had left a thousand trained Maglan rats in place of the fresh corpses they sought. He enjoyed the privilege of beheading an Ilyssa courier bearing an offer to end the feud when the twins pointed out that he was also bearing a dormant strain of plague that would burst forth as soon as he set foot inside the manor. Ockeed, the head of the Ilyssa clan, narrowly avoided blindness and death when his daughter-in-law impulsively opened a cursed communiqué that appeared to be from his only surviving son.

Virot had never felt more alive. His face was unknown to most of the city, and it was relatively easy for him to move among the network of taverns, gambling dens, and docks that the two families were feuding over. If anyone confronted him or asked too many questions, he simply touched the nearest part of that person's body, whispered his incantation, and left them dead where they stood. He left Ilyssa corpses in his wakelike footprints.

On this night, he brought Vinya with him when he slipped out through his secret passage. She hated being apart from Val, who nearly wept as he watched them go from his window, but there was no other option. The twins required a very specific person for a very specific augury, and she needed to identify the victim herself.

"Is this what you do at night?" Vinya asked. Virot thought she sounded more lucid and focused on her own.

"I've become something of a student of human nature," Virot said. They were well clear of the manor and had reached the edge of Docktown, the epicenter of the feud.

"Really? What for? Is it part of a new ritual?"

"Something like that. I'm trying to understand what people value most."

"So you can take it from them." Vinya smiled slyly.

"So I can obtain it for myself. There's a slight difference."

"Bosh. You just want to find out what hurts the most when you take it away. Oooh!" she squealed suddenly and pointed to a street vendor. "Buy me a snack, little brother. I'm famished, and I haven't any money."

The pair went over to the vendor's booth, and Virot pointed to a roasted meat kebab. "Two." He put a gold coin on the counter. Virot handed one to his sister, and the Maglans strolled on. Vinya eagerly tore into her food, but Virot carried his at arm's length as if he found it distasteful.

"If you're not learning how to hurt people on these little jaunts," Vinya said through a mouthful of meat, "what are you learning?"

"I thought you'd never ask. Come this way."

He led his sister closer to the docks, where the street lights were fewer and the dangers more numerous. There were more people there, not less, as anyone who wanted to survive traveled in packs for protection. Burly stevedores and enslaved brutes lugged huge crates on their shoulders. Rodentlike men with valises skulked nervously between armed bodyguards. Gangs of thugs loitered on corners, looking for a fight or a whipping boy to pass the time.

Virot turned down a narrow alley and motioned for his sister to follow. She tore the last bit off her kebab and tossed the stick aside. Virot pointed to one of the semiconscious street people propped up against the dirty bricks. The man was malnourished, ragged, and filthy. Vinya wrinkled her nose.

"A starving person," Virot said, "will beg for food." He waved his kebab down in front of the transient's face, and the man's rheumy eyes creaked open.

"Please," he croaked. Virot dropped the kebab onto the man's lap and ushered his sister back out to the street. His charity had not gone unnoticed, and a handful of other street denizens groveled up to him.

"Alms, sir," one of them said. "Enough for some bread? I've got a sick child. . . ."

"A poor person," Virot scattered a handful of gold onto the street, and the shabby group fell on them, "will beg for coins."

Vinya paid no attention to the scrabbling bodies at their feet. "You've been thinking about this a lot, haven't you?"

Virot nodded. He tilted his head and flicked his eyes, and Vinya turned to see what he was looking at. A tall, elegant man with dark skin and braided hair walked proudly beside a beautiful canary-skinned woman atop a huge black dog. Behind the couple walked a cold-eyed man with at least a dozen knives belted across his chest, and a seven-foot-tall insectoid with spiked limbs and serrated mandibles.

"A rich man begs for power," Virot said. "That handsome fool can't protect himself or his woman, but he hires those who can. And then he parades himself through Docktown to prove that he is not afraid, that he controls his own destiny."

Vinya yawned. "Are you going somewhere with this, little brother?"

"I am. In fact, I think we've already arrived." They had come to the porch outside an Ilyssa tavern. The zombie makers' standard hung over the door, and some of the toughs lounging outside also wore the standard on their shoulders. "My errand for the evening," he explained.

Vinya's boredom vanished. Now she glared angrily at her brother. "I've had enough sightseeing for one night, Virot. Take me home now."

"Hey," one of the toughs said. "Isn't that the Maglan bitch who sees the future?" Some of the others grunted in reply, and one of the group dashed indoors, presumably to tell the owner. The toughs rose and began to move toward Virot and Vinya, drawing their knives as they came.

"What does a powerful man beg for?" Virot was caught up in his lecture, seemingly oblivious to the approaching danger. "It seems that no matter how much one has, there is always something more. Something one wants. Something one treasures above all else. I think I've figured out what that is."

Vinya stepped away from him. The toughs now had them partially surrounded. "Can't you tell me what it is after we get home?"

"You've made your last mistake, Maglan." The owner of the tavern stood in the doorway. "Kill them both." Virot recognized him as a nephew to the Ilyssa patriarch, and he smiled. Perfect, he thought.

In a flash, Virot drew his sword and lopped off the nearest tough's arm. He shoved the maimed man toward his sister and said, "Defend yourself for a moment while I make my point." The other toughs sprang forward at Virot, but his sword kept the gang at bay, parrying a blow here and slashing a torso there. As he fought, Virot made sure to touch each one of his attackers.

Vinya, meanwhile, had sunk her long black nails into the wounded man's neck. Her eyes rolled back in her head, she bunched up her fists, then screeched like a brace of banshees. Her hair stood on end as she wailed, and then each strand erupted from her head, doubling, tripling, quadrupling in length. Guided by Vinya, spikes of her hair skewered the two toughs closest to her, pinning them to the brick wall then withdrawing in the blink of an eye. The toughs gurgled and fell with only the vaguest notion of what had killed them.

"Bravo!" Virot cheered. Then, without speaking, he thought the words of Kuberr's spell. All around the Ilyssa tavern owner, his toughs staggered, clutched their throats, and crumpled painfully to the ground. It's getting easier and easier, Virot thought. Soon I won't need the words at all.

The tavern owner found himself alone and facing two sworn enemies over the broken bodies of the men he had just sent to kill them. He turned to flee back into the tavern. A coiled strand of

Vinya's hair speared through his shoulder, spinning him around and dropping him heavily onto his rump.

"Don't kill me," he cowered and held his good arm in front of his face. "Please, Maglan. Please!"

"Let me guess," Vinya said. She was mopping the gore from her hair with her red silk sash. "A powerful man begs for his life."

"Correct," Virot said. "Listen closely, corpse-grinder." The man whimpered and tried to staunch the flow of blood from his shoulder. "Your life is mine. I've killed so many of you over the last few days that I'm losing count. Do you want to survive?"

"I do," the man bawled. "Anything, I'll do anything, please!"

Virot leaned down and whispered in the man's ear. "Renounce your family," he said. He traced a finger across the man's damp forehead. "You belong to me, now. When I call, you will answer. When I beckon, you will come. Agree now or disappear forever."

The tavern owner choked, glanced frantically at Vinya, then let his face fall. "I am yours," he said.

Virot tapped the man on the head and stood up. "I have marked you, so I can kill you with a word," he said. "With the merest thought, really. If you ever displease me, I will."

"Yes, Master."

"Oh, there's no need for that. Just remember whom you serve. Now. Get up and get out of my sight. You will hear from me shortly."

As the man ran off, Vinya smoothed her hair back into shape. "Why did you let him live?"

"Because it's time for us to change our thinking. Mother was right about the Ilyssa. They can't risk destroying us all at once, and they can't kill us one by one so long as I'm around. Dead, they're of no further use to us. Alive and fearful, there is no limit to what we can make them do."

"You sound like you have a plan. That's not like you."

"It's more like me than you realize. I plan to create a community of people who think like I do. A society of shared concern. Mutual obedience, mutual benefits. Care to be a part of it?"

Vinya considered. "Not without Val."

Virot gallantly offered his elbow. "My plan has always included you and Val both."

Vinya took her brother's arm, and they walked together through city streets that became deserted as they approached.

* * * * *

"So you have finally learned," Kuberr said. "Life is the most precious treasure there is."

In his dream, Virot nodded. "I think I always knew. I just didn't understand."

"One's own life is to be savored. The lives of others are to be cultivated."

"You are wise, Kuberr. I have marked a score of my enemies but let them live. They serve me now, as I serve you."

"Then you are pleased with our bargain so far?"

"I am. And more, I am ready to extend it."

"Outstanding. What do you propose?"

Virot smiled. "To expand the family fortune, my personal power, the number of your followers. The best way to amass wealth is to generate it ourselves."

"I approve, Virot Maglan." Kuberr's multiple eyes flashed. "Do it."

* * * * *

In a converted warehouse on the edge of the waterfront, a small gathering had formed. People and monsters stood in small groups, muttering to themselves and glaring at each other. Some had been invited to attend. Most had been compelled.

A servant, hand-picked for his booming voice, walked to the center of the huge room and raised his hands for silence.

"Thank you for coming," he said. "You are among the select few who will witness something new. An entertainment not found in the taverns or the bawdy houses. And though it costs you nothing to watch, your attendance is not free. When we are done, you will go out and spread the word about what happened here. Your master expects to see you all again next week. And each with no less than three paying guests." There was a murmur through the small crowd, and the servant waited for it to subside.

"Place your bets. We are about to begin."

The servant introduced Vinya and Val Maglan as they came from a corner dressed in matching purple leather. The crowd muttered, and some even gasped. The twins were not often seen together outside the manor. Val looked confused and intimidated by the attention, but Vinya was calm and smiling. From his hidden seat high above the floor, Virot felt a rush of confidence. He had prepared the twins for a week beforehand, and he knew he could rely on his sister not to disappoint him.

"Friends," the servant called, "also welcome Cato Ilyssa and her . . . ah, pets . . . to this special inaugural event." Virot had caught the eldest Ilyssa daughter en route to a tryst. She was notoriously proud and haughty, but she had surrendered easily when she saw what Virot did to her bodyguards. Now she rode a huge black hound into the center of the room, a saw-beaked raven perched on her shoulder and a pair of zombified tigers trailing behind her.

Vinya turned to Virot's elevated chair. "For Kuberr," she said. She prodded Val, who echoed her words, then dropped lightly into a sitting position and began to meditate.

Cato Ilyssa raised her short sword. "For Kuberr," she spat. Virot had promised her freedom only if she was the last person standing at the close of the evening's entertainment.

The servant announcer spread his arms wide. "When the horn sounds," he said, "begin." He bowed and quickly retreated from the center of the room.

Val was rocking and chanting on the floor, his eyes tightly shut. Vinya stood behind him with her hands on his shoulders, her chants forming a dialogue with her brother's. Their hair grew as they spoke, Val's climbing up and Vinya's trailing down until the ends met and intertwined. Cato Ilyssa spurred her giant dog forward a pace, then brought the two undead tigers up, so that they all stood in a straight line. She held her arm out, and the raven hopped from shoulder to elbow to wrist, waiting for the signal to take flight.

Virot leaned forward on his chair. His heart was racing, and he was grinning foolishly in anticipation. His voice rang out over the assembly.

"For Kuberr," he said. "Begin."

The horn sounded. Cato's bird and her tigers leaped forward, making straight for the twins. She glared witheringly at Virot and spat on the floor. Then she dug her heels into the dog's flank and she, too, sprang to attack.

The twins' chants had begun to overlap and combine, their voices rising. The raven reached them first and slashed Vinya across the face with its claws, but she did not break contact with her brother, and she did not interrupt her chant. Instead, she and Val both opened their eyes to reveal a terrible yellow glow from within. Val screamed and Vinya roared, and from their mouths poured a great cloud of gelatinous light. The formless blob engulfed the raven in midair, rose toward the ceiling, then slammed into the floor hard enough to crack the boards. The crowd fell back against the walls of the warehouse, but the doors had been barred, and there was no way out.

Cato's tigers plowed straight into the huge greenish blob and became stuck like insects in amber. They struggled and coughed, but the glob hunched up and over them like a thing alive. Once they were entirely within its mass, the glob contracted in on itself, and the horrified assembly watched as the raven and two tigers were crushed together at its center.

Cato struggled to control her dog and to keep it clear of the amoebic shape. Guided by its master, the dog bounded safely around the undulating heap and charged toward the twins. Val and Vinya continued to chant, arcane energy sparking from where they touched each other.

When it was a mere twenty feet long, the grisly mass shuddered and pseudopods lashed out from its front, rear, and top. Cato steered her dog away from the glob's new appendages as the thing itself began to roll together and stretch itself out. The lower pseudopods became burly arms and thick legs, and the ones on top began to flap like wings. The thing's newly sprouted head snapped at Cato, and her dog reared. Val and Vinya kept chanting.

The thing was now recognizably a winged quadruped, an unholy melding of tiger and raven. Its beaked, feline head screeched. Its tail lashed, and its wings fluttered as it padded forward. Cato's steed finally panicked and threw her off, bounding through the crowd and trampling some of the spectators. Cato herself cursed the dog, then cast a searing black bolt of light into the tiger-thing's face. Greenish flesh split where the light touched it, but the thing did not stop stalking.

"Hold," Vinya called, and the twins' monstrosity stopped with Cato Ilyssa between its paws. Virot nodded in satisfaction. Vinya had remembered his injunction to keep their foe alive if at all possible.

Vinya waved her hands, and the tiger-thing melted in a noisome wash of protoplasmic slime. Cato was carried back on the tide and slammed into the nearest wall. She rose, coughing the vile stuff from her lungs, and drew her sword.

"Kill you all," she croaked. "I'll kill each and every last one of you."

Val held his hands palm-up over his shoulders, and Vinya placed her hands on top of his. She helped him to his feet, and, still connected by their hair, the twins exhaled together. A stream of stinging flies poured out of their mouths, buzzing across the room and swarming around Cato's face. Hundreds of the savage insects tore into Cato's flesh, and she staggered, waving her sword feebly, before falling face-first onto the floor.

Half the crowd cheered. The other half was too stunned to speak. Vinya waved her hands, and the swarm of flies disappeared like smoke, leaving the ravaged and unconscious form of Cato Ilyssa lying in the slime.

At a signal from Virot, the announcer stepped forward.

"This concludes tonight's entertainment. Remember—next week, bring guests who like spectacle and have money."

* * * * *

Dreaming, Virot stood on the endless plain of black rock once more. He waited silently, patiently listening to the wind howl and waiting for the moon to slip out from behind the cloud.

"You have returned," Kuberr's voice boomed. Virot looked up, and the bowing mountain of gold with Kuberr's outline was visible against the moonlit sky.

"The feud is over," Virot said. "Ockeed Ilyssa himself is coming tomorrow to prostrate himself at my mother's feet." He smiled thinly. "The cost to his family turned out to be greater than he was ready to pay. He will submit. For now."

"So you have conquered. You are victorious. Why then do you sound so unhappy?"

"You know why. This is not what I want," he said. "Mother intends to take complete control, as it was generations ago. The Ilyssa will become vassals of the Maglan. Their zombies will be put to work on our behalf, for our glory. And though my idea of exhibiting blood sports has proven quite profitable, I," he snarled in pure disgust, "am to become the general in some sort of zombie army."

"But your family will rule. You will be the undisputed masters of the entire city."

"Who wants to rule?" Virot spat. "Politics is all ebb and flow, compromise and concession. Let others wield power. I am content to improve my own position. Content to amass real wealth."

Kuberr chuckled. "Are you, now? So you have learned what the most valuable treasure of all is?"

"I have."

"And you are ready to pay the price for it."

"Any price."

"Tell me what you have learned, and then name your desire."

Virot grit his teeth. "Wealth is not property, or currency, or even power. These things are derived from true wealth. There is only one prize that can guarantee all the rest will follow."

Kuberr's mountain brought him closer, down to where Virot could see each individual massive eye. "And that is?"

"Time," Virot said. "I wish to live forever. I wish to serve you for a hundred lifetimes and beyond. A man could gorge himself to death on the crumbs from your table. I want a seat at that table, for all eternity."

"Immortality." Kuberr's smile thinned, then stretched wide. "The price is high. And those who serve me forever, serve me to the exclusion of all others."

"I understand. Have I not served you well so far? Tell me. What is the price?"

Kuberr spoke three words. Virot nodded. He had anticipated the cost of Kuberr's gift and was ready to pay it.

"Done," he said. "When?"

"Today. Tomorrow. It matters not, so long as it is done. And lest you think me a fool, remember this—my gift goes on forever. You cannot possibly receive it all at once. The longer you serve me, the longer you will live. If you renege on our deal, or fail to obey me in the future, our bargain is void."

"I understand."

"There are details. Matters of form to be observed. Your name, for example. Cast it aside. I shall give you a new one. Are you ready?"

"I am."

Kuberr stretched out his massive arms, each as long as a river. "Then come to me, and be the first to join my family."

Virot closed his eyes and felt himself being swallowed up by a power so profound that it was indistinguishable from joy.

* * * * *

The Maglans stood in their manor's great hall, each of them clad in their finest clothes and most expensive jewelry.

"How much longer till they arrive?"

"Not long, Vinya." Mother's copper hair glowed with reflected candle light.

"I have something to say before they do," Virot said. "Something important."

"Of course you do," Vozama muttered. He was fidgeting and uneasy, unable to keep his eyes off the scepter in mother's lap.

"Hush," Lady Maglan said. "Make it quick, Virot. I don't want our guests to find us unready."

He tossed his cloak off his shoulders. "That's part of what I have to say, my dear. I am Virot Maglan no longer. I reject the name you have given me, as completely as I reject the role I have played. I am done. I am leaving."

Val gasped and Vinya's eyes grew wide. Vozama sputtered and fumed, struggling for words. Mother picked up her scepter and passed it back and forth from her left hand to her right.

"Leaving, my son? Where will you go? Your family needs you."

"This is a ploy, Mother," Vozama broke in. "He wants the scepter for himself. He's always wanted the scepter."

Virot's eyes never even flickered toward Vozama. He spoke only to the woman in the chair. "You're not listening. I am no longer your son."

Mother waved her scepter in annoyance. "This is ridiculous. You cannot simply declare yourself out of this family. We are blood. We are inseparable.

"But I do not have time to indulge you now, Virot. Go, if you must. We will accept the Ilyssa's surrender, and we will enjoy the fruits of our victory. You are invited to join us. And no matter what, in a year from now, or ten, you will come back to us. I know this to be true. There is nothing you can do to destroy the bonds between us."

"Come back soon, traitor," Vozama spat. "For if I hold the scepter when you come, you will not be welcome."

Virot stepped forward to the foot of his mother's chair, but he did not sit there. Instead, he bowed his head and waited.

"You are an irksome and troublesome boy, Virot," his mother said. She extended her hand, which he kissed. He held onto her for an extra moment, looking deep into her cold yellow eyes. Then he turned.

"Vozama," he said. "Will you bid me farewell? For all the time we've spent together." Vozama stepped forward and threw a wild slap at his brother's face. Virot caught the slap and stared hard at Vozama. Then he released him and faced the twins.

"Farewell," he said. He opened his arms, and Vinya leapt into them.

"I don't believe you're going," she whispered against his neck. "But when you get there, send for me. I'll come visit."

Val's mismatched eyes were wary as Virot took his hand and shook it.

"I've always been afraid of you," Val said. When Virot let go, Val rubbed his hand as if it'd been squeezing something sticky.

Virot walked to the entranceway of the great hall, then stopped. He turned, placed a hand on his saber, and cleared his throat.

"There is one last thing I have to say." His former family members watched him with a wide range of emotion. Anger and sadness, love and fear.

I understand, he had said in his dream. *What is the price?*

Kuberr had spoken three words, and Virot had nodded. Virot had anticipated the cost of Kuberr's gift and was ready to pay it.

What is the price? he had asked.

The Maglan family, Kuberr had replied.

"Suffer," Virot said to his family.

Vozama was the first to scream, a fact that surprised Virot. He had thought Val would buckle before the others. In fact, as they writhed ignobly on the floor, Vozama and Val were the only ones to cry out. Virot felt a new rush of respect for his mother and sister.

The Maglan women had always been tougher than anyone thought. Vinya herself would be very difficult to replace.

"Wither." Mother suffered the least dramatic effects, as her body was already dried and emaciated. Veins blackened, rose to the surface, and burst. Skin hardened and flaked away. Copper wire and white hair alike crumbled to dust.

There was a knock from outside the chamber. "The Ilyssa have arrived," called a servant's voice.

"Bring them in directly," Virot answered. He marched over to the throne of bone, past the wretched husks of his former family, and took up the scepter, the symbol of Maglan power for ten generations. He spared it but a single glance, then snapped the ancient hardwood across his knee. With both hands, he raised the splintered wood and the black crystal globe high over his head.

"Die," he said, and the sound of the glass globe shattering on the floor was loud enough to be heard at the farthest end of the city.

* * * * *

Ockeed Ilyssa wore a beard even bigger and blacker than his second-born son's. He came at the head of a procession of ten, mostly distant relatives with a handful of trusted retainers. They all coughed and gagged as they came into the Maglan great hall.

"Nine hells, what's that stench?" Ockeed peered at the tall man standing at the far end of the room. "Maglan?" he said. The man wore a black cloak, and his eyes were clouded over by a ghastly white film. He stood beside a pile of bleached and broken shards of bone that had once been a chair. "What is the meaning of this? Where is Lady Maglan?"

"There are no more Maglans," the tall man said. He gestured. "Come forward, Ockeed Ilyssa."

Ockeed slowly approached with his hand on his dagger. "Who are you?"

"My new name is a secret. But you may call me Pater."

Ockeed sneered. "My father died long ago, boy, and you're half my age. I'll call you 'fool' until you tell me your name."

"That's Virot Maglan," Danske, Ockeed's eldest son hissed. "Their pet killer. I recognize the sword."

"Where's your mother, boy? What sort of game are you playing?"

"There are no more Maglans," the tall man repeated. "Just as there will soon be no more Ilyssa. Or any other family but Kuberr's."

"Look, I've come to discuss terms. I expect to be humiliated, but I will not be ignored." He turned to his entourage. "We're leaving."

The tall man sprang across the room before Ockeed Ilyssa could take a single step. He clamped onto the bearded man's face with both hands, and with a terrifying expression of calm, turned a two-hundred pound man into a pile of ashes and grit before any of his fellows could so much as draw a blade.

"What's your name?" the tall man barked at Ockeed's son. His saber was out and at the younger man's throat. The entire delegation found themselves unable to move, pinned to the floor by a spell they never saw their tormentor cast.

"I am heir to the Ilyssa fortune," Danske said. His eyes were wide and his face damp with fear as he looked at the remains of his father. "And there is no need—"

"Your name."

"Danske Ilyssa," the man blurted, and the tall man ran him through.

"What's your name?" He oriented on a new target, not caring who it was. The woman hesitated, then said, "Whatever you say it is, Pater."

He lowered his sword. "Very good." He pointed the sword again. "And you?" In turn, each of the defeated Ilyssa rejected their given names in favor of whatever the madman with the saber chose to call them.

"Outstanding," the tall man said. "Again, there is only one family left in this city. I am currently its only member. You will all join me shortly.

"There will be no more feuds. There will only be the docks, and the gambling houses, and the blood-sport pits. We will serve Kuberr, the god of wealth, and he will make us strong and rich beyond our wildest dreams."

"How will we serve him, Pater?" The woman was fast, he realized. He would find the best place to put her quick mind to work.

"I will teach you. There are forms to be observed." He smiled, remembering the words Kuberr spoke in his dream. "And we shall observe them. To start, you all need names. Line up," he pointed to the woman, "behind her. There are a few simple rituals and oaths you will perform.

"And then—" he smiled broadly—"we will visit the other noble houses in the city and explain the benefits of joining our new family. And they will join us or die. Is that not wise, my children?"

"Yes, Pater." Others were starting to follow the woman's lead, answering correctly.

"Then tell me so. The First is wise."

"The First is wise," they all chanted.

The man who had been Virot Maglan sheathed his sword. He felt the familiar rush of a well-won victory, but it was paler, muted compared to the anticipation of the greatness that lie before him.

* * * * *

Though he grew closer and closer to his god each day and dreamed of him often, the First only had one dream of Kuberr, over and over, for the next three hundred years. In it, he was on the field of black rock once more, sitting on a throne of bones in the moonlight. Kuberr's mountain of wealth was a short march away, but it had grown so high that its peak was out of sight, beyond even the moon. Thousands, perhaps millions of beings walked past the throne in a single file toward the mountain's base. Humans, non-humans, spirits, and beasts alike all paused at his throne and bowed. Then they scratched the tiniest fleck of black rock from the ground and held it tight between both hands.

When they rose, their eyes were hollow sockets weeping ebon tears.

He shifted uncomfortably in his seat. The ulna bone that served as his armrest had a hairline crack near the wrist, right where adolescent Valdim Maglan's arm had been broken during a particularly violent seizure. But for that crack, the matching ulna on the other side was a mirror opposite, smooth and slender like the bone from a vivacious and mysterious lady. The legs of the chair were bowed slightly, as Vozama's had been, and the headrest was the small but durable skull of a wizened old women.

The line of supplicants continued to file past. He peered down the line toward the mountain. Though the figures were tiny in the distance, he could see each folding, melting, and reforming around their bit of rock, shrinking and hardening until they were indistinguishable from the coins they approached. With each transformation, the hoard became incrementally larger.

The first member of Kuberr's community looked in the opposite direction, down the line that stretched past the horizon. There was no end in sight, but he knew that when the last adherent came and contributed to the pile, he would see Kuberr again. The god would call his secret name and praise the work he had done.

And then Kuberr would force him to rise from his throne, scratch a bit of rock from the plain, and join the rest of the cabal he had created. The wealth god feasted on life, after all, and the First knew that he must either feed Kuberr or become his food.

In his dreams, and in every waking hour, he vowed to keep the line of cabalists going for as long as possible.

About the Authors

Philip Athans, the David Hasselhoff of computer game novelizations, has lately been dealing with the petty nuisances of advancing age. Hair loss and bursitis aside, he's heard of no one currently being played on MTV (except Aerosmith, of course), and was left in stunned silence when he realized that babies born when he was in high school can now buy beer. He is a father, husband, author, editor, gamer, and all-around swell guy.

Jim Bishop lives in Edmonton, where he works for BioWare and writes stories. He'd like to thank his editor for making him use his powers in the service of Good.

Cory J. Herndon is a Seattle-based writer, editor, and game designer. His written work has appeared in the pages of *Amazing Stories*, *Duelist*, *TopDeck*, *Star Wars Gamer*, and *Dragon*. He is also the author of the *Magic: The Gathering Encyclopedia Vol. 5* and the *Official Strategy Guide to The Magic Starter Set*. His editing credits include the STAR WARS ROLEPLAYING GAME® (including sourcebooks such as the *Alien Anthology* and *Secrets of Tatooine*) and THE WHEEL OF TIME RPG. He designed sections of *The Rebellion Era Sourcebook* and *The Dark Side Sourcebook*, both for the STAR WARS RPG. Cory is currently working on a fantasy novel and a box of donuts, not necessarily in that order. Spiders and teenage elf girls scare the bejeebers out of him.

When **J. Robert King** was asked to write for *The Secrets of Magic*, he replied, "Secrets? What secrets? I have no secrets. I tell you everything, Jess. I'm offended you even asked. We both know those rumors are false. Yawgmoth is, well—dead. Why would I lie? Why would I fake something like that? Where would I even hide him? Sure, I was rooting for him, but you told me to kill him, so I made sure . . . What . . . ? An anthology . . . ? Oh, forget I even brought up—How much money . . . ? Sure!"

Nate Levin is a freelance rock-and-roll critic, a serious amateur photographer, a part-time revolutionary, and an ersatz role-playing geek. He likes his free time and spends it wisely. Currently, he delivers bread to pay the bills. He lives in Seattle, Washington.

Will McDermott is a freelance writer living in snowy Buffalo, New York, with his scary-smart wife, three scary-silly children, and one scary-big dog. He also appeared in *The Myths of Magic* with his wife, Daneen, and wrote the MAGIC novel, *Judgment*.

Scott McGough grew up in New Jersey and has been recovering ever since. This volume marks his third straight appearance in MAGIC fiction anthologies, and he loves things that happen in threes because then he gets to refer to them as "hat tricks." He also wrote *Chainer's Torment* and is currently at work producing a hat trick of MAGIC novels (AKA a trilogy) for publication in 2003. And yes, when he said he watches "any movie with a monster in it," he meant *any* movie with a monster in it.

Vance Moore was born in Sunnyside, Washington, in 1967. He learned to read at an early age and devoured the childhood classics of the fantastic—Dr. Seuss, fairy tales, Dr. Dolittle, Oz. He is an avid theater patron and regularly pilgrimages to Ashland and San Francisco. He lives in Bellingham, Washington. His other interests include singing, history, and a smattering of debate. He has written the novels *Odyssey* and *Prophecy* as well as several stories for Wizards of the Coast.

Chris Pramas desperately needs a vacation. By day he is the Creative Director of Miniatures R&D at Wizards of the Coast. He co-designed WotC's first miniatures game, DUNGEONS & DRAGONS CHAINMAIL®, and created the game's setting, The Sundered Empire. By night he runs Green Ronin Publishing, a market leader in the d20 field. He authored the RPG adventure *Death in Freeport*, which won a prestigious Origins Award in 2001. In his "copious free time" he foolishly takes on freelance writing projects and occasionally tries to relax.

Paul B. Thompson is the author of more than a dozen novels, including the recent "Barbarians" trilogy of DRAGONLANCE® books, and *Nemesis*, a MAGIC: THE GATHERING® novel. Though he freelances in many fields, he always returns to his home base in fantasy and science fiction. He loves old movies, obsolete technology, and his wife Elizabeth. Paul lives in Chapel Hill, North Carolina.

Continue the journey into the depths of a reborn and frighteningly hostile world with the two newest titles in the ODYSSEY™ Cycle

As the people of Dominaria struggle to survive in a brutal
post-apocalyptic world, an artifact of frightening might is
discovered. All those who lust for power, whether wizards,
fighters, or kings, are determined to own it at any cost.
Little do they know that their actions have consequences—
consequences that will determine the fate of the world.

Chainer's Torment
Book II
Scott McGough

January 2002

Judgment
Book III
Will McDermot

May 2002

Now available:

Odyssey
Book I
Vance Moore

The MAGIC® Legends™ Cycle Continues!

Explore the danger and intrigue
behind some of the most popular
MAGIC: THE GATHERING® characters
with these new titles:

Hazezon

Legends Cycle, Book III
Clayton Emery
The last in this exciting trilogy

Full-scale war seems imminent as Johan continues
his march into the southlands. Hazezon, Jedit, and
Adira must stop him at any cost.

August 2002

Assassin's Blade

Legends Cycle Two, Book I
Scott McGough
A new cycle begins

The head of the emperor's assassins plots the death
of several regional monarchs, kings, and leaders. The
emperor's champion disagrees with this dishonorable
tactic and works to stop the assassins. In the midst of
this turmoil, war seems inevitable.

December 2002